D1235216

BANDIT COUNTRY

A Joe Johnson Thriller

ANDREW TURPIN

The Write Direction Publishing

COPYRIGHT

First published in the U.K. in 2018 by The Write Direction Publishing, St. Albans, UK.

Copyright © 2018 Andrew Turpin
All rights reserved.
Print edition ISBN: 978-1-78875-005-9

WELCOME TO THE JOE JOHNSON SERIES!

Thank you for buying **Bandit Country** — I hope you enjoy it!

This is the third in the series of thrillers I am writing that feature Joe Johnson, a US-based independent war crimes investigator. He previously worked for the CIA and for the Office of Special Investigations—a section of the Department of Justice responsible for tracking down Nazi war criminals hiding in the States.

The other books in the series about his various war crimes investigations are all for sale on Amazon. In order, they are:

Prequel: *The Afghan*
1. ***The Last Nazi***
2. ***The Old Bridge***
3. ***Bandit Country***
4. ***Stalin's Final Sting***
5. ***The Nazi's Son***

If you enjoy this book, I would like to keep in touch. This is not always easy, as I usually only publish a couple of books a year and there are many authors and books out there. So the best way is for you to be on my Readers Group email list. I can then send you updates on the next book, plus occasional special offers.

If you would like to join my Readers Group and receive the email updates, I will send you, **FREE** of charge, the ebook version of another Joe Johnson thriller, ***The Afghan***, which is a prequel to the series and normally sells at $2.99/£2.99 (paperback $11.99/£9.99).

The Afghan is set in 1988 when Johnson was still a CIA officer. Most of the action takes place in Afghanistan and Washington, DC.

To sign up for the Readers Group and get your free copy of *The Afghan*, go to the following web page:

https://bookhip.com/QHCLTZ

If you only like reading paperbacks you can still sign up for the email list at that link. A paperback of *The Afghan* is for sale on Amazon.

Andrew Turpin, St. Albans, UK.

To Alexa and Ross

"The Rose Tree"

By William Butler Yeats

"O words are lightly spoken,"
    Said Pearse to Connolly,
    "Maybe a breath of politic words
    Has withered our Rose Tree;
    Or maybe but a wind that blows
    Across the bitter sea."

"It needs to be but watered,"
    James Connolly replied,
    "To make the green come out again
    And spread on every side,
    And shake the blossom from the bud
    To be the garden's pride."

"But where can we draw water,"
    Said Pearse to Connolly,
    "When all the wells are parched away?
    O plain as plain can be
    There's nothing but our own red blood
    Can make a right Rose Tree."

PROLOGUE

Wednesday, December 19, 1984
  Crossmaglen, Northern Ireland

Dessie Duggan felt his heart rate slacken as he exhaled slowly yet again. Time seemed to stand still as he squinted into the high-powered telescopic sight and squeezed his finger, light as a lover's caress, on the trigger of the forty-three-inch sniper rifle.

Even through the scope, the target he was aiming at looked tiny. There was no margin for error here. The physical effort required to pull the trigger was minimal, but every time he took a shot, his head seemed to burst outward under the mental pressure, the concentration.

The explosive sound of the weapon firing carried unimpeded across the flat, rain-swept fields. A quartet of crows that had only just settled at the top of a leafless oak tree to Dessie's left took off again, squawking in alarm, and headed south toward the border with the Irish Republic.

Dessie, who lay prone on a short length of tarpaulin,

remained still and glanced up and down the smooth matte-black metal casing of the FN FAL semiautomatic rifle, its twenty-one-inch barrel pointing toward a small copse almost five hundred yards away at the top of a slight incline.

He removed his earplugs, turned his head, and looked at his father, Alfie, who stood behind him, peering through a powerful spotting scope mounted on a monopod, toward a sheet of white printer paper pinned to one of the distant trees. After a few seconds, Alfie nodded. "Hit."

"About bloody time," Dessie said, his voice low and soft. He ran his hand through his cropped black hair.

"You control that breathing, son, you control your gun. Simple as that," the older man said. "Otherwise it controls you. And then you're finished." He scratched at the gray and black stubble that sprouted under his chin and began to remove the scope from the monopod.

"Are we done? No time for another?" Dessie asked.

Alfie looked at his watch. "No. Been here twenty minutes already. It's way too long. I need to disappear, and anyway, Patrick's car will be here in a minute. We don't want to make him late for the airport. Then my car won't be far behind."

He inclined his head toward the very tall, angular figure of Dessie's oldest friend, Patrick McKinney, who stood behind him, arms folded. His hair had grown long and he'd recently dyed it black. He had a new beard and was wearing a pair of black-framed glasses. They'd been in the same junior school class and had grown up with a republican fire inside them that wouldn't go out.

It was just past three o'clock in the afternoon, and the dregs of the pale winter sun, now down near the horizon, were casting long shadows.

Dessie stood, pushed the FN's safety up, and removed the empty magazine. He slid the rifle into a long black case, together with the remaining cartridges, and zipped it up.

Then he picked up the spent cartridge cases and quickly folded the tarp. "Okay, let's go."

The three men walked around the clump of rhododendron bushes that had hidden them from view and went back along the rough farm track toward Coolderry Road, the single-lane road four hundred yards away.

By the time they reached the road, a blue Ford Cortina that had pulled onto the shoulder next to Alfie's Land Rover stood waiting, its engine running.

Dessie paused for a moment. The hour just spent with his father had been their longest time together in the previous thirteen months. It had been the same ever since the old man and Patrick had gone on the run, ducking and diving, following their escape from Long Kesh, the Maze prison southeast of Belfast, along with thirty-six others. Most of the escapees had long since been recaptured.

Alfie and Patrick stood on the wet grass and faced each other in silence. Alfie held out a hand and Patrick shook it slowly, then scratched the scar that ran down the right side of his face, below his cheekbone.

"Go well, Patrick," Dessie's father said. "I hope Boston is kinder to you than Belfast. A new life. We'll all three work together again soon, I know it. Don't let the bastards get to you."

Patrick turned to Dessie and briefly embraced him, then stood back and nodded before climbing into the Cortina. "Tell the council I'll still be looking to help. Funds, weapons, whatever." He looked at Dessie. "And you," he said. "Keep practicing. I'll miss you, big man."

With that he pulled the door shut and was gone.

Dessie and Alfie watched the Cortina head east toward Larkins Road and the back route past Thomas "Slab" Murphy's farm over the border into the Republic. No sooner had it disappeared around the bend than another car, a green Rover 3500, came toward them from the same direction.

"Okay, time to go again," Alfie said. "I'll see you next month then, son, all being well." He pointed toward the small copse of trees. "I want you getting four out of five by then. And you'd best go get that target."

The Rover drew level with them and stopped.

"Try and enjoy your Christmas. Tell your mother I love her." Alfie hugged his son before reiterating his usual parting refrain. "And if I don't see you again, keep up the struggle. No surrender. Okay?"

Alfie eyed his son steadily. Dessie hesitated, looked down, and finally nodded. Only then did his father climb into the front passenger seat and close the door.

It was pointless asking his father where he would be for Christmas. He wouldn't have been told yet. Shuttled from one safe house to another, usually by night, he slept on mattresses in back bedrooms, attics, and basements. Probably no more than a couple of days in each place, at most. It was no life for a fifty-two-year-old. Dessie's mother, Megan, was on Valium to cope with the stress of it.

The driver slotted the Rover into gear and accelerated quickly westward along Coolderry Road.

Dessie stood next to the long wheelbase Land Rover, which belonged to the family farm, and watched the car until it was around the corner behind the woods and out of sight.

He looked at his watch and eyed the rough track that headed north off the lane through the fields toward the copse. He'd better do the sensible thing, as his father suggested, and take down the piece of paper he'd been aiming at.

That was when it happened.

From behind the woods, where the Rover had disappeared, came the insistent clatter of semiautomatic gunfire. Not just from one weapon but several.

Then a pause. Followed by more gunfire.

Then silence.

A cloud of dark smoke climbed from behind the trees into the winter air and drifted slowly in the breeze as Dessie sank to his knees.

PART ONE

CHAPTER ONE

Thursday, January 3, 2013
  Belfast International Airport

"We're going on a detour first, before I take you to the apartment," Michael Donovan said. He wedged himself into the driver's seat, started the engine, and rapidly accelerated out of Belfast International Airport's pickup zone.

"Where?" Joe Johnson said. He yawned. It had been a tedious twenty-hour journey from his home in Portland, Maine, via Boston and Amsterdam, and he'd only managed a fitful sleep on the plane.

"South Armagh," Donovan said in his lilting Ulster brogue. He glanced from beneath a set of spiky black eyebrows across to Johnson in the passenger seat.

"South Armagh?"

"Yes, I want to show you Crossmaglen and Drumintee. Just a quick visit."

Johnson raised an eyebrow. "That was a trouble spot, years ago, wasn't it?"

"Yep. It's still not exactly a safe haven."

Johnson looked at his host. "So why are we going there?"

"You need to get a feel for this place. It'll help explain why I've brought you over here," Donovan said. He swung right at the traffic circle and headed south down the A26 toward Craigavon and Armagh County, instead of east toward Belfast as Johnson had expected.

"I thought you'd done that. You've said what you want me to do, roughly."

"Yes, but some more background would be useful."

Johnson had been getting emails from Donovan for several months urging him to head to Northern Ireland. Donovan ran his own business, matching foreign investors with companies in Northern Ireland that needed funds to grow.

Several of Donovan's emails had mentioned continuing attacks by dissident Republicans on police stations, homes, vehicles, and individuals and especially the economic damage they were doing.

Donovan's focus had been on how money was being driven elsewhere, which was hurting his business, and the police were not doing anywhere near enough to deal with it.

Johnson's interest had been partly piqued by Donovan's background as a former senior intelligence operator with the British army in Northern Ireland. He'd been a handler for informers within the Irish Republican Army, he'd said. For Johnson, an ex-CIA officer who'd played a similar role in Pakistan and Afghanistan, it had struck a chord.

The other attraction was that Donovan was offering 20 percent more than Johnson's normal fees. And he'd paid for Johnson's airfare.

Donovan's large, fleshy left hand grasped the gear stick as he pushed his Audi 4x4 up into fifth.

"I thought the peace process had sorted out most of the

problems, Michael," Johnson said. "Isn't it just a small group of nutters now, with no future?"

After decades of war between nationalist republican forces—who wanted Northern Ireland to be part of a united Ireland—and British security forces, the 1998 Good Friday Agreement had led to the apparent decommissioning of weapons. As part of the agreement, the British government consented to a new arrangement in Northern Ireland that allowed the Irish Republic a say in what happened there.

Donovan laughed, causing the jowls of his double chin to wobble. "You can call me the Don, like most people. No need for Michael. And you're joking. It's smoke and mirrors, mate. The old IRA leaders, like Gerry Adams and Martin McGuinness, might be wearing suits and ties these days, sitting in these fancy new Northern Ireland Assembly seats, but down at grassroots level, people still feel the same. The Catholics, the Republicans still want the British out of Ulster. These dissidents have still got guns, rocket launchers, and grenades stashed away in huge quantities. What they decommissioned in '98 was the tip of the iceberg, a PR stunt. Forget it."

He drove down the long, straight road past Maghaberry and onto the M1 divided highway, where he headed west toward Craigavon.

"Not far from here," Donovan said, "down near Craigavon, a prison officer from Maghaberry jail was shot dead as he got out of his car at his golf course a few weeks back. Long-distance job by a sniper from high up on a hilltop. They think from around three-quarters of a mile away. Back in September, a guy who runs his own security company was also shot. That was another long-range job from a cliff top while he was walking his dog. A nasty business."

Johnson frowned. "So the victims were Protestant, were they?"

Donovan nodded. "Yes, Protestant unionist guys but not

particularly flag-waving types. Beyond that, there was no
clear motive for either. We've had other killings, bombings of
government offices, kneecappings. You name it. I mean, don't
get me wrong; it's nothing like the dark days of the Troubles.
We're not going back to the '70s, nothing like that, but it's
getting worse."

Johnson glanced out the car window. "I've read about
them forming a merged republican organization." Prior to
flying to Belfast, he'd gone through several high-level
specialist reports on the Northern Ireland situation. All of
them had mentioned a merger toward the end of the previous
year between the Real IRA and other republican paramilitary
groups, including Óglaigh na hÉireann, to form a larger entity,
the New IRA.

"Yep," Donovan said. "They were fragmented, but they're
becoming more organized. And it's showing. Attacks are
becoming more frequent and more aggressive. Make no
mistake, there's hundreds of them in the group now."

"And who's doing what about it?"

"That's the issue," Donovan said. "In some parts of
Northern Ireland, like south Armagh, the police are still
reluctant to police a lot of the time, though they'll deny that.
And of course, there's been no army presence since mid-2007.
As a result, it's like the Wild West in some parts. That's my
problem. It's shit for business. People don't want to invest
with all this crap still going on. I had an American guy over
here in early November from California, looking at putting
money—big money—into an aircraft components factory, a
new venture to supply Airbus and Boeing. Would have
created hundreds of jobs. Then the prison officer gets taken
out. There's a bomb attack on a police station. He gets the
jitters and jumps on the next plane back to San Francisco.
And you can't blame him."

"So it's a money issue for you?" Johnson asked.

"Partly. I spent years as an intelligence guy in the army," Donovan said. "It was interesting, but I got paid peanuts. I'm making up for it now, as a businessman. But I also don't like people getting away with stuff they should have done time for, no matter who they are, which side of the fence they're on. Guess I've changed my view on that over the years. When I was younger I looked the other way when it involved my own side. Anything went back then."

Donovan glanced at Johnson. "That's why I called you in. I've tried talking to the police, but they seem reluctant to act unless someone's shooting at their officers. I've tried talking to journalists, but none of them have time to investigate stuff anymore. They're all tied to their desks, under orders from their editors to write a couple of thousand words a day, and they're scared of this republican lot, anyway. I've tried politicians, but they're just bullshitters." He shrugged.

"The journalists weren't interested?" Johnson asked.

"A couple of them were actually very interested, in principle. They said that if I could bring them something concrete —names, evidence, and so on—they would have a look at it," Donovan continued. "So again, that's why I brought you in. I'd like to use the media to embarrass the authorities into action. But we need to make it easy for the journalists, so I want someone to do the spadework first."

Now they were in County Armagh, and Donovan turned off the divided highway, heading south past Portadown and into the flat, rural countryside, punctuated with leafless winter trees, gray farm buildings, and isolated houses.

Donovan had interrogated Johnson thoroughly on his track record investigating historical war crimes, via email and during various phone calls, prior to flying him to Belfast. The Irishman had been particularly impressed with his work chasing down former Nazis and mass murderers from the Yugoslav civil war.

Johnson ran his hand through the short-cropped semi-circle of graying hair that surrounded his bald patch.

"If you've got a passion for justice, then there's a lot you can get stuck into here," Donovan said, as he continued to drive south.

The Irishman continued driving along the A29 until they reached the Crossmaglen turnoff. Donovan pointed to a memorial on the other side of the crossroads. "That's for the hunger strikers, the 1981 lot. Remember Bobby Sands?"

He swung the car right onto the B30: four miles to Crossmaglen, according to the road sign.

Johnson did remember the hunger strikes. He was only nineteen at the time but recalled the television pictures beamed from outside the Maze prison, southwest of Belfast, as Sands and several other IRA prisoners eventually died after weeks of refusing food and demanding special treatment, such as the right to wear their own clothes, arguing they were political prisoners, not criminals.

A few minutes later, they passed a petrol station and came to a dip in the road on a bend left, just before a dense clump of trees. Two cars were stopped in the middle of the road, one at a forty-five-degree angle, which meant there was no way to get around them.

Donovan braked and came to a halt behind the nearest of the two cars. "Looks like somebody's broken down here. Or has there been an accident?"

As he spoke, a blur of movement in the trees at the side of the road ahead of them caught Johnson's eye.

Suddenly, three men ran out from the shadows into the road about a hundred yards in front of Donovan and Johnson. The men were dressed all in black, each wearing a balaclava, two of them carrying handguns.

One of them held out his palm in front of Donovan's car in a clear signal to remain still.

Donovan grasped the top of his steering wheel and jerked his bulky body forward. "What the hell's going on here?"

Into their hearing came the distinctive high-speed clattering and thumping of a helicopter, drawing rapidly nearer.

One of the men in balaclavas crouched behind the farthest car, his gun pointed straight at Donovan's Audi, another likewise from behind the nearest one. The third man strutted in a no-nonsense fashion right up to Donovan's driver's side window, carrying a sheaf of papers in one hand.

He jerked his thumb forcefully back, signaling Donovan and Johnson that they should get out of the car.

* * *

Thursday, January 3, 2013
　Crossmaglen

The Police Service of Northern Ireland helicopter cruised in at a brisk 120 miles per hour over the random collection of green fields that spread across the County Armagh landscape like the shapes of a patchwork quilt.

The man sitting on the left side of the cabin, Eric Simonson, the chief constable of Northern Ireland, fingered his silver hair and looked out the window.

Clearly visible in the distance was the immense mass of Slieve Gullion, the ancient volcanic mountain that dominates south Armagh like a medieval fortress. The aerial view of sunshine splashed on the purple and gray rock and the green countryside reminded Simonson of an oil painting and always lifted his spirits.

Up front, the pilot, Steve Richardson, was focused on his instruments as he navigated the Eurocopter EC145 toward the village of Crossmaglen. To his left sat the copilot, Ben Trench.

Richardson turned his head toward Simonson and his four co-passengers who sat in the rear seats, including the assistant chief constable, Norman Arnside.

"Five minutes to landing," Richardson said into his microphone.

Simonson heard the words clearly over the intercom connecting the passenger and crew headsets, despite the din generated by the aircraft's twin engines. He caught Richardson's eye and nodded.

Simonson was responsible for policing the six counties that make up Northern Ireland, and this was a big day. He had mulled long and hard over the decision to bring the man now sitting on his right, the British government's secretary of state for Northern Ireland, Bryan Long, on a walkabout in Crossmaglen village center.

Decades ago, such a visit would not have been possible. During the dark days of the Troubles, south Armagh was a no-go zone for outsiders, an isolated place where well-organized, well-equipped IRA republican operators slugged it out on an almost daily basis with the British army and the Royal Ulster Constabulary, rebadged in 2001 as the Police Service of Northern Ireland.

Simonson, now fifty-nine, had seen soldiers and police killed on a regular basis by sniper bullets, car bombs, booby traps, and other devices. A considerable number of IRA fighters also had died in the fighting. It had been an exhausting, intensely brutal conflict: a nimble, surprisingly well-equipped guerrilla force on one side had often caused havoc among the well-trained but more regimented British security forces.

Now, almost fifteen years after the Good Friday peace agreement, Simonson had agreed with Long that he should see at ground level how his force was trying to change the face of community policing to engage with local people rather than push against them.

Nevertheless, Simonson still had concerns, deeper ones than he was prepared to share publicly. Chief among these was rising activity among the so-called dissident Republicans, the ones who refused to accept the political, peaceful solution to Northern Ireland's future backed by former proponents of violence such as Gerry Adams, the leader of Sinn Féin, the republican political party.

The helicopter descended gradually and slowed sharply as it continued in a southeasterly direction toward Cross, as the locals called it, where it was scheduled to land at the police barracks, a base protected by high corrugated steel walls and electric fencing that stood next to Crossmaglen Rangers Gaelic football club's ground.

Long looked at Simonson through heavy black-rimmed spectacles, then gave him a thumbs-up sign and smiled.

As he did so, a series of thuds came from underneath the helicopter, which lurched sharply to the right and dropped a little.

Richardson swore loudly over the intercom. "Bollocks. Think we've got some sort of mechanical problem."

Simonson instinctively grabbed the side of his seat. He could see both Richardson and Trench leaning forward and staring frantically at their instruments, trying to work out what was wrong.

Seconds later, a series of thuds and bangs emanated from the rear of the helicopter.

The chopper then lurched sharply to the right again.

"I'm losing one of the bloody rotors, the rear one. We're losing RPMs, the power's down," Richardson yelled.

There was another bang, this time at the front of the aircraft.

Simonson looked forward past Richardson at the left-hand side of the large curved glass windshield at the front of the helicopter.

Right at the edge of the laminated glass was a hole with a spiderweb of cracks spreading outward.

"It's not a mechanical failure, there's a bloody bullet hole. We're being fired on," Simonson yelled.

Another series of bangs came, and more holes appeared in the windshield.

The helicopter went into a slow spin that sped up as it passed 360 degrees.

"Can you control it?" Simonson shouted into his microphone.

"Yes, I can control it," Richardson responded. "It's the bullets. They've hit the back. The bastards. I'm going into autorotation, else we'll spin like a top. I'm lowering the collective pitch control on the rotor blades. It'll keep the revs up. Stop the spin."

Ten seconds later, Richardson came over the intercom again. "I'll have to put her down in a field."

"In a fecking field?" Simonson asked, his body now rigid with anxiety.

"Yep. There's no way we'll get over the houses to the barracks like this."

There were three more bangs as bullets slammed into the fuselage.

"Dammit, they're maniacs," Arnside said over the intercom.

"That's a bloody machine gun they're using," Simonson said. "The gunman's over to the right somewhere."

Another ten seconds passed, which seemed to Simonson like an eternity, but there were no more bullets.

They passed over Newry Road, the B30, which ran into Crossmaglen. Simonson briefly noticed a couple of cars stopped in the middle of the road next to some trees, with men standing nearby, but had no time to consider the implications.

Now the spinning had stopped. The chopper seemed stable once again and was facing back toward Crossmaglen. Richardson appeared to have got the Eurocopter into a controlled slow glide.

"I'm going to put her down in that field over there," Richardson yelled and pointed over to his left. "Get yourselves in brace position. We'll be down with a bump. We'll get out as quickly as we can. Remember to duck down; the blades will be spinning. Wish me luck."

Simonson and the other four passengers leaned slightly forward, hands over their faces, elbows wedged into their hips, as they had been instructed in the routine safety briefing carried out by Richardson and Trench before they left Belfast.

Simonson had seen the field Richardson was aiming for. The stretch of grass, just a few yards from the road leading into Crossmaglen, wasn't flat but was just about level enough, he thought. In any case, it was the only obvious option.

He felt the aircraft's nose rise a little, flatten out, and then there was an almighty bump and a thud as the skids made contact with the turf.

Simonson bounced hard in his seat, forcing his shoulders painfully upward against his seatbelt.

They were down.

"Thank God," Simonson said out loud over the intercom.

But already his mind was racing ahead. "We'll need to head straight for cover. Once we're out, run for that stone wall over to the right, next to the road."

CHAPTER TWO

Thursday, January 3, 2013
Crossmaglen

As machine-gun fire echoed distantly across the south Armagh countryside, the stricken helicopter dipping and spinning slowly, Dessie Duggan thought the job was done.

As he peered through his scope, Duggan could see the chopper rock and pitch as the bullets hit home.

But after a few minutes, it became obvious that the pilot had regained some control and was going to get it down.

Duggan swore softly. His boys sitting on the other side of Newry Road with their DShK heavy machine gun had been detailed to bring the chopper down. They'd started the job but hadn't finished it. Maybe their gun had jammed again.

"He's doing an emergency landing," Duggan said. "Looks like Plan B, then."

His spotter, Martin Dennehy, crouched to his right, peered through a powerful spotting scope on a small tripod. "Yeah, you should be able to reach him from here, depending on where the chopper comes down. Maybe you'll have a chance when they get out," Dennehy said.

"Slim chance."

It was Duggan's way of taking the pressure off. He let his torso sink onto the small tarp spread over the damp ground between two bushes and tucked the recoil butt pad of his beloved Barrett M82A1 rifle—his Light Fifty—snugly into his shoulder. Then he went through his relaxation routine.

It was a mild day for January, thanks to warm air that was drifting in from the south, in contrast to the four previous days that had frozen the ground. Duggan was thankful for that.

The pair were on an area of farmland three-quarters of a mile south of the field where the helicopter was about to land. Behind them, out of sight behind some trees at the end of a track that led to Monog Road, east of Crossmaglen, was a dark green Honda Civic, stolen before dawn that morning from a driveway just outside Newry and now carrying false license plates.

Duggan exhaled slowly, breathed in, and then exhaled again. His rifle felt like an extension of his arm, balanced perfectly on its bifold support.

Through his Schmidt & Bender telescopic sight, set to a maximum twenty-seven times magnification, he saw the chopper touch down. "The bastard's landed it," Duggan said.

It was going to be a long shot.

After checking his weather meter, he had already amended his scope settings to allow for the slight north-to-south breeze.

"You'll have to just confirm to me who's who," Duggan said. "I think I can pick 'em through this, but not 100 percent sure. It's too far." He reached into his pocket, removed two yellow earplugs, and inserted them into his ears.

"Okay," murmured Dennehy. "Just wait." He also inserted

earplugs, pulled his scruffy blue anorak straight, and reapplied his right eye to the spotting scope.

Seconds later, Duggan saw five figures emerge from the helicopter, all bent double. They moved quickly across the field toward a stone wall that marked the entrance to a farmer's field.

"The chief constable's on the left, definitely him, and the secretary of state's second left," Dennehy said.

"Definitely?"

"Yeah. The cop's the one with the white hair, on the left. The Brit's got black-framed glasses."

"Okay, got 'em."

There were five large fields between Duggan and the helicopter. He had a narrow angle of vision past some bushes a couple of hundred yards in front of him. A rise in the ground at the same place, forming a slight ridge, also limited his field of vision in the vertical. But he could see just enough.

He tweaked the position of the reticle just fractionally, watching the crosshairs fall, then rise with his breathing, focusing on the small figure on the left of the group of five, who were now crouching behind the wall.

They probably thought that with the machine-gun fire having come from the other side of the road, they were safe, Duggan mused.

Despite the earplugs, Duggan could hear muffled sounds all around him: the hum of distant traffic, a mooing cow, birdsong. But now he blocked them out. He even blocked his thoughts, everything, apart from the target he was focused on.

His body was rock-solid but relaxed. He exhaled once again, lowered his chest, and then lay motionless; his index finger began almost imperceptibly to move backward.

The Light Fifty fired, with a bang that sent a pheasant over to their left squawking up into the sky. The half-inch diameter, .50-caliber BMG bullet left the barrel at about 3,000 feet per second. The rifle's butt recoiled an inch or so into Duggan's shoulder, the spent cartridge case was thrown out, and the semiautomatic mechanism fed a fresh round into the chamber.

A few seconds passed.

"Nope," Dennehy said. "Try again."

"Bollocks," Duggan said.

"There's seven of them there now. The pilot and copilot have joined the others," Dennehy said. "Secretary of state's still second left."

"Okay. I can see the cop's still on the left, Brit still second left."

"Correct."

Duggan went through his routine again, settled his breathing, settled his crosshairs on his target, and then settled his mind once more.

A couple of seconds later, another explosive bang sounded as Duggan's index finger pulled the Light Fifty's trigger.

Another few seconds passed. Duggan kept his right eye glued to the scope. He saw the white-haired man on the left suddenly keel over and fall to the ground. The man next to him looked around, then dived to the ground. A second later the others also flattened themselves to the ground.

"You got the cop, not the Brit," Dennehy said in a low voice.

Duggan showed no visible reaction. He stood up quickly and flicked the rifle's safety catch horizontal.

"Right, let's get out of here," Duggan said. "The shit's gonna hit the fan."

"What about the feckin' Brit?" Dennehy asked.

Duggan paused. "I can't. He's hit the deck." He calmly removed the magazine and the remaining cartridge from the rifle chamber, bent down, picked up the two used cartridges off the ground, and folded his tarp.

Then he started walking back toward the green Honda.

* * *

Thursday, January 3, 2013
Crossmaglen

The man in the balaclava ordered Johnson and Donovan around to the front of the Audi and told them to flatten themselves on the hood, facedown.

The raucous sound of an oncoming helicopter grew rapidly louder behind them.

Johnson felt his stomach turn over. With two men behind him, both pointing handguns, he had no choice but to comply. He leaned over the car, his hands out in front of him, spread wide.

Donovan did likewise but then asked, "What the hell's this all about, guys? We're having a quiet day out here."

His words were interrupted by the staccato sound of automatic gunfire coming from somewhere farther along the road, through the woodland.

Johnson jumped and raised his head. Above them was a black-and-yellow-painted helicopter with the word *Police* emblazoned in yellow along the side.

The aircraft lurched to the left and dipped a little; and after a few seconds its tail began to spin slowly around.

"Shit," Johnson muttered. "What's going on?"

There came another burst of gunfire, after which the tone of the helicopter's engines lowered, then rose again, but now sounded quite different.

"Bloody hell, it's coming down, the chopper's had it," Donovan said, his voice rising rapidly in pitch.

"Shut it, both of you," the man said. He quickly frisked first Johnson, then Donovan.

"Okay," he said. "This is an informational roadblock organized by the IRA, the New IRA, fighting for a united Ireland. That's us. Take this and make sure you read it. You can go in a minute." He handed both of them a leaflet.

By now the helicopter was a few hundred yards farther up the road ahead of them and descending rapidly. But the gunfire appeared to have stopped.

"Get back in the car, then don't move until I tell you to. Don't even think about trying anything else, or you'll be crow's meat," the man in the balaclava ordered.

Johnson and Donovan climbed back into the Audi.

They sat in silence for a minute or two. The faint sound of a single gunshot from the direction of Crossmaglen could be heard, followed a minute later by another one.

A car pulled up behind them, and Johnson turned around to see the IRA man in the balaclava repeat the procedure with the driver and a woman passenger in the second car, spread-eagling them over the hood, searching them, then handing them leaflets. The woman screamed but was silenced by one of the men in balaclavas who yelled a stream of obscenities at her.

Johnson glanced at the leaflet.

It was a plain typewritten sheet headed "Óglaigh na hÉireann—The New IRA," and contained two densely written paragraphs.

The New IRA is a combined republican force under a unified leader-ship that abides by the constitution of the Irish Republican Army. We are committed to the armed struggle in pursuit of Irish freedom through the removal of British military presence and British political

interference. The people of this country have been sold a phony peace
by a false political legislature that represents a failure of leadership of
Irish nationalism. The ideals and principles set down and enshrined
in the Proclamation of 1916 are what drive our unified organization.
Nothing will divert us from this path.
Anyone passing on information about republican activity to the Police
Service of Northern Ireland, MI5, the Gardaí, or Sinn Féin will be
dealt with severely.

Donovan glanced at the sheet. "Now you see what we're up against here."

Johnson looked up as the three men in balaclavas ran back past Donovan's Audi and jumped into the two cars that had been blocking the road ahead.

Seconds later, they shot off, back in the direction of Newry, away from Crossmaglen.

"We'd best get out of here, quickly," Donovan said and started the engine. He accelerated forward.

As they passed the trees that lined the road, the police helicopter came into view on the left, resting in a field screened from the road by a stone wall. Two men could be seen standing on the other side of the wall.

Donovan continued to accelerate up a slope in the road and over a ridge. The village of Crossmaglen was now visible ahead of them, with its gray- and white-painted houses, a gas station, and a church spire.

He braked to a halt behind a line of cars at a junction. To the right was a large Roll of Honor sign with the pictures of twenty-four volunteers from the IRA's south Armagh brigade. Johnson assumed they had died for the cause.

Four men dressed in black jeans and sweatshirts ran across the road in front of them and jumped into a car. Johnson noticed Donovan's white-knuckled grip on the steering wheel.

Underneath the photographs was a quote attributed to a woman called Máire Drumm. "We must take no steps backward, our steps must be onward, for if we don't, the martyrs that died for you, for me, for this country will haunt us for eternity," it read.

The traffic began to move again, and the Audi passed through the village square. Donovan turned down Cullaville Road. "You'll see the police barracks in a moment," he said. "Ugly place; it'll be like an ant colony that's been set on fire right now."

In front of them on the left lay a tall corrugated steel structure topped with several strands of electric fencing, with a communications tower rising inside. As they approached, two double vehicle gates opened, and a trio of police cars poured out, tires squealing, sirens blaring. Donovan braked hard to a standstill.

The three cars screamed past them toward the village square, their blue and red lights strobing the white-painted house walls at the junction. Two more cars followed a few seconds later.

Johnson was tempted to contrast the action playing out in front of them with Donovan's earlier comment about police being reluctant to police but held back.

Donovan flicked on the car radio, which was set to BBC Radio Ulster, then accelerated away again. A business news program was underway, with a slot about the economic problems plaguing Northern Ireland.

After several minutes, the program was interrupted by a newscaster. "Apologies for interrupting the business news, but word has just reached us of a major incident in south Armagh. A police helicopter carrying the chief constable of Northern Ireland, Eric Simonson, was shot down just outside Crossmaglen. Police sources have told us that the helicopter managed to make an emergency landing, but Mr. Simonson was shot dead, seemingly by a sniper, as he escaped from the aircraft. The secretary of state for Northern Ireland, Bryan Long, was on the same helicopter but is understood to have been unhurt. We're expecting to get official confirmation and more details of this incident very soon, and of course we'll bring those to you as soon as they come in."

"Unbelievable," Johnson said.

Donovan glanced at him and pushed his head back into the headrest. "Bloody hell. I might as well flush my business down the toilet."

CHAPTER THREE

Thursday, January 3, 2013
Belfast

The mug of tea was sweet and hot. Brendan O'Neill sipped it slowly and looked around the snooker club bar.

He glanced at his watch again and removed his scuffed brown leather bomber jacket. It was almost noon and GRANITE was three-quarters of an hour late. True, the man wasn't the most punctual individual on earth. But normally he could be relied on to turn up when he said he was going to.

Still, it gave O'Neill time to think things through, a rare commodity.

O'Toole's Snooker and Pool Club, just off Falls Road in West Belfast, near the huge Milltown Cemetery, had been a fertile recruiting ground for O'Neill and his team of agent handlers at MI5 as they had tried to keep themselves up to speed with the sometimes random activities of dissident republican terrorists in Northern Ireland.

He had found three decent informants at the club, right in the middle of a Catholic republican stronghold, during the nine years he had been at MI5, to which he'd transferred from army intelligence. That was good going, he thought. So much so that he'd had to stop recruiting there for fear that if one agent was blown, it could bring down the others.

Of the three, GRANITE had been the toughest to recruit; it had taken three years of effort, off and on, and he had only come on the payroll a year or so ago. But he had established himself as a trusted lieutenant of the OC—the officer commanding—in the Real IRA's south Armagh brigade, the group O'Neill was particularly focused on. MI5 was tasked with gathering intelligence to combat the growing threat from dissident Republicans who were happy to use violence to further their objectives.

Snooker was one of many plausible covers, a viable excuse for a meeting, although the serious business of passing over information was normally done at either Black Lake or Grey Dog, the code names for two safe houses in the area.

Only two months earlier, over a hurried sandwich lunch at Grey Dog, O'Neill had received a tip from GRANITE that a number of pipe bombs were due to be transported two days later in a certain car from Derry and were to be used to attack a police station south of Portadown, in County Armagh.

Police, operating on the pretext of a routine check for uninsured drivers, had checked the vehicle, discovered four large bombs in the trunk, and arrested the driver. Almost certainly, that information had saved lives.

O'Neill's hope was that information from GRANITE would enable him to nail one of the big fish, namely the OC, the quartermaster, or the IO—the intelligence officer—of the brigade.

But he had found GRANITE difficult to handle. He was inscrutable and to O'Neill's annoyance was often selective with the information he passed over. So far, the leads had led to the arrests of only minor RIRA volunteers.

GRANITE occasionally passed on information but first insisted on O'Neill committing to not using it or giving it to anyone else in MI5 or the police, usually because there was a threat that he might be compromised, given the small number of people with that particular knowledge.

There had been a few of those situations recently. GRANITE seemingly wanted to put O'Neill to the test, check him out, make sure he could trust him. That was how it felt, anyway.

That wasn't good, O'Neill felt, given that he was supposed to be the one controlling the relationship.

In most cases O'Neill discussed the situations that arose with his boss, Phil Beattie, who headed the team of agent handlers in Belfast, but not always.

Three days earlier GRANITE had briefly mentioned a plan for some guns to be shifted north over the border from the Irish Republic into south Armagh. GRANITE was one of the drivers responsible for the transfer. Again he'd requested no action on O'Neill's side and had claimed that the circle of knowledge was too small and that the OC, Dessie Duggan, would finger him immediately. He had claimed he didn't know what the weapons were intended for anyway.

O'Neill had agreed. He reasoned to himself at the time that he couldn't risk putting one of his agents at risk of a kneecapping, torture or even death. That was the first law of agent handling.

Now as always, the violent Republicans showed no mercy to a tout, or informer. So-called six packs were still relatively common—bullets in the ankles, kneecaps, and elbows—as were broken fingers and toes, sometimes arms and legs. The abuse was a warning to others.

The threat to handlers was almost as great. O'Neill had worked in Northern Ireland for well over three decades in different army and security roles. When he had started, O'Neill had followed the advice of an army colleague and took to sleeping with a fire extinguisher in his bedroom and a pistol under his pillow. Even now he followed the same routine.

Given all that, O'Neill often wondered at the motivation of some touts. Sometimes it was the money; he was paying GRANITE more than one thousand pounds a month. Sometimes it was a desire to take revenge on a superior inside the organization. Occasionally it was because touts did not agree with what was being done but were too scared to get out or object.

In the case of GRANITE, O'Neill guessed it was money.

O'Neill rubbed his chin, which was covered with a day and a half's worth of stubble, and looked at his watch again. Ten past twelve. One more cup of tea, then he would have to leave. Something had clearly gone wrong.

He walked to the bar and asked the young blond girl behind it for another mug. On the other side of the bar the rolling satellite TV news was on, so O'Neill moved around and sat near the flat screen on the wall.

That was when he noticed the moving ticker across the bottom of the screen: "Breaking news: Ulster chief constable shot dead in south Armagh after helicopter comes under fire."

O'Neill felt his chest tighten and his forehead start to sweat.

The girl behind the bar was looking at the screen and saw the ticker. "Shit, those guys are going one step too far." She turned toward O'Neill. "Did you see that?" she asked.

He nodded distractedly, but his mind was already focused elsewhere.

Then O'Neill's phone rang. He knew who it would be before he even pulled it out of his pocket.

* * *

Thursday, January 3, 2013
Forkhill, south Armagh

Duggan carefully placed all his clothing into a large black plastic bag.

One of the brigade's volunteers was waiting in the hallway of his farmhouse south of Forkhill to take it away to be incinerated. Duggan didn't want to risk leaving behind any traces of the gases and minute particles of propellant and other gun matter thrown off when he fired the Barrett.

Then he eased his angular, slightly stooped frame into the shower in his en suite bathroom and began to systematically soap himself down, cleaning his skin thoroughly. Then he shampooed himself three times, running his fingers carefully through his close-cropped dark hair, now flecked with gray.

The Barrett and the unused ammunition had been offloaded to another volunteer whose job it was to return the gun to the cache, located south of the border in some woodland down near Dundalk.

Downstairs, drinking coffee and waiting in his living room, were the guys with whom he had worked and operated for the past fifteen years, since the catastrophic Good Friday agreement.

Apart from Duggan himself, who had the OC title, there was Danny McCormick, the quartermaster, Liam McGarahan, who was the intelligence officer, Dennehy, and Kieran

O'Driscoll, the finance director and brains behind the operation.

They all saw the political settlement as a sellout by Sinn Féin politicians Gerry Adams and Martin McGuinness, not least because it removed the historic claim of the Irish Republic on the six counties of Ulster and instead gave the people of Northern Ireland the right to decide whether they should be part of the UK or Ireland.

Not long after the peace agreement went into effect, Duggan's group disentangled themselves from the Provisionals. They saw themselves as a separate entity altogether—a splinter group that was part of the Real IRA. More recently, there had been more cooperation with others, particularly the coalition of other republican entities under the name Óglaigh na hÉireann, following a merger agreement to form the New IRA.

Duggan knew that Óglaigh na hÉireann members had been handing out republican leaflets at a roadblock outside Crossmaglen while the operation to bring down the PSNI helicopter had been going on.

All the groups in the New IRA were firmly committed to a united Ireland—and to the armed struggle as a means of achieving it. They believed that sooner or later the peace agreement would fall apart, leaving them in the driver's seat of a new armed, violent republican movement.

This often left them at odds with the Provisionals, the old guard, at national and local levels. In south Armagh, the Provisionals had been a highly organized group that operated with almost military discipline, so Duggan trod with care and with as much secrecy as possible.

Duggan toweled himself off, dressed in jeans, a T-shirt, and sweatshirt, and headed downstairs carrying the clothes destined for the incinerator. He handed them to a young man who sat on a chair in his hallway and then watched as the man went out and climbed into a waiting car.

Then he walked to the living room door. He knew what was coming.

"All cleaned up?" O'Driscoll asked. He watched Duggan as he walked to an armchair and sat down.

"Yeah, spotless. Good job I was there to mop up Pete's mess," Duggan said, referring to the machine gunner Pete Field, whose job it had been to down the helicopter. "Went to plan, though. That was the obvious spot they'd land it. We chose well."

Duggan looked at McGarahan. "Your man Fergus came up with good info there. Spot on. Timing was just as he told you."

McGarahan nodded but didn't smile. The information the IO had received in advance—of the chief constable's visit to Crossmaglen and the fact that the secretary of state would be accompanying him—wasn't the first valuable tip from his mole in the chief constable's office, a public affairs officer named Fergus Kane.

"We spent a long time cultivating that guy," McGarahan said. "Paid off now, hasn't it?"

There was a short, awkward silence.

"So, Dessie. You did well with the cop. But what about the Brit?" asked McCormick.

There was a distinctly hostile note in the quartermaster's voice.

"What do you mean, Danny?"

"You took down the right man first, did you?"

Here we go, it's started. "Took down the one I could get best sight of. I was three-quarters of a mile away. I knew it was the chief constable. I was after the Brit next, but he'd hit the deck immediately, and the angle was too tight. We had to get out of there quick as possible."

There was silence in the room.

"Anyway," Duggan said, "None of you knows how to handle a Barrett, do you? What other OC is out getting his hands dirty, lying in the mud waiting for hours, looking through the crosshairs. None of 'em, I tell you. They're all tucked up inside giving orders over their cocoa. I do it because none of you lot know how."

He knew he was right. None of them could handle a sniper rifle. There was another silence.

Dennehy broke the silence eventually. "He's right. He did well to hit the cop from that distance. Then the Brit was on the ground straightaway. Saw him through the scope." He glanced at Duggan.

O'Driscoll butted in. "It makes little difference. The chief constable was a good hit. I mean, the shit's hit the fan, it's already causing chaos. The Brit would've been better, we're agreed on that. But I've heard the radio news. They've no idea where the bullet came from. And there's already been some rent-a-quote on the radio saying that at this rate the Brits'll have to put the army back on the streets if the police can't protect their own chief constable. Beautiful, if you ask me."

Duggan nodded. "He's right. Normalization's out the window now."

They all knew that their unwritten objective was to prevent the establishment of normal policing operations in Northern Ireland, which would put the province on a similar footing to the rest of the UK. The biggest step by the British government to that goal had been removing the army from the streets in 2007, when the ugly, symbolic army watch-towers had been torn down.

"That's three you've done in the past few months, Dessie," McGarahan said. "I don't see the rationale behind all of them, but okay, I'd suggest taking a breather now until the dust settles."

"I'd disagree," O'Driscoll said. "Better to keep up momentum, actually. But if we're going to keep it up, we'll need more funds—a lot more. And soon. Dessie, you'll need to speak to Patrick over in Boston about that."

"Yeah, I've got to speak to him," Duggan said. "I need another M82 as a backup now that we're down to just one. I'm not happy with the one I've got—it's a very old piece of kit."

The biggest issue he had was that occasionally the bolt wasn't chambering the next round properly; it wasn't going into battery and engaging the lock ready to fire again. He couldn't afford for that to happen when he was on a big job.

"If I had a new one," Duggan said, "it'd also mean that Martin here could use the old one. We could get him trained up, make us a lot more effective." He glanced at Dennehy. "Besides, it's too much of a risk having just one gun in the locker. That okay, Kieran? It's gonna cost a few bob."

The other Barrett M82 rifle the brigade owned had been discovered by police in a cache in woodland near Armagh City during a raid a year earlier, along with a batch of other weapons. To replace it with another in good condition would probably cost US$6,000 to $7,000.

The finance director grimaced. "Yeah, okay, but like I said, we need more cash coming in if we're going to spend that amount."

McCormick laughed. "You're full of shit, Kieran. How many millions have you got stashed away?"

O'Driscoll ignored the jibe.

"What we need, if we're gonna keep momentum up, is a real 'spectacular,' in my view," Duggan said. "And it needs to be us, this group, who does it, not one of the other brigades, and definitely not one of the other republican groups."

"You wouldn't count the chief constable as a 'spectacular,' then?" McCormick asked. "You had the chance. You had the secretary of bloody state in your crosshairs. Why didn't you take him out? You're the Dentist after all . . . aren't you?"

After a few seconds Duggan said, "I'm thinking higher up the food chain than him."

He leaned over the side of his armchair and picked up the previous day's copy of the *Belfast Telegraph* and threw it down on the coffee table in the center of the room.

"There, take a look at that," Duggan said.

The front-page headline, in large bold capitals, read, "Police Crank Up Security for G8."

Below it, the story referred to a major security initiative by the Police Service of Northern Ireland ahead of the annual meeting of leaders from the eight main industrialized countries.

For the first time, the story continued, the G8 meeting was being held in Northern Ireland, at a hotel resort complex near Enniskillen. In an editorial, the paper said the choice of Northern Ireland was "a move intended to signal to the world that Northern Ireland was now demonstrably a safe place for tourists to visit and businesses to invest in."

"You've got no chance there," McGarahan said. "There'll be a ring of steel around that resort. And after this chief constable thing, they'll probably cancel the whole thing now, anyway."

Duggan picked up the newspaper and turned to page 3, where the front-page story continued. He picked up a pen and circled a paragraph about halfway down. "They definitely won't cancel. That'd be seen as bowing to terrorists now, wouldn't it? There, read that."

He passed the paper across to O'Driscoll, who read out loud, "US President Barack Obama and UK Prime Minister David Cameron are expected to carry out a community visit, possibly to a factory, library or school, during the two-day G8 summit meeting."

O'Driscoll lowered the newspaper and stared at Duggan, as did McCormick and McGarahan.

"You're joking, Dessie, aren't you?" McGarahan said.

Duggan shook his head.

CHAPTER FOUR

Thursday, January 3, 2013
Belfast

A group of men were gathered next to an enormous mural of Bobby Sands painted on a wall on the corner of Falls Road and Sevastopol Road in Belfast.

Donovan braked to a halt a short distance away, giving Johnson a clear view of the full-color mural, two stories high, across the road from Falls Road Library. It showed a portrait of Sands, who was just twenty-seven when he died after his hunger strike in the Maze.

Donovan ignored the men.

"This is the block. You're on the third floor," Donovan said, pointing up at a newish block of flats. "My tenant shifted out last month, and I'm waiting to get another, so you're lucky. More privacy than a hotel, hopefully. All furnished. Should do you while you're here. No charge of course."

Johnson nodded. The block stood in contrast to some of

the older, grubbier terraced properties they had driven past farther west along Falls Road, the main road that runs through West Belfast. It had been the scene of some of the fiercest fighting between British troops and republican forces during the Troubles.

Johnson got out of the car and removed his small suitcase from the trunk.

As he did, the group of men standing next to the Sands mural, which Johnson now realized was painted on Sinn Féin's office building, burst into song, delivered in a raucous, high-speed, staccato style.

Craigavon sent the Specials out,
To shoot the people down,
He thought the IRA were dead,
In dear old Belfast town,
But he got a rude awakening,
With cannon and grenade,
When he met the first Battalion,
Of the Belfast Brigade.

After they had finished singing, they all burst out laughing and two of them high-fived each other. "Chopper down. C'mon guys, time for another beer," yelled one of them. They'd clearly had a few drinks already, and their performance seemed well rehearsed and coordinated—hardly the first time they'd sung the song that afternoon.

"Locals seem to be happy at events down in Crossmaglen," Donovan said. "It's one in the eye for Sinn Féin's peace strategy. That's why they're singing outside their offices."

"What was the song?" Johnson asked.

"It's called 'Belfast Brigade.' An old rebel song. Follow me. Could be a bit of noise tonight around here after what's happened."

A TV news crew was unloading camera and sound gear from a car just outside the Sinn Féin offices. One of the crew walked over to the group of men and appeared to be trying to persuade them to repeat the song on camera.

Donovan strode toward the block of flats, unlocked the front security door, and went in, Johnson close behind him. They headed up the stairs.

"We need to have a chat," Donovan said as they reached the apartment door. He opened it, held the handle as Johnson walked through, and then closed the door behind him.

The two-bedroom apartment was fully furnished, modern, and clean. Johnson leaned against a black granite countertop in the open-plan kitchen area, folded his arms, and looked around. One of the bedrooms had an en suite bathroom, and there was another bathroom off the hallway. Outside the living room was a small balcony.

"Nice place. I'll be fine here," Johnson said.

"Good. Listen, after what you've seen today, you'll have some idea why I'd really like you to get stuck into this job," Donovan said. "These bloody dissident Republicans. You've had a flavor of it—not planned by me, I have to say, in case you were wondering."

Johnson looked at Donovan and pursed his lips. "So you think an American investigator like me can make headway coming cold into a place like this when the police, intelligence networks, the army can't? Come on, Michael. Get real. My specialty's investigating stuff where none of those kinds of organizations are interested, or it was too long ago, where they can't be bothered any more. Historical stuff. What I've seen today is real-time crime. The police'll be on it, probably MI5 too, from what I know of British intelligence. Everyone'll be all over it like a red rash."

Donovan shook his head. "Ha! I wish. That's the problem. They'll try, but they won't get anywhere. I don't think so. The communities around here, especially south Armagh, are still as watertight as a duck's backside, mostly. People are still running scared of passing on information to officialdom. When it comes to police, they hear nothing, see nothing, know nothing, say nothing. There's still that stigma about being a tout. It's still dangerous, they think, and probably they're not wrong."

He tugged at his chin. "In the meantime, my business goes bust. What d'you think tomorrow's headlines are gonna look like to my investors in Frankfurt, Hong Kong, Singapore? They'll laugh. I'm wasting my time. Until a year or so ago, they were all optimistic, thinking things were on the upturn around here, that the Republicans had all gone quiet. Now it's all going pear-shaped again with all the shootings that have happened."

"So why don't the police come and talk to members of the old intelligence community like you, or anyone else who might be able to help?" Johnson asked.

"They try, up to a point, but there's too many old rivalries, too much bad blood."

Johnson was feeling a little confused. "Or why don't you do your own investigation, given you know the issues and the territory so well? You're ex-army intelligence. It's right up your alley, isn't it? Or why not get a local guy to do it?"

Donovan shook his head. "I'm too busy with this business. I'm working eighteen-hour days as it is. I need a pro to do it. Besides, too many people know who I am, know my background, and would never talk to me, not if it were an IRA issue. Same goes for all the decent local investigators, the good ones anyway. Most of 'em have army or police backgrounds. It scares people."

That must undoubtedly be true, Johnson thought.

"Okay, so what d'you want me to do?" Johnson asked. "I'm scheduled to fly out of here Saturday evening, so I've got two more days. You're going to have to persuade me by then."

"Dig up the gang who did today's job down in Crossmaglen, for starters," Donovan said, his voice rising a little. "I'm assuming that whoever shot the chief constable was probably the same guy who did the prison officer and the security company guy in recent months, the ones I mentioned to you. There'll quite likely be a group of 'em, probably all hardliners, old IRA stock, who can't let go of the past."

"So actually," he continued, "you'll probably find there is a historical link to all this. It might be your bag after all. It's probably a cleanskin, a guy who's not been convicted of anything before. There's still a few of 'em around. I'm speculating a bit, but that's what I think."

Johnson scratched his ear. "Why d'you think it was the same guy who did the other jobs?"

"It's got all the same hallmarks. There's not that many militarily active dissidents—probably a few hundred. And out of them, a sniper who can operate successfully from very long range and has the equipment to do it? A rare breed. Probably no more than one or two of 'em at most."

"And you don't have any names?" Johnson asked.

Donovan shook his head. "Not really. Although that said, following today's shooting something rang a bell at the back of my mind. Remember, I worked in army intelligence in the '80s and '90s, so I picked stuff up. The name I recall was a guy called Dessie Duggan. He was the son of another legendary IRA sniper, Alfie Duggan, who ended up in Long Kesh—they never pinned him for his sniper killings but for something else—might have been smuggling or something. Anyway, he escaped."

"What, the father you mean?"

"Yeah—the father, Alfie, escaped from Long Kesh in '83. The Maze mass prison escape. Legendary. Thirty or so prisoners got out. He and one of his big IRA buddies were on the run for over a year. They nearly recaptured him a couple of times—he took risks and resumed his sniper operations. There was one job during that period, near Belfast, where he was apparently planning to take out an army patrol. He never completed the job—got wind of soldiers closing in on him and got away a few minutes before they arrived. His buddy was never caught; he disappeared off the face of the earth. But finally Alfie got shot."

"Shot? By whom?"

"Nobody's sure. Word was that some loyalist gang got him. It was vague."

"And the son?"

"He's still out there," Donovan said. "He's never been caught or nailed for anything. They never got anything on him. A slippery fish, as they say."

"Where does he live?" Johnson asked. "Do you know where he came from in Ulster? Background? Family roots and so on?"

"I don't know exactly where he lives—never had a reason to find out previously—but I think in south Armagh. One thing I do know is that when he was a kid his family lived in a street not far from here. I've forgotten the name of it. Just off Falls Road though, farther west. I went down there when I was in intelligence, trying to find someone who'd talk, a sympathetic neighbor. Never got anywhere. Wall of silence."

"You can't remember the address or the street?" Johnson asked. "The number?"

"Not off the top of my head. I might have it in a notebook at home. I've still got my old files. I'll check." Donovan looked at his watch. "I need to go. I've got a business meeting down in the city center in half an hour. And I doubt I'm going to see you much tomorrow—I'm driving down to Dublin for more meetings with investors and bankers. Might possibly be back in the evening in time for dinner, but I'm not sure. Sorry."

Johnson shrugged. It was fine, he said. He'd maybe check out the city center and visit the old neighbor, if Donovan could get the details.

"Okay," Donovan said. "You get yourself sorted out here. There's a shop around the corner if you need food, or there's plenty of restaurants. Don't walk too far tonight, though. Could get lively. And whatever you do, if you see any fights, scuffles, just walk the other way. Don't get involved. I'll be in touch later."

With that, Donovan was gone.

Johnson opened the door to the balcony and stepped outside. He sat on a hardwood patio chair, looked out across Falls Road, and pulled out his pack of Marlboros.

It was almost dark now. A different group of young men walked along the opposite pavement, also singing what sounded like a rebel song. They turned into the doorway of a pub on the corner.

Johnson lit a cigarette and took a deep drag.

Two police vans roared along the road, their lights flashing but sirens turned off.

The Catholics and the Protestants. The Republicans and the loyalists. Johnson shivered in the cold January air. He was suddenly feeling jaded.

He thought back to the Roll of Honor sign he had seen in Crossmaglen and wondered who Máire Drumm was. He took out his phone and found an article that described how Drumm, a Sinn Féin vice president and republican martyr, had been shot dead in her hospital bed in the '70s by Protestant unionist paramilitaries—one of hundreds of killings carried out by groups such as the Ulster Volunteer Force (UVF) and the Ulster Defence Association. It seemed that each side had been as bad as the other.

Johnson wondered what it was about sectarian and religious differences that generated the most bitter and violent of conflicts. His feeling was that often the differences were simply an excuse for a small minority of war-minded people to do what they'd always wanted to do. He had seen it in many parts of the world. In the end it boiled down to power —who controlled it and who prospered from it.

Should he get involved here? Johnson remained skeptical.

His phone rang. It was Donovan, who had just arrived in the Belfast city center. He had remembered where the Duggan family used to live, he said.

Johnson stubbed out his cigarette and moved back indoors. He grabbed his notebook from his pocket and wrote down the address.

Then, after ending the call, he checked the location on the maps app on his phone. The road, Cavendish Street, was no more than half a mile away, right in the republican heartland, just off Falls Road. A short walk from where he was staying.

Maybe he would go and take a look. The neighbors might remember something.

* * *

Thursday, January 3, 2013
  Belfast

"Why the hell didn't we get a sniff of this? Not a sniff. Nothing." Phil Beattie threw his pen against the wall of his office and stood up. "We're gonna be absolutely strung up over this, you realize that. A damned laughingstock. That's the third sniper victim in the past few months, and the biggest, and we've not had a whisper of any of them."

"Tell me about it," O'Neill said.

Beattie walked over to the window of MI5's modernistic office building inside the Palace Barracks army complex at Holywood, just northeast of Belfast.

O'Neill remained in his seat as Beattie, head of the agent-handling team, turned and stared at him.

O'Neill had driven back to his office from O'Toole's snooker club, taking one of his random surveillance avoidance routes, as soon as he'd heard about the shooting of the chief constable. While driving, he had listened to nonstop coverage of the incident on the radio.

At least two senior politicians had already called for an inquiry and accused MI5 of an intelligence failure, which they said was clearly the root cause of Eric Simonson's death. The news journalist covering the story mentioned that this had happened despite MI5 employing more than a thousand people in Belfast.

The senior policeman who had been given the difficult task of fronting up for media interviews was Assistant Chief Constable Norman Arnside, who gave journalists a brief description of what had happened based on his firsthand experience on the helicopter that had been shot down.

However, Arnside refused to speculate on exactly who had been responsible, other than to say that the incident had all the hallmarks of an attack by dissident Republicans. He confirmed that a major inquiry had been launched and that more detail would be available in due course.

"I don't think anybody saw that one coming," O'Neill said. He coughed, as he often did when feeling stressed. "Not that they'd take out the chief constable. Neither GRANITE nor any of the other agents have given me anything that would've pointed to that." He brushed his hand across his forehead, which was already covered in droplets of sweat, hoping that Beattie wouldn't notice.

Beattie turned around and faced O'Neill. "You're looking like you've just seen a ghost. Are you all right?"

"Yeah, just came as a shock, frankly."

Beattie exhaled noisily. "You could say that. That lot had a bloody Dashka by all accounts; that's what got the chopper into trouble. A big machine gun. They sprayed it with bullets. Then a .50-caliber sniper's rifle got Simonson. Somebody knew those guns were being moved around."

Beattie shook his head. "The whole of Holywood is going to come under scrutiny over this. We'll cop a ton of flak. You know how the police take every chance to throw shit at us. They'll be briefing every journalist this side of Westminster. Those guns are huge pieces of kit. We're not talking dinky handguns you can slip in your pocket, are we?"

O'Neill tried to focus on what Beattie was saying. As usual, he was right. Someone must have retrieved the weapons from a cache and probably driven them to a pickup point. From there they would have been taken to the site of the shooting and back again afterward. They had probably come from over the border; that was his guess.

"That's a big operation," Beattie said. "And we don't hear a word. How did they know about Simonson and the secretary of state visiting Crossmaglen, anyway? It was all kept confidential. They must have someone planted in there, at police headquarters somehow."

O'Neill winced and soaked up the tirade. To say MI5 would cop a ton of flak was probably the understatement of the year.

"We've had a good run, right? You know that," O'Neill said. "The past few months especially. There's been the pipe bomb at the police station down near Portadown. Got that one and stopped it. There was the Semtex down in Lisburn. We got that. All from good intel and all from GRANITE."

"Yeah, but we've missed a few, too," Beattie said. "And the

people who've been nicked are all low level—none of the top guys. We need to pull in the brigade chiefs, not the small-fry volunteers and the message boys."

He jerked with his thumb toward a large handwritten chart stuck to the wall behind him, showing the hierarchy in the south Armagh brigade. There were several gaps, partly because of changes in personnel but also partly because it was notoriously difficult to get information from members of a traditionally tight-knit organization, even including those who had been jailed.

O'Neill paused and twisted around in his chair. "It'll come, it'll come. The one I'd like to nail is the OC. There's been the odd chance, but . . ."

"But what?" Beattie demanded.

"Well, it's the same problem we've always had and always will have," O'Neill said. "We can't put our agents in jeopardy, otherwise we're finished. Nobody will talk to us. We've always agreed that's the last thing we'd do." He could almost feel the guilt creeping across his face like a rash.

Beattie stared at him. "What *do* you mean? You're trying to tell me you did know something?" He walked over to within a couple of feet of O'Neill, bent down, and put his head close.

"It was GRANITE, wasn't it?" Beattie demanded. "You had something about a hit on Simonson. Was it from him?"

"Look, there was nothing about Simonson, nothing. Believe me," O'Neill said. "But three days ago I did have a vague word from him about some arms being moved over the border. The thing was, GRANITE would be three feet under by now if we'd done anything. It was kept very tight. Four of them knew, apparently: him, the OC, the quartermaster, and the IO. It'd have been obvious who had leaked it. I think he was the driver."

"A vague word? Shit, man." Beattie signed heavily and put his hands on his hips.

O'Neill stared at the ceiling. "Oh, bollocks, this job's impossible. It's like playing God. Who lives or dies."

It had always been hard to know exactly how much risk informants were at from their IRA colleagues when passing on intelligence to police, given the lack of subsequent control over what police might do with it. A heavy-handed approach to stopping an IRA operation might easily see the agent end up the victim of a reprisal killing instead.

Sometimes it was easier and safer not to say anything, despite clear and strict guidelines from senior leaders in both organizations that intelligence and information should be shared between MI5 and police—in both directions.

The issue had always existed but had become more complicated in 2007, when MI5 took over responsibility for agent handling from the police.

O'Neill often imagined the police weren't that sorry to lose their intelligence-gathering function. It was a tough job. The IRA operational structure, with small cells of maybe four or five people who were given information on only a need-to-know basis, was designed to prevent touts leaking details and blowing operations. It worked, mostly. And when intelligence did come through, O'Neill often felt it placed him in the nightmarish situation of taking responsibility for either the target's life on one hand or his agent's on the other.

Beattie walked around the table. "We can't say anything, not on this one. They'll kill us. Seriously."

"Well, yeah. Both sides would," O'Neill said.

"Did you put anything in GRANITE's file on this?"

"Obviously not."

Beattie breathed a sigh of relief. "Okay, we keep it quiet. We point to the intelligence we've passed over in recent months that has saved lives and leave it at that."

A knock came at the door and the deputy director walked in. "Phil, sorry to interrupt, but the director needs to speak to you urgently," he said, looking alternately at Beattie and then O'Neill. "He's got a conference call with Downing Street in twenty minutes. The prime minister's going to be on the call, and the home secretary. He needs a briefing—says they're going nuts over in London. Nobody can understand how this could have happened without some sort of heads-up on it. Sounds like the PM's going to have to make a statement in Parliament sometime soon. The director's shitting himself, thinks his head's on the block."

Beattie swore loudly. "Okay, tell him I'm coming."

It was never a good move to irritate Jeff Riordan, who headed MI5's operation in Northern Ireland.

"Also, I've had a call from Norman Arnside," the deputy director said. "He wants to speak to you."

"Okay, tell him I'll call him back after I've finished with the director," Beattie said.

Once the man had gone, he turned to O'Neill. "We need to talk to GRANITE. Both of us. And we need to sort this out. I'm really minded to drop him right in it over this one. We can't be seen as soft. We've got to send a message out to the rest of 'em: these touts can't have their cake and eat it."

CHAPTER FIVE

Friday, January 4, 2013
Belfast

Johnson came out of the newsstand, stuffed a fresh pack of Marlboros into his coat pocket, and continued along the busy Falls Road until he came to St. Paul's Catholic Church on the corner.

There he turned right onto Cavendish Street, all neatly terraced houses with tiny front gardens bordered with low brick walls.

There were a couple of large republican murals painted on the end walls of some terraced homes, and Irish flags were draped in several upstairs windows.

Johnson stopped, looked around, and tried to imagine the scenes in the 1970s, when the British army, with its riot shields and CS gas, ended up in long-running gun battles with IRA paramilitaries in the streets around that area.

Now the only evidence of scuffling was a couple of

teenage boys pushing each other and fighting over possession of a mountain bike.

A couple of women pushing strollers made their way toward Falls Road, lined with shops and busy with the flow of cars, buses, and taxis.

Johnson walked on, checking the house numbers as he went, until he found the one he was looking for. He continued straight past and turned the corner, where he found a bench to sit on.

He mentally rehearsed his planned doorstep strategy one more time. He also took the opportunity to double-check that he wasn't being followed.

Despite being tired by the long journey from his home in Portland, he'd struggled to fall asleep in Michael Donovan's apartment. It was two o'clock before he finally overcame the effects of jet lag and tuned out the periodic bouts of singing outside in the street, and a stream of busy thoughts.

Johnson took out the Marlboros, ripped off the wrapping, and lit one. The nicotine flowed through his veins and perked him up.

The job that Donovan wanted him to do still seemed to be more of a police investigation, not something in which he could really use his experience to add value. Or was he just trying to talk himself out of it?

At heart, Johnson was a flag-waving American. Although he liked international assignments and was thoroughly committed to achieving justice and righting wrongs, he lost a little of his enthusiasm if there were no links to his homeland.

His sister, Amy Wilde, was looking after his teenage children, Carrie and Peter, as well as Cocoa, the family dog, while he was away. She often said jokingly that he was a glory hunter. Maybe there was a grain of truth in what she said. He did, admittedly, enjoy basking in the US media coverage when he pulled off a successful investigation with an American angle that won him headlines and plaudits at home.

Maybe that was the problem here, he mused.

He finished the cigarette, ground out the stub on the pavement, and stood up. *Enough thinking, time for action.*

Johnson strolled back toward the front door of the house he had pinpointed earlier, pushed open the gate, which had decorative wrought iron work, and rang the doorbell.

A man wearing a cloth cap, who was raking dead leaves in the postage stamp–size front garden next door on the left, straightened up and stared.

The door in front of Johnson opened, and a woman in her thirties peered out. A crying toddler clung to her right knee, and a dog barked somewhere inside the house.

"Hello, don't know if you can help," Johnson said. "It's a bit of a long shot. I'm over here from America on holiday—my family used to live down the other end of this street before I was born, and my mother often talked about the Duggans, who she said used to live next door to you here." Johnson gestured to his right. "Do you know what happened to them?"

The woman looked at Johnson. "No idea. Only lived here for a couple of years. Sorry." She shook her head.

"Okay," Johnson said. "No problem. Is there anyone else nearby, other neighbors, who have spoken of them or might know them?"

The dog inside the house yelped, then barked, and the toddler's wailing stepped up a few decibels.

"No, sorry," she said and shut the door.

Johnson pulled the gate open again and walked out onto the sidewalk. He had gone about ten yards back up the road when he heard her calling after him. "Mister, you should try Ryan, the old man, lives on the other side. He's been here for decades."

Johnson turned around and smiled at her. "Thanks. I'll do that."

He retraced his steps, nodded at the man in the cloth cap, who was still staring at him, and went up to the brown door with peeling paint on the other side of the Duggan family's old house. There were two windows upstairs, while downstairs there was a bay window and the front door.

An old man with white hair and hunched shoulders answered the door. His feet pointed out at forty-five degrees and a small terrier hovered quietly behind him.

Johnson introduced himself as Philip Wilkinson, which was one of the two aliases he adopted when required, the other being Don Thiele. Both legends encompassed completely false and thoroughly backstopped identities, including US passports, credit cards, bank cards, driver's licenses and birth certificates. He even had fake LinkedIn and Facebook accounts. Everything checked out.

All the papers and cards were linked to the addresses of two different uninhabited houses in the middle of rural New Hampshire. The whole arrangement had been made through a contact who was a former police officer. As long as Johnson paid off the credit card bills and the bank accounts stayed in the black, he never encountered a problem.

His preferred option was the Wilkinson legend—that of a single man with no dependents who was a sales representative for an American industrial pumps business. Thiele was a reserve. However, this was the first time he had used Wilkinson operationally since his search for an old Nazi in 2011.

Johnson carefully shook the slightly trembling hand that was held out toward him.

"Ryan's the name. Ryan Worrall," the man said.

Johnson ran through his carefully crafted explanation for the second time.

"The Duggans? You've come all this way looking for the Duggans? From America?" Ryan croaked.

"Er, yes, guess so."

"They're long gone from around here, long gone. Years and years ago. Probably in the '70s. Come in, it's freezing out. I can't stand here and pay to heat the street."

Ryan stepped back and held his door open. Out of the corner of his eye, Johnson could see the man in the cloth cap still looking. He stepped through the door and Ryan closed it.

"I'll make you a cup of tea, seeing as you've come all this way. Come through here."

Ryan led the way through to his kitchen, which seemed to Johnson like a museum piece. The electric cooker had coiled ring elements, the fridge was yellowed and rusty, and the glass fronts on three of the four overhead cupboards were missing. The kitchen countertop, made of some kind of laminated chipboard, was swollen and cracked where water had seeped into it.

But Ryan's stainless steel kettle worked, and within a few minutes, he pressed a mug of tea into Johnson's hand.

"Philip Wilkinson, did you say? Which number did your family live at?" Ryan asked.

"It was 120 something, down the other end. Or was it 130? My mother did tell me, but I've forgotten exactly. Stupid. I wrote it down, then forgot to bring the piece of paper."

"But you remembered the Duggans' old number?" Ryan said. He put his tea on the table and glanced at Johnson over the top of his metal-rimmed spectacles.

"Yes, I did, somehow. So the Duggans moved away. You lost touch with them?"

"Yes, I lost touch." He ran through the family members. There was Alfie, a quiet man but a hotshot with a rifle, who'd ended up in Long Kesh, and his wife, Megan. Then there was the son, Dessie, who'd been just a youngster when they moved.

"Is there any word on what happened to them?" Johnson asked.

"Any word? Yes, last year I spoke to an old friend in the pub up on the Falls Road who knew the Duggans. He said he'd heard from another friend that Dessie had a daughter, called Moira. Actually, she might have been his stepdaughter. Anyway, she was training to be a nurse at Queen's."

"Queen's?" Johnson asked.

"Yes, the university. Sorry, that's all I know. That was the only thing I've heard about them in years." Ryan finished his tea and put his mug down.

"Well, if I can't find Dessie, then maybe I could try and find her," Johnson said.

"Give it a try, give it a try. Send my wishes if you ever find them. Tell them old Ryan Worrall says hello, down on Cavendish Street."

Johnson nodded. He would do that, he promised, and thanked Ryan.

On the way out five minutes later, Johnson walked past the man in the cloth cap, who was sitting on his garden wall, a cigarette in his mouth. He was holding up his cell phone and tapping away at the screen as Johnson walked by.

* * *

Friday, January 4, 2013
  Belfast

Half an hour after the American left, Ryan Worrall made himself another cup of tea, gave his dog a biscuit, and sat at his kitchen table to read his copy of the *Belfast Telegraph*.

The doorbell rang.

Ryan was surprised to see his near neighbor, Donal Wilson, standing on the doorstep. The two men spoke only rarely.

Wilson peered at Ryan from beneath his cloth cap. "I'm sorry to bother you and all that, but I heard that American guy's story. Looking for the Duggans, right?"

"Yep. He was. His family used to live down this road, years back. He wanted to know about the Duggans, where he might find Dessie, and Dessie's daughter, or might be his stepdaughter."

"You know who the Duggans are, don't you? Don't you think we should report him?"

Ryan felt a little confused. "Report him? What for, and to whom?"

"Are you completely out of touch, Ryan? Report him to the brigade, who d'you think? To intelligence. If he's looking for Duggan, then I think they need to know. Might just be coincidence, but then again it might not be."

"Sorry, I don't follow you," Ryan said. "I would have done twenty years ago but—"

Wilson opened his mouth and looked as if he was about to launch into an explanation, but then he checked himself.

"Okay, don't worry about it," Wilson said. "I'll do it. I know who to call. What was the American's name?"

"I think he said Wilkinson. I can't remember what his first name was. Oh, I think Philip," Ryan said. He looked at his neighbor. "Old habits, eh?"

Wilson nodded and raised his hand in acknowledgment. "Yep, old habits." Then he turned and walked back to his house.

* * *

Friday, January 4, 2013
   Boston

The view across Boston Harbor from the top floor of the office block attached to the Shipright Global Logistics warehouse usually inspired Patrick McKinney. He could see right across the main channel to the stretch of blue-gray water beyond, with planes landing and taking off from Logan International Airport.

Beyond that were Spectacle Island, Long Island, and out in the distance, the Atlantic Ocean.

But most importantly, he could see the container shipping terminal. From there, the ubiquitous rectangular steel boxes holding his cargo, his sales, were dispatched to destinations all over North and South America, Europe, and the Far East.

Today, though, he had already gone through almost half a pack of his favorite Camels, and it was only eleven o'clock in the morning. That was roughly triple his normal rate of consumption. Each cigarette involved a walk down to the ground floor and a lap around the warehouse. And it was cold outside.

Cigarettes were big business. Each forty-foot container held about a thousand cases of smokes. And in each case there were fifty cartons, each holding ten packs of twenty cigarettes. Therefore, half a million packs, or ten million cigarettes, would normally be crammed into each container.

The warehouse that Shipright operated in Boston's Seaport District loaded and dispatched many such containers each day. All of them were filled with cigarettes from SRS Tobacco, the global manufacturer that had an exclusive distribution arrangement with Shipright.

And it was McKinney's job, as sales director, to find the

customers, keep them happy, and ensure that his company's revenues remained on an upward trend each year.

Achieving that, at a time when tobacco consumption in many developed countries was falling due to steep increases in taxes imposed by federal and state governments—not least in the US—was difficult. The huge burden on health care budgets from tobacco-related diseases and the need to try and cut consumption was the driving force behind those increases.

It meant that many tobacco manufacturers and distributors had to become increasingly inventive and innovative in finding new ways to boost their sales.

And McKinney, a tall, fifty-two-year-old Irishman with the gift of the gab, considered himself to be nothing if not inventive.

Now he was anxiously awaiting an email to confirm the delivery of one particular order. Hence the heavy smoking.

He returned to his seat, hunched his slightly rounded shoulders even further, glanced across the harbor and then back to his computer screen. Was it there yet? He clicked away from a spreadsheet that detailed the contents of shipments to and from Boston and went back to his email inbox. He refreshed the screen, but still there was nothing.

A week earlier, he had dispatched eight container loads of cigarettes, seven to destinations in the US, Spain, Canada, Singapore, and Brazil.

The recipients would move their purchases on to warehouses, supermarkets, shops, and other outlets, ready for sale.

The eighth container had gone to a customer based at a warehouse in the Colón Free Trade Zone, at the Atlantic, or northern, entrance to the Panama Canal in Central America.

It was a duty-free zone, which meant there were no import customs duties to pay, either for McKinney's company or for the customer, a business called Panama Tobacco Distribution.

McKinney ran his fingers through his receding, mainly gray hair and checked the schedule. Once it had left Boston, the container ship normally took seven days to arrive in Colón. It should be there by now.

Once there, the ship would be unloaded and the container of cigarettes taken to Panama Tobacco Distribution's small warehouse, a nondescript gray steel structure, one of hundreds like it in the sprawling free trade zone area.

He sipped a cup of coffee and pictured the scene. It wasn't difficult, as he had been there several times, most recently just six months earlier.

Right next to the Panama Tobacco Distribution unit was a similar warehouse belonging to a timber company, Pan-American Timber Products, which bought and sold hard and soft wooden beams, gateposts, fencing posts, panels, and other similar items for export, mainly to the US, the UK, and Continental Europe.

There were no obvious synergies between the two companies.

But they were owned by one man, also Irish, called James Caffrey. McKinney knew him from his junior school days in Forkhill, south Armagh. Along with Dessie Duggan, they had been the three live wires among a serious bunch of children.

Since then, they had all steered a course through life that had never been easy.

Indeed, McKinney had only felt safe to abandon his long-standing alias and resume using his real name in recent years, long after the 1998 Good Friday agreement. The subsequent amnesty for paramilitary republican prisoners meant there was no longer any danger of him being extradited to Northern Ireland and sent back to jail. But he never felt tempted to return—America was now home.

McKinney sat on the board of Caffrey's company as a non-executive director and often visited its sales warehouse in Boston.

He decided he couldn't wait any longer for the confirmatory email. He picked up his phone and called James instead. It was answered almost immediately.

"Paddy, you sly old dog."

McKinney laughed, running a finger down the scar on the side of his face. "I thought you'd gone off to the pub and forgotten me. I've been sitting here like an idiot waiting for the email. What's happening . . . has it arrived yet?"

"Yeah, ship came in a couple of hours ago. We're expecting the container soonish. Sorry, haven't had time to send you the email. I've only just got back to my desk."

"Okay, nice one. I'm on my way to the airport shortly, so I'll see you this evening."

It was part of the routine. Every time he sold a container load to PTD, McKinney would book himself on a plane down to Colón's Enrique Adolfo Jiménez Airport, via Panama City, at his employer's expense.

I just need to keep the customer happy, he'd tell his chief executive; he's a big buyer, I'll take him out for dinner, sweet-talk him—you know the routine. And because Patrick delivered the goods, it would never be a problem.

He might even combine the trip with a visit to meet a couple of genuine trade contacts who ran a cigarette import agency that operated in a number of South American countries.

It usually involved a night or two in a hotel and a flight back a day or two later.

He finished the call with Caffrey, turned off his computer, and put on his coat.

It would be hot down in Panama, a jarring change from the freezing early January temperatures in Boston.

That was another good reason to get out of town.

But while he was there, McKinney knew that, as always, he would be working damn hard.

And it wouldn't be for the benefit of Shipright Global Logistics.

CHAPTER SIX

Friday, January 4, 2013
Belfast

"Moira? Actually, we don't give out personal information about our students, no. I'm sorry." The woman sitting at the second-floor reception desk of Queen's University Belfast's Medical Biology Centre scrutinized Johnson from above her rimless spectacles.

He tried to withhold his almost instinctive sigh. "I'm not asking for personal information. I'm just wondering where I might find—"

"I said no," she said. The stare was one of finality. She folded her arms.

"Okay, no problem," he said and turned to leave.

He went around the corner, but instead of exiting the building, Johnson cut through some double doors and down a corridor past a large sign that read Lecture Theatre.

After descending two flights of stairs to the ground floor, he found himself in a large, brightly lit student lounge area.

At the far end of the room, at least one hundred students, most of them holding wine glasses, were gathered, facing toward two much older men and one woman. One of the men was giving what looked like an impromptu speech. The crowd frequently burst into laughter.

Johnson quickly realized it was a farewell party for one of the lecturers.

A girl carrying a tray of wine glasses stepped toward him and offered one. He accepted and made his way to the back of the group. This looked more promising. Maybe Moira was here.

"The future of nursing in Northern Ireland will be in good hands, if you lot are anything to go by," the man said. "And on a more serious note, judging by what happened yesterday down in Crossmaglen and events elsewhere, you'll all be in high demand."

He paused. "But I can tell you I've had a great twenty-five years here at Queen's, despite the political ups and downs and the turbulence going on around us. I hope you enjoy what time you have left as students, and who knows, maybe one or two of you will stay on and become lecturers yourselves. I'd like to thank all of you. Now, there's free wine to be had and some snacks at the tables. Go carry on drinking, eat, enjoy, chat some more, and I'll catch up with you all over the next couple of hours. We'll be here until seven."

There was a loud round of applause.

The crowd broke up. Most headed straight for the two tables at one side of the room, one with filled wine glasses and the other with a selection of canapés.

It was Friday night, and Johnson assumed that most of the students saw the party as a chance to freeload before setting out for the city's bars and nightclubs.

He worked his way around the room, which was furnished with large red modern sofas and yellow chairs. Feeling conspicuously old among the twentysomethings in the room, he tried occasionally to chat to female students who were not part of larger groups.

His first few attempts to inquire about the possible whereabouts of a Moira, on the pretext of being an old family friend who was meant to be meeting her there, met with blank stares and shakes of the head.

Then, ten minutes later, one of the girls he had previously approached walked up to him with a friend who had a large grin on her face. "Excuse me, she knows a girl called Moira," the girl said, nodding toward her friend.

"Yes, we've only got one Moira here," the friend said. "Moira McKittrick. Is that the one?"

Johnson remembered the old man's lack of certainty over whether the girl was Duggan's daughter or stepdaughter.

"Yes, that's her." He hoped it was.

"Okay, she's not here. She'll be working tonight. She started at five," the other girl said, brushing her long blond hair back over her shoulders. Then she looked at her friend and giggled.

Johnson asked where she worked and whether he could speak to her there.

"If you like seedy bars with even seedier clientele, I could tell you where she works," the girl said. She winked at Johnson and took a long sip from her glass of wine.

Johnson half-smiled. "Well, I'm not particularly seedy, but tell me anyway."

"If you're a family friend . . . er, are you sure you want to go there?"

"It's fine," Johnson said. "I'm not squeamish."

"It's a bar called Akimbo. She serves drinks or works behind the bar. It's basically a strip joint. Just to warn you."

Johnson nodded and asked for directions. It was on Union Street, a twenty-five-minute walk through the city center, the girl thought. "Good luck—with Moira, I mean, not with the walk," she added as she turned and walked away.

Despite a hint of drizzle and darkness that accompanied him as he walked down Lisburn Road toward the city center, Johnson was feeling more upbeat. He pulled up his coat collar, thought momentarily about hailing a cab, then decided to walk and get a feel for the place.

The route took him past an array of shops, offices, restaurants, and bars, and finally the CastleCourt Shopping Centre.

Outside a newsstand, a *Belfast Telegraph* billboard screamed in handwritten thick black felt-tip, "Sniper Fears after Top Cop Killed."

A hundred yards farther on, another one, this time for the *Irish Times*, read, "Police Step Up Chief Constable Death Inquiry."

Johnson walked on. The investigation teams must be all over it—police, MI5, probably MI6, even the army, all chipping in. Like an ants nest under an upturned stone. He struggled to see what value he was going to add.

Union Street was a distinctly seedy-looking narrow road that smelled of lamb kebabs, engine oil, stale beer, and cannabis smoke. It had a tattoo parlor, an intricate array of graffiti on the closed steel shutters across shop windows, a couple of derelict buildings, and then a coffee bar and the Sunflower pub, which had a green steel wire security cage outside the front door. Johnson assumed the cage was a legacy of the Troubles.

"No topless bathing, Ulster has suffered enough," read a large sign on the pub's outside wall.

Halfway up the street, on the right, Johnson finally spotted the modest illuminated purple and black sign. Akimbo, it said, printed in a sprawling handwritten font. A logo, featuring the silhouette of a dancing girl with her right leg kicking high up to shoulder level, appeared at both ends of the sign.

Below the sign, a black-painted double door, which was open, led down some steps from street level.

Two fleshy bouncers, arms folded and dressed in black jackets, white shirts, and bow ties, watched Johnson as he approached but didn't speak or smile as he walked between them and descended the stairs.

The throb, throb, throb of electronic dance music rose from the basement to meet Johnson as he went down.

He recognized the track that was playing, by some band whose name he couldn't remember, because Carrie had played it incessantly, full blast, in her bedroom the previous year for two months solid. Then, thankfully, she had moved on to something else.

Already he was feeling out of place, and he hadn't even gotten through the door. The strobing lights—green, yellow, red, blue—came up the stairwell with the music to meet him.

On the wall an Irish flag hung proud, next to a slogan embroidered into some cloth. United Ireland, Never Surrender, it read.

What am I getting into here?

By the time he'd reached the bottom of the stairs the music was drilling deep into his skull.

A girl with short blond hair wearing a tight white sleeveless dress opened the door to the bar for him, and then he was inside.

The colored lights splattered from revolving mirrored balls across a black dance floor. It was busy. Groups of men, some suited, some in jeans and T-shirts, drank around tables or sat on huge leather sofas.

Girls dressed to match the music—all with clinging, shimmering black, red, or white dresses, with high heels and lipstick—hovered around the bar and the sofas. Three of them gyrated slowly on the dance floor.

There were no strippers. Perhaps that happened later in the evening or in another room. Or maybe Moira's friend at the university had exaggerated.

Johnson wandered up to the bar, which was all shining chrome and black granite. Behind it a young man in a bow tie and a white shirt stood to attention and raised his eyebrows. "Evening, sir. What can I get you?"

Johnson could hardly hear him above the music. He hesitated. "A beer, please. Make it a Stella."

The man turned, extricated a bottle from a fridge behind him, and theatrically poured it into a glass. That would be five pounds and ninety-nine pence, he informed Johnson.

Johnson handed him a ten pound note. "I'm looking for someone," he shouted. "You know Moira? She works here."

"Moira? Did you say Moira?"

Johnson nodded.

The man handed Johnson some change, then turned and looked around the bar. He walked to the other end, dodging past colleagues who were pouring beers and mixing cocktails, and surveyed the other side, which was out of Johnson's sight.

He beckoned Johnson, who navigated around a kissing couple and moved to the corner of the L-shaped bar. The man pointed. "There," he mouthed.

A slim, statuesque woman, clad in a sparkly black cocktail dress that stretched at most halfway down her long thighs, was making her way toward a sofa in the corner, a tray of drinks in her hands.

Her jet-black hair, which was tied back in a ribbon behind her head, fell neatly three-quarters of the way down her back. Dark, almost black lipstick and thick mascara stood out against her white skin and high, sculpted cheekbones.

Johnson inhaled sharply and paused. Where to catch her?

He moved toward a hatch at the far end of the bar, where the drinks girls were collecting orders.

The music now seemed louder, the lyrics more grating.

Johnson sipped his beer. She was coming back. She was young. Twenty? Twenty-one? And she must be five feet ten inches tall, at least.

She didn't look at him but put her tray down on the bar and stood there, waiting.

"Excuse me . . . Moira?" he asked after a few moments.

She turned her head. "Yes?" She was almost inaudible.

He paused. Before coming in, he had decided not to give his Wilkinson cover name, given that he badly needed to forge some sort of link with this girl. Now he had momentary second thoughts but dismissed them.

"I'm Joe Johnson. Sorry, could I—"

"I just serve the drinks here, I don't—" She stopped, then coughed, a thick rasping, phlegm-filled cough.

"No. I know. I just wanted to have a chat. About your father. It's Dessie, yes?"

Moira jerked back and stood upright, unsmiling. "No, he's not my father. My stepfather, you mean. What's he done? Who are you?"

Always the difficult part. "I don't know if he's done anything, has he? But I was trying to find him."

"You police?"

"No, not police. Private work. I'm an investigator, though." His gut instinct was to be honest with her.

A barman began loading up her tray with more drinks behind her.

She stared at him, her dark eyes steady. "I can't talk. Not about my stepfather. Okay?" She spoke in a low-pitched Irish burr.

Johnson pursed his lips. "It'd be all confidential, nothing official. Nothing to worry about. You don't know me from Adam, I'm aware of that. But I can promise you—"

"No." She exhaled and shook her head.

Johnson nodded. "All right. Here, take my number. If you change your mind, just send me a text. But I'm due to fly out of here Saturday evening, so you don't have long."

He took out his wallet and removed a business card, which carried his contact details and a quote in smaller print from Martin Luther King Jr. The quote read, "Our lives begin to end the day we become silent about things that matter."

She scrutinized it but said nothing. Then she picked up the tray and walked off.

Johnson suddenly realized there had been no word from Donovan. Not a call, not a text. He reconciled himself to dining alone. He continued to sip his beer and perched himself on a barstool when one became free.

The place was humming, the dance floor was livening up, and the sign said that the bar was open until two in the morning. Moira was facing a busy night.

Another track started. Johnson knew this one, "Wild Ones," by Flo Rida. It was another of Carrie's favorites.

Moira came back several times to collect trays of drinks, but not once did she glance in his direction.

After half an hour, Johnson decided he'd given Moira enough time. He drained his glass and looked one last time at a skimpily dressed blond girl who was twirling increasingly manically around a pole on the dance floor, leaving little to the imagination. Maybe she was the stripper? Or maybe not.

He headed toward the door. What was the point?

* * *

Friday, January 4, 2013
  Belfast

. . .

Although it was only about half a mile from his own place, it had been ten years since Donal Wilson had been to the house on Waterford Street, opposite Dunville Park in the Lower Falls area.

He walked past the green facade and black shutters of Boyle's Bar on the corner, where he stopped momentarily, wondering whether he should bother, especially this late into the evening. But then he continued down to the terraced house at the bottom of the road.

Wilson went back a long way with the intelligence officer for the Belfast brigade's second battalion, Wes Monaghan. In fact, right back to the gun battles of 1970, when thousands of British soldiers poured into the area and imposed a curfew.

They still met up from time to time to reminisce but only ever for a beer at Boyle's, or sometimes over a coffee at St. Paul's after mass.

So Monaghan did a good-humored, slightly mocking double take when he saw Wilson on the doorstep.

A thickly built man with a beard that was more salt than pepper now that he was into his sixties, he had, like many in the area, never come to terms with the Good Friday peace agreement.

"I'll make you a cuppa, we can have another chew over the sellout," he told Wilson as he let him in.

Those who supported Gerry Adams and his cronies mocked Monaghan these days and told him he was past his sell-by date.

But no, he saw his role as critical, he often told Wilson, given that so many Real IRA initiatives were being stymied by leaks, by touts who thought themselves loyal to Sinn Féin's political processes and solutions. There were too many dissidents ending up in Maghaberry jail because of it.

"So what can I do for you?" Wes asked as he poured boiling water into his teapot. He glanced at his watch. "It's late. So I'm assuming you haven't just popped in for old times' sake, have you?"

Wilson fiddled with his cloth cap, which he'd placed on the kitchen table. "True, there is something I need to discuss."

Monaghan sat up straight when Wilson mentioned Dessie Duggan, and detailed how an American, Philip Wilkinson, had been looking for him and his stepdaughter, Moira.

"It might be nothing," Wilson said. "It might be true that this Wilkinson guy is just trying to dig up an old connection from his family's Irish roots. But it seems a bit odd."

Okay, Monaghan said, he'd pass on the information and make sure it got to the south Armagh brigade. He knew the IO down there, Liam McGarahan. No problem.

"Did you get a good description of Wilkinson?" Monaghan asked as he passed over a steaming mug of tea.

"Ah, yes, I can do better than a description. I took a photo of him on my phone as he walked out. Just had a gut feeling, so I snapped him," Wilson said.

CHAPTER SEVEN

Saturday, January 5, 2013
  Forkhill

It was never a simple process to speak to Patrick McKinney. But then Duggan was a cautious man, a loner who deliberately made it complicated. That was why he'd survived unscathed and uncaptured for so long, in his view.

He was a cleanskin, to use the Ulster slang for someone who didn't have a criminal record. Unbelievably lucky, some people called it. Duggan thought that the more careful he was, the luckier he got.

And that caution was why his old schoolmate McKinney had remained free too, as he often reminded his fugitive friend.

Every time they spoke, he made McKinney call him from a burner pay-as-you-go cell phone. And he always had to take the call at a different location. A friend's house, somebody's empty office, a farm, even occasionally a pay phone.

He didn't know if the police were tapping phones or not.

It certainly wasn't like the old days, but he assumed they probably were. Better to err on the side of caution. They couldn't tap every phone in south Armagh. That was his theory.

So he'd sent an encrypted WhatsApp text message containing the number that McKinney should call. Now he was waiting for the phone to ring.

Today Duggan was sitting in a corner of a drafty, freezing barn belonging to one of his volunteers, Pete Field, the brigade machine gunner who had been responsible for forcing the chief constable's helicopter into an emergency landing. Field's farm was on the edge of Forkhill village, just two miles north of Duggan's home, which sat literally on the borderline with the Irish Republic.

The phone he was sitting next to was an old one, with a curly coiled cable that connected the handset to the main body, and stood on a rickety oak desk that was covered with water stains and dust.

Out of the filthy, cobweb-covered barn window, across the wintery fields, he could see the hulking dark gray mass of Slieve Gullion towering over the countryside in the distance.

Then it sounded with a bell-like double ring that reminded Duggan of phones when he was a kid.

After the usual preliminary banter, McKinney got down to business.

"You'll be pleased to know we're sorted with the shipment," he said in his deep and slightly intimidating south Armagh burr. Even to Duggan's ear, it had been only slightly diluted by his years in the United States.

"You're in Cólon now?"

"Yeah, with James here. I flew in last night. We're packing the container, and it should be out of here tomorrow, heading your way. Should be into Dublin Thursday the twenty-fourth.

It'll be a combination of half smokes, half timber beams to hide them."

"That's good," Duggan said. "We're running short of cash, so that should keep number cruncher O'Driscoll happy." He paused. "But there's something I need to ask, big man."

"Go on," McKinney said.

"Sorry about the late notice, but I need a few things added to the cargo. Top of the list is a new Barrett. We're down to one here, as you know, and the one I've got sometimes doesn't work properly. I can't afford for that to happen on a big job."

Duggan ran through a short list of other weapons that he needed, including handguns, ammunition, and mortar shells.

There was silence at McKinney's end. "Where the feck d'you think I'm going to get a Barrett from here? I'm in Cólon, remember? Can't it wait until the next shipment? And what do you need it for, anyway?"

"No, it can't wait. There might be a chance to do something big coming up. I can't discuss it on the phone. So I need a new one—this one might need to go in for a repair."

"Something big. Bigger than the chief constable?"

There was silence for several seconds. "I'm not saying anything on the phone, Patrick. Not even to you."

Another silence.

"Okay," said Patrick eventually. "It's probably going to mean a delay getting the container to you, then. I'll talk to James, but I think I'll have to reroute it through Boston. I can try and get what you need there. It'll be easier. And I'm not promising anything, either. It's not just locating the rifle, which will be tough enough, it's about shipping it safely. We'll have to hide the hardware in the timber beams."

"Obviously, but you've done it before."

Duggan's cell phone rang in his pocket. He pulled it out and looked at the screen.

"Patrick, I need to go. I've got the IO calling on the mobile here. See what you can do. Keep in touch. Let me know."

He put the handset down and answered the incoming cell phone call.

"Liam," he said, not giving the caller a chance to speak. "I've just been on the phone to Patrick. He's in Cólon. I've given him the instructions," Duggan said. "The good news is he's already got a shipment ready. Now he just needs to get the hardware to add to it."

"That's good to hear," McGarahan said. "But there's something you need to know about. Might be nothing, but I had a message this morning, first thing, from the IO up in Belfast."

"You mean Wes?" Duggan asked.

"Yeah, Wes. Says there was someone looking for you down near your old place, Cavendish Street. And asking where your daughter was, too."

"Who? What's that all about?" Duggan demanded.

"An American guy apparently knocked on the neighbor's door just down from one of our guys and said his family used to live there years back before emigrating to America and knew your family, when you were a kid. He was trying to track you down. Sounds suspicious to me."

"Yeah, that's bullshit—we must have left that road when I was only nine or ten. I can't see anyone popping up out of the blue from the States like that, suddenly deciding they want a catch-up. I don't even remember anyone going to the States. No way. And asking about Moira as well?"

"Yeah, apparently."

"Is he police? Intelligence?"

"No idea yet. I need to find out."

Duggan paused, thinking quickly. He wasn't surprised at what he had just been told. It had long been a concern that his stepdaughter might at some point say something

damaging to the wrong person. They had a fractious relationship.

"Okay, Liam," Duggan said. "Whoever he is, I want you to
arrange to sort him out, head him off. Do we have a name?"

"Philip Wilkinson."

"Right. Well, you and Wes between you find out who he
is, do whatever it takes to put him off," Duggan said. "Moira's
the last person I want anyone talking to, especially at the
moment, with everything going on. I don't have time to waste
on that kind of stuff."

"Right boss. Will do."

"And I'll take care of Moira. Right?"

"Right."

Duggan hung up.

CHAPTER EIGHT

Saturday, January 5, 2013
  South Armagh

Down where the remote south Armagh hillside climbed gently toward the border with the Irish Republic and the rain sheeted at forty-five degrees in the wind, a farm lane led right off the single-lane road, up behind some woodland.

As one of many alternatives to O'Toole's snooker club and some of the safe houses they used as meeting locations, it had its advantages. It was possible to park a car in a place that was invisible from the road and out of sight of any building.

But GRANITE knew that in the remoteness lay other dangers. In this lightly populated area of countryside, there were dissident Republicans who knew every unmarked footpath, every farm track, and every copse.

It was hard enough to move around anonymously amid the crowds of Belfast. Here, out in the wild, it was just as risky but in a different kind of way.

One sighting by the wrong person that linked him with

the MI5 man Brendan O'Neill, and GRANITE would be hauled in for a meeting with the OC, the IO, and others.

There was a zero tolerance policy toward touts. There would be a beating, a kicking. Eventually a hood would probably go over the head. There would be an order to confess to a camera or a microphone.

Then bullets might go through the elbows or the ankles or both. Or, if he was unlucky, through the temple.

The chances of being pinpointed these days were much higher than in the leaky old days of the '70s, when everybody in the Provisionals knew everyone else and their business and information was exchanged far more freely. Now new recruits might be lucky to know any more than seven or eight others. There were small cells of people, and information flowed on a need-to-know basis. It was almost corporate in its approach.

GRANITE sat and waited. The gunmetal-gray clouds scudded low over the hillside, the rain streamed down the windshield, and the wind whistled through some tiny gap in the window seals of his car.

Although it was half past ten in the morning, GRANITE found it difficult to read his *Belfast Telegraph* in the gloom. Or was it that he just had difficulty concentrating this particular morning?

Why do I do this?

It was a good question. The answer lay in the three years with no regular employment. Since the economic crisis struck in 2008 and the Northern Ireland property market nose-dived, demand for electricians had vaporized.

But his family still had to eat, and he still had to pay the mortgage he'd taken out in the boom times of 2006.

More than one thousand pounds a month, paid straight into a special bank account, made a huge difference.

Fear had driven him to do what he did, and now it was

fear that made him want out. Getting out, though, was proving a lot harder than getting in.

Finally, half an hour late, a dark blue Ford Mondeo station wagon nosed around the edge of the trees. It pulled up next to his car, and a familiar figure got out and climbed into GRANITE's passenger seat.

O'Neill usually smiled. Today his mouth was fixed in a thin, grim line. "We need to talk."

Out of the corner of his eye, GRANITE saw another dark figure in a raincoat emerge from the Mondeo and move fast across to the rear door of his Astra. The door opened and the man slid in.

"This is Phil Beattie, my boss. I've mentioned him before," O'Neill said. "He wanted to meet you."

GRANITE turned around. "Two of you. What's going on?"

"So, why didn't you bloody tell us, you stupid asshole?" O'Neill began. "Vague bloody talk of guns crossing the border, can't talk because you're driving, bollocks. Then the chief bloody constable gets taken out. Bloody hell."

"I didn't know it was going to be him. I—"

"Balls," O'Neill said. "You're talking balls. How can we trust you anymore?" He pushed his chest out, eyes wide.

"Pity we have to meet like this," Beattie said from the back in a slow, level voice. "But you work for us, you get paid by us, and we keep you alive. That's in return for you telling us what's going on. You obviously forgot that part."

The car windows were already misting up with the warmth and wetness of O'Neill's and Beattie's breathing in the cold air.

"Listen," O'Neill said. "You must think I'm soft or something. But if that happens again, your OC and your IO will get anonymous notes telling them you're a bloody tout. Don't worry, there'll be a bit of proof, not much but enough. They'll carry out an inquiry. You'll get the bag over the head. Your wife'll become a widow and your kids will be fatherless. Touts still don't go down well in south Armagh, do they? Nothing's changed on that front, has it?"

GRANITE clenched his fists and clamped them tight against the sides of his thighs. "You bastards. Feck you. You know nothing. You don't know what it's like, with your soft government jobs and fancy pensions. I run the risk of dying every day for you. Every bloody day. That's what it feels like. I want to get out. I've had enough of this."

Beattie shook his head. "Not possible right now. We're the ones who tell you when you can get out, when it's finished."

O'Neill cut in. "We need you to start performing much better for us. Singing like a diva. Understand? We're paying you well, and we've put a lot of effort into you. But we only protect you if you're of value to us. Otherwise, what's the point? You look after us, we look after you."

"And it won't be just your OC and the IO who get to hear. It'll be the police," Beattie said. "You'd be doing a fair stretch in Maghaberry for what you've done, no problem. That's if your OC doesn't serve sentence on you first."

There was a pause. GRANITE's chin sank down onto his chest.

"Now, what's next?" O'Neill asked. "What's the next operation? I need to know. Has there been any talk of activity around the time of the G8 summit, because that's only three weeks away. We need to know."

GRANITE closed his eyes. "No, nothing," he said.

O'Neill's voice rose in pitch. "So what, then? Come on, it seems to me there's no shortage of action on your side."

After a long pause GRANITE said, "Tomorrow. There'll be a pipe bomb hidden in a moped seat, parked outside

Lurgan police station. Church Place. A volunteer's bringing it from Derry at lunchtime tomorrow."

"Time?" O'Neill said.

"One-thirty."

Now GRANITE was singing. Singing when he didn't want to sing. When all he wanted was to get out. His head felt like it was going to explode.

That'll be another good man gone to jail, come Monday, he thought.

GRANITE felt the pressure hemming him in from all sides—from Duggan and the others in the brigade, from O'Neill. And also from his wife and the bills she ran up.

Now he had to go and face Duggan, who had another job for him to do that afternoon. One that he also wasn't going to tell O'Neill about.

* * *

Saturday, January 5, 2013
  Belfast

Johnson hovered over his open suitcase. He picked up his laptop, took it to the table, and flipped open the lid. He was still undecided about whether to stay or whether to take the flight out of Belfast that was booked for that evening.

There was a typically brief email from his son.

Dad, are you back by Tuesday? I have a school game, state championships. Home v. Bangor. We need support! Love, Peter.

Peter always liked his father to watch his high school basketball games. He brought him luck, he always said, and with reason. Peter, an industrious point guard with increasingly silky passing skills, had won every game Johnson had watched so far that season.

He tapped his pen on the table and sipped from the cup of coffee that he had just made. Now he really didn't know which option to take.

Five minutes later, the text message arrived.

I've decided to chat. Working Akimbo's tonight at 5. Can meet in pub down road. Sunflower, 4.30. Moira.

Half past four. And his flight was due to leave at half past five.

Johnson laughed to himself. *What the hell . . .*

He drained his coffee, went out onto the balcony of Donovan's apartment, pulled out his pack of Marlboros, and lit one.

He sat down on one of the chairs and smoked it slowly, watching the passersby below, the buses rumbling up the road, the buzz of taxis.

Then he sent a reply.

Good. Looking forward to it. See you there. Joe

The response came straight back.

OK. Will help if I can, but have to be careful. Can't afford for my stepfather to find out.

CHAPTER NINE

Saturday, January 5, 2013
  Belfast

Johnson turned the corner past the tattoo parlor onto Union Street. It was dark now, at twenty past four, and the butcher's and thrift shops on the right had their steel shutters pulled down.

His phone beeped. It was a text message from his sister, Amy, telling him everything was well with his two children back home. Her husband, Don, had taken them to the movies and then to lunch at their favorite burger joint. Did he know yet when he was heading back to Portland? No rush, but she needed to plan.

Johnson smiled. Nothing had changed there then. Since they'd been kids, she'd always planned and diarized everything; he never did.

Ever since Johnson's wife, Kathy, had died in 2005, Amy and Don had helped him when necessary by looking after Carrie and Peter. It was a real blessing when he had important extended work trips, such as this one, which lasted some time.

He put the phone back in his pocket, took out his pack of Marlboros, and lit one. He wasn't even sure why he was smoking; he rarely did at home—normally just on work trips away. Maybe it was a comfort of some kind.

There were few street lamps on Union Street, but he could see the lights from the Sunflower's windows reflected in the wetness of the road next to it and the silhouette of the steel security cage at the door.

Johnson leaned against a brick wall and looked toward the bar, past a small parking lot on the left with a steel security fence separating it from the road and the graffiti-covered wall of a tall warehouse building on the right.

On the pavement outside the Sunflower, three people were involved in a scuffle. It looked like a woman and two men.

Johnson's first instinct was to go and look, but then he heard Donovan's voice in his head.

Whatever you do, if you see any fights, scuffles, just walk the other way.

He hung back and waited.

The woman screamed and shouted at the two men, one of whom slapped her hard across the face. She fell to the ground and screamed again.

"You bastard," she shouted and sat up on the tarmac. "I'll bloody kill you, I will. That's it. You're finished."

The taller of the two men shaped to kick her on the ground, and she curled herself up into a fetal position as the impact came, straight into her buttocks. Then she shrieked again.

That was too much for Johnson. His instinct was about to shout at the two men and intervene, but at the last moment he checked himself. Being identified as an American in a dark

Belfast back street by two thugs might not be the smartest move right now, he calculated.

The two men, both wearing black leather jackets, left Moira and turned and walked quickly in Johnson's direction. The one who had done the kicking was tall, angular, and slightly stooped; the other was thicker set with a mustache.

For a moment, Johnson thought they were going to start something, and he braced himself. The shorter man glanced briefly at Johnson as they passed, but they both walked on and disappeared out of sight around the corner.

Johnson stubbed out his cigarette on the pavement and walked toward the woman, who had picked herself up. Now that she was in the light cast from the windows of the Sunflower, Johnson recognized her.

It was Moira.

Her hair had partly escaped the ribbon that held it back, and blood was dribbling from a split in her lip where she had been struck. Her black dress had muddy streaks from where she had landed on the road, and lipstick was smeared across her right cheek.

The contents of her small handbag had spilled all over the road. Lipsticks, a hairbrush, a hair clip, a red ribbon, two credit cards, a few bank notes, and a tin of home-rolled cigarettes, from which the lid had become detached.

She scrambled to stuff her belongings back into her bag.

Johnson reached her just as she tucked the bag under her arm and limped onto the sidewalk.

"Moira, it's Joe. Are you all right? I saw what happened."

She looked at him with a blank expression. Then recognition dawned.

"Oh, no, I'm not all right. Would you be all right if you'd just been beaten up by your bloody stepdad and his thuggish mate?" Her right heel had slipped halfway out of her shoe, and she tugged it back into position.

"Come on, let's go sit down," Johnson said. "You can tidy yourself up. Can you walk?" He indicated toward the pub with his thumb.

Moira looked at the pub. "No, no, definitely not in there." Her voice rose sharply. "He might come back. I can't go to work looking a mess like this—they'd fire me. I'm going to have to text and tell them I'm ill, then go home. Can you help me to my car? It's not far."

Johnson nodded, thinking his chance of speaking to Moira had just gone south. "Sure."

She tapped a message into her phone, then looked up and down the street carefully in both directions before beginning to limp heavily in the opposite direction from Akimbo's. After a few paces she stopped.

"Do you want a hand," Johnson asked. "You're hobbling."

She hesitated. "No, I'm fine . . . actually, yes. My hip's hurting, my back, my foot."

Johnson slipped his left arm around her waist, and she put her arm over his shoulders. He took her weight, her body pressed tight into his, and they continued slowly on. She was almost as tall as he was; her dark hair blew across his face, and he noticed she was wearing a delicate perfume that he vaguely recognized that only partly camouflaged the whiff of tobacco on her.

"Him and his bastard friends, they think they own Northern Ireland," she said.

"IRA, yes?" Johnson asked.

She nodded. "Yeah, but dissidents, living in the past, all of them. Dinosaurs. They think violence is the only way to sort things out. They kill and beat people up, and they get away with it. Most people have moved on from that. The police are useless."

Johnson knew then he had to get Moira to talk while her

outrage still burned hot, before the shutters he'd seen in her eyes the previous day descended again.

"So what was that all about? With your stepdad, I mean?"

Moira stopped briefly and looked at him. "You, I think."

"Me?"

"Yep," she said. "He said he'd heard some American investigator had been sniffing around, trying to find out where he was and where I was, and I was to keep my mouth shut, otherwise he'd seal it for me. I told him to piss off. I talk to whom I want to talk to. That's when he hit me. It's not the first time he's done it, by a long way. Disagree with him, and next thing you know, wham. First time I'd seen the bastard in six months. He hates me, really does."

She winced and rubbed her hip, then looked at Johnson. "But I don't care anymore. He can beat me up all he wants. I'm not going to let him win."

Moira paused. "Can you drive? I'm not sure I can like this."

"Your car, you mean?"

"Yes, back to my place. It's a clapped-out Corsa, piece of crap, but it just about works. I'm gonna tell you a few things."

The Corsa, once a vivid purple, was parked two streets away and was indeed clapped-out. Its bodywork was dented, scratched, and chipped, and inside it reeked of stale cigarette smoke. The floor was covered in mud, chocolate bar wrappers, and empty drinks cans.

Johnson was surprised that a young woman who seemed to take such care over her appearance would own such a messy car.

"I know what you're thinking. I bought it off a friend a couple of months ago," Moira said. "A hundred and ten quid. It was all I could afford. Fifteen years old. Haven't had time to clean it since."

However, the engine started the first time, and she directed him to the end of the road.

"Who are you, actually?" she asked suddenly.

"I'm an investigator, I told you. I specialize in war crimes but not just that. I used to work for the CIA, years back, then became a Nazi hunter for the US government. I run my own business these days."

"What are you doing here in Belfast?"

"I was called in by someone."

"Who?" she asked.

"Sorry, can't say. Someone concerned about the dissidents, the killings, because it's affecting him and his business. He thinks the police are a waste of time. I don't actually know if I'm going to do the job. Just thinking about it." Johnson steered around a sharp corner.

"And how did you find me?"

Johnson told her about the old neighbor in Cavendish Street and the farewell party at Queen's.

She turned her head and looked at him. "Persistent bastard, aren't you?"

Johnson shrugged.

"You should bloody do it," she said.

Johnson struggled to keep a straight face at this beautiful but foulmouthed twentysomething. "You're a straight-speaking bunch here, aren't you?"

They stopped at some traffic lights and she gave him further driving directions.

"Just to warn you," she said, "my house is just as bad as the car. I share with two other nursing students. Both girls. They're both away, though, so we're okay to talk there."

The journey back to Moira's house took just ten minutes. It was a small redbrick terraced house in St. James Crescent, in an area wedged between the M1 divided highway and Falls Road.

"Catholic area here, I'm assuming?" Johnson asked.

"Yeah, this is nearly all Catholic. But you go the other side of the M1, over there, and it's Protestant. That's the problem in this city."

Johnson couldn't logically see why having two different groups of Christians in one city should be a problem at all. The line of Scripture that his mother often used when he was a kid, quoting Jesus' words at the Last Supper, sprang to mind. What was it? *A new commandment I give you: love one another.* Something like that.

He shook his head but said nothing and carefully parked the Corsa half on the sidewalk, half on the road, at Moira's direction.

"I was meant to be on a flight heading out of Belfast now, going home," Johnson said. He looked at his watch.

She gave a small laugh. "I think you should stay."

Again he supported her as she got out of the car, his arm around her waist and her arm around his neck. He could feel her body heat against his side, even through their coats, and her breath on the side of his cheek.

It had been a while since Johnson had been that close to a woman. He saw her glance down at his ring finger, which was bare.

"Good thing your wife can't see you, taking a young woman home in this state," Moira said.

"My wife died in 2005," he said. "I'm a single dad, with two teenagers back home. My sister looks after them when I'm away."

"Ah, sorry to hear that. My mother, Ann, was a single mom—my father died when I was two, and my mother married Dessie when I was four. She died when I was fourteen, eight years ago. So I know a bit about that kind of stuff."

They made their way into the house. She was right. It was

a mess inside, a typical student house. Piles of unwashed crockery in the sink, cereal packets on the countertop, jam jars, empty baked bean tins, and a half-eaten baguette.

She sat in the living room on a battered black faux leather sofa, the padding of which was emerging through various splits and tears.

"If you go into the kitchen, you'll find a bottle of Jameson," Moira said. "Can you bring it here with two glasses? And a pack of painkillers from the cupboard above the fridge."

Once he'd found them among the detritus in the kitchen, she poured two large measures of Jameson into the glasses.

Johnson sat at the other end of the sofa. "So what's your stepfather's story?" he asked. "What's he done and why's he so against you?"

She took a couple of tablets from the pack, popped them into her mouth, sipped the whiskey, and sighed.

"In my view? He's just angry with everyone," Moira said. "I think it's partly about his dad. He was shot dead by somebody—I never exactly knew who."

"So nobody knows who did it?" Johnson asked. He took a large sip from his glass.

"No." Moira took another slug of whiskey. "I can't stand Dessie's violence, the killing. His republicanism I agree with, always have done—I'd like a united Ireland. But it has to be a political, democratic route, not his route." She shivered.

"But he gets away with it?"

She snorted. "He's a careful bastard. They've never pinned anything on him. He's like a leopard—you never see him, but when he strikes he's deadly."

Moira stared up at the ceiling, searching for the words to sum up her stepfather. When it came to killing, he'd rather do it from a distance, she said, where everything was emotionally detached, where he could somehow separate himself from the outcome.

"His mates called him the Dentist," she said.

"Why?" Johnson asked, as he drained his glass.

"Because they said he was so accurate with a rifle he could take out a tooth from a mile away."

She reached across and refilled his whiskey glass, then her own.

Johnson sat back and sieved through what Moira had told him.

"So the sniper killings that have happened recently—"

Moira interrupted. "That'll be him, no doubt about it."

"How do you know that?"

"There's nobody else who could do that. Not from such long distances. Look at that chief constable. The TV reports said it was done from three-quarters of a mile away." She threw up her hands. "Bloody obvious, isn't it? But he'll get away with it. He won't have left any traces behind. There'll be no proof."

There was silence for a few seconds.

"You don't talk?" Johnson asked.

"I've left him behind," she said. "I came up here to Belfast when I left school at eighteen; I couldn't wait to leave. I messed about for a couple of years, worked in a supermarket, then decided on this nursing course. I'm going to plow my own furrow. I don't like the job I do at Akimbo, but it pays better than the supermarket, the tips are bloody good, and I fund my uni course that way."

Moira grabbed a road atlas of Ireland from the bookshelf at her elbow and shuffled across the sofa next to Johnson. She winced as she moved, rubbed her hip, then spread out the map over her knee, balancing half of it on his thigh.

Their knees touched underneath the map.

"Here, this is where he lives. It's where I grew up. Willows

Farm," she said, unselfconsciously leaving her leg in contact with his. She pointed to a spot on the map right on the border between Northern Ireland and the Republic, south of Forkhill.

She took another large sip of whiskey.

Her stepfather's farm spanned the border, she explained. Half was in the Republic, the other half in south Armagh.

"But he doesn't make most of his money from the farm," she said. "The land is more handy for other things—like moving weapons from one side of the border to the other, smuggling from south to north, escaping after jobs, you name it."

"Smuggling?" Johnson said. "What kind of stuff?"

"Cigarettes and diesel, mainly. They're lethal, the smugglers down on the border. They'll run you off the road if you get too close to a drop. We often used to have lorries coming to the farmhouse in the middle of the night, delivering cigs and stuff. I think his friend Patrick sends the smokes, from the States."

"From the *States*? Who is Patrick?"

"Yes, Patrick McKinney. That's where he escaped to. He smuggles cigarettes in from there, certainly used to, so I presume he probably still does. I think he lives in Boston. How d'you think they fund their operations? He escaped from the Maze prison along with my stepdad's father, and they never found him."

At least it was cigarettes and not hard drugs, Johnson thought. That was one thing about the Irish Republicans: most of them hated drugs, he knew that.

Johnson tugged at his right ear. "Look, have you told anyone about all this before?"

"No. I've been too worried about stirring it all up, worried about what my stepfather might do. But after today? He can go to hell."

She yawned deeply. "I'm dozing, need my bed. I can tell you more about all this another time. I'm not going to get up the stairs to bed by myself. Can you . . . ?"

Johnson looked at her. Her low-pitched Irish burr was irresistible. "Okay, I'll give you a hand. But I don't want to—"

"It's not an invitation, don't worry, Joe." She smiled.

Oh, God.

"I mean, I *do* want to," he corrected himself. "But you're young enough to be my—"

She interrupted before he could complete the cliché. "Don't say that. That's a killer. You can borrow my car tonight to get wherever you need to go. Bring it back tomorrow or Monday, okay? It won't be any good to me for a day or two, not in this state."

She stood and held out her arms for support. Johnson also stood and slipped his arm around her waist again. On the way up the stairs he found himself pausing for breaks every two steps, when in reality there was no need.

But once out of the house and behind the wheel of the battered old Corsa, his mind was instantly elsewhere.

Johnson pulled out his phone and began to type in a message to an old contact, a friend, an old lover, in fact, dating back to his time in Afghanistan, well before his marriage. It was to Jayne Robinson, a former British intelligence officer with the Secret Intelligence Service who had helped him on a couple of big freelance assignments in the previous eighteen months.

He knew that Jayne had done at least one stint in Northern Ireland while at the SIS, otherwise known as MI6.

And Moira had made his mind up for him: he was going to stay and do this job in Northern Ireland. What he now needed was Jayne's help.

PART TWO

CHAPTER TEN

Sunday, January 6, 2013
Belfast

The Union Jack bunting crisscrossed the road, and Ulster Volunteer Force flags and stickers adorned the lampposts. Johnson clamped the phone to his left ear and eyed the Great Eastern pub, which was on the other side of Newtownards Road from the bench he was sitting on.

The Great Eastern was deep in the heart of unionist, Protestant unionist East Belfast. Donovan had summoned him there for a lunchtime "livener" to celebrate after Johnson had called him first thing that morning to say he had decided to take on the job.

But before going into the pub, Johnson needed to get hold of Jayne Robinson. There had been no reply to his text message the previous night, so he decided to give her a call.

She answered almost immediately. "Joe! I'm in Tanzania. How are you doing? I only just got your message half an hour ago," she said.

Jayne had just gotten back to her hotel following a six-day ascent of Mount Kilimanjaro as part of an expedition to raise funds for an African schools charity, and she was due to head back to London on Monday.

Kilimanjaro? Typical of her, Johnson thought. Just two months older than Johnson, at fifty-one, she was probably fitter. Unconsciously, he patted the pack of Marlboros in his jacket pocket.

He gave her a quick summary of the task facing him in Northern Ireland and asked if she was interested in helping.

"Quite possibly," she said. "I've got nothing else on right now. I think Northern Ireland will have changed a lot since I was there with MI6, though. Ulster reminds me of one of those maze of mirrors things we used to get at fairgrounds. Nothing's what it seems, nobody's who you think they are."

She promised she'd think about it while heading home.

But he'd have bet the wad of twenty pound notes in his wallet on her coming. He somehow knew she'd drop everything if there was a chance of a stimulating job at hand. That was what motivated her. That was why she'd left her boring desk job at the Secret Intelligence Service's London headquarters the previous year to go freelance. Jayne loved being out in the field, he told himself. She'd do it.

Johnson hung up and lit a cigarette—he felt he needed one before going into the Great Eastern. He'd been in Belfast for not much more than two days, and already it felt as though he was being sucked in, slowly but surely.

An ex-army businessman with a slightly opaque background, an aging sniper with a grudge and a violent streak, yet who was wily enough to have escaped prosecution. And a bunch of dissident Republicans unable to let go of their guns and bombs. It was an interesting mix.

And that's not to mention the sniper's stunning, feisty stepdaughter.

He would also need someone to do some checks at the US end, given the link to McKinney, and he knew exactly who to call on for that job: Fiona Heppenstall, an investigative reporter based in Washington, DC. Another one he'd had a brief fling with, the year after his wife had died.

Why do I do these things?

If it were indeed a US-based fund-raising operation for the Real IRA, then it would be a good one for Fiona. She was a fearless operator—she'd proved that when helping him out on the hunt for the old Nazi fugitive a year or so back, during which she'd been shot and badly injured.

Johnson threw the remnants of his cigarette on the ground, crushed it with his foot, and crossed the road toward the pub. After a few months of relative inactivity back home in Portland, he recognized the old familiar rush in his system once again.

When he walked into the bar, Ulsterman Van Morrison's new album was playing over the music system. There were Union Jacks and St. George English flags on the walls, and a huge man stood at the bar wearing a Manchester United football shirt; he had a Union flag tattoo on his forearm.

There was no mistaking the politics and the sentiment here.

Johnson spotted Donovan sitting at the back of the pub with another man, their heads together, deep in conversation. He paused for several seconds, uncertain about interrupting what was clearly an intense discussion. But then he carried on.

As Johnson arrived at the table, Donovan looked up, a worried expression on his face. But it cleared immediately, and he pushed a full pint of Guinness across the table at him, its creamy head spilling slightly down the outside of the glass. "Joe, there you go, sit down. I got that for you. When in Ireland . . ."

Johnson thanked him. "I don't normally start drinking midmorning, but this once."

Donovan gestured toward his companion, a man who looked to be in his late fifties. "Meet an old friend of mine, Brendan O'Neill. We go back to the '80s. We used to drink in this bar back then, even," Donovan said. He lowered his voice. "He's also ex-British army and interested in what I'm interested in, but he's coming from a slightly different angle—he does what you used to do."

Johnson raised his eyebrows. "Oh, yes?"

"Intelligence. Works for MI5. You can trust him, he knows what I'm trying to do. He's behind me with it, unofficially."

"Right." He looked at O'Neill and inclined his head toward a Union Jack hanging on the wall. "Safe ground for you around here, I guess?" Johnson knew that MI5, the British security service, had a large base at Holywood, in East Belfast.

"Probably not totally safe, but safer than some places, yes." O'Neill shook Johnson's hand.

Donovan explained that he would be out of Ulster for much of the following two weeks talking to investors in London and Berlin and that he'd invited O'Neill along today because he might be able to help Johnson. "Information, equipment. Whatever."

Johnson nodded. "Yes, that would be useful."

"I'm pleased you're going to do this job," Donovan said. "We both are. Brendan here runs informers, agents, but despite his experience he battles to make headway too, believe it or not."

O'Neill sipped his beer. "Might seem odd, but it's sometimes easier for an outsider to come in and ask questions, get in through closed doors, than someone who's part of the system and is treated with massive suspicion. It's hard work around here. Fresh pair of eyes and all that. I gather you've made a bit of headway already?"

Johnson nodded. He'd already briefly told Donovan about Moira but now filled the two men in on the rest of the details, including her car.

He also briefed them about Jayne, at which point O'Neill raised his eyebrows a fraction.

"Do you really need to bring someone else in here?" O'Neill asked. "I mean, between us, me and Michael here should be able to give you all the help you need. Plus, we've got agents in south Armagh, of course. We get good information from them. Taken together, I think we've got sufficient resources."

"No," Johnson said. "If I'm doing a proper investigation, I want to have someone here with me I've worked with before and trust. That's not a problem, is it?"

O'Neill looked at Donovan, who nodded.

"If you think it's important, I agree," Donovan said to Johnson. "I'll pay for her."

"Great. That's a good decision, you won't regret it," Johnson said. Feeling relieved, he leaned back in his chair and turned to O'Neill. "So your agents in south Armagh, how are they working out?" Johnson asked him.

"It's working," O'Neill said. "Though still some way to go, if I'm honest. There's not a hundred percent flow of information always."

"As we saw in Crossmaglen with the chief constable," Johnson said pointedly. "Guess the shit's hit the fan over that one?"

"You could say that," O'Neill said. He folded his hands behind his head. "The way it's shaping up, I'll be lucky to keep my job, frankly. But the least said about that the better."

"I've been there, got the T-shirt," Johnson said. "Lost my

job with the CIA in Pakistan once. Less said the better about that, too."

Donovan raised an eyebrow. There was a short silence. "Was that where your ear was injured, as well?" he asked.

Johnson self-consciously tugged at the old wound. "Afghanistan, actually. Stray sniper bullet in Jalalabad, years back. I was lucky."

O'Neill nodded. "Yes. As long as you make sure the Republicans don't give you a matching deal for the left ear while you're here, you'll be fine."

Donovan laughed, causing an elderly man at the next table to turn around and stare.

When Donovan's guffawing ceased, Johnson told them he was thinking of heading back to south Armagh to quietly look around, hopefully with Jayne, if she was able to join him.

He drained his pint of Guinness.

Donovan tapped the table with his fingers. He could let Johnson use his wife's car, he said, so Johnson could avoid driving a rental car and be less conspicuous. "She's away in Hong Kong visiting her sister for the next three weeks, so it's not being used." The car, a Toyota Avensis, also had the advantage of a specially fitted magnetic bomb detector, he said.

"Bomb detector?" Johnson asked.

"Yes, it lets you know if anything magnetic's been attached to your car, whether it's a bomb, a tracking device, anything really. It works with an app on your phone and sends you a message if anything registers. It detects any change in the magnetic field in the car bodywork, or something like that. I've got one on my car too."

Donovan showed Johnson how to download the app onto his iPhone, saved the company's contact details into Johnson's contacts list, and then activated the app for him using his own email address and password.

O'Neill took a long drink from his glass. "Look, my friend, I don't want to teach my granny to suck eggs, but here's a bit of advice from me. Tell yourself you're in a war zone and take the same precautions you would if you were somewhere like Kabul or Baghdad or wherever. Check for everything. If you're getting in a car, look underneath every time you get in. Make sure you're not followed. I can get you a gun, if you need one."

"Okay, thanks. I appreciate the advice. And if you can get me an M9 or a 950, that'd be great. Same as I have back home," Johnson said. "If you can get a Walther, too, that would be helpful. That's what Jayne uses."

"Right, got it. Beretta man. Should be doable. Hopefully I'll have them both over the next few days."

"Thanks," Johnson said.

"You need to be damned careful around here," O'Neill said to Johnson. "You need to remember one thing, dealing with these dissident Republicans. They may not be quite as well organized as the IRA of old, but there's enough of the old stagers left to instill discipline into the others, at least in some brigades. South Armagh's one of those. Underestimate them at your peril. They're well armed too. But you've seen that already. The politicians like to dismiss them and down-play the threat. Don't make the same mistake."

CHAPTER ELEVEN

Sunday, January 6, 2013
   Belfast

The three men were dressed in anonymous woolly hats, waterproof jackets, and thick gloves. The tallest of them, Duggan, pulled his zip up to the top around his neck, pulled his scarf tight, and nodded at the other two.

It was time to go for a walk.

They left their cars and spoke only intermittently as they hiked from the parking lot next to the coffee shop up the single-lane road toward the TV transmission station on Black Mountain, high above Belfast.

The brisk January morning wind bit hard, despite the sunshine. The shortest of the men, Fergus Kane, a wiry, bearded figure, took a pair of prescription sunglasses from his pocket and put them on.

A pair of female joggers, both clad in pink and black Lycra with thick gloves and earmuffs, came back past them in the opposite direction, and a falcon cruised high above.

Just before they reached the tall transmitter masts, which carried several satellite dishes and radio transmitters, the hikers cut down a footpath to the right, signposted Ridge Trail, which led across the treeless, boggy moorland.

Patches of snow were still visible from the storm that had come just before the New Year, and the trio crunched across frozen puddles on the path.

The walking route, in Divis and the Black Mountain National Trust area, was one of several the group used at random. It was safer than meeting in the city.

Finally, when they were well away from the masts, the silence was broken.

"So, I guess there's a shitstorm going on?" asked the third man, Dennehy.

"Shitstorm?" Kane said. "That's one way of describing it. There's a bloody witch hunt started; they're after whoever leaked it."

"But there are no fingers pointing in your direction?" Duggan asked.

Kane shrugged. "Doubt it. Thing is, it was quite a long list of people in the know by the end, and not just in Simonson's office. Officers in Crossmaglen had to be told, a few people at MI5, helicopter staff, not to mention the secretary of state's office."

"Could have come from anywhere," Duggan said. "Cross would have to be the favorite, I guess?"

"Yeah, definitely, they think it came out of Cross."

"Right, well, it was good info, bang on," Duggan said. "You're earning your money, so far."

"Yes, well, I'm getting so bloody stressed over all this I'm not sleeping well," Kane said. He walked with his eyes to the ground, head bowed.

The three men fell back into silence again. They continued along the gravel path as two other groups of walkers, all laughing and joking, full of nodded acknowledgments for Duggan's group, came past them in the opposite direction.

Now they were near to the 1,275-foot-high peak of Black Mountain, which offered spectacular views over the entire city of Belfast.

As they walked on, the scenery unfolded in front of them: Lough Neagh in the west over to Strangford Lough in the east, the streets, tower blocks, and factories sandwiched between.

"There's one more piece of information I need," Duggan said. "Then you can relax for a while."

The diminutive police public affairs officer glanced up at Duggan, at least half a foot taller, who strode along at his right-hand side. Kane adjusted his sunglasses. "What do you mean?"

Duggan gave a thin-lipped smile. "It's for a big job, potentially. So it's quite urgent."

Now Kane stopped walking. He put his hands on his hips and turned to face Duggan, his forehead below his woolly hat deeply creased with horizontal lines.

"What, the G8?"

Duggan said nothing.

Then Kane gave a nervous laugh. "You've no chance. Security will be tighter than a duck's backside, especially after the chief constable. You won't be able to get near it. There'll be checkpoints, helicopters, rooftop snipers, men with binoculars, hundreds of them."

Duggan took off his gloves and pulled a cutting from the *Belfast Telegraph* out of his pocket. "There's something I'd like to know. Here, look at this." He pointed to the same circled paragraph he had shown to his brigade colleagues at his home near Forkhill. "There's this community visit Obama and Cameron are going to do, at some as-yet-unknown location in Ulster. It says so in the *Telegraph*, so it must be right."

Kane grimaced. "I must be a mind reader. As it happens, I brought something that'll give you an outline of that. A preliminary schedule, which came in yesterday, so I brought a copy. Be careful with it. Only about seven people are on the distribution list, so it'll be a short witch-hunt if they know that one has leaked."

He reached inside his jacket and took out a red and black plastic USB flash drive in a small, clear plastic bag, which he held out to Duggan.

Duggan took the bag and put it into his trouser pocket. "Thanks," he said. "That's what I like about you. You're always one step ahead of the game. This schedule is just preliminary, you said. Does it say which school or other location it will be at?"

"No. They don't know yet. They're working out the options. I'll let you know when I hear more."

Duggan slapped Kane on the back. "You make sure you do, little man. You want your money, you get me everything you can put your hands on about that community visit. I want to know exactly where it's going to be, I want timings down to the millisecond, I want to know vehicles, activities, exact locations. Who's sitting on which side of the car. Who's driving. Who's gonna greet them, meet them. Everything. When will you get them?"

Kane shook his head. "I don't know. Probably much nearer the time."

"Okay," Duggan said. "Soon as you can, Fergie boy. Otherwise there'll be a note into the deputy chief constable's office, typewritten, anonymous, telling them where to refocus that witch hunt that's going on." It was the usual threat. He knew that Kane was never sure whether he meant it or not.

Duggan took a small brown packet from his trousers and

rammed it deep into Kane's jacket pocket. "There you go, that's another seven hundred and fifty. That's January's payment. Covers your rent for another month on that nice flat of yours, and your Sky TV subscription, doesn't it?"

Kane nodded, and Duggan gave a faint, almost imperceptible grin.

They were at the top now. Duggan stood near the concrete triangulation point marking the peak of Black Mountain. He looked southward over the city stretching out far below him, lit up by the winter sun glinting off a pair of construction cranes and a glass-fronted office block.

"Are we done?" Kane asked. "Anything else?"

"Done?" Duggan pointed toward Protestant East Belfast. "We won't be done until those Union flags are down over on that side."

CHAPTER TWELVE

Monday, January 7, 2013
Washington, DC

Fiona Heppenstall was deep into writing a story about a senator caught in an insider trading racket: his wife had purchased half a billion dollars' worth of shares after a tip-off he had received from a friendly investment banker in return for the nod on a massive property development deal just outside the capital.

Two days later, the wife sold the shares after a 60 percent spike in the share price, caused by the company's biggest rival announcing to the New York Stock Exchange that it was launching an all-cash hostile takeover bid.

The senator had pocketed a near $300 million profit from the deal.

It had taken Fiona six weeks to dig out all the transaction details, but she was finally there.

All being well, *Inside Track*, the online news organization where she worked as political editor, would publish the story the following morning.

Fiona was confident the senator would not only have to step down but would be pilloried from all sides, given that only the previous year he had spoken strongly in the Senate in favor of a new bill—which had since become law—designed to clamp down on exactly that kind of activity.

She took her hands away from her computer keyboard, paused for breath, and sipped her third coffee of the morning. Two hours of intense concentration had sapped her energy in a way it never used to, not before her injury. She was feeling exhausted after an intense few weeks at work and only two days off at Christmas.

The large newsroom was busy, humming with the noise and chatter of phone calls, people shouting at each other, printers whirring, fingers bashing away on keyboards. It was a typical day at *Inside Track*.

Her cell phone rang. Initially she let it go. There was no time.

But then she noticed the caller ID, smiled, and picked up the phone.

"Joe! Hi, how you doing? Where are you?"

"I'm all good. I'm in Belfast, chasing work, potentially. How are you? Are you fully fit and back to normal again?" Johnson asked.

The truth was, she was still suffering occasional pains in the upper part of her left arm where she had been shot while working with Johnson in pursuit of an elderly Nazi and his son in Argentina over a year earlier. The bullet had nicked a nerve on the way through, and the surgeon warned her the pain could take a very long time to disappear fully, if ever.

But all that detail could wait for another time. "Yeah, I'm back at work, nailing crooked senators as we speak," she said.

"But let's cut the crap—is this a social call, or do you have a story for me?"

She listened as Johnson explained his situation and the few brief details he'd gotten from Moira about Patrick McKinney's background.

"Patrick McKinney? An Irishman, tobacco guy? That rings a bell. I think he's quite well known, got some senior job with one of the big smokes distribution companies. In fact, I remember now. I had him on a list of people I was going to interview a couple of months ago, for a story about a strike by port workers in Boston. The longshoremen's union walked out, and his business was being hit hard because no containers were being loaded onto ships. Then he pulled out of the interview, and I spoke to some other company instead."

Fiona paused. "Listen, if he's really who you say, IRA escapee, fund-raiser, smuggler—that's a great story. I'll have a look at it, do a bit of digging. We'd be interested, for sure."

"I thought so," Johnson said.

She knew that Boston, with its big Irish community, was still a focal point for IRA backers, fund-raisers, and arms smugglers and had been for decades.

They agreed to touch base a couple of days later, and she hung up.

Then her deputy, Penny Swanson, piped up.

"Did I hear you say Joe Johnson?" Penny asked, a gleam in her eye. "The guy you had that fling with a while back? You can't leave him alone, can you?"

Fiona grinned. "Penny, shut it. That was years ago. Then we worked together a year or so ago; remember the hunt for the old Nazi—and nothing happened between us then, just to remind you. Anyway, he called me. He might have another job for me, a good story."

"Dunno about a good story," Penny said. "You two seem

to be a never-ending story. I thought you were feeling exhausted? You seem to have perked up a bit."

Fiona crumpled a sheet of newspaper into a ball and threw it at her sidekick, who sat opposite her. The two had moved together from *The New York Times*. Penny neatly ducked as it sailed past her head.

But she smiled as she threw it.

* * *

Monday, January 7, 2013
  Belfast

Johnson took a circuitous route to drop the purple Corsa back at Moira's house. He cut off Falls Road north and onto Cupar Way on the edge of the Protestant area, checking his mirrors continuously for any sign of a tail.

He cursed the fact that the car, in its battered condition, was more conspicuous than he would like.

BBC Radio Ulster, on the car radio, was running a news analysis program about dissident Republicans; the previous day a plot to attack the police station in Church Place, Lurgan, had been uncovered. According to the presenter, a pipe bomb had been found in the pannier of a moped parked outside the station.

The program included a short interview with assistant chief constable Norman Arnside, sounding very pleased with himself, who said that the plot had been uncovered after receipt of information from intelligence sources and that many lives had undoubtedly been saved. News of the incident had only just been made public because police had been carrying out further investigations overnight.

The BBC also reported a story from political sources at

Westminster who said the prime minister was going to launch an inquiry over the next couple of days into the circumstances surrounding the killing of chief constable Eric Simonson, particularly given the need for increased security ahead of the forthcoming G8 meeting in Belfast.

The G8 was certainly a possible target, Johnson reflected, given that Barack Obama and other world leaders would be there, and it was only three weeks away.

He continued past the enormous graffiti-covered Belfast peace wall, a monstrosity of corrugated steel sheet and mesh which ran at above-house height to his left, separating the Protestant unionist community centered around Shankill Road to the north from the nationalist Catholic Falls Road area to the south.

For Johnson, the giant peace wall brought back memories of the Berlin Wall, which he had seen a couple of years before it was finally torn down during the momentous events of 1989. He turned left at the end of the road and drove through steel security gates that could be closed by police in times of trouble.

"There was never a good war or a bad peace," ran a slogan painted on the rusting gray gates.

After another couple of left turns, he was back near where he had started. Only then, satisfied he was not being followed, did he head in the direction he had originally intended.

Ten minutes later, he pulled up at the end of Moira's road and parked the purple Corsa. He looked carefully up and down the street before moving. It was empty.

Johnson got out and walked the remaining hundred yards or so to her house. He went up the path and knocked.

Moira opened the door and greeted him with a broad smile. "Joe! Good to see you. I'm pleased to say I'm in a slightly better state than I was the last time you came, and so is the house."

"I'm glad about that," Johnson said. "You youngsters definitely have greater powers of recovery than I do." She looked a lot better: a purple blotch on her upper lip was the only evidence of the street fight with her stepfather. She led him through to the kitchen, which had indeed been tidied since his previous visit.

"I've decided I'm going to do this job," Johnson said. "I've got an old friend coming in from the UK who's going to help me."

"What's his name?"

"Her name's Jayne."

Johnson could have sworn that Moira's face dropped a bit. Or was he just flattering himself?

"It's fine," Johnson said. "She's good. We've known each other for years."

He paused. "By the way, I was thinking about something you said the other day, about your stepfather's rifle. Do you know what gun he uses and where he keeps it?"

Moira swept her long black hair over her shoulders. "I'm not sure, but I remember he used to call it a Light Fifty. He used to talk about it when I was younger as if it were his favorite pet dog and he looked after it like a family heirloom, which he probably thought it was."

She looked at Johnson, her deep brown eyes full of intensity. "He loved it more than he loved me, that's for sure. But the cache where he keeps it—do you really think he's going to tell me that? Probably just him and the quartermaster know that. One thing I do know; he mentioned once that they were expensive, thousands of dollars, and I'm certain he's got only one of them. I heard from a friend in Forkhill he had two, but one was found a year or so back by police. So if you find the gun, you put him out of action, at least temporarily."

Johnson tugged his ear. "Hmm. We could look for the gun first. Thing is, if we find the cache and remove the gun, he'd know straight away he'd been compromised. Then he'd go underground and we'd never nail him. Not for a long time. No, we need to catch him in action so we get the evidence. Although then, of course, there's the risk he hits someone before we trap him. It's a high-risk approach but high reward if it works."

"Tricky choice," Moira said. "It'll be even more difficult to catch Dessie actually with the gun. Those guys have a chain of people who bring it in and take it back to their cache. That's why he's survived so long."

She told Johnson how originally there were two sniper gangs in south Armagh that both used Barretts in the '90s, which they had smuggled in from the US and had been used to kill several British soldiers. The gang in Cullyhanna was caught in a Special Air Service ambush in 1997. "They were careless, and a tout gave them away. They were all jailed, and their guns were taken. But my stepfather's gang, in Drumintee, was never caught."

Johnson nodded. "You know a lot about all this."

She shrugged. "I've got friends who tell me things, keep me updated, even though I'm not living down there anymore. It's part of everyday life around here. This is Northern Ireland. I grew up with it, watching him deal with all this stuff all the time, even after the peace agreement. Look, I'll help you as much as I can, but you'll have your work cut out, Joe. I'll wish you good luck because you'll need it. Especially if you start nosing around down in south Armagh. You'll need someone to guide you around. You can't go in cold. Down there, a stranger stands out like—well, you might as well walk around in a fluorescent jacket with a flashing light on your head."

"Could I talk to any of these people safely?" Johnson asked.

Moira pondered. "My mother kept in contact with a friend of hers, a builder, Ronnie Quinn, who might be able to help. He lives by himself in Forkhill, not far from the farm, and knows the land around there as if it were printed on the back of his hand."

Ronnie had done some of the building work at Willows when she was a child, she knew that. He had always been there, digging, mixing cement, and laying bricks. He got to know her mother and had always been friendly back then, always ready with a joke. He didn't like Dessie, though, despite doing a lot of work for him.

"I wouldn't be surprised if Ronnie hadn't done a bit of touting in his time," Moira said. "He never came across as a hard-core Republican, though he went to the right places and said the right things." She had heard him criticize the bombs-and-guns approach repeatedly, she added.

"The other option is I come and help you myself," Moira said. "Tell you what. I'm going to talk to Ronnie and we'll make a plan. I trust him. He'll know what to do."

Johnson nodded. The girl seemed more mature than her twenty-two years.

He scribbled a few lines in his notebook, including Ronnie's name. Was there anything else about her stepfather that might help, Johnson asked, such as passwords, cell phone numbers, that kind of thing?

Moira thought for a moment. He had often used the names of two legendary heroes of the 1916 Easter Rising against British rule in Ireland for his passwords, she said, Padraig Pearse and James Connolly. But she didn't know if they were still current, and she couldn't think of any others. Johnson wrote them down, along with a cell phone number for Duggan, which Moira showed him in her phone directory.

"Great. Now, can you do me a favor?" Johnson asked. "I need a lift, to pick up the car I'm borrowing while I'm here. It's in East Belfast, out near Holywood, that direction," Johnson asked.

Moira nodded. "No problem. Now?"

"Yeah, need to get moving, really. I've got to get to the airport to pick up my colleague."

She looked sideways at him. "Ah yes, you'd better not keep *her* waiting."

Moira put on her coat and led the way out the front door. Johnson followed and then waited at the end of the short path while she locked her front door.

Their hands brushed as she went past him at the gate, on the way back to her car.

* * *

Monday, January 7, 2013
Belfast

"There's someone coming out," the man said.

Monaghan looked out the window at the house directly opposite, on the other side of St. James Crescent. "Shit, you're right."

He grabbed his Olympus OM-D camera, which hung around his neck, quickly extended its telephoto lens to its full 300 mm, put his eye to the viewfinder, and concentrated hard.

Moira, followed by a man he knew as Philip Wilkinson, had emerged from the front door of her house, and both were standing on the path.

Click, click, click.

Monaghan captured several shots of Moira shutting the

door of her house and turning around. Now he could see both of their faces through his viewfinder as they walked together down the short path.

Click, click, click.

The intelligence officer for the Belfast brigade snapped fifteen frames of the pair from his vantage point at an upstairs bedroom window as they walked down St. James Crescent to Moira's purple Corsa, which was parked at the end of the street.

When they had driven off, Monaghan quickly checked the pictures on the small monitor screen at the back of his camera.

"Did you get what you needed?" asked the brigade volunteer standing behind him.

"Yeah, no problems. Thanks for the use of your bedroom," Monaghan said. He chuckled. "I wasn't expecting to get them in the bag so fast."

"Pleased to help. Anytime," the man said.

Monaghan looked at the flask of hot tea and the plastic container of sandwiches that he had brought with him. They lay next to his black leather jacket on the bed. "Don't know why I wasted my time making that lot this morning. Half an hour, job done."

"I won't ask why," the man behind him said.

"No," said Monaghan. He scratched his salt and pepper beard. "Never ask why. See nothing, hear nothing, know nothing. That's the way."

CHAPTER THIRTEEN

Tuesday, January 8, 2013
Belfast

Carrying the same dust-covered backpack she had taken to the top of Kilimanjaro, Jayne Robinson emerged from the arrivals hall at Belfast airport.

The pack, along with her khaki top, newly acquired African tan, and wide smile, looked somewhat incongruous among the pasty-faced, miserable, briefcase-carrying business commuters who jostled around her.

Johnson smiled as he watched her walk through the crowds. Still the same slim athletic body, narrow waist, and great legs. *How does she do it?*

"You're going to have to get rid of that gear," Johnson joked, embracing her. "I need you to go native here; it's not a safari guide look-alike competition."

"Don't worry," she said, "I've got the boring clothing packed in the bag, and this is Northern Ireland, so the tan'll be gone inside two days."

"Hope it's not just boring stuff in the bag?" He raised an eyebrow.

She grinned and shook her head. "Sorry, Joe, I left my box of toys at home under the bed. You don't change, do you?"

He put on a disappointed face and took the bag from her as they walked to the silver Toyota Avensis borrowed from Donovan.

Johnson briefed her on what Donovan had employed him to do as they drove the fifteen miles back to the apartment, via Falls Road.

He talked her through the recent upsurge in attacks by dissident Republicans, the pipe bombs and then the sniper attacks, and the background to the chief constable's death.

Jayne listened attentively. "So, it's simple. All we need to know is who's next on the hit list," she said.

He glanced at her. It was her usual dry-witted attempt at a joke, but it cut right to the chase.

"That might help," Johnson said. "First, I want to check the background of the guys he's taken out."

That was where Johnson hoped Jayne might be able to help, he explained. Did she, from her time at MI6, have any contacts who might access files held on people by, say, MI5, the army, or the police?

Jayne pondered for a moment. "I've still got a couple of old friends working at MI5 headquarters who might be able to help. Both of them are going back to my time here from '92 to '95, but I've kept in touch, and we meet up occasionally if they're in London."

She explained that one of them, Noreen Wilson, had worked for the Royal Ulster Constabulary, now called the Police Service of Northern Ireland, before joining MI5 and had done a lengthy stint at the secure police archives unit at Carrickfergus, just outside Belfast, where many of the old files were stored.

"So she might know where to find what we need," Jayne said.

"Okay," Johnson said. "Maybe for starters she can get names and addresses of the wives or relatives of the men who have been shot by the sniper."

"Sure, I'll ask," Jayne said. "But first, the important stuff. Have you got me a gun?"

Johnson nodded. "Always your first request. Yes, I've asked O'Neill for a Walther for you and a Beretta for myself. Hopefully he'll get them today."

Johnson parked the Toyota, as instructed by Donovan, a few minutes' walk away from the apartment block down a side street full of redbrick terraced houses near the local college.

Shortly after arriving at the apartment, Jayne had her laptop out on the table and had dug out phone numbers of her old MI5 contacts.

Then she got on the phone. That was what Johnson liked about working with her. She didn't waste any time.

Johnson left her to it and went outside onto the balcony, where he could hear her side of the conversation.

"Hi, Noreen, it's Jayne Robinson here . . . yes, been a long time . . . no, I'm freelancing these days . . . I left Six, yep, had enough . . . But I'm in Belfast for a short while, a work job . . . Look, I need a favor: we need some information on a couple of people, files if possible. I know it might be tricky but . . ."

Johnson lit a cigarette and tried to think through some sort of plan.

They could stay in Belfast and try to ferret out what they could from their contacts. Or they could take the direct approach and go back to where Donovan had taken him on his first day, down to south Armagh, and try and find out more about Duggan there.

He took a deep drag on his Marlboro.

They weren't going to make much headway sitting in Belfast, that was for sure.

He looked out across Falls Road.

On the other side, a man came out of the newsstand. There was a newspaper billboard on the sidewalk that read, "Mystery Armagh Sniper Still at Large."

The man removed the sheet and put a new one on the board in its place.

"PM Launches Chief Constable Killing Inquiry," it read.

When Jayne got off the phone, Johnson finished his cigarette and went back inside.

"I see you can't get off the cigs."

Johnson coughed. "It's only when I'm away working. I don't get the urge at home. Think it's a stress thing."

"Sure, sure. Anyway, my friend Noreen's on the case. She's going to chase up those files. If she can't get them, nobody can," Jayne said.

"Great," Johnson said. "Look, go and put your bags in your bedroom. I'd like to head down to south Armagh. If we're going to make any progress here, we need to know the lay of the land, what this guy Duggan's farm looks like."

"I don't need to go there to tell you the lay of the land. It's bandit country."

"Sorry?" Johnson asked.

"Bandit country. It was Merlyn Rees, the British government's Northern Ireland secretary, who gave it that tag. That must have been in the mid-'70s. But everybody called south Armagh that when I worked here in the '90s. Seems like not much has changed."

Johnson gave an ironic laugh. He looked at Jayne's backpack. "You got a flak jacket in there?"

"No," she said, grimacing. "But anyway, you're talking about a sniper with a .50-caliber rifle in his bag. You think a flak jacket's going to stop a fifty? No chance. You might as well pin a sheet of cardboard to your chest."

* * *

Tuesday, January 8, 2013
  Forkhill

Duggan was slouched in a black leather armchair in the living room of his white-painted farmhouse, a MacBook laptop resting on his thighs.

It was the property that his father had bought when the family moved there from Belfast in the '70s. One advantage of owning a farm was the space it offered to build whatever he needed. And over the years Duggan had built a number of facilities, some visible, others less so.

The new four-bedroom place was smart but functional. Granite kitchen, underfloor heating, hardwood stairs, three en suite bathrooms, a spacious office. He had it all to himself.

Duggan opened the file he had just downloaded from the USB flash drive that Kane had given him.

It turned out to be a very simple document indeed.

Draft Community visit Mon 28 January
School TBD
2:30 p.m.—BO and DC arrive with Chief Con + dignitaries.
2:40 p.m.—Activity
2:50 p.m.—Talk by BO/DC and QA
3:10 p.m.—Depart for G8

Duggan read through it a couple times and leaned back to think. This looked very promising.

Eventually he closed the MacBook, placed it on the floor, and looked over at McGarahan, his broad-shouldered IO, who sat on the other side of the room, his large frame hunched over his own laptop, which was perched on the dining table.

But before Duggan could speak, McGarahan stroked his chin, coughed, and glanced up at Duggan.

"You ain't going to like these," McGarahan said. "Come over here and have a look at these photos."

Duggan waited a few seconds. He didn't like being told what to do. But the serious tone in McGarahan's voice was clear. He walked over to the table and peered over his colleague's shoulder.

The photograph almost filled McGarahan's laptop screen, a series of small thumbnails down the left-hand side of the screen telling Duggan that there were several others to view.

There was a pause as Duggan took in the detail. "Shit. Is that the American again? That's outside her house. When were these taken?"

"Wes just emailed these photos down from Belfast," McGarahan said. "He took them this morning. Doesn't look good."

"Taken this morning! And after the kicking we gave her the other night. Bloody hell. How many are there? Scroll through them."

McGarahan flicked slowly forward through the series of photographs, which showed Duggan's stepdaughter emerging from the front door of her house with Philip Wilkinson and walking down the road to her car.

What the hell is she doing with that guy? Duggan thought.

"Go back to that second photo," Duggan said, when McGarahan had circled through all of them.

He scrutinized it more closely. It showed Wilkinson and Moira at the gate of the house, facing each other, standing very close.

"Are they bloody holding hands there, or is it my imagination? Enlarge the photo. Is he in with her or what?"

McGarahan zoomed in on the picture.

"Nah, you can't see properly from this angle whether they are or not," McGarahan said. "I don't know, chief, he's got to be way too old to be her sort. He's got to be late forties, fifty or so."

Duggan swore. "I want you to find out everything you can on that guy. I want him tracked. When he blows his nose I want to know about it. And I want you to put him off. If we can't put him off, then . . ."

"Yeah, got it, chief. I'm going to put a couple of the volunteers on him."

Duggan's phone beeped as a message arrived. It was from Fergus Kane's private burner cell phone number, which clarified the key remaining question from the document Duggan had just downloaded. *Venue likely to be the new White-field Integrated Primary School. Will call you soon,* the text message said.

Interesting. So the school visit was going to happen.

Duggan looked up at McGarahan. "I need to get moving with things. We've got a lot on our plates now, a lot on our plates. I'm going to head over to Belfast this afternoon now."

"Okay. What's that for?"

"I'm going back to class, checking out schools." He winked at the IO.

Duggan walked back to his armchair and picked up his MacBook. He had acquired it from a lower-level volunteer in the south Armagh brigade the previous spring. The volunteer, known to be a small-time house burglar, had approached him with the computer and presented it to him, telling him he had acquired it at a garage sale and that Duggan might be extremely interested in one of the documents he had found on it.

Well, the line about acquiring it in a garage sale was clearly bullshit. He'd obviously stolen it.

But Duggan needed a laptop at the time, and the volunteer had been spot on in his comment about the significance of the document on it—in fact, to Duggan's astonishment, it was sheer dynamite.

CHAPTER FOURTEEN

Tuesday, January 8, 2013
Forkhill

There was definitely something not right about the large, architect-designed new houses, built on extensive grounds with balconies, patios, floor-to-ceiling picture windows, separate granny annexes, and huge garages.

They looked oddly out of place amid the battered farm cottages, small white bungalows, and gray steel-roofed barns.

As they drove, Johnson slowed down and scrutinized a couple of the houses, which stood amid a backdrop of rolling hills that rose green and brown over to the east, crowned by dense woods and gorse bushes.

The narrow lane, splattered with tractor mud and lined with leafless hawthorn hedges and ivy-covered trees, ran straight south toward the border with the Republic. The low-hanging gray clouds almost seemed to touch the tops of the trees where the land rose up.

Johnson repeated to Jayne what Donovan and Moira had

told him about the cross-border smuggling of cigarettes and diesel to cash in on the differences in duty between the Republic of Ireland and the UK to fund dissident republican activities.

"These big places are probably diesel mansions, no doubt paid for in cash," Jayne said. "Reminds me of the marijuana mansions I used to see when I was in Mexico."

They noticed a number of large unmarked fuel tanker trucks parked near various farm outbuildings. Johnson pulled over to the side of the road near one of them, and he and Jayne scrutinized the map Moira had given him.

"Willows Farm must be the next property down this road on the left," Johnson said. "I'll just drive past and we'll take a quick look."

He set off again. A couple of hundred yards farther on the right was another large house with outbuildings. As they drew near, a large white van careered out of the driveway to the house and accelerated straight at Johnson's car on the single-lane road.

Johnson slowed, thinking the van would do likewise. But it gathered speed instead. At the last second, Johnson slammed on the brakes and swerved sharply left onto a muddy grass shoulder as the van flew past, missing the Toyota by no more than a couple inches. He got a quick glimpse of the driver, a bald man with a black beard, peering out of the van's side window straight at them.

"Shit, that was close," Jayne said. "What the hell was that all about?"

"I don't know, but Moira did warn me that the smugglers don't like visitors driving around and run people off the road if they get too close to a drop. Maybe it was something like that. Or maybe they were just checking us out. Not going to be too many strangers driving around here; it's the back end of nowhere."

Johnson eased back onto the road and continued at a more sedate pace.

They came over the brow of a small hill, and as they descended on the other side, saw Willows Farm on the left side of the road, right at the point where the speed limit signs switched to kilometers per hour, signifying the border with the Republic.

"Just pretend to make a phone call," Johnson said. "There might be cameras. Couple of glances, I'll slow down a bit as we go past. You know."

Jayne nodded and put her cell phone to her left ear.

There was an array of buildings. Johnson eased off the accelerator as he passed and glanced sideways a couple of times, just enough to register three large green barns, set well back from the road, plus a few smaller outbuildings.

In front of them, next to the road on the southern side of the site to their right, stood a white-painted house. He caught sight of a gatepost next to the road with a slate sign that said Willows Farm.

"Trespassers will be shot," Jayne said.

"What?"

"There's a sign next to the gate—that's what it says. Smart place he's got there. I spotted a security camera outside but couldn't hear any dogs barking."

Now in the Republic, they drove on for a mile before Johnson was forced to pull into a gateway as two fuel tankers, both painted plain white with no company logos, headed toward him up the single-lane road in the direction of the Northern Ireland border.

Jayne looked at him. "And not a cop in sight, five days after the chief constable's been shot dead," she muttered.

It had been half an hour since they had left the M1 that ran between Belfast and Dublin, yet they hadn't seen a single

police car, neither from the Police Service of Northern
Ireland nor the Irish police, the Gardaí.

* * *

Tuesday, January 8, 2013
  Belfast

Just as Johnson and Jayne were navigating the narrow country
lane in County Louth, more than forty miles to the northeast,
a middle-aged man in dark-rimmed glasses and a baseball cap
pulled on a large backpack, opened the rear door of a blue
Volkswagen Passat station wagon, and grabbed the black
Labrador inside by the lead.

Duggan was about to take a dog for a walk.

Jet belonged to one of the men who helped Duggan look
after the few sheep that grazed in the fields surrounding his
house down near Forkhill. The man had been happy to allow
someone else to volunteer to walk him for a change.

"Come, Jet, out you get. We're going on a long walk,"
Duggan muttered as the dog, frustrated by a seventy-five-
minute car journey, bounded out, pulling the lead and almost
jerking him off his feet. "No, not that way, you stupid bloody
animal, this way."

Duggan set off from the spot where he had parked. He
walked along the busy Springfield Road for a short distance,
then took a left, heading toward Black Mountain, which
towered high above the city.

After about a third of a mile, he came to the site that he
was interested in: Whitefield Integrated Primary School, a
new school built only a couple of years earlier on the border
of the neighboring Catholic and Protestant communities,
with pupils from both sides of the sectarian divide.

Duggan stood and absorbed the detail of the school site.

The ubiquitous eight-foot blue steel fencing that many schools now used as a security barrier encircled the premises, its sharp triple spiked tips acting as a deterrent to potential intruders.

Beyond that was a large parking lot for staff and visitors and then a series of smart brick, steel, and glass two-story classroom blocks, administration offices, and what looked like a gym. To one side lay a large playing field, including two football pitches.

Anyone knowing Duggan, if that person had recognized him behind his glasses and incongruous cap, might have wondered why a single man with a grown-up stepdaughter was so interested in a primary school at the other end of the province from his home.

But the answer had come in a short phone call to Duggan earlier in the day from Kane, made from a phone box outside a pub in the Holywood area of the city.

The call lasted no more than thirty seconds and added a little more detail to the draft document and short text message Kane had supplied earlier. But it told Duggan most of what he needed to know at that stage.

During the G8 summit, US President Barack Obama and UK Prime Minister David Cameron were now definitely scheduled to visit the Whitefield school to highlight the progress made in normalizing society in Northern Ireland.

The idea was to spin the visit by the two world leaders to the school, located between the Catholic Whiterock area and the Protestant Highfield area of Belfast, as a massive statement of optimism for Northern Ireland's future.

But to Duggan, and other dissident Republicans, it was an exercise in political bullbaiting. He saw it as a proverbial red rag by the British to those who had never abandoned the idea of a unified Ireland.

The schedule, as it presently stood, involved the two political leaders joining in a ten-minute game of soccer with the pupils before going indoors for a quick tour of the main building, a short activity session with pupils, a short speech for the benefit of TV crews, and a photo op. The visit was due to last for around forty-five minutes, Kane had reported. His voice had sounded nervous to the point of trembling, and he had cut off the call off before Duggan could ask any questions. They would have to wait.

A ten-minute game of football . . .

A jolt had gone through Duggan at that news. He had been expecting the window of opportunity to be far smaller, probably restricted to the short walk between a car and the school buildings. To have ten minutes outdoors, on an open playing field, was a significant bonus indeed.

Duggan walked slowly around the perimeter of the school site to the road that ran along the south side, allowing Jet to stop and sniff the fences, lampposts, and grass shoulders as he went. Jet cocked his leg whenever he found evidence of another dog's presence.

As Duggan walked, he saw a group of five dark-suited men emerge from the school building and walk around the school playground and parking lot. Two of them were making notes, and one man, clearly in charge, was pointing at the various buildings on site. They looked like security of some kind, maybe the US Secret Service preparing for Obama's visit, Duggan wondered.

From near the school, Duggan found he had a good line of sight up to the top of Black Mountain, where he had been walking only two days before with Dennehy and Kane.

There was nothing that would obviously interrupt that line of sight, short of rain, fog, or other bad weather. And in those circumstances, the football would likely be canceled anyway, and with it would probably go his opportunity.

All that would be out of his control. He shrugged to himself.

Years of experience told him that from where he was standing to the ridge near the summit was around a mile. It was a hell of a distance but just about within his range—on a good day.

Duggan looked around. There were a few blocks of high-rise flats back toward the city that he could conceivably use, but they were even farther away, and the angle of fire would be far shallower and the line of sight more unpredictable. That would be a more complicated option, too, involving procuring a flat in advance to test the visibility, and was definitely a riskier option. He ruled it out.

He tugged at Jet's lead. Now it was time to go and check out the top of the mountain.

"Come on, Jet boy, we've got a bit of climbing to do," he said.

Duggan returned to Springfield Road and followed it until he reached Whiterock Road, where he turned right. After a short distance the road began to climb steeply, and once he was beyond the houses, it narrowed immediately into a single lane.

Duggan turned off to the left after a couple of shacks and made his way across a field and through some trees. He let Jet off the lead, and the dog bounded ahead, up an overgrown limestone path that dribbled water downward like a ministream.

There was no well-defined path here. But Duggan had climbed this way before.

By the time he finished his scramble across heather, stone, and scrub and reached the concrete triangulation marker at the peak, he was sweating heavily, despite the temperature being only a few degrees above freezing.

He turned and looked back, then gave an ironic smile. It

had been only a few years since, while out walking, he had been ordered off the mountain by a couple of British soldiers. He'd told them to get lost but had gone eventually. That was when the entire mountain was an army training area and observation station, not National Trust land, as it was now.

The idea of striking a major blow for the republican movement from that exact same location seemed to him like poetic justice.

The problem was, at the spot where he would need to be, up on the top of Black Mountain, there were no trees, just heather and grass. In short, there was no decent cover.

That was why Duggan had brought the backpack with him. He undid it and took out a black padded carry case, which he unzipped. Inside was a small drone, about fourteen inches wide and long, with four circular blades to power it in flight.

He took an iPad from the backpack, tapped on an app, and a control screen for the drone loaded.

Within a couple of minutes, Duggan was using the iPad to control the drone as it hovered slightly farther down the hillside from where he was standing, flying at a height of no more than twenty feet. Using a high-definition camera mounted to the base of the drone, he clicked off a series of photographs of the ground below it: pictures of heather, grass, and scrub. An onlooker, if there had been one, would probably have looked at him in some bewilderment.

Once he had around thirty photographs and was satisfied they contained what he needed, he landed the drone and packed it away again in his backpack.

He took out a new large-scale Ordnance Survey walking map of Black Mountain and the Divis area, which he had bought that morning, and used it to check the shortest pathway from his current spot to the coffee shop parking lot, well over a mile away in the opposite direction to the city. That was an important detail, and speed would be essential.

Next he took out his range finder, a small but high-powered Vectronix Terrapin laser model, which could calculate distances of at least one and a half miles, maybe two, if he needed it.

He checked the yardage down to the Whiterock school playing fields far below. It was showing 1,610 yards, just under a mile, allowing for the downward angle from the mountaintop. That was very long, but he was confident it was doable. The good news was, there was a perfect line of sight from this piece of ground down to the school. In any case, it was his only option.

Duggan was replacing the range finder in his bag when from behind him came the chugging sound of an engine. Duggan turned and watched as, a couple of hundred yards or so away, farther along the path back toward the huge TV masts, a man arrived on a large quad bike, streaked with mud.

The vehicle had a storage box mounted on the back, behind the driver's seat, from which the man removed a shovel and other tools.

Ignoring Duggan, he began carrying out maintenance work on the gravel path, starting at the point where he had obviously left off the previous day. There were piles of gravel spread at intervals along the path, waiting to be spread and compacted. Behind the workman, the wide expanse of wet moorland stretched out like a green and brown carpet.

Duggan stared at the man and his quad for a couple of minutes. Gradually, an idea began to take shape.

CHAPTER FIFTEEN

Wednesday, January 9, 2013
Forkhill

"Chief, we've been going through the unknowns up and down the lane from yesterday," McGarahan said, his chest heaving a little as he tried to catch his breath. "There were eight of them, and seven look harmless. But there's two bits of film I want to show you, one from Dave's van dashboard cam, the other from your own security cam."

Duggan frowned, led his IO into his office, and motioned to him to put his laptop on the desk. It was only ten to eight in the morning and still dark outside. McGarahan was not normally up and about this early.

McGarahan voluntarily kept a daily check on any unknown and unrecognized vehicles and people driving within a couple of miles of Willows Farm, using the feeds from various fixed cameras mounted outside volunteers' properties over a wide radius as well as video footage uploaded by those who had dashboard cameras.

The various video feeds had proved a valuable precaution; already two raids by customs officials had been foiled as a direct result, allowing time for incriminating evidence to be cleared up with plenty of time to spare.

Duggan peered at the laptop screen as McGarahan tapped on the play button. The first bit of film, from Dave's van, showed the vehicle from which the video was taken rushing along a narrow country lane straight toward a silver Toyota Avensis, which swerved onto the grass shoulder with only seconds to spare.

Just before the Toyota disappeared from camera range, McGarahan pressed the pause button. "Now look at that. What do you see?" he asked.

Duggan scrutinized the screen. "It's on the road down from Forkhill. Apart from Dave's normal shit driving, I see a man and a woman." Then it dawned on him.

"Bloody hell, is that the American Wes photographed with Moira?"

McGarahan didn't reply. He switched to a second video clip, this time in higher definition, and again pressed play.

This time the scene was the narrow single lane outside Willows Farm, and the film was from a fixed camera. The video showed the same silver Toyota approaching down the lane, then slowing a little as it reached the farm. The woman in the passenger seat, who appeared to be using a cell phone, and the driver could be seen briefly glancing at the farm buildings as the car moved forward.

Again McGarahan froze the film before the car passed out of view.

"And again," he said. "Same car, same two people."

Duggan had another closer look. "Yeah, it's definitely him. And who's the woman? She's got a tan, so she can't be from around here. Could be another investigator."

"We don't know who she is yet, chief, but we'll find out."

Duggan stood up and walked slowly across his office to the window. "Moira must have told that American about the farm, the stupid cow, even after that warning we gave her. She's not one of us, Liam. She's a liability. She'll take us all down if we're not careful. Who knows what she's saying to these people. She's not much different to a tout—actually no different at all. What do you think?"

McGarahan shrugged. "Don't know, chief, that's your call. It's your stepdaughter."

"I know. Unfortunately." Duggan grimaced, then looked up at the IO. "You've got the plate number from the film, I'm sure. I want a trace on the American. I want to know who owns the car, whether it's private or rented. You can probably get that from Kane or use the volunteer at the police station over in Dungannon."

McGarahan nodded. "I've already done all that, Dessie. The Dungannon man did the check. Car belongs to a guy called Michael Donovan, runs an investment business of some kind up in Belfast. I've got a couple of guys out now on the motorbike looking for it—we've put the word out. It's a matter of time."

Duggan turned around. "Michael Donovan?" he said sharply.

"Yeah, you know him?"

Duggan looked away. "The name definitely rings a bell." He paused. "Also, do you know where Martin is? I can't get hold of him. I wanted to talk to him about that Lurgan job, the police station. I was going through my list. There were only six people who knew about that job, and Martin was one of 'em. You were one and I was one. The others were Kieran, the OC in Derry, and the guy on the moped who had the device."

"As far as we know," McGarahan said pointedly.

Duggan folded his arms. "Yeah, as far as we know," he conceded. "But I want to make sure I've gone through everyone. I don't want any touts around here—we've never had touts in this brigade, not when I was in the Provos and not since, and I'm proud of it. We've lost a few jobs of late—this Lurgan one and then the pipe bomb at the police station up near Portadown and also the Semtex, which was found up in Lisburn."

"Think we've a tout?"

Duggan shrugged. "Three jobs, three intercepted. What else can I say?"

"But we got the chief constable. And you've got two others recently without a problem."

"Yep, I know. But if I find there's a tout on this patch, the payback will be the same as it's always been. You can put that word around."

"Might be someone who's turned, who's thinking the other way might be better now?"

Duggan snorted. "The other way? The Sinn Féin way? All talk, no tackle?"

He despised the way of Gerry Adams and Martin McGuinness: the sellout, the taking of the political shilling, and the smart suits and the seats in power, and betraying the memory of those who had died in the cause over the past few decades. No. If he bought into that, then those volunteers died in vain. Many of them, brave men, had died in agony, leaving their children fatherless and their wives penniless and frantically worried about how they'd cope. Those were the ones who'd acted, who'd achieved, in the name of a united Ireland. They were true martyrs, all of them; that was his view and he was sticking to it.

After McGarahan had gone, Duggan made himself a strong double espresso and sat on a barstool in his kitchen, nursing the blue mug with both hands, feeling its warmth and enjoying the sensation as the caffeine worked its way into his system.

Duggan knew he needed to root out whoever in his brigade was leaking his operations to the PSNI or maybe MI5, and he needed to do it quickly. He couldn't afford to have the next operation he had in mind leaked to anyone.

He began mentally listing the potential points of vulnerability. In his long experience, leakages sometimes emanated from the source that seemed most obvious, but that wasn't always the case, and it would be a mistake to prejudge matters.

Of the group, Danny McCormick, the quartermaster, would be seen by many as above suspicion. He had managed the brigade's armory of weapons and ammunition for a long time. But Duggan had never built a close personal bond with him. There was always something between them, and they had exchanged angry words after Duggan's spare Barrett M82 had been seized during the police raid on the weapons cache near Armagh city a year earlier. Who had touted its location to the cops? That remained an unanswered question.

McGarahan, as intelligence officer, spent more time than anyone in contact with those on the other side of the fence, both PSNI and MI5. He was often evasive about the identity of his best sources of information, and Duggan assumed there must have been times when he had done a trade to get what he wanted—it couldn't just be a one-way street.

Then there was Kieran O'Driscoll, the finance director. Although the gray-haired academic talked a good game, Duggan always had it in the back of his mind that as the boss of a house-building company, he had more to lose in financial terms than most did from the economic uncertainty caused by ongoing dissident terrorist activity. You never could tell.

There was also Martin Dennehy. He had worked tirelessly for the cause, more so than the others, which was why he had been brought increasingly into the inner circle. He was a trusted spotter, too, on operations. But despite his private regard for the man—something he deliberately never showed publicly—Duggan had a nagging uncertainty about him. He had financial problems, and Duggan occasionally felt that he had never fully bought into a continuation of the armed struggle once the British Army had been removed from the streets of Ulster. So Dennehy needed to be on the list too.

There were one or two others who might have to be included, such as Pete Field, whose barn Duggan sometimes used for phone calls to McKinney and who was at the center of many operations.

Duggan drained his coffee. Maybe he should set a little test, a rat trap, to see who ended up biting the cheese.

A planned operation was coming up, and he would need to tell McCormick about it. He could then concoct a few other fictional operations, the details of which he could drip-feed to others in the brigade on a confidential need-to-know basis.

Then, having set the trap, he would sit back and see what happened.

* * *

Wednesday, January 9, 2013
Forkhill

Dennehy was watching the morning TV news at home in his kitchen when the text messages came through. Short ones and to the point.

"Who are they from?" his wife, Tess, asked as she busied herself cleaning up the breakfast pots.

"Duggan, as usual. Wants to see me. Like now. Usual

language, too. Get my ass down there quick, you know. Doesn't sound happy about something. Then again, he never does."

"No, but I think he likes you, actually. Can't it wait until you've taken the kids to school?"

"No, best not. I don't want to upset him."

Tess stopped what she was doing and smoothed her long dark hair back behind her ears. Although she was firmly republican in outlook, she had never liked his involvement with the dissidents. She saw them as a bunch of mavericks and had a particular dislike for Duggan.

"Have you thought about trying for proper work again?" she asked. She ran her fingers through her hair, looking stressed. "Maybe you could register with some of the new housing developments up in Belfast. They must need people. Or even in Dublin?"

"I've registered, just waiting to hear, but there's so many people like me. It's tough competition."

Tess looked down at the floor. "I don't know, then, Martin. Why don't you go and talk to Arthur; he's always good for advice, and he's on your side. He's almost an uncle to you. He might even be able to give you some work?"

Arthur Higgins, an old-school Republican who ran a welding business in West Belfast, had been a close neighbor of Dennehy's several years previously. Higgins always took an interest in Dennehy's fortunes, even after they both moved and saw less of each other.

Dennehy leaned back in his chair. "Yeah, you're right. Good idea, I'll do that. I'll go and look him up. Are you okay to take the children? I'd better get across to Duggan's place."

Tess nodded and started toward the stairs. Then she stopped and took a step back again, looking at him.

"Martin, is everything all right?"

Dennehy closed his eyes momentarily. He could feel a headache coming on.

"Yes, I'm fine. He's just difficult to work for. A few jobs have gone tits up, like the Lurgan police station moped thing, and Dessie gets angry and has an inquiry each time."

Tess walked over and leaned against the kitchen counter-top. "Look, just you take care of yourself. I worry about you working with Duggan and that crew."

He nodded, took his phone from his pocket, and tapped in a text message to tell Duggan he was coming. "Don't worry. I'm okay. See you later," he said.

Dennehy put on his blue waterproof jacket and made his way out to his car.

The one-and-a-half mile journey down to Duggan's house on the borderline took only a few minutes. Dennehy rehearsed his lines. He knew what the routine would be. A chat in the kitchen, a cup of tea, then through to the office, and the questions would begin.

He was right. He had half of his cup left when Duggan moved through to the office. "Martin, we've got a problem. A shitty tout in the camp."

"The Lurgan job, you mean, the moped?"

"Yeah, correct, but the two others before that as well. There were six who knew about Lurgan. Me, Liam, Kieran, those two in the Derry brigade—their OC and the moped rider—and you."

He paused and looked Dennehy straight in the eye. "I need to find out who leaked it."

Dennehy looked straight back. "You're not accusing me, Dessie, are you?"

"Should I be?"

"You're right to suspect anyone and everyone. I know that, given what's been going on. But you can strike me off your list. Also, you need to remember there were more than six who knew about Lurgan. What about Marcus, when he came to that meeting last month to talk about cigarette disposals? He was hanging around outside the room for ages afterward waiting for his lift. And then Annie, remember, it was a long meet, and she brought in that plate of sandwiches and a pot of tea and probably waited outside for quite a while until we finished the agenda. Just saying, it wasn't as watertight as you seem to remember."

Duggan scowled and tutted. "You may be right. Anyway, I want you to know. I like you and I've trusted you, and I'd like to keep on trusting you, but I've got to be careful."

Dennehy relaxed a little. "Sure, Dessie. We all need to be careful."

"I've been wondering whether we should get a full inquiry going," Duggan said. "Bring in people from outside the brigade to handle it. That wouldn't be fun for any of us."

That was the understatement of the year. An outside inquiry, involving hard men from one or two of the other dissident brigades, would be nasty. Dennehy nodded. "But if it clears things up, might be worth having at the back of your mind. Do you need me to work on anything?"

"A couple of things," Duggan said. "There's a job coming up that I'm telling you about as you might be needed to help out. It's a pipe bomb, two weeks from today, the Wednesday night, against a Prod copper at his home in Woodside. Plan is to stick it under his car before he goes off for night shift."

Dennehy nodded. Woodside was a neighborhood in the mainly Protestant—Prod—and nationalist Poleglass area of West Belfast. That would definitely cause a major stir.

"Good. Let's keep it tight, then," Dennehy said.

"Yeah, and I've got another job in mind that I'd like you to do. Just you and I are in on this. It's a private one."

"What is it we're looking at, then?" Dennehy asked.

"Right, I'll explain," Duggan said. "It's in upper Falls and needs to be done soon. I want to take a backseat on this. You've done a lot of admin jobs over the past few months but not much action. Don't want you to get rusty, do we?"

Dennehy nodded. There was something in the tone of voice. He knew Duggan of old. Was the OC about to put him to some sort of test or put him in the firing line? Or possibly both? It was hard to tell.

"Okay, then," Dennehy said. "What's the detail?"

Duggan started to run through a list of instructions and then gave the name.

Dennehy recoiled. "You're joking? Tell me you're joking."

But it was immediately obvious that his boss wasn't joking. He was deadly serious.

CHAPTER SIXTEEN

Wednesday, January 9, 2013
  Belfast

Johnson looked up sharply from the three sheets of paper that Jayne had put down on the breakfast bar in front of him.

"I was kind of hoping for a little more than this," he said. "But I guess you've done well to get this much out of her, realistically."

Jayne had come back to the apartment on Falls Road just after ten o'clock following a breakfast meeting with her old friend at MI5, Noreen Wilson.

"The girls in the basement wouldn't let her see the file on the chief constable," Jayne said. "It's restricted while they're working out what to do following the shooting."

The sheet on Eric Simonson included his address and his wife's name. The files on the other two were only slightly less thin, comprising only their wives' name, brief work history, addresses, and a few other sketchy details.

Jayne shrugged. "Noreen was a bit apologetic."

Johnson sighed. "Okay, in that case we need to do some legwork. I think we'll go and visit the wives. I need a shave."

He stood up and stretched, then headed into his bedroom.

An hour later, they were in the silver Toyota, edging cautiously along Union Street, Portadown. The Beretta and the Walther, which O'Neill had delivered to them the previous evening, were safely stashed in the glove compartment.

A giant Ulster Volunteer Force mural, painted on a house end wall across the road from a Methodist church, underlined the area's unionist and Protestant credentials.

Johnson steered around the corner and parked fifty yards down from the house where the assassinated prison officer, Will Doyle, had lived prior to being shot at his golf course.

They walked back and knocked. The man's widow, Beth, was a fragile but well-groomed lady in her mid-fifties, with short gray hair and glasses. She was hesitant, but Johnson explained the reason for their visit, and eventually she agreed to make them a cup of tea.

"We've had a very tough year," she said. "First there was the burglary, not long after New Year's last year, when my husband's laptop and credit cards and some books and papers were stolen. Will was on edge after that, anxious and worried."

Then the shooting had come out of the blue in late October and had destroyed the family. Their adult children were still in shock, she said, and their six-year-old grandson couldn't understand where his grandad had gone.

"I still cry every day, many times a day," Beth said. "It's a sadness that won't go away. The police have got nowhere with it, so we've no idea who did it. The dissidents, I guess, but why him?" The bags under her eyes and lined forehead told their own story.

"They shot him from the top of a hill overlooking the golf course—high up, and must have been three-quarters of a mile away," Beth continued. "The police think whoever did it got away down a country lane. I mean, nobody knew where to look because it was from so far away." She put her head in her hands.

As a prison officer, he saw himself at risk to some extent, but he'd done that job for eighteen years, ever since he left the army, she said, and had never had a problem previously.

Johnson sipped the hot, sweet tea and leaned back on Beth's sofa. He felt sorry for her but also slightly mystified.

"Terrible. But you know, you're living here, in County Armagh, which is republican territory. How risky did you think that was for an ex-army man?" he asked gently.

She looked out the window. "We moved here a few years ago to be near our daughter and our grandson after he was born. Before that we were up in Antrim. Nobody around here knew he had been in the army. We never spoke about it."

Jayne leaned forward in her seat. "Which part of the army was he in?"

"He worked in intelligence," Beth said.

"Army intelligence? Which unit was that?"

"It was the 14th Company, the Det, they used to call it," she said. "What do you know about them?"

"I worked in Northern Ireland years ago," Jayne said. "So I do know a bit. Did he talk much about it?"

"No. Never."

"And that burglary you mentioned. What was the laptop they took?" Johnson asked.

It was a MacBook Pro, Beth said, with a pale blue cover. "He'd been slowly typing up his journals, his old diaries, into it and had been annoyed because, stupidly, he had no backup, and he then had to start all over again."

"Do you know what was in the journals?"

"No. I never read them," Beth said. "I think they went years back to his army days. He was thinking of writing a book or something eventually; that's why he wanted to get them all on the computer. He'd nearly finished the job, actually. He told me he only had a few weeks of entries still to copy. There was a ton of material there. My son, Archie, has the journals now, in London where he lives, for safekeeping. He's going to get them typed up as a keepsake for all the family."

Johnson moved forward and sat on the edge of his seat. "Do you think I might be able to see the journals? There could be some useful leads in there that could help with the background to this case."

Beth looked doubtful. But she eventually promised to ask Archie and see if he could get some photocopies or scans made. "I'll find out and let you know," she said.

After that, Beth said little more. Johnson realized they were going to make no further progress.

In the car afterward, as Johnson accelerated down the road, he glanced at Jayne. "The Det. Wasn't that Special Forces?"

"Yep. Tough bastards, would have made good prison officers, I guess," Jayne said. "I had to deal with them quite a bit when I worked over here. Never could get anything out of them. They worked behind closed doors."

The next stop, back up the M1, was the home of the deceased security company owner, Gary Joyce, who had lived in a substantial 1960s-style brick home in Upper Road, in Greenisland, a mainly Protestant village just east of Belfast.

Johnson and Jayne drove through the village, which overlooked the waters of Belfast Lough, where ferries to England and Scotland were cruising past in the distance.

The house was on the main road.

Joyce's widow, Susan, was a robust, stocky Scotswoman.

She sat them down in a chilly glass conservatory at the back of the house, with views over the garden.

"It was in September when it happened. He had only just left the house with the dogs," she said, nodding toward two mongrel-looking animals who lay, ears pricked, on beanbags behind them in the living room. "He was taking them for his usual walk after work. It was routine. Got shot from somewhere right up there at the Knockagh war memorial. That's what the police told me when they'd worked out the angles and everything."

She pointed through the conservatory window to the top of a cliff that rose up high over the fields at the rear of the house. "You can see it up there," she said, referring to the silhouette of a pointed obelisk that was visible against the skyline.

"The monument's at least two-thirds of a mile away from here, and high up, over 1,200 feet," she said. "Some bloody gunman that was, if they're right. The police said it was the routine that did it for him. They tell you not to do the same things at the same time every day, don't they? They always say vary it, but—"

"Yes, easier said than done, I guess," Johnson said. He went through a similar set of questions to those he had put to Beth Doyle earlier in the day.

However, Susan was far more forthright than Beth had been.

"He was thirteen years out of the army," Susan said. "He left after the Good Friday agreement when it became obvious they were going to downscale his team. Since then he'd kept his head down and had built his security company from scratch. I was proud of him. He had no trouble."

"What army unit was he in?" Jayne asked.

"It was the 14th Company, the intelligence detachment.

He hated it, couldn't wait to leave. He never said why, but I can guess it wasn't easy work." Susan shook her head.

But after a few more questions, it became obvious she knew little about the work her husband had done. The Official Secrets Act meant he wasn't able to discuss much of it, even with his family.

After a while, Johnson glanced at Jayne and raised an eyebrow. She nodded, signifying they might as well leave.

How many widows were there like Susan, he thought, as they walked down the garden path. Republicans, British army, nationalists, Catholics, Protestants. Hundreds. Thousands, even? In every city and town across the province, in many villages too. The human, living and breathing flotsam and jetsam of the conflict that seemed to have no end.

Johnson lit a cigarette before getting back into the car and took a couple of deep drags. He leaned against the side of the Toyota.

Jayne stood next to him, her arms folded as protection against the stiff breeze.

"So, do we go for the hat trick?" Jayne asked.

"The chief constable's wife?"

Jayne nodded.

He took another deep drag. "She won't talk. Of course she won't."

It was obvious she wouldn't. The place would be crawling with detectives, intelligence officers, minders, bodyguards, you name it.

But what was it his old boss at the Office of Special Investigations, Mickey Ralph, always used to say? *Never die wondering, son . . .*

"We'll give her a try," Johnson said.

Jayne walked around and got into the passenger seat.

Thirty-five minutes later Johnson parked the car on a side road that led off Whinney Hill in the upmarket Cultra suburb of East Belfast, just down the road from Holywood, and with views across to the northern side of Belfast Lough, where they had just come from their meeting with Susan Joyce.

They walked a hundred yards or so around the corner and Johnson pressed the button on a security communication device built into a brick gatepost at the end of a secluded driveway.

There were no police cars in sight. All was quiet but for the distorted sound of a refined female Ulster accent crackling at them from the loudspeaker.

It took several minutes of explanations, showing passports to the security camera and passing over phone numbers and addresses, before Norma Simonson felt confident enough to let them in. They were lucky to catch her at home, she said. Her life had been spinning out of control since the shooting.

As they reached the end of the driveway, a heavy wooden front door opened, and there stood a well-coiffured silver-haired woman wearing a maroon silk scarf and a navy blue jacket.

She shook hands with Johnson and Jayne, without smiling, as she looked them up and down from beneath lowered eyebrows and a furrowed forehead.

"Thank you very much for seeing us," Johnson said. "I know this has been a very difficult time, and you would have been well within your rights not to talk to us. I'm sure your husband's police colleagues have been taking up a lot of your time too."

Norma led them through into a sitting room, talking as she went. "I don't mind telling you this whole thing has been handled in a most appalling way. I was initially minded to tell you to go away when you rang the bell, but frankly, somebody definitely needs to look into it," she said. "Eric should never have been put in that dangerous situation. I asked him the night before the helicopter trip whether he was sure it was safe to take a cabinet minister down there, and he reassured me. He said things were under control and it would be fine."

The sitting room was lined with bookcases, and a sofa, two armchairs, and a hi-fi stood in the corner. "Eric always read his books in here with his music on, when he had the time. I'm sorry, I don't want to criticize Eric's force publicly," she said, "but . . ."

"It's fine, Mrs. Simonson," Jayne said. She sat down on the sofa while Johnson sat on the settee, and the chief constable's widow on the other armchair. "We're not really delving into what happened at the PSNI end—that's somebody else's job. We're more interested in who killed him and why they did so. He was the third person to be shot by a sniper from long range in the past few months."

"Well, it's obvious, isn't it?" Norma said. "The top policeman in Northern Ireland, he's bound to be a target. I'd been afraid of something happening ever since he was promoted into that job. It's like being a lightning conductor for those dissidents." Her face crumpled a little, and Johnson thought she was going to cry.

Johnson let her recover before he continued with his questions. Her husband had originally been in the army, then joined the police in the late '80s, he understood.

"Yes, that's right," she said, recovering herself. "That was just as nerve-racking a time for me as now is, if not more so. We got married while he was in the army, and every day I worried he wouldn't come home. It was at the peak of the Troubles, and there was a lot of pressure, worse than now."

Norma gazed up at the ceiling for a couple of seconds, then back at Johnson. "That's why this came as a shock. Things are meant to be better than back then, but it's been obvious for some time that that's not completely true."

The questioning routine with Jayne by now felt well rehearsed.

"Which army unit was he in back then?" Jayne asked.

"Oh, it was intelligence. That's where he cut his teeth."

"Was it the 14th Company, by any chance?" Johnson asked.

"Yes, that's the one. It was tough going. Seems a long time ago now, a very long time." She spoke a little about how the strain of working for the 14th had made her husband less communicative and more withdrawn than he had ever been, before or since. She thought that was why he had decided to leave the army and join the police.

"It really was a relief when he moved across to the police, which I think must have been 1987. He was based at Carrick-fergus, at the secure police facility there, along with one or two of his other army friends who also joined the Royal Ulster Constabulary. Those were much more relaxed times, before he started getting promotions in the police. Then the stress level went up again."

She looked at her watch. "I'm sorry, we've got the funeral on Friday, and I need to get to the church to speak to the vicar before four-thirty."

Johnson's phone pinged as a message arrived, but he quickly silenced the device and put it into his pocket. He needed to concentrate on what Norma was telling him.

"That's fine, Mrs. Simonson. Look, we'll let you go. I might like to get back in touch though, if that's okay?" Johnson asked.

She nodded and gave him a cell phone number and an email address. "I'm sorry to cut you short," she said, "but there's so much to get through. It's going to be a huge funeral. All the political people will be there, from both Stormont and Westminster, as well as the media and all the paraphernalia they'll bring. It's going to be an ordeal—me and my two children are dreading it all, frankly."

She looked at Johnson and Jayne. "I wish we'd had longer to speak. Good luck with your inquiries. Please keep me updated."

They exited the driveway and walked back up the hill toward the car.

"So. The 14th Company connection," Johnson said. "The big, obvious common linkage."

"Yes, maybe," Jayne said. "A lot of army people spent time in the 14th. But you're absolutely right. We need to look into it further."

They rounded the corner, Johnson clicked the door remote to open the car, and they both got in. Johnson was about to put the ignition key into the socket when his phone pinged again to remind him of the previous unread message. He took the phone out of his trouser pocket and read it.

Johnson stared at the phone and said nothing for several seconds.

"Magnetico Alert: Driver's Side Front. Danger. Do Not Enter Vehicle," the message read.

"Everything all right?" Jayne asked.

"No, sonofabitch," Johnson said. "Don't move."

"What?"

"I said don't move."

* * *

Wednesday, January 9, 2013
Crossmaglen

By early evening, Duggan had finished working his way through his list of meetings and conversations.

He had contrived a lunchtime pie at the café in Crossma-glen with Kieran O'Driscoll on the pretext of a discussion about arranging the funding transfer to McKinney for the new Barrett.

As they left the café he had casually dropped into the conversation that a pipe bomb hit was planned for the following Wednesday against a Protestant policeman at his home in the Culmore area of Londonderry. He was telling O'Driscoll, he said, because there might be an operational need for the brigade to provide backup if the volunteer involved needed quick transport across the border after the hit.

During the afternoon Duggan dropped in for a cup of tea with Danny McCormick to chat about drawing up a fresh inventory of the weaponry and ammunition the brigade currently held and to discuss what new equipment might be needed once additional finances were in place following the shipment due imminently from McKinney.

Duggan also wanted to know where they would store the new Barrett once it arrived. He was keen, he said, to try and keep it north of the border if possible and ideally in a fresh, previously unused location.

As he left McCormick, Duggan mentioned that a pipe bomb hit was planned for Wednesday in two weeks time, the twenty-third, first thing in the morning, against a Prod copper at his home in Irvinestown, Enniskillen.

"I might need you to go and fetch the fireworks from the Dundalk cache," Duggan told him. "I'll let you know."

On his way back home, Duggan called in to see Pete Field. Just a catch-up, he said, as they hadn't had a proper chat for a while. Pete poured him a bottled beer, and they sat in his living room and spent more time talking about a couple of new players acquired by Crossmaglen Rangers than about the brigade.

As Duggan stood to leave, he mentioned a planned pipe bomb attack on a policeman's house in the Ballymacash estate in Lisburn, scheduled for the following Wednesday evening. The volunteer who would carry out the attack was expected to head through Forkhill and across the border afterward, Duggan said. He was letting him know for information only.

Field nodded. Duggan thought, as he left, that the farmer was the least likely of the brigade members to be the tout. He wasn't financially driven and he wasn't a political thinker but rather someone who was involved because he loved the camaraderie, the trenches spirit, and the action of the brigade.

The cheese was well and truly planted in the trap now. All Duggan needed to do was keep his ear close to the ground for the sound of rats underground.

In fact, only the details he had given McCormick were factual; he would indeed need explosives to be retrieved from the Dundalk cache, and the hit on the officer in Irvinestown was a go. All the other purported operations he had mentioned to Dennehy, O'Driscoll, and Field were entirely fictional. He decided not to include Liam McGarahan in this particular exercise; if it turned out he needed to investigate him, that could wait until another day.

So, if the Irvinestown operation ended up going wrong or if word got back to him of police and army technical experts running in the direction of Londonderry, Poleglass or Lisburn, Duggan would know the reason why.

CHAPTER SEVENTEEN

Wednesday, January 9, 2013
Belfast

"There's a magnetic device detector fitted to this car," Johnson said. "I've had a warning text. It says something's been attached underneath, below the driver's seat. It says do not get into the car."

"*What?*" Jayne asked.

"Just stay still a second. Let's think this through," Johnson said. He wiped his forehead on his jacket sleeve. "I unlocked the car door with the remote. Nothing happened."

He paused. "Then we both opened the doors, got in, nothing happened."

"No. So it's not the remote," Jayne said. "Just don't put the key in the ignition."

"Don't worry, I'm not going to. And I haven't touched any of the pedals, either."

Johnson realized he was clenching the car key so tightly in his right hand that his knuckles were showing white.

"Right," said Jayne. "So if we now open the car doors again and get out, we should be okay?"

Johnson looked at her. Her brow was furrowed, her lips pressed. "Wait, wait, wait. I don't friggin' know, Jayne. I could call Donovan, but he's not going to be any help."

Then Johnson's phone rang. He jumped, turned it over and looked at the screen. The caller ID showed *Magnetico*.

"Answer it," Jayne said.

Johnson tapped the green button and flicked on the loudspeaker so Jayne could hear. "Hello, Joe Johnson here——"

But it turned out to be a computer, not a person, on the line. "This is an automated message from Magnetico Services. Warning, a magnetic device has been detected attached to your vehicle. Location is driver's side front. Repeat. Location is driver's side front. Do not enter vehicle. Repeat. Do not enter vehicle." The call ended.

"Shit, I say we just open the doors and get out. We can't just sit here—could be a timed bomb," Johnson said.

"Agreed. Let's do it—slowly."

Johnson pulled the door handle. There was a slight click as the door mechanism disengaged. He cautiously opened the car door until there was just enough room to squeeze out.

Nothing happened.

He turned to Jayne and nodded. She did likewise on the passenger side.

Johnson eased himself carefully out of the seat, turning sideways so he could plant both feet on the ground at the side, then slowly stood up, closed the door, and moved away from the car. Jayne mirrored his movements on the other side.

They both walked along the road until they were about two hundred yards away from the Toyota.

"Thank God for that," Jayne said. "Now what?"

"I'm going to call Donovan," Johnson said.

He rang and quickly explained what had happened. Donovan was in Berlin but wasted no time coming up with a plan.

"Joe, if we call the police first, they'll get army technical people in straightaway, and all hell will break loose," Donovan said. "The street will be full of army vans, there could be a controlled explosion, residents evacuated, you name it. It'll take hours. I'll tell you what I'm going to do. I'm sending one of my ex-army bomb disposal mates around to have a quick look underneath. He does private work for me as needed. If it's a bomb, it'll almost certainly be a tilt fuse device—that's what they use. It'll only detonate if the car moves. So he'll tell us straightaway what it is. If it looks anything remotely like a bomb, then yes, we have to get the army guys in to deal with it. So be it. But it could be a false alarm or even something else. I'm trying to stay below the radar. I don't want you, me, my car on the evening TV news unnecessarily. Got it?"

Johnson hesitated. "You're joking? Doesn't sound like the safest approach, Michael. There are houses nearby, people walking past."

"It'll be fine. You stay well away from the car and wait there." He took the location details from Johnson and hung up.

Johnson relayed the conversation to Jayne, who threw up her hands. "Bloody hell, he sounds like a total maverick, that guy." She turned around and looked at a bus stop forty yards away. "We'll go and sit at the bus stop. If it goes up, we'll deny all knowledge. Not our car, nothing to do with us."

While they were waiting, a text message arrived. It was from Moira, who had been in touch with her mother's old friend down in Forkhill, Ronnie Quinn. He would be around the next morning. If Johnson could pick her up at around ten in the morning and drive, she'd take some time off from her studies and go with him. She thought he'd be a useful contact, a man who was on her side.

Yes, that would be a good step forward, Johnson replied. He didn't mention the car issue that was currently unfolding.

After twenty minutes, a large, unshaven man in an unmarked black Land Rover rolled up next to the bus stop. He jumped out, nodded unsmilingly, and introduced himself as Zach. "Michael sent me down to have a look at his car. That's it there, I guess? He said the alert was saying driver's side underneath?"

Johnson nodded. "Yeah, that's what the alert I had said." He showed Zach the message from Magnetico.

"But you're not just going to stick your head under the car, are you?" Jayne asked.

"This is everyday life around here, lady," Zach said. "Nothing's changed. Personally, I've only found a couple of actual viable devices in, oh, I'd say the past two years. A few false alarms. But you read the paper, watch the TV news, and every week the army guys, the technical people, are removing bombs, doing controlled explosions. Often it's policemen; the dissidents target them but others, too."

From his Land Rover, Zach took a mirror on an extendable pole and an eighteen-inch blue electronic device with a nozzle at one end.

"Portable explosives detector, very reliable," Zach said. "Does a vacuum vapor test, and I can do a swipe and a particulates check with it as well, if needed. I check my own car every day with this gear, and I serve VIP guests who are in the province, like some of Michael's investor mates. You two just stay here and wait."

He put on a pair of cotton gloves and walked slowly to the Toyota.

Johnson and Jayne watched from near the bus shelter as Zach eased the mirror under the car on the driver's side and scrutinized the reflection, moving it slightly to one side, then the other. Then he appeared to press a button on the blue device, bent down, and worked it under the car.

After a short while, Zach lay down on the tarmac and put his head under the car.

"This is ridiculous. I can't look at this," Jayne said.

But then Zach stood up and began walking back toward them, his phone in his hand.

"It's a magnetic tracker device, not a bomb," he said, as he showed Johnson a photograph he had taken of the device on his phone. It was a small black box that was fastened to the underside of the car. "Someone put it on the chassis. Do you know who might have put it there?"

"No, not exactly," Johnson said, "But I've got a reasonable idea."

"I didn't remove it because a short, odd movement like that might alert whoever put it there. But if you want, you can just pull it off and do whatever you want with it. It's perfectly safe to do that." He wished Johnson and Jayne good luck and left.

Johnson called Donovan to let him know what had happened.

Donovan was stunned into silence for a few seconds. "Shit, that's unbelievable. They didn't waste any time. Somebody must have somehow clocked my car when you drove it down to Forkhill. But I don't know how. I told you, don't underestimate those guys. The south Armagh mob was always as organized as the army ever was, if not better. Still seems to be the case."

"Yes. But it now means I can't take the Toyota back down that way, can I?" Johnson said. "I'm going to have to rent a car, although I'd like to keep the use of your wife's as well, for the time being."

Donovan paused. "I'm just thinking, if you want to give

whoever put it there the real runaround, you can put the tracker under a bus or a taxi. Let them follow that around Belfast. Or even better, one of those Romanian haulage lorries. Otherwise, take out the battery and bin it."

Johnson looked thoughtful. "Hmm. Although it might come in handy if I keep it."

"How do you mean?"

"I can deploy it more usefully," Johnson said. "As a decoy."

CHAPTER EIGHTEEN

Thursday, January 10, 2013
  Belfast

Johnson parked the black Ford Focus at the end of Moira's road and walked with Jayne up to her house. He was looking forward to seeing her again.

He had earlier driven Donovan's wife's Toyota to the huge CastleCourt shopping center in central Belfast and had left it on the second floor of the main multistory parking lot—complete with the magnetic tracking device.

Then they had taken a taxi to the offices of a small, local Ulster car rental company, where the Focus seemed the most anonymous and unobtrusive vehicle available.

Johnson rang the doorbell at Moira's house twice, but there was no reply.

"She's probably in the shower or something," Jayne said.

"She knew we were coming at ten." Her purple Corsa was parked outside, half on the sidewalk, half on the road. He rang again. But there was still no reply.

Johnson pressed down on the front door handle; the door swung open. "Good security," he said. "She should be more careful around here."

He led the way into the small hallway. "Hi, Moira?" he called. "Joe here. Anyone at home?"

There was no reply. He called again. Silence.

"She's got two housemates, apparently," Johnson said. "I never met them. They're not around either. Maybe she's walked down to the shop or something. Let's look in the kitchen."

The kitchen was again in an untidy state. The sink was filled with dirty cereal bowls and teacups. There was a half-eaten slice of toast and jam on a plate, together with a very brown banana skin. It was the remains of several hastily eaten breakfasts.

"Think I'll give her a call, find out what she's doing." Johnson said.

He rang her number and clamped the phone to his ear.

"It's ringing upstairs," Jayne said immediately, pointing her index finger at the ceiling. "Her phone's up there."

Johnson removed his phone from his ear, and sure enough, the faint sound of a ringing phone could be heard from above.

He cancelled the call. The ringing upstairs stopped and he looked at Jayne. "I'll go up," he said.

Johnson slowly climbed the stairs to the landing and then headed for the bedroom he recognized from helping the injured Moira the previous Saturday night. The door was slightly ajar.

He knocked. There was no reply.

Johnson pushed the door open slowly.

He recoiled at what he saw. Moira's body lay on the bed, her head twisted away from Johnson, and the pillow and sheets were stained crimson from blood that oozed from a large, ragged bullet exit wound at the back of her skull.

"Shit," Johnson said. He felt his legs buckle momentarily, and he leaned back against the wall.

Moira's arms and legs were spread-eagle, her jeans unbuttoned at the top as if she had been getting dressed. She wore a green T-shirt, which was saturated with blood, and a blue sweatshirt lay neatly folded at the bottom of the bed on the duvet.

The wallpaper behind her bed was sprayed with blood over a wide area, and there was a gash in the plasterwork, probably where the bullet had hit after exiting the back of her head, Johnson assumed.

"Jayne, get up here quick," Johnson called. "The bastards have shot her."

Jayne ran up the stairs and into the room behind him. "Bloody hell. Is that the stepfather who's—"

"It's got to be, him or his cronies. And it's only a short time ago; the blood's still oozing, hardly started to congeal."

He clasped his hands behind his head and took a couple of breaths. "That's obviously the price you pay for opening your mouth around here. This is my fault—if I hadn't tracked her down and started nosing around, it probably wouldn't have happened. Her stepfather warned her off talking to me."

"It's appalling. What a bastard. We'd better call an ambulance, although it's obviously far too late," Jayne said.

"What do we say?"

Jayne turned on her heel in clear frustration. "Don't know. It's going to sound callous, but I really don't think we want to get caught up in a murder investigation here. That'd be hugely complicated, trying to explain what we're doing and why we were here. Police would probably stop us doing anything more. We'd be finished." Jayne's face had gone pale behind the remnants of her tan.

Johnson said nothing. He stared at Moira's body, unable to take his eyes off her, this girl he had spent just a few hours with but had felt a great deal of empathy for and could not help feeling attracted to, despite himself.

Eventually, he shook his head. "We've got to tell them, though. We can't just leave her like this for her housemates to find."

Jayne hesitated. "I agree. But let's get out of here, then call anonymously. Say we were passing and heard gunshots."

Johnson looked around the room. He walked to her dressing table. There was a yellow sticky note there. On it was scribbled the name Ronnie Quinn, together with an address in Forkhill.

Next to it lay her cell phone, her open handbag, and an array of lipsticks and tubes and tubs of makeup, brushes, and bottles. There was a radio and a Bluetooth music speaker.

Johnson glanced at the cell phone. He took a paper tissue from a box on the table and used it to pick up the phone and press the call button to activate the screen. No password had been set, and the screen immediately showed a string of text messages. His hair prickled on the top of his head as he realized the message conversation showing was with him.

Shit. Who's seen this? Johnson stood rooted for a few seconds, his mind in a whirl.

"What's up?" Jayne asked.

Johnson looked grim. "She's got my text messages on her phone here, using my real name. Which means whoever killed her might well have read them. I should have told her to be careful and stay somewhere else. She was knocked around in the street by her father last Saturday when I was going to meet her, remember? I should've seen this coming, and she should have too. I should never have involved her."

"Don't blame yourself, Joe," Jayne said.

Johnson put the phone down and picked up the yellow

sticky note. "This is the guy she was taking us to see today, Ronnie Quinn." Johnson pocketed the note and the tissue.

"Joe, don't touch anything. I really think we should get out of here, even if it goes against the grain. Any minute somebody could come home, and then we're deep in it," Jayne said.

Johnson nodded. "I know, you're right. Dammit. What a mess. Come on, let's go."

He headed down the stairs, Jayne right behind him, and they went out the door. Jayne removed a handkerchief from her pocket and wiped the door handle.

"I'm going to call the police from that phone booth at the bottom of the road, near where we parked the car," Johnson said.

"I'll do it," Jayne said. "A British accent's more anonymous than an American around here."

She headed into the phone booth, her hand wrapped in her handkerchief, and dialed 999. She wanted to report gunshots heard on St. James Crescent, she told the call handler. She'd been walking past a house and heard them. She didn't want to intervene. No, she'd rather not give her details, she didn't feel safe. Then she hung up.

They got into the Focus, and Johnson drove to the end of Donegall Road, then right onto Falls Road.

A short distance in front of them, a police car was parked outside a pub. As they got nearer, its siren started up and its blue lights flashed. Then it did a quick U-turn and shot off in the direction Johnson and Jayne had just come from.

Johnson pounded his hand on the steering wheel as he drove. "I'll tell you what, that does it for me. I'm gonna nail the bastard who did this. And I know who did it. I think a good place to start would be this guy Moira was meant to take us to visit, Ronnie Quinn. I don't want to waste any time."

* * *

Thursday, January 10, 2013
  Forkhill

Ronnie Quinn's house was one of many white-painted houses with gray slate roofs scattered across the countryside on the south side of Forkhill village. It had a view over the valley to the stony peak of Croslieve Hill and was tucked away next to a couple of other houses at the end of a gravel lane. Johnson felt grateful for the cover as he pulled up behind a row of conifer trees, out of sight of the road.

Despite mentioning the fact that he'd been sent by Moira, Johnson was forced to parry a handful of penetrating questions, accompanied by a suspicious stare, before Ronnie finally let him and Jayne in through the back door.

"We get hardly any Brits, let alone Americans, coming down this way. Not if they've got any sense," said Ronnie, a slight but wiry man in his sixties. "Feelings are still running high around here. But if you know Moira, then that's fine. A good girl. I'm surprised she didn't call to let me know you were coming. And why's she not with you?"

"Ronnie, you'd better sit down. I need to tell you something, about Moira," Johnson said.

The older man stopped still and glanced at him. After a couple of seconds he said, "It's bad news, isn't it? We're used to bad news around here."

Johnson told him quickly about events from that morning.

Ronnie sank onto a wooden chair next to his kitchen table and ran his hand through his silver-gray hair. "She was always on the wrong side of that family. Her stepfather never liked her; she spoke her mind too much. She hated the violence."

He looked up. "Is it him and his gang who've done it? Must be. Doubt she had any other enemies."

"Don't know," Johnson said, "but I saw him and another man give her a bit of a kicking in the street near the club she worked at a few nights ago. I'm struggling with that. I should've done something more."

"Another man? What did he look like?"

"Thick-set, dark hair, had a mustache, wore a black leather jacket."

"That's Martin Dennehy." Ronnie said. "I've known Moira since she was about four. Her mother was a sound woman, married the wrong guy."

Ronnie leaned forward and tapped his fingers on the table. "Look, if your aim is to nail Dessie Duggan, I'll help you as much as I can. Okay?"

Johnson nodded. "Whatever you can do will be helpful. Especially if you've got any inside knowledge of Willows Farm."

Ronnie stood up and filled his kettle. While he was waiting for it to boil, he disappeared upstairs, then came back a few minutes later carrying a thin cardboard folder.

He removed two folded sheets of paper, his hands shaking a little, and spread them out on the table. They were photo-copies of a set of building plans, which had been drawn by an architect.

"Nobody knows I've got this," Ronnie said. "It's a drawing of the project I worked on at the farm going back, what, twenty-five years. I did other work there after that, as recently as ten years ago. I was often down there, but this was the original one. All very hush-hush. No proper builders involved, just mates. Or mates as they were at the time. Mates no longer in some cases, not that we've argued or anything, just drifted. I used to feel a bit sorry for him because of the way his dad died, but never liked him."

Ronnie made three mugs of tea, without asking whether Johnson or Jayne actually wanted any, and piled a large spoon of sugar into each. Johnson knew that Jayne didn't have sugar, but she didn't say a word.

Ronnie sat down again.

"Just on the subject of his dad dying," Johnson said. "What happened there?"

Ronnie wrinkled his face. "A bad business. He got taken out in an ambush over in Coolderry Road, near Cross. Nobody ever knew for sure who'd done it, but probably one of the unionist gangs, the Prods."

"Yes, I heard that from Moira."

"A real mess, apparently. I never saw it myself, but I've heard the stories from Dessie and others."

Ronnie exhaled, then picked up a pencil and used it as a pointer to tap on the drawing in front of him. "Right, back to this. It's not what you can see above ground that's of interest. It's the part below ground."

He stabbed at two oval-shaped outlines, each with a rectangle drawn around them, and a separate slightly smaller rectangle, all linked by parallel sets of lines.

Ronnie explained that the oval shapes were two huge diesel tanks buried beneath the concrete farmyard floor. One was on the Republic side of the farmyard, one on the Northern Ireland side. He stabbed at the paper again. Linking them was a pipe through a small tunnel, with just about enough room to crawl through. He wasn't sure if there was a pump or whether it was a gravity feed. But it allowed the diesel to flow from the Republic to the other side, or the other way.

Then from both underground tanks there were pipes that led to other tanks above ground in the barns, from where the fuel could be pumped straight into vehicles or into large fuel tankers. The tanks above ground were in two barns, one north of the border, and one south.

Ronnie took a deep breath. "What it means is that Duggan could make a mint from the differences in diesel duties north and south of the border. They've made millions from this, must have, over the years. Along with the cigarette smuggling, it's funded their weapons and plenty more besides."

Johnson was skeptical. "But surely someone would have picked up on this and investigated it?" he asked. "I mean, if he's making a fortune by smuggling diesel on his own farm property? Don't the police or the local authorities or the customs people just come in and close the whole thing down?"

Ronnie sighed. "There were lots of inquiries. The problem was, there was little proof. Duggan used to buy the diesel in the Republic, stick it into his tank on that side of the border, then move it to the tank on the Northern Ireland side. From there, he'd sell it, for cash, to people whom he trusted not to drop him in the shit with the police. Unless they caught him in the act, there was little they could do."

Most of the customers came at night, Ronnie explained, and in any case, Duggan's network of informers meant they could just close down any diesel loading operation well before any police or customs people could get anywhere near the place. He just told them it was for his own use on the farm.

"Is that sort of thing common around here, then?"

"Frankly, he was a minor player. Others did the same thing on a much bigger scale."

Johnson shook his head. "Sounds like the Wild West." As he said it, he realized he was echoing Donovan's words to him a week or so earlier.

"A few have been prosecuted over the years but not that

many. There wasn't much policing going on. They were too terrified—same with the customs authorities. They thought, quite rightly, they'd get beaten up or worse. So they often just let Duggan and the others get on with it."

Ronnie turned back to the drawing and stabbed at the other rectangle with his finger. "That was a storage room, a den, a guns and weapons cache, you name it, linked to the tanks by other small crawling tunnels. Dessie kept his secrets in there, in special hiding places."

He leaned back in his chair and folded his arms. "Word has it the brigade used it as a torture chamber. Anyone suspected of touting was hauled down there. When they came out—if they came out—they were never the same again. Most people didn't come out, at least not alive."

"So you escaped that fate?" Johnson asked.

"Who's saying I was a tout?" Ronnie asked. He gave Johnson a hard look.

"So how do you get in and out of this underground chamber thing?" Jayne asked swiftly, clearly trying to change the subject.

"Not straightforward," Ronnie said. "There's a manhole cover in one of the barns—this one here." He tapped on the plan, pointing to the outline of a building on the southern side of the site.

"Then you have to climb down through the manhole into what looks at first glance like a big sewer. Then there's a hidden tunnel that goes sideways. You crawl through, straight into the den. From there you can access the tanks via more tunnels."

He laughed. "It's like a rabbit warren down there. But that's where all the toys will be, and the secrets. It's all wired up—proper power supply, lighting, water, taps, everything, even if it is like some sort of medieval underground dungeon.

He had electric heaters in there because it was freezing in winter. It's all made from breeze blocks."

Johnson nodded. "Cinder blocks, we call them. So there's only one way in and out?"

Ronnie drained his mug of tea.

No, he said. It was also possible to get into the tunnel via the basement in the house, which meant another crawl, but it was an alternative to using the manhole cover in the barn. Going the other way, it was also possibly a way into the house.

"There's also an emergency exit from one of the diesel tank structures out into a field," Ronnie said. "It used to come out through a drain cover in a concrete block underneath a cattle drinking trough."

However, he wasn't sure if the trough exit was still functional. In fact, he would put money on the route not having been used since the tunnels complex was built, he said.

Johnson took his phone from his pocket and carefully photographed the plans on the table.

"What about security systems and dogs at the farm?" Johnson asked. "Do you know what he's got there?"

Ronnie tapped the table with his fingers. "He's got a large Rottweiler named Rex, I know that. An aggressive beast. Security systems? Hmm. It's funny, I remember having a conversation with him about that when he built the complex. I said I thought he should get it all wired up. But he said the best security system was his rifle; then he wouldn't need cameras. And everyone knew he was handy with a rifle."

Johnson raised his eyebrows. "Yes, but that's not much use if he's out somewhere."

"No. And I think he does have some cameras, actually. But the word is that if he's out, he arranges for someone else to be in. It might not be someone with his level of expertise, but it's always someone who knows which end of a rifle to hold."

"And has it worked?"

"There were two burglars in the early days, going back fifteen years, who I know for a fact didn't make it out. Word got around after that, and I don't think he's had a problem since."

Johnson raised his eyebrows and opened his mouth, as if to say something.

But before he could do so, Ronnie cut in. "It's Northern Ireland, lad. Get used to it."

* * *

Thursday, January 10, 2013
Forkhill

"Well, that was useful," Johnson said after they left Ronnie's house. "I wonder if he'd have been so forthcoming if Moira hadn't been killed the way she was."

He shifted into fifth gear and accelerated down the on-ramp onto the divided highway back to Belfast.

"I'd like to keep a close eye on what Duggan's doing in that house and underground bunker," Johnson said. "Speaking of which, you know that box of toys you keep under your bed?"

Jayne grinned. "Yeah, the one you have fantasies about, you mean?"

"Yep. That's the one," Johnson said with a straight face. "I think we might need a few items out of it. Like some computer monitoring software, a few wireless microcameras, and so on. I want to watch it closely. It sounds like his center of operations."

"Good idea in theory," Jayne said. "But then there's the small matter of installing them. Are you happy to take that job on?"

Johnson shrugged. "I guess so. That's where I've got an advantage over official investigators. I'm not exactly going to be applying for a warrant before going in there. Given what happened to Moira, I'm feeling fairly fired up about this job. I want to get stuck in and sort it out."

"That's a dangerous way of thinking," Jayne said.

"What?"

"Letting your feelings rule the roost."

"Yes, but it's not just that."

"What is it, then?" Jayne asked.

"Everything going on here. It's just another pointless, inward-looking sectarian clash. These people can't see the bigger picture."

Jayne didn't disagree. She folded her arms and gazed out the side window as the Armagh countryside flashed past.

"I've just remembered," she said. "There's a guy I know who used to work for the SVR until a couple of years ago and before that for the KGB—a guy called Vladimir Timmer. I met him at an arms conference and we kind of clicked."

The SVR—Russia's foreign intelligence service and successor organization to the KGB—had been the focus of Jayne's attention for years. She described how she and Vladimir had both been thinking of going freelance, ended up in a deep conversation about it, and agreed to keep in touch on the basis that they might be able to help each other at some point.

"A Russian? And you kind of clicked?" Johnson threw Jayne a sideways glance.

"Not clicked in that kind of way, you idiot. Professionally, I mean. And no—he wasn't trying to recruit me. At least I don't think so."

"He probably was. And how did you click, exactly?"

"He wasn't. It's like how I help you out. But he's got good sources for the kind of kit we need. He might even have some in stock himself. I can get in touch. How does that sound?"

Johnson chuckled. *"Fantasticheskiye, bol'shoy."*

Jayne turned in the passenger seat and narrowed her eyes. "Good to hear you haven't forgotten your Russian, but I think you need to do something about that accent."

"Really? I thought it was still quite authentic."

Johnson paused. If Jayne was going to request some equipment from her Russian friend, then she could add a few other items to the order, he told her. He gave her a short list, including a pair of infrared night vision goggles, a handheld thermal imager, and some microchip GPS tracking devices.

For what he had planned, all of them might be useful. He suspected that getting into the underground complex might not be a straightforward task.

CHAPTER NINETEEN

Friday, January 11, 2013
Belfast

Duggan nosed his white Volkswagen Transporter van into the yard of a plastics and specialist vinyl manufacturing company on a small industrial park in West Belfast.

Among its best-selling lines was a range of thin vinyl wraps, superimposed with computer-designed artwork, which car enthusiasts used to transform the look of their vehicles.

On his last visit, Duggan had watched, fascinated, as a brand-new Ford van was transformed into a highly convincing rust bucket, with realistic orange and brown streaks and holes all over the body, in the space of a few hours.

His requirements had nothing to do with his van, however, but with a Yamaha Grizzly quad bike, stolen from a dealership on a country road halfway between Omagh and Ballygawley, and also with something of a more personal nature.

Duggan knew the business owner, Francis Conaghy, a staunch republican activist now in his early fifties. He had several British army scalps to his credit, dating back to the 1970s, but had long since retired from active service. Nevertheless, he remained supportive of the cause.

Francis's real skill set and passion lay in camouflage. He had two businesses. One was the vinyl company, a more recent venture. The original business, which he still operated, provided handmade camouflage equipment and suits for a large variety of customers, including birdwatchers and photographers.

However, an unadvertised sideline to his main range of products was camo garments, known as ghillie suits, used by snipers to conceal themselves from view while working out in the open. He used a variety of both man-made and natural materials and designed the suits so that they could be adapted quickly in the field by adding local vegetation to special netting that was stitched to the suit material.

Francis had learned his craft from an American friend who worked at the US army sniper school in Fort Benning, Georgia. And he had gradually built up a below-the-counter client list that included a motley bunch of mavericks and mercenaries who operated in some of the darkest corners of the globe, particularly Africa and the Middle East.

During the '80s and '90s, Francis had occasionally provided the south Armagh sniper gangs with ghillie suits, including Duggan's father, Alfie, which was how the two men had come to know each other.

There were two items on Duggan's shopping list. One was a ghillie suit, the other a vinyl cover for the Grizzly in the back of Duggan's van.

For both items, Duggan provided Francis with a flash drive containing several photographs he had taken on Black

Mountain with the high-definition camera mounted on his drone.

Francis led Duggan through his vinyl wraps showroom to an office at the rear of the building, made him a cup of tea, and closed the door.

He loaded Duggan's photographs onto his laptop and scrutinized them carefully. "Good pictures," he said. "Can I ask, where did you take them?"

Duggan studied the older man carefully. "You don't need to know that," he said.

Francis shrugged. "Of course."

After Duggan left Francis, he steered his van off Falls Road and through another industrial park until he reached a small, run-down cluster of units that housed various businesses, some of them legitimate, others that he knew were less so.

Now he was onto the next job he had scheduled for that morning, which he expected to prove a little trickier.

Arthur Higgins Welders, said a weather-beaten painted sign on a piece of plywood above the fifteen-foot-wide steel roller door that formed the main entrance.

Duggan parked and walked through the door. He paused for a moment to allow his eyes to adjust to the gloomy interior of the workshop, which was lined with workbenches, oxyacetylene equipment, tanks, masks, pails of paint, and other paraphernalia.

Over in the corner, a thin, wiry gray-haired man in an oil-stained blue boilersuit was bent over a workbench, wearing a pair of plastic safety goggles.

Arthur Higgins had run his three-man welding business in that particular area of West Belfast for many years. His normal stock-in-trade consisted of customized steel beams for home additions, metal gates, and made-to-measure steel staircases, all of which he supplied to local building companies.

But, like Francis, Arthur also had a sideline. For years he had acted as welder in chief for whichever IRA units required his services. No matter the equipment requested of him, Arthur had found a way to manufacture it all: from under-car weapons concealment devices designed to look like part of an exhaust system, to platforms for heavy machine guns on the backs of farm trailers, and hidden containers on trucks that could be used to transport explosives around the province.

Known to his friends as Hurricane because he worshiped onetime Northern Ireland world snooker champion Alex "Hurricane" Higgins—who was ironically a Protestant Unionist—Arthur still spent an inordinate amount of time hustling for money against all comers in the snooker hall near the Milltown cemetery.

For that reason, persuading him to take on new jobs was often extremely difficult.

Duggan stood in the center of the workshop until Arthur looked up from his bench and raised a hand in greeting. He slowly limped over, which reminded Duggan that the old man had taken a bullet in the leg during some long past street battle with a bunch of unionist paramilitaries in the early 1980s.

"Long time no see," Duggan said. "How's business?" They shook hands.

"Hectic," Higgins said. "There's not enough hours in the day. Too much work from those rich folk in the posh houses over in Holywood and Cultra, all wanting fancy metal fences."

"Are you still doing much work for the brigades?"

"The odd job, but not like the old times."

Duggan nodded. "The fire's gone out of the Provos' belly, but we're still up for the fight. I still have the same dreams that Pearse and Connolly dreamed in 1916." He grinned.

"Glad to hear it," Higgins said, a doubtful expression on

his face. He removed his safety goggles and peered at Duggan. "And how's Martin?"

Duggan knew that Higgins was an old pal of Dennehy, going years back, when they had lived a couple of doors down from each other somewhere in West Belfast.

Duggan's face tightened. "He's okay."

"I hope you're looking after him," Higgins said in his slow Ulster burr. "Anyway, what can I do for you?"

Duggan waved a cardboard folder he was holding. "Got something here I want to show you."

"Well, I've got a list of work as long as my arm, to be honest."

"Can I just show you?" Duggan said.

Higgins hesitated, then turned and led the way to a small office in the corner of the workshop. He pointed toward a desk and sat on a chair behind it.

Duggan removed a few sheets of paper from the folder and laid them out on the desk.

"Four-wheel drive quad bike?" said Higgins as he picked up the first sheet, printed from a website. "That's a big beast. Yamaha Grizzly. What you gonna do with that?"

Duggan felt like asking Higgins why he needed to know but reined himself in. "I've bought one of these buggers for a job I'm planning," Duggan said. "It's in the back of the van." He jerked his thumb toward the van, parked outside. "What I need now is some work on it."

Duggan went on to explain in some detail what he would need Higgins to do to the quad bike.

"Fine, but like I said, I'm snowed under right now," Higgins said.

Duggan picked up the next sheet. "This is the other part."

"What is it?" Higgins asked.

"More customization work," Duggan said. "The van this time."

"Right," said Higgins. "Presumably you're not converting it for deliveries of coleslaw and baguettes to the local deli?"

Duggan made an effort through gritted teeth to laugh at the attempted joke. "There's two things I need," he said. "First, I need to be able to get the Grizzly into it as fast as I can, to make it secure in the back, and get away, quick. Real quick. So, I need a set of ramps and some anchoring points installed in the back of the van so the Grizzly doesn't start sliding around inside. And I also need you to do some other modifications to the high-roofed part of the van."

Higgins rubbed his chin, hemmed and hawed for a few seconds, then said, "I can do it, but the issue is, do I have time to do it. And the answer is no."

"Arthur, I know you're really busy, and the reason is because you're damn good at what you do. What's your current hourly rate?"

"Forty-five."

"Okay, I'll pay you sixty-five. In cash."

Higgins scratched his chin again, looked Duggan in the eye, then nodded almost imperceptibly.

"Good," Duggan said. He reeled off a further list of instructions and grabbed a pen and carefully drew a diagram on the sheet of paper, showing detailed specifications and dimensions for what he had in mind.

Higgins nodded. "Okay, that's also doable, I think. We'd need to cut part of the bodywork away, put a hinge or something in there, and tidy it all up, but yeah. Shouldn't be a problem."

"Good stuff. Right, I'll leave the van and the Grizzly with you now. I'll need both of them back within a couple of weeks, absolute maximum. Okay?"

Higgins pulled a face but nodded.

"Now, can I order a taxi? I need to go and pick up my car."

After he left Francis, Duggan's phone rang as he was climbing back into his Passat. It was McGarahan.

"Yes, Liam. What you got for me?"

"Just something I found out when I was with Dennehy, when he did that job for you, boss. The American guy who's been nosing around. I found his details on Moira's phone when we were in her house. A load of text messages between them, arranging to meet up and so on."

"Okay, that confirms what we knew from the photographs," Duggan said.

"Yeah, but there's more to it. He's been using a false name. It's not Philip Wilkinson. She had him listed on her phone as Joe Johnson."

"Joe Johnson?"

"Yes. I've found out a bit already, done some Internet research on him. He runs his own investigations business, based in Portland on the East Coast. He's no mug. Ex-CIA, worked for the Office of Special Investigations for years tracking Nazis on the run around the States. Got a few big scalps under his belt."

Duggan climbed slowly into his driver's seat and shut the door, the phone still clamped to his ear.

"Shit," Duggan said. "So if this Johnson is ex-CIA, what's his story? Is he some sort of pro killer?"

McGarahan ran through his findings. It seemed that Johnson was definitely not a paid killer but simply an investigator, although there had been deaths during his investigations, according to press clippings.

"He seems to specialize in getting people into court in cases where mainstream law and order forces haven't been able to," McGarahan said.

Duggan wrinkled his forehead. "What kind of cases?"

"War crimes—he's done an old Nazi commander, did a guy from Yugoslavia. Put them both behind bars."

Duggan stared up at the car roof. "So what the hell's he doing here? Who would've brought him in?"

"No idea, chief. It can't be anyone official. They're too proud, they don't bring in outsiders. Unlikely to be the Prods. They know who you are, anyway, and they're not going to hire some gun investigator from the States, are they?"

"So who, then?"

McGarahan paused. "I've no idea."

Duggan leaned forward and stared out the windshield, his hands clasping the steering wheel.

* * *

Friday, January 11, 2013
Drumintee

It was the first time Dennehy had been to Danny McCormick's house and, in fact, the first time any of the brigade had called him in to do an electrical repair job.

McCormick had been complaining for some time that his electrical fuse board was always tripping, throwing his house into darkness and cutting off his broadband connection for no apparent reason.

Perhaps the quartermaster was taking pity on him for having no regular work at present, Dennehy thought, as he went through a series of tests on the electrical circuit to try and pinpoint the fault.

Whatever the reason, he had received a call from McCormick the previous evening and had gone around to his house the next morning.

It was a sprawling five-bedroom, single-story bungalow, probably no more than ten years old, built on an elevated one-acre plot of land on the edge of Drumintee village. It was just down the road from the Three Steps Bar and Lounge, which achieved notoriety when British army officer Robert Nairac was abducted from there and killed by the IRA in 1977 after an undercover operation went wrong.

Gentle green hills rose to the east and west, and to the north, the formidable mass of Slieve Gullion stood black and inscrutable, looking down over the straggly ribbon of white houses that formed the village.

McCormick, whose chiseled, craggy features and mop of graying hair reminded Dennehy of the nearby mountain, made them each a cup of tea and stood watching as Dennehy changed the fuse board.

"This is your problem: the board. Whoever put this in went for the budget option," Dennehy said. "Buy cheap, buy twice."

"Thanks," McCormick said, sipping his tea as Dennehy packed his tools back into his carry case.

On the way out, McCormick stopped as he was about to open the front door. "I might need your help again, week after next, on the Wednesday," he said.

Dennehy looked at him. "What's that about—another electrical job?"

"No. Operational reasons this time. Dessie wants me to fish some gear out of the cache down at Dundalk that day, but I might need to take the missus into Belfast for a doctor's appointment, and I can't get out of that. Could you step in?"

"Probably. What's the job?"

"Pipe bomb for a hit on a Prod copper at his home in Irvinestown. You'd just need to do a drop-off in Hannahstown. A volunteer will pick it up from you and do the rest. Easy. No need to tell Duggan we're swapping roles. He might not like it."

Dennehy nodded. The quartermaster was correct.

Duggan certainly wouldn't like members of his brigade swapping jobs, given his strict operational rules.

"Sure," Dennehy said. "I'll do it. Won't say a word."

"Good. I'll be in touch."

* * *

Friday, January 11, 2013
Belfast

After persuading Arthur to do the job, Duggan had another task to complete before going home: a round of golf.

He drove to East Belfast and headed toward Holywood Golf Club. All sports fans in Northern Ireland knew it as the home club of Rory McIlroy, who won the US Open a couple of years previously and had grown up in the area.

The course, built on a hillside with views out over Belfast Lough toward the Antrim coastline across the water, was one that Duggan knew reasonably well. It was also only a stone's throw from Palace Barracks, the British army and MI5 headquarters.

Duggan had played the odd round there over the years with a farming friend who was a member and also sometimes met up with him for a drink at the bar. No republican talk on those visits—there were far too many police and army types in the clubhouse.

But today he was planning a solo round. And his true purpose had little to do with golf.

Duggan pulled into the club parking lot and hauled his bag of clubs and golf cart out of the back of the car.

There he stopped and checked the phone app he had set up to monitor the location of the GPS tracking device placed under the silver Toyota Avensis, which he knew Johnson had borrowed from Donovan.

He was becoming certain that something was wrong. According to the GPS device, on Thursday, the Toyota had been parked for the whole day at the CastleCourt shopping center. Today it hadn't moved from a backstreet just off Falls Road. He decided to assign one of the volunteers to keep a physical watch on it the following day. It was frustrating that he didn't have enough men to do everything he needed.

Duggan shook his head and walked into the pro shop, where he paid his fee for nine holes. That would be enough to cover the area of the course he was interested in.

Five minutes later he was on the first tee. The only other people on the course were a couple of fast-moving youngsters who were two holes ahead of him. *Perfect*.

He deliberately pulled his tee shot a little left on the first hole, toward the trees, then grabbed his cart and set off to find the ball.

When he got down toward the green, well away from the clubhouse, he walked to the fringe of the trees, which gave him some cover.

From there, Duggan could see down to the northwestern boundary of the course, where there was a curved row of mainly semidetached houses that formed Demesne Road.

He unzipped a compartment in his bag and took out a piece of kit not carried by many golfers—his Vectronix Terrapin range finder.

He quickly applied the range finder to his right eye and focused. There, 355 yards away, was the house in Demesne Road, its front cleared of bushes and trees, presumably to improve security. He expected it to have plenty of illumination after dark—security systems, infrared beams, movement sensors, and other toys in place—given what he knew of its owner.

But sophisticated systems designed to deal with burglars weren't Duggan's concern. He was more worried about getting a clear line of sight. And from there, near the first green, things looked good.

He guessed his target would be a similar distance away to that which young McIlroy would hit his driver on a good day.

Not that anybody would be out on the course at the time he had in mind, though.

Because he was planning a night strike.

CHAPTER TWENTY

Saturday, January 12, 2013
  Belfast

The Russian Vladimir Timmer had moved quickly.

Before Johnson and Jayne had finished their breakfast, a courier delivered to the apartment on Falls Road a box containing the equipment Jayne had requested from the former SVR operative only two days earlier.

"Express courier from Moscow. Looks like he's trying to impress you for some reason," Johnson said as he glanced up at her from his coffee.

Jayne slit open the box and spread the contents across the table.

There were fifteen microcameras, each about three and a half inches long and not much fatter than a pen, that held a tiny lens and a microphone, a wireless transmission unit the size of a cigarette pack, and a matchbox-size signal booster. The kit was identical to a system Johnson had successfully used a couple of times before that fed footage to a server where it could be viewed live and also recorded and stored for easy access online at any time.

All the cameras had ultra-long-life batteries that would last around seventeen days, according to the blurb.

Also in the box was a small USB hard drive with a printed sheet of paper wrapped around it.

The note on the sheet said that spyware had been copied to the hard drive. If installed on a computer, it would allow complete remote monitoring of activity and files, including emails, without the user being aware that it was happening.

The sheet also included installation instructions—a simple setup that could be used if the PC could be unlocked and accessed and a more complicated method if a PC were locked with a password.

There was also a thermal imager with an 80 mm lens, which was roughly the size of a small telescope or camcorder. According to the instructions, it would allow covert night viewing up to a mile and a half away without any likelihood of the user being detected.

The other item was a small pack of GPS microchip tracking devices, which could monitor the location of any item into which they were inserted.

Johnson walked to the coffee machine, made another cup, and turned on the radio Donovan had left in the apartment. A BBC Radio Ulster news program was underway.

He looked up the PC monitoring software brand, Total-AccessSpySoft, online and began to read up on its capabilities. The package looked comprehensive and had many good reviews from corporate users.

Johnson's phone rang. He looked at the display. It was Ronnie.

There was no exchange of pleasantries. Ronnie got straight to the point.

"Word's got around the village," he said. "Duggan got

picked up this morning by police. We think for questioning about Moira. They took him up to Belfast."

Johnson instantly felt a jolt go through him. It was hardly surprising, though. "Has he been charged with anything?"

"No idea. That's all I know. They've picked him up and apparently two others in as well. I don't know who the others are. My bet is that he's got alibis up to his armpits, but you never know."

Johnson thanked Ronnie, ended the call, and turned to Jayne. "Did you get that?"

"I picked up that Duggan's been taken in for questioning," Jayne said. "That's standard procedure, I'd have thought, to quiz him."

"Yes. I'm just thinking—"

"He's going to be held for at least a day or so, that's my guess. The house'll be empty."

That was what he liked about Jayne—always on the ball. "Right. Unless he somehow arranged for someone to sit in at short notice, as Ronnie suggested. Unlikely. Or is it?"

"Don't know, but it's our best chance. We'd best get moving," Jayne said. She would get Noreen Wilson to use her network to check on how long police might keep Duggan for questioning or at least to give Jayne a heads-up when he was going to be released. That would hopefully give them enough time to make a quick exit if needed.

Johnson nodded. He certainly didn't want Duggan to catch him breaking into Willows Farm.

The usual butterflies fluttered in his stomach, as was always the case before he set out on something that either was dangerous or on the wrong side of the law.

Or both.

* * *

Saturday, January 12, 2013
 Forkhill

Dusk was falling rapidly, and a relentless north wind was buffeting the sparse branches of a tall pine when Johnson and Jayne arrived at the wooded area he had pinpointed, about three-quarters of a mile south of Willows Farm.

This time they drove up from the Irish Republic side, having earlier traveled south across the border on the divided highway, rather than take the route through Forkhill. There was less chance of being spotted by the wrong people that way.

Jayne drove the black Ford into the gateway to a field, cut behind a large stack of silage bales wrapped in black plastic, well out of sight from the road, and killed the lights. The plan was already agreed, so there was no need for further discussion.

Johnson and Jayne would head toward Willows Farm, but only Johnson would go in. Jayne would wait a suitable distance away in case things went wrong. If he didn't return within an hour or send her a message, she would go in and search for him. He had given her a copy of Ronnie's map of the underground complex.

Almost unconsciously, Johnson patted the Beretta, which he had stuffed into his belt, under his jacket. Hopefully he wouldn't need it. They both got out of the car and set off.

Dressed entirely in black, from his woolly hat to his waterproof jacket to his leather boots, Johnson moved quickly behind the hedge separating the field from the straight single-lane road. Jayne, similarly attired, followed behind.

Up to their right, to the east, lay a slope that rose to a large wooded area on a ridge beyond the fields. Johnson quickly calculated that if they could work their way up to the trees, they could make their way along a ridge and get within a third of a mile of Willows Farm without breaking cover.

They walked up the side of the field next to the hedge until they reached the densely planted conifers and pine trees, then turned north and, hugging the darkness of the wood, followed the curve of the field.

Fifteen minutes later they reached the end of the tree line. Looking down the slope away to his left, Johnson could just about make out the outline of the three barns, the farmhouse, and the other outbuildings that made up Willows Farm, about half a mile away.

Johnson took out the thermal imager from his backpack and focused on the farm below, which instantly became clearly visible on the viewfinder as a series of white-gray images against the dark background of the field behind it. The whitest of them, indicating it was the warmest, was the farmhouse, next to the road.

There was no sign of life.

Johnson turned and pointed the imager toward the neighboring field, where several cows grazed. They showed up as clear white or pale-gray images. A fast-moving smaller white shape suddenly appeared from the bottom of a hedge and ran up to the wood. A fox.

"I think you should stay here," Johnson said. "You can see everything, and you're within range if I need you."

"Yes. Perfect," Jayne said. "See you soon, and good luck."

Johnson nodded, returned the imager to his backpack, and made his way down alongside the hedge toward the farm.

After a few minutes he was within a couple hundred yards of the three barns that stood between him and the farmhouse and the road. The barn he needed was on the far left, southern side of the farmyard, on the Irish Republic side.

Johnson moved up behind a clump of gorse bushes, which provided him with good cover as he resurveyed the farmyard with his thermal imager. Again all appeared quiet apart from a cat that strolled out of one barn and sauntered slowly to the next.

Where was the Rottweiler Ronnie had mentioned? There was no sight of him in the farmyard and neither had he heard him barking. In any event, Johnson was prepared for the animal with a pack of dog treats. In his experience, they were worth a try. There weren't many dogs he couldn't charm, unless they were particularly vicious, rigorously trained animals.

Johnson checked carefully for surveillance cameras through the imager. The only one he could see was mounted on the outside of the barn he needed to access, above large double doors that faced north.

But he could tell from the angle the camera was pointing that if he stayed flat to the barn wall he should be safe. It was positioned to capture people coming into the farmyard from the road, not the field.

Johnson decided to make his move. He edged his way to the end of the gorse bushes and climbed over a wire mesh fence that separated the field from the farmyard. Then he bent double, ran across the rough concrete yard to the wall of the barn he needed to enter, and hid around the corner from the double doors and the security camera.

He dropped to his haunches and listened. There was only silence.

Then he put on a pair of thin rubber gloves and, after a minute, peered around the side of the barn, again checking the camera, which was pointing away from him. Then he rounded the corner, flattened himself against the corrugated steel wall, and moved swiftly toward the huge double barn doors twenty yards ahead. The large doors were closed, but to his surprise, a single inset door appeared slightly ajar. Was someone inside?

Johnson visualized the map of the underground complex in his mind. The manhole leading down into the tunnel must be at the rear of this barn. But where exactly?

He peeked through the slight gap where the inset door was open. It was pitch-dark inside, and there was no sound. He pushed the door slightly, and the rusty hinges squeaked loudly in the still air. Johnson immediately stopped and winced. But again there was no sound from inside, and he needed to open the small door farther to get in. So after waiting a minute, he pushed again. There was another squeal of metal on metal.

Johnson stopped again and listened, his right hand resting on the Beretta at his side. But there were no shouts, no alarms, no running footsteps across the farmyard, no dogs barking.

He slipped through the gap into the blackness within.

Once inside, Johnson felt in his bag, took out the imager, adjusted the lens to wide angle, and slowly surveyed the interior. On the screen, he could now see the ghostly gray outlines of two tractors parked over to the right, a trailer, and a stack of hay bales. Occupying a large area to the left were two enormous fuel tanks mounted on cinder blocks with pipe systems emerging from the top and hanging down. Presumably they were used to fill or refuel vehicles or tankers.

But he couldn't yet see what he was looking for.

Johnson took several steps toward the rear of the barn and again slowly moved the imager from right to left.

There it was. Right in the corner, next to a stack of cinder blocks, a slightly lighter gray circle stood out against the blackness of the floor that surrounded it. A manhole cover, elevated a little from the rest of the barn floor on a cement base, presumably to ensure that no water would drain into the cavity below.

It looked like a simple drain cover. But Johnson knew it wasn't.

He walked to the manhole, replaced the imager in his backpack, and briefly flicked on a mini flashlight that he took from his pocket.

There were two handles on the metal manhole cover. With considerable effort, he grabbed them to lift it up and put it to one side. Below was a shaft with a metal ladder attached to the side.

Another quick flick of the flashlight, and Johnson could see the bottom, which he estimated was about fourteen or fifteen feet down. It looked dry. Above it were two openings to the right and the left, each perhaps four feet square, just as Ronnie had described. Anyone who didn't know would simply assume it was a large drainage or sewer pipe.

The problem here was that he would have to leave the manhole cover off. It was just too heavy to maneuver back into place from below once he was in the shaft.

Before going down, Johnson took one of the microcameras, turned it on and wedged it into a small gap between two of the cinder blocks in the stack next to the manhole. The camera would be virtually invisible unless someone made a close inspection of the stack or moved the blocks. He could see by the flashlight that the blocks were covered in dust and hadn't been touched for a long time, so a disturbance was unlikely.

Next he took the 3G transmitter unit and placed it out of sight between two other cinder blocks.

The cameras would connect wirelessly with the transmitter, if necessary via the booster unit he planned to place in one of the tunnels. In turn, the transmitter would send the pictures and sound via a 3G wireless connection to a secure website where Johnson could monitor the outputs, using either his laptop or the Internet connection to his phone.

He knew from experience that barring some unforeseen disaster, the system would provide decent pictures of whatever was going on in the barn or the other locations where he positioned the remaining microcameras.

Johnson removed a headlamp from his bag, strapped it onto his forehead, and began to descend into the blackness.

CHAPTER TWENTY-ONE

Saturday, January 12, 2013
  Forkhill

At the bottom of the shaft, Johnson turned on his headlamp and climbed into the right-hand tunnel, which he knew led to the farmhouse.

To his relief there were squares of dark green foam-backed carpet along the tunnel floor to make crawling more comfortable.

He set off slowly. The tunnel, built from cinder blocks, ran in a straight line. The floor on either side of the carpet squares was littered with pieces of cement and other building debris that had never been removed. Cobwebs filled every crevice. Ahead of him, a mouse appeared briefly, then vanished into a hole.

Johnson crawled on. He had never grown used to enclosed spaces, and he could feel his stress level rising, his heart rate increasing. Sweat stung his eyes, and he brushed it away with his hand.

After about fifty yards, Johnson saw a plywood hatch door in front of him. He took his Beretta from his belt and turned off his headlamp. Then he pulled the handle slowly toward him, a fraction at a time.

The hatch door opened, but behind it was only darkness. He felt with his hand to discover another flat wooden board.

Johnson turned his headlamp back on and scanned the board. At the top left-hand corner was a small brass catch. He pulled the catch gently open, clicked off his headlamp, and pushed very slowly on the board. Gradually it opened a couple of inches.

Was this a door into the house? Now Johnson was braced for the Rottweiler.

He found himself having to apply some pressure on the door to persuade it to move. It felt very heavy.

On the other side was more darkness.

Should he risk the headlamp?

The imager would be a better option.

Once he removed the imager from his bag and had a quick look, he could see the opening led into some kind of storage room filled with old wooden chairs, floor lamps, a mattress, and other furniture. The door on the far side of the room was closed.

Still there was silence from the dog. Strange.

Johnson turned the headlamp back on, eased his way out of the hatch, and stood.

The second door he had just come through, behind the hatch, was actually a bookcase on hidden hinges, designed to prevent anyone in the house from seeing the hatch door to the tunnel. It was filled with books, which explained why it had been so difficult to push open.

He moved slowly to the storage cupboard door, the Beretta in his right hand, and opened it fractionally. In front of him was a short passage, with two other doors leading to the right and the left, and ahead of him, a wooden staircase.

Surely a dog, if there were one, would have come running by now.

What he really needed was to find Duggan's computer. But would it still be in the house, or would the police have removed it?

Johnson turned the headlamp off again and moved to the staircase. Planting his feet at the sides of the steps to minimize any creaking, he went up. He emerged in a utility room, then stepped through it to a kitchen.

Johnson took out his mini flashlight and turned it on, with a finger over the lens to minimize the light. He could see that the kitchen had been fitted with granite countertops and several top-of-the-line appliances.

There, lying on the countertop next to a pile of unopened letters and a copy of *The Irish Times,* lay a laptop with a pale blue cover, its small white standby light winking slowly in the gloom.

Johnson felt some relief that he wasn't going to have to go through a prolonged search for the device. He flipped open the lid. As he had expected, the machine, a MacBook Pro, was password protected.

There were ways around that. Johnson considered trying to restart the machine with the bootable USB drive he had brought in his backpack and then copying the contents of the laptop's hard drive. But he decided it would take far too long, and time was probably short, so he closed the laptop. It was better to spend his time ensuring that the cameras were in position.

Was there anything else of interest in the kitchen? Johnson began opening the drawers below the counter. There were spare light bulbs, batteries, and some matches in the top drawer. The next one down contained utility bills and a bunch of shopping receipts. In the bottom one was a spare laptop charging cable, a small radio, and a couple of electrical extension cables. Johnson was about to close the drawer when he noticed, half-covered by the charging cable, a small red and black USB flash drive in a clear plastic bag. He hesitated for a second, then picked up the flash drive and popped it into his pocket. If he couldn't take the computer or copy the contents, then maybe there was something of interest on the drive. Hopefully it would be some time before Duggan spotted that it had disappeared.

At the other end of the countertop, next to a sophisticated-looking coffee maker, was a battered copy of a novel Johnson had once read years earlier, *Trinity*, by Leon Uris, which he remembered as a deep study of Irish nationalism. Beside it was a new-looking large-scale walking map for the Belfast Hills, Divis and the Black Mountain. On the cover was a photograph of Black Mountain, rising up above the city of Belfast below.

Johnson turned around. Hanging on the wall was a framed photograph of a large Rottweiler. Underneath was a printed caption, "Rex: Aug 8, 2005–Oct 7, 2012, R.I.P." That explained that, then. Duggan clearly hadn't found a replacement.

He pursed his lips and looked around. Then he placed a microcamera on top of the shelving that ran around the kitchen wall, hidden between two dusty saucepans. In the absence of computer monitoring software, that was probably the next best option.

Next Johnson stood on a kitchen stool and worked another camera into the cavity behind a downlight in the ceiling, wedged in the gap between the stainless steel rim and the movable center housing for the bulb. He made sure it was almost vertically above the laptop, knowing there might be a need to record keystrokes as Duggan typed. That was assuming he always used his computer in the same place—which was probably unlikely.

He moved into the living room, then a small study, and the hallway, carefully placing the tiny cameras in each area in the most unobtrusive locations he could find. The shelves were spotless, which concerned him a little. He hoped Duggan didn't have a daily cleaner who might come in and find them.

Johnson moved upstairs and also placed cameras in the master bedroom and the next largest bedroom, which showed signs of having been recently occupied. A sudden sense of voyeurism came over him as he placed a camera between two cardboard boxes on top of a wardrobe in the main bedroom. But at the same time he doubted that Duggan was involved in a relationship with anybody, based on what Moira had told him.

Nowhere were there any papers, notebooks, or anything remotely interesting in sight that might give a hint or be useful evidence of Duggan's past or future plans in relation to his Real IRA activities.

The strange thing was, apart from the messy basement room, the place was spotless. Only a handful of photographs, few trinkets, no fridge stickers, no clutter. Johnson hadn't expected to see pictures of Moira or even Duggan's ex-wife. But equally, he hadn't envisaged the place looking like a show home, either.

Hanging on the living room wall was a large framed black and white photograph of a devastated Dublin city center during the 1916 Easter Rising, seen as the birthplace of modern violent Irish republicanism.

He gazed at the photograph for a few moments, then shook his head. He had now been in the house for twenty minutes. He realized it was time to move, so he turned and headed back down the stairs to the basement.

He reentered the tunnel via the hatch and paused to place another camera in a crack between two cinder blocks near the entrance. That might be useful in the future.

After crossing the vertical shaft where he had entered, Johnson paused to place the wireless booster unit in another crevice near where the shaft met the two horizontal tunnels. That should ensure that signals from the cameras in the tunnels would reach the transmitter in the barn.

Johnson continued along the tunnel on the other side of the shaft until he reached another hatch. He pulled it open with his left hand, his right poised to grab the Beretta if needed, and emerged into a room about twenty-five feet long and fifteen feet across, again made of cinder blocks, with a normal-height ceiling. It had two deeply recessed areas the width of a large double bed stretching back at least another twenty feet on both sides of the main room. There was another hatch at ground level at the far end.

Johnson stood and looked around in astonishment. There was a a desk, a chair, and a computer monitor screen, together with a swivel chair and a desk lamp. He flicked a light switch on the wall and two bare bulbs came on, dangling from wires at either end of the room.

Five more wooden dining chairs stood against a wall, and there was a low coffee table in the center of the room.

Next to the desk was a small fridge, which hummed away, and in the far corner was a white sink and a single tap with a small countertop on which stood a kettle and three mugs.

In one of the recessed areas a dartboard was screwed to the wall. A piece of paper next to it had a series of seemingly random letters written on it in thick felt-tip pen across the page, with some of them crossed out in red ink.

Opposite the dartboard, on the floor, stood a car battery with a set of jump leads, an electrical extension lead with bare ends, cut back to the copper wire, together with a pair of rusty handcuffs, some rope, and a set of sharp knives. He looked up. Above him, screwed into the ceiling, was a meat hook. There were several deep brown stains, obviously blood, engrained in the concrete floor beneath the hook. Johnson gave an involuntary shiver.

At the back of the other recess sat a dirty old double mattress. There was also another smaller recess with a rough, thin plywood door that had a squatter toilet built into the concrete floor.

The whole thing looked like an emergency wartime bunker. It was dark and gloomy but functional.

There was no time to waste. Johnson quickly found gaps in the mortar that bound the cinder blocks and wedged in two microcameras, one at each end of the main room.

He began opening the drawers in the desk. The top and middle ones were empty. But the bottom one contained a cardboard box holding three huge .50-caliber cartridges, each of them nearly four inches long.

Johnson took a deep breath.

This was doubtless what Duggan used to feed his favorite Barrett M82 rifle.

He photographed the shells with his phone camera and replaced them in the drawer, then took additional photographs of the underground chamber, the torture equipment, the furniture, and the exit hatches.

It was time to go. Johnson switched off the lights and, relying on his headlamp again, crawled back along the tunnel toward the shaft where he had entered.

As he drew near to the shaft he stopped still.

A loud metallic scraping noise echoed clearly along the tunnel. After about ten seconds it stopped. There was a pause and then another similar noise, which also lasted several seconds.

Johnson knew immediately what it was. Somebody above him was opening the giant metal doors to the barn.

Sure enough, several seconds later, there was the sound of a heavy diesel engine revving up and getting louder.

Shit. Now what?

The engine stopped.

Then came the muffled but audible sound of a man's voice. "Can I leave it there, Dessie?"

A pause. "Yeah, that'll do. Come on, let's get inside. I'm just going to stow these boxes."

There was another pause. Then the same voice, clearer this time. "Have you been down in the den? The cover's off."

"No, not for weeks."

"Weird. I'd have sworn I left the fecker in place. Has Dennehy been down?"

"Dunno."

"Okay, I'm just going to go down and check."

Johnson swore to himself. He was trapped underground. And someone, probably Duggan, was heading down the shaft.

CHAPTER TWENTY-TWO

Saturday, January 12, 2013
Forkhill

Johnson thanked God that he was slim and still flexible enough to turn in the tunnel and scuttle back the way he had come.

As he did so he remembered Ronnie's words about the emergency exit from one of the diesel tank structures out into a field, beneath a cattle drinking trough.

Johnson pictured the hatch at the far end of the cinder block underground room. That was where he needed to head.

Johnson crawled as fast as he could, back into the room through the hatch, which he closed behind him.

He strode to the other end of the room, yanked open the other hatch, and scrambled through into another similar tunnel. He pulled the hatch closed behind him. As he shut it, he was certain he heard the sound of the hatch at the far end of the room scrape on the floor as it began to open.

Johnson began to crawl again at speed. Within fifteen

seconds he reached another hatch, from which he emerged into another underground room, this time filled almost entirely with a massive green polypropylene tank. The entire room stank of diesel.

Now he needed to find the way out.

Johnson walked around the side of the tank. There was no sign of an exit. But on the left side of the tank at the northern end of the room there was another hatch door. This one was raised up off the ground to allow two thick plastic pipes that came from the base of the diesel tank to pass underneath.

He opened the hatch: another straight tunnel. Johnson crawled again, this time with more difficulty and major discomfort because there was no carpet cushioning and he had to place a knee on either side of the twin pipes that ran along the tunnel.

Soon he emerged into yet another room, identical to the previous one, with another large green tank. This must be the tank located on the Northern Ireland side of the border.

Some fuel smuggling operation. There was clearly fraud on a large scale going on here. And it must pay handsome dividends, to make this kind of investment worth it. But again, he couldn't afford to waste time thinking about that now; it was a secondary issue for local police to deal with—or not, as seemed to be the case.

Johnson didn't need to take out the map of the underground complex from his bag. He had memorized it. Drawing also on Ronnie's description, he knew that in theory there should be another tunnel heading to the right, going east, which should then pop up in the field underneath the cattle water trough.

He walked around the side, and there, sure enough, was another hatch.

This time the door wouldn't budge. It took all his

strength to shift it, and even then it opened barely a foot. The hinges were rusted and the plywood swollen with damp, which prevented it from moving any farther. There was just enough space to squeeze through.

Johnson quickly realized the floor of this tunnel was covered in water and mud. Or was it something other than mud? It had the distinctive smell of cow muck.

Once he started crawling, the wet mud came almost over his knees, plastering his trousers, boots, hands, and arms. But there was no going back.

The tunnel stretched for at least forty yards, Johnson guessed, before he came to a shaft similar to the one in the barn. This time the bottom of the shaft was filled with a stagnant, foul-smelling mix of animal urine, dung, and water. Water dripped down the sides of the shaft, which was covered in green slime, and the rusty rungs of the ladder were similarly coated.

There was no alternative.

Johnson crawled out of the tunnel, managed to grab the second bottom rung of the ladder, and hauled himself across without falling down into the foul mixture below.

He clambered up. He could see by the light of his head-lamp that above him was a circular metal manhole cover—which he now needed to shift in order to escape.

Johnson began by trying to push the cover up with one hand while hanging onto the ladder with the other.

It wouldn't move.

He paused for a few seconds, then lowered his head down into his chest, raised his shoulders, and, adrenaline pumping, used them to lever the heavy metal cover upward, pulling with his hands and arms on the metal ladder to gain leverage.

The cover lifted an inch. But it wouldn't move farther. Maybe Ronnie was right. This cover probably hadn't been moved in a quarter of a century—and it felt like it.

He tried again, a third attempt. This time Johnson somehow summoned up the strength to lever the cover upward and sideways.

The cold outside air on his face felt good. Johnson turned off the headlamp and eased his way out of the shaft. He realized as he banged his head hard on the base of the metal water trough above that there wasn't much headroom.

A second later he realized something else. All he could see, in both directions, was a forest of cattle legs. The trough was surrounded by a stinking, steaming herd of cows busy drinking.

Johnson had on several occasions heard of people being trampled to death by stampeding cows.

But there was no option. He knew Duggan must be after him down the tunnel. He wriggled sideways then pulled the metal cover back over the entrance to the shaft.

He was going to have to crawl out, through the thick sludge of urine and cow shit, get to his feet fast before the cattle went for him, and just hope for the best.

* * *

Saturday, January 12, 2013
Belfast

The car stank from the cow shit covering Johnson's clothing, and Jayne drove all the way back to Belfast with the windows open, despite the temperature being only a few degrees above freezing. Her attempts to protect the car seats with a few sheets from the *Belfast Telegraph* failed miserably.

"Do you think he realized someone was down there?" Jayne asked.

"He knew someone had been down there because the

manhole cover in the barn had been moved, and I heard him talking about it. I'm hoping he thought one of his sidekicks had done it. He certainly didn't see me, but he might have heard me moving ahead of him, especially when I was opening and closing those hatch doors. And if he went into that last tunnel, he'd see my trail in the mud, for sure," Johnson said.

When they got back to the apartment in Belfast, Johnson went into the bathroom and looked in the mirror. His hair, face, and most of his body were plastered in brown slime.

But he felt satisfied with his evening's work.

As soon as Johnson had showered and changed, he opened his laptop. He needed to check that the eleven microcameras he had put in place were operating properly. This was the moment of truth. The thought that they might not work after all that effort was just too much.

The website hub, through which the video and sound links from the cameras were channeled, took a while to load the different feeds. But gradually they filled the screen in a grid pattern, three across, until there was a black and white image, a little grainy but clear enough, from each of the cameras Johnson had placed.

He leaned forward and studied them closely. As he clicked on each one, a new inset window opened on his laptop to give him a larger picture, and the sound feed also went live.

There was nothing happening in any of the images until he got to the one in the study. In that one, a man with short dark hair, heavily flecked with gray, was sitting at the desk, his back to the camera, working on a laptop.

Duggan.

All Johnson could hear was the faint sound of fingers tapping on the keyboard, interspersed with a few crackles and momentary interruptions as the sound feed came and went.

After a few minutes, Duggan's cell phone rang.

Johnson jumped. Then he reached for his keyboard and flicked on the screen sound recorder.

Hearing the action, Jayne came from the kitchen area and looked over Johnson's shoulder at the computer screen.

"Hey, Patrick, what's the craic over there?" Duggan said to the unseen caller.

That must be Patrick McKinney, Johnson thought.

A few seconds later, Duggan told his caller to ring back using Skype. Johnson guessed that was because, being encrypted, it was more secure than an open cell phone connection. Johnson was hoping they would now use a Skype video connection on the laptop, so he could see and hear the caller as well as Duggan, but the conversation resumed via a voice-only link on Duggan's smartphone.

Duggan sounded tinny and distant over the link from the remote camera, and the picture froze at regular intervals. However, to Johnson's relief, the sound quality improved and remained consistent. His transmitter unit was functioning as it should.

There was a pause while Duggan listened to his caller for a few minutes. He swung his chair around a little so that Johnson could see his face, serious and focused.

Then Duggan said, "Are you still putting it in the timber as we discussed?"

He listened again for a few moments, then said, "Sounds good. So what's the timetable? It'll be into your place from Colón on Tuesday, yes?"

Definitely McKinney on the line.

A quick pause. Then Duggan spoke again. "Okay, a two-day turnaround, fine. But then how long?"

Again Duggan listened. "That'd work fine, but you can't let it go any later, else it'll be too late."

Any later than when, and too late for what? Johnson wondered. *Is he talking about the G8 and Obama?*

A further lengthy pause and then a chuckle. "The Green Dragon, eh? Okay, well I'll raise a glass to you Tuesday night then. Wish I was joining you—I went there last time I was in Boston. Long time ago, but a lovely old pub."

The call continued for a few minutes—inconsequential chat about the social side of a trip that McKinney had recently made to Colón. After ending the call, Duggan resumed tapping away on his computer keyboard.

Johnson felt he had made a breakthrough of sorts, although annoyingly, several key pieces of information had been missing from the conversation.

He turned back to Jayne with the hint of a smile on his lips. "Useful," he said. "Just about made it worth rolling around in the cow shit. So whatever they're shipping in is coming in a timber cargo via Boston from Colón. Pity they didn't say which Irish port it'll come to or when—not sure how we find that out. I'm going to fly out there and check it out. I might even get there in time for a drink at the Green Dragon on Tuesday night. I know it well. I wonder who our friend McKinney's meeting there. And why."

The Green Dragon, a small but historic downtown watering hole, had been one of his favorite haunts as a student at Boston University, where he had majored in history thirty years earlier, prior to moving to Germany to study for his doctorate on the economics of Hitler's Third Reich at the Freie Universität Berlin.

The idea of revisiting his old stomping ground now, for the first time in many years, was appealing. And he suddenly had a good excuse.

"It's a good starting point," Jayne said. "I agree. Get over there and tail McKinney from the Green Dragon—that's the best option."

Johnson took out his phone and called Fiona Heppenstall. She was in a coffee shop on Capitol Hill talking with one of her political contacts but broke off and stepped outside the café to take Johnson's call.

As he had anticipated, she was intrigued by his briefing.

"I've been trying to do a little digging on McKinney since we spoke last Monday," she said, "but he's not been around. His PA said he was out of town."

"Yes, he's been down in Colón, arranging the shipment," Johnson said. "We need to know what he meant when he said they were putting it in the timber like before. Putting what in the timber—are we talking guns, bombs, grenades? And what does he mean by timber? Logs? Furniture?"

"No idea," Fiona said. "But I do know that Colón is a transit point for all kinds of shady goods."

Johnson told her his plan was to fly to Boston before Tuesday and suggested that she persuade her editor to let her join him.

"Yes, great idea. I'll talk him into it; leave it to me," she said.

Jayne looked up sharply from scribbling in her notebook.

When Johnson hung up, Jayne folded her arms. "Sounded like the old flame was heating up when you mentioned you were heading over there."

Johnson gave her a glare. "I'm not rising to that bait."

He felt in his pocket and took out the red and black USB flash drive he had removed from Duggan's kitchen and slotted it into his laptop. A few seconds later, he was looking at what appeared to be the only file on the tiny device: a document entitled "Visit," with just five lines of text.

Draft Community visit Mon 28 January
School TBD
2:30 p.m.—BO and DC arrive with Chief Con + dignitaries.
2:40 p.m.—Activity
2:50 p.m.—Talk by BO/DC and QA

3:10 p.m.—Depart for G8

"Shit," Johnson said. He realized immediately the significance of what was on the screen in front of him. *BO and DC: Barack Obama and David Cameron.*

He clicked on the Properties tab of the document to look for an electronic trail back to the author, but the metadata segments were all empty.

CHAPTER TWENTY-THREE

Sunday, January 13, 2013
Belfast

"You went into Duggan's *house?*" Michael Donovan's eyes widened a fraction. He shook his head and handed Johnson a glass of whiskey. "There you go. Tullamore Dew, Ireland's finest."

He walked across his living room and sat on a black leather armchair, opposite Johnson, who was on a matching sofa.

"I'm not going to make progress sitting here in Belfast," Johnson said. "At some point, to get proof, you've got to take a risk. I'm not exactly going to apply for a search warrant, am I, so what other option is there?"

He raised his glass and nodded at Donovan. "Anyway, cheers, my friend."

It was the first time in over a week he'd had a chance to sit down with Donovan and run through progress. The man seemed to be constantly on the move, talking to investors across a series of European capitals.

Indeed, it was the first time Johnson had been to his house. He arrived just as it was starting to get dark.

Johnson updated him on events, including the meetings with the sniper victims' wives, Moira's death, and the visit to Ronnie Quinn who had effectively provided him with the key to Willows Farm.

"Police have obviously failed to catch Duggan doing anything wrong and haven't found any evidence," Johnson said. "And that's clearly gone on for years and years. He's either very clever or lucky. But the question is, are police really trying to nail him? And if not, why not?"

Donovan shrugged and paused a few seconds before answering. "I don't know. I don't see it. That's why I brought you in."

"Sooner or later, unlike the police, I'm going to nail him," Johnson said. "Then we can take the evidence to them, and if they still ignore it, we'll go to the newspapers and TV."

There was a copy of the *Belfast Telegraph* on Donovan's coffee table. A story on the front page reported that the Northern Ireland assistant chief constable, Norman Arnside, was now in charge of the inquiry into Eric Simonson's shooting.

"You know this guy, Arnside?" Johnson asked.

"Yes, a little."

"Any good?"

"I guess so," Donovan said.

He showed Donovan the photo he'd taken of the three .50-caliber shells in Duggan's underground desk drawer. "That's for starters. He's not using them for paperweights, is he? We need to find the rifle he uses them in, too."

Johnson told Donovan about the journals on the laptop that had been stolen from prison officer Will Doyle at the beginning of the previous year and that he had asked to see copies of them.

"How exactly is that going to help nail Duggan?" Donovan asked, wrinkling his nose.

"I won't know until I see it. Why not? It might give an insight into why he was a target. It's worth a try."

Donovan didn't reply but inclined his head from one side to the other, as if to say maybe.

"I'd like to know what Duggan's strategy is," Johnson said.

"Like many of these dissident Republicans, there's no obvious strategy," Donovan said. "It looks random to me."

He stood and held up his whiskey glass. "Like a refill?"

Johnson nodded. "Yes, it's a nice drop, that Tullamore Dew."

Donovan took his glass and disappeared into the next room at the front of the house.

Johnson stood and followed Donovan. The front room had been set up with a projector, a large pull-down screen, a small bar and a drinks fridge, a satellite TV, and two sofas. It was a real man's den. He stood a couple of yards behind Donovan and surveyed the bar. There were four different whiskeys and an array of other spirits.

Donovan turned around. "Go and sit down. I'll bring it to you. Relax."

Johnson nodded his thanks and looked out the window for a few seconds. It was now pitch-dark outside except for the distant lights of the parking lot at the golf course across the road.

He turned and went back to the living room, then sat and placed his hands behind his head. He needed to think.

There were a few things he needed to discuss with Donovan, not least the tracker device found under his wife's car. So far he hadn't had a chance to do so because Donovan had been away. He would be interested in Donovan's thoughts on why the tracker had been planted—was it to follow Johnson, Donovan, or his wife, and why?

There was a call from the other room. "D'you want it on the rocks?" Donovan shouted.

"Yes, please, but only one cube," Johnson called.

Seconds later, all hell broke loose.

There was a deafening bang, followed by an explosion of bricks, dust, and plasterwork, followed by another massive bang, and a ragged hole the size of a fist appeared in the wall between the living room and Donovan's den next door.

Another eruption of noise sounded, a third bang, and a larger chunk of the wall fell into the living room with a crash, taking wall paper with it. Brickwork and other debris scattered across the carpet, the armchair in which Donovan had been sitting and the sofa where Johnson was.

Something hard hit Johnson on the side of the head, and the air was heavy with a fog of pink and white dust.

The dust particles filled his lungs, and he began to cough violently. Johnson could see very little and felt as if he were going to choke.

He managed to regain his faculties and instinctively threw himself to the floor and rolled toward the door into the hallway.

He put his hand to his head, where the object had hit him, and looked at it. His hand was covered in blood. "Shit," Johnson said.

There was another explosion, and the wall at the back of the room behind the TV disintegrated in a firework display of brick fragments and dust.

At least out in the corridor the dust cloud was less dense.

"Sonofabitch," Johnson yelled as he jumped to his feet and ran down the hallway toward the kitchen at the rear of the house.

Behind him, another enormous bang and an explosion

rang out, followed by a loud fizzing noise. Then the house was plunged into darkness.

Whoever was firing on Donovan's house—and Johnson's immediate thought was Duggan—was definitely using something more than an ordinary rifle. This had to be a heavy-duty semiautomatic weapon.

Johnson's immediate concern was for Donovan, given that he had been in the front room, where the firing was focused. He assumed that the Irishman's silence meant he must have been hit.

But there was no way Johnson could venture in there without putting himself right in the firing line for the next round.

Johnson took out his phone and flicked on the flashlight, his finger over the beam to minimize the light emission. His cream-colored sweat top was flecked with red stains. It certainly wasn't his own blood. He swore out loud again, his suspicions about Donovan confirmed, and turned off the light again.

Now there was silence. Johnson waited in the back of the house.

His instinct was to get out. The noise outside must have been incredible, and it was a certainty that neighbors would already have called the police.

What to do?

After another minute, with no further gunshots, Johnson dropped to his knees and crawled back down the hallway toward the front door, knowing he was taking a major risk.

He had calculated that the gunman would almost certainly be moving away from the scene. A quick strike and out. Hanging around in a residential area would hugely increase the risk of arrest.

His eyes now adjusting to the gloom, helped by the faint orange glow from the street lights outside, Johnson passed the doorway to the living room and continued another ten feet or so to the doorway to the front room. The door was splintered and hanging off its hinges.

Johnson peered around the doorframe.

He had seen plenty of gunshot victims in his time, but that never made it any easier. He turned his head away and vomited.

* * *

Sunday, January 13, 2013
Belfast

Duggan shoved the Barrett M82 into its slim case and pushed the whole thing into his golf bag, which he had adapted to take the weapon. A handful of irons were positioned around the opening so it appeared to be a normal bag of clubs.

Then he pulled a toweling cloth over the end of the rifle case, slung it over his shoulder, and headed back through the trees at the rear of the first green.

Any onlooker would probably assume that he was a golfer carrying his clubs through the woods on a shortcut home after a couple of beers at the clubhouse.

After an opening shot, which came in slightly left of target, Duggan knew for certain that his second round had hit Donovan.

The man had loomed large in Duggan's beloved Schmidt & Bender scope and Duggan had seen his head explode in a pink mist, as if in slow motion, when his second shell struck home. There was no doubt about that. The red stain was clearly sprayed all over the white wall behind him.

The third and fourth shots had been superfluous.

But at the same time, Duggan was cursing himself for not

acting more quickly to be sure of also getting Johnson, the American investigator.

Johnson had entered the front room and had even glanced out the window into the darkness for several seconds, staring as if he knew Duggan was out there.

The curtains were pulled wide open, so Duggan had a perfect view through the powerful scope from his slightly elevated vantage point about 350 yards away.

But crucially, he had waited a couple of seconds, undecided about who to go for first amid a nagging concern that Donovan might dive for cover if he hit Johnson first. And in that time, Johnson had turned and exited the room.

"Bastard. Why did I do that?" Duggan muttered to himself. He stamped the ground as he walked and slapped his thigh in frustration.

His only hope was that one of the shells he had seen rip through the back wall of the room, punching a large hole in it, had somehow hit Johnson.

The ammunition he had chosen to fill the ten-round magazine was the devastating Raufoss Mk211 shell, which meant there was some chance he had hit Johnson if he had happened to be in the vicinity.

But he knew that realistically, the odds were long.

Duggan walked swiftly through the trees until he reached a path that led down past a lane next to the cemetery.

There he had parked a Ford stolen by one of his young volunteers from a secluded driveway on the edge of Craigavon the previous night. The car had fresh license plates Duggan had put on only four hours earlier.

Before long Duggan was on the A55 heading southeast, which would connect with the M1.

He estimated he would be back home and cleaning himself up in the shower inside an hour and forty minutes.

Duggan turned on the car radio and smiled briefly to himself.

* * *

Sunday, January 13, 2013
Belfast

Johnson pulled his woolly black hat well down over his head, zipped up his black jacket, and left Donovan's house by the rear kitchen door. He glanced at both neighboring houses, chose the one that was in darkness, and vaulted over the fence onto a path.

From there, he bent double and, clinging tight to the shadows of some conifer trees, made his way out onto the road. His car was parked about forty yards away, as was his usual habit.

The road was deserted and silent. He was completely certain, though, that behind the lace curtains was a frenzy of activity.

Johnson glanced up the hill, where he could see the outline of trees against the night sky. That was most likely where the unseen gunman had struck from.

He jogged to the car, quickly started it, left his lights off, and accelerated away in the direction of the A2 divided highway that ran back toward Belfast city center. He prayed as he left that nobody was able to see his license plate in the darkness.

It was only as he got well away from Demesne Road that he turned his headlights on. He had no wish to get roped into the formal, interminable process of a police murder investigation.

Johnson drove down the on-ramp onto the A2 just as two

police cars, sirens blaring and lights flashing, raced in the opposite direction, toward Donovan's road.

As he drove toward Donovan's apartment, the initial relief Johnson felt at escaping intact was overridden by a rising wave of despair.

It had been a sickening sight. Donovan had been left completely unrecognizable, his features destroyed and the entire back of his skull missing, splattered widely over the walls and carpets behind the bar.

What should he do now? He could just walk away. He'd been paid half the money promised by Donovan, which was enough, and he knew his kids would love to have him back earlier than expected.

But he felt the same driving force inside him that had pushed him on for his whole career: a fierce need to see justice done.

Slowly, the despair turned to determination to get to the bottom of what was going on. And it was a determination driven by anger.

He knew who was behind the trail of carnage. First Moira, now Donovan. Collecting the firm evidence necessary to bring Duggan to justice was clearly going to be tough. He was dealing with a pro.

The big question was, why was he doing it?

The following morning Johnson was due to fly to Boston from Dublin airport, which was a good two-and-a-half-hour drive away. Hopefully there he would get to the bottom of how Duggan's dissident republican campaigns were being financed.

Then he might be in a better position to nail him for what he was doing on the ground.

Johnson parked the black Ford Focus in its now familiar spot, down a road that led off Falls Road, and ran up the stairs two at a time to Donovan's apartment, where Jayne had stayed in watching TV.

She turned around as he burst into the living room.

"Donovan's just been hit by a sniper in his house while I was in the room next door," Johnson said.

"*What?*" Jayne's eyes widened, and she jumped to her feet to face him. "Hit? You mean killed?"

"Yep. It's got to be Duggan. He shot Donovan through the window. A huge mess, you wouldn't have recognized him."

Jayne grimaced. "Bloody hell. Another one."

"Yes, it was bloody hell all right. Duggan must have been using that damn Barrett of his, judging by the damage. It blew a couple of holes in the living room wall. I was lucky to get out of there."

He tugged at his right ear. "We need to pack and get out of here. It's a matter of time before police turn up and we get caught up in a massive murder investigation. That would hold us up for days, put the brakes on everything. We'd make no progress. Let's just get out and distance ourselves."

Jayne walked to the other side of the living room. "Yes, agreed. But hang on a minute. If it's Duggan, why did he hit Donovan? I can't see why. Unless he knew he had brought you in?"

"Maybe that's it, maybe he does know. Duggan's aware that I've been nosing around—Moira told me that. And that's why she was killed, I'd guess, because he thought she was talking to me. So maybe he also knows that it was Donovan who brought me in. It's my fault again."

He silently cursed himself. He was playing the self-blame game once more. His favorite.

After a few seconds, he gathered himself. "But how would Duggan link Donovan and myself? I was going to ask Donovan whether he thought that tracker device was intended for him and his wife or for me. But he was shot before I could ask the question. I don't know, Jayne; it's an odd one."

Jayne squinted at him. "But you think there's more to it?"

"Yes, I do think there's more to it. And I'm going to find out what."

PART THREE

CHAPTER TWENTY-FOUR

Tuesday, January 15, 2013
  Boston, Massachusetts

The snow had already started to fall as Johnson turned the corner and stood still for a moment, looking across the road at the Green Dragon Tavern. He was instantly uplifted to see it hadn't changed dramatically on the outside since his last visit to Boston.

The pub, on the ground floor of a battered three-story wedge-shaped block on cobbled Marshall Street, still had the same old-fashioned lanterns, which glowed invitingly in the late afternoon gloom, and ancient wooden windows.

A couple of shamrock stickers in the windows and the Irish flag flying outside gave away its heritage. Clearly McKinney hadn't lost a sense of his roots if this was his favorite watering hole.

Headquarters of the Revolution, it said on the sign outside, referring back to the plotting and planning that went on in Boston to overthrow the British in the 1600s and 1700s, although Johnson knew well that the original Green Dragon Tavern had been on a different site.

He gave a wry smile as the parallels to his current task in Northern Ireland struck him and then walked in through the old swinging doors.

There, sitting at one end of the long wooden bar, perched on an old stool, sat Fiona, nursing a beer.

It had been over a year since he'd last seen her in northern Argentina. He'd had to leave her at a hospital for repairs to her shoulder, which had been injured in a shoot-out as she helped Johnson track down an aging Nazi fugitive.

Judging by the way she raised the glass with her right hand upon spotting him, she'd recovered from the bullet injury.

Johnson walked up to her and kissed her on the lips, then gave her a tight hug. He always forgot how tall she was. Her long dark hair and her skin still smelled the same, and she wore the same subtle but distinctive perfume.

"Joe, you're looking good—still running? In between the odd smoke, no doubt?" She chuckled, that same seductive laugh, and tapped him briefly on the abs.

Fiona did this every time they met after an extended period. But Johnson always felt flattered, probably because he did make an effort to stay fit, despite his cigarettes when traveling.

"Looking good yourself," Johnson said.

He glanced at her taut thighs, snugly encased in a pair of tight-fitting jeans that also showed off her slim waist.

He sometimes wondered why he hadn't continued things with her after their brief affair in 2006, the year after his wife had died. But at the time he'd wanted to move back to Portland, whereas she had been entrenched in her reporting job in DC.

Also, she was ten years younger and gave the occasional hint that she might like to have kids. That had never felt right to Johnson. He wasn't sure how his two children might react.

They had never discussed it again.

"So are you fully mended now? The shoulder's okay?" Johnson asked, placing his hand lightly on her right shoulder.

"A lot of rehab and gym work later, yes, pretty good," she said. "I can write, take notes, and type. So I can earn a living. That's the important thing."

Johnson nodded. He felt hugely relieved that she had recovered since he held himself responsible for placing her in a dangerous situation he should never have allowed to happen. Although, he told himself, he'd tried to dissuade her, but she had refused point-blank.

"That's great, but enough of the small talk. Is there any sign of our tobacco magnate?" Johnson asked, looking around the pub.

"No, not yet. How definite was it that he was coming here?"

Johnson had to admit it wasn't definite, simply a line he'd picked up on the telephone conversation with Duggan that he had overheard, and the timing had been nothing more specific than Tuesday night. It was now five o'clock, and the bar was open until two in the morning.

The two of them sat facing the door at a wooden table underneath a frame that contained an ancient musket, a couple of pistols and other artifacts and drank a couple of beers while Johnson briefed Fiona on events in Northern Ireland.

He had brought a copy of the previous day's *Belfast Telegraph* with him, which had a big front-page headline, "Investor Firm Boss Dies in Sniper Terror."

The story included a photograph of Donovan. The newspaper was pinning the blame firmly on dissident Republicans but gave no explanation why Donovan had been targeted.

"This is the guy who brought me in," Johnson said. "I'm struggling to make sense of it at the moment."

Fiona read the story with interest. "Keep digging. I'm guessing things will become clearer if you can do that."

The snow had continued, off and on, since Johnson had arrived and was now starting to settle on the cobblestoned road outside. Johnson took a look at the weather forecast on his phone. Heavy accumulation was expected overnight.

Around seven-thirty, just as Johnson and Fiona were starting their main course, a band came in to set up in the front corner of the bar and was soon working its way through a series of Springsteen cover versions.

Fifty minutes later, after dessert, Johnson had just ordered coffees when a man walked in by himself.

Johnson noticed him immediately. He was very tall, probably six feet four or five, with graying hair and slightly rounded shoulders that looked as though there was a coat hanger inside.

Fiona immediately nudged Johnson. "That's him, McKinney, the tall guy. I checked out the photos we've got on file," she muttered.

McKinney, who wore a suit under his overcoat, had a scar down the right side of his face, under the cheekbone. He joined a shorter, stockier man with a shaved head, wearing jeans, a blue sweat shirt, and a fleece jacket.

They shook hands and ordered beers, then made their way to a table in the far corner, where they immediately began an intense conversation, their heads close together.

They drank as quickly as they talked, and as soon as the beers had gone, they stood, put their coats on, and headed for the door.

Johnson looked at Fiona. "Okay, we need to follow." He had parked his rental car around the corner on Union Street, where McKinney and his companion now headed.

The falling snow had deposited a thin white layer over the rooftops and parked cars.

Johnson and Fiona, trailing some distance behind, watched as the two men climbed into a black four-door Ford pickup, McKinney in the driver's seat. There were so many cars jammed onto the road that Johnson and Fiona had plenty of time to reach his rented white Toyota Camry and follow, separated by a couple of vehicles.

A quarter of an hour later, McKinney's pickup rolled into a small parking lot next to an industrial unit in the Seaport district and pulled up next to a Honda.

Johnson parked across the street, about two hundred yards away, and killed his lights.

Under the eerie glow of a couple of street lamps, which illuminated the snowflakes being driven sideways by gusts of wind, they watched as the stocky guy jumped out and opened the Honda's trunk. He took out a long, thin box.

Then the man opened a rear door of McKinney's pickup and shoved the box onto the floor.

"Might as well write rifle on the box," Fiona said.

Johnson nodded but said nothing.

The stocky man climbed back into the front seat of the pickup, and they drove off. Johnson followed at a distance, waiting until the pickup had turned a corner before turning his lights on.

A short distance farther on, near the Conley shipping container terminal entrance, the pickup pulled into a timber merchant's yard, which housed a warehouse in the center and high stacks of different types of wood products around it.

A sign outside read Pan-American Timber Products. The complex, which was dimly lit by a few lackluster orange security floodlights, was surrounded on all sides by a heavy-duty chain link fence.

A guard on duty at the gate came out of a prefabricated

hut, lifted a security barrier, and waved McKinney through. The pickup left tire tracks in the fresh snow. It was nearly nine o'clock, and a sign said that the yard closed at six-thirty.

"Shit. Now what? We can't pretend to be customers. They're closed," Johnson said as he drove past.

"Screwed if I know."

"There's only two choices, I think," Johnson said.

"What?"

"We can wait, then follow when they come out, or—"

"No, we need to know what they've done with the gun," Fiona said.

"Agreed. So we find a way to get in."

Johnson drove around the corner, on the far side of the timber merchant, and pulled over to the side of the road. He scanned the neighboring buildings: an old brick office block on one side and a factory unit on the other.

"There's only one way that I can see," said Johnson.

* * *

Tuesday, January 15, 2013
  Boston

Johnson waited behind a truck that was parked just outside the timber yard gates while Fiona walked quietly through the vehicle entrance and around to the front of the security guard's hut.

Her plan was to tell the guard that there was a problem with her car battery and to ask him if he might have a quick look at it as she knew nothing about cars and was late getting home.

A few minutes later he caught a glimpse of Fiona and the guard emerging from the vehicle entrance and walking on the other side of the truck toward the car, the hood of which was lifted.

"I'm sorry about this," he heard Fiona say to the guard. "I'm just worried about this snow. I don't want to get stuck."

"Don't worry, lady," he replied. "Hopefully I can get you on the move so you can get home."

Johnson edged his way around the side of the truck and poked his head around the corner. The security guard, a rough-looking guy, was standing with his back to Johnson, looking at the engine.

The man bent over and put his head under the hood.

As he did so, Johnson emerged from the shadow of the truck, moved swiftly toward the Toyota, and lifted the heavy lug wrench he had removed from the trunk of his rental.

The guard must have caught a glimpse of Johnson in his peripheral vision. He gasped slightly and had just begun to turn when Johnson brought the wrench down hard on the side of his temple.

The guard collapsed to the ground, facedown.

Johnson turned him over so he faced up, grabbed underneath his armpits and began to pull him toward the yard entrance, thirty yards away, his feet dragging across the pavement. "Quick, get that hut door open," he told Fiona.

She complied, and Johnson pulled the guard through the gate and into the hut and dropped him on the floor. He grabbed a cloth from the small countertop, stuffed it in the guard's mouth, and secured it with several rounds of duct tape from a roll on the desk.

He bound the guard's hands behind his back and then his ankles, all with the duct tape. Then Johnson pushed the guard into the corner behind the fridge, where he was out of sight of anyone peering through the front window or entering through the door, and pulled down the window blind.

"Dammit, Joe, is he okay there?" Fiona asked.

Johnson checked the man's pulse and nodded. "He's fine. Let's get going. He's not going to be out for long."

There was a printout from a spreadsheet on the desk, which Johnson saw was an agency staff list divided into three shifts starting at six o'clock in the morning, two in the afternoon, and ten in the evening.

That helped, if it was an agency, Johnson figured. It meant the guards on duty were less likely to be recognizable and familiar to McKinney or any other official figure. The night shift list had only one name on it, Callum Wright, whereas the other two daytime shifts had four names. He noted the name listed for the night shift and also the site supervisor's name, Tom Kurtheim, listed at the top.

Johnson began pulling out drawers in the security guard's desk and tipping the contents on the floor: a jumble of paper clips, pens, staplers, scissors, rubber bands, and other supplies.

"What are you doing, Joe?" Fiona asked.

"The security office has unfortunately been burgled," Johnson replied.

He scattered all the papers that were neatly stacked on the desk, and he emptied cardboard folders filled with paper invoices, dockets, receipts, and other random notes all over the floor.

Then he stood back and admired his work for a few seconds. That should do the job, he figured. If anyone came in, it would be fairly obvious why the security guard had been knocked unconscious and trussed up like a Thanksgiving turkey.

Johnson turned to see Fiona looking at several pairs of company-branded overalls hanging on a hook next to the door. She grabbed a pair and held them against her for size, then looked at Johnson. "What do you think?"

"Brilliant," Johnson said. "Pass me that large pair." He

grabbed a black baseball cap with a Pan-American Timber Products logo on the front from another of the hooks, jammed it onto his head, and grinned.

A couple of minutes later, overalls now over the top of their jackets, they walked out of the hut. Johnson lifted the security barrier in case anyone needed to come in or out, and then went over to the Toyota and closed the hood.

He led the way toward the warehouse in the center of the complex.

"Just keep it quiet and go slowly," Johnson said.

He edged his way along the left-hand wall of the warehouse until he reached the corner, then slowly put his head around it until he could see what was happening.

A line of parked cars and vans stood close to the far side of the building. Good for cover, Johnson thought.

About halfway along the building was a high, wide truck entrance, and on the other side of that stood a shipping container, the doors open.

Johnson and Fiona crept behind the cars to within forty yards of the container and squatted behind a pickup.

He could see that McKinney and the stocky guy were standing at the door to the container, which was filled floor to ceiling with very large, heavy-looking square wooden beams, each of them several feet long. One of the beams stood on the floor, leaning against the side of the container.

Six men emerged from the warehouse, went to the container, and picked up a beam, which they carried with difficulty into the warehouse.

A few minutes later, the loud squeal of what Johnson assumed was an electric saw or drill came from inside.

"I'm going to take a look," he said. "Wait here."

Johnson walked around in front of the cars, pulled his cap down low over his forehead, and strode purposefully into the warehouse, his phone clamped to his left ear as he went, pretending to carry out a conversation. It was his method for checking for surveillance and avoiding being challenged when entering places he shouldn't.

He looked up. The extensive floor space of the warehouse was covered with pallets and racks stacked with timber products of various types and sizes, ranging from decking to fencing to trellises, gates, and beams. At the back of the warehouse Johnson saw a long, low glass-fronted office, which looked empty.

To the left of the office, McKinney and his colleague had the wooden beam, which Johnson estimated must have been a good foot and a half square, on a horizontal drilling machine that was boring a large hole into its base, effectively hollowing it out.

Johnson headed to the right side of the huge warehouse, away from McKinney, and within seconds was hidden from sight behind high stacks of pallets holding wooden fences, posts, and other products.

Once Johnson made his way to the right side of the office, he realized it had entrance doors at both ends, meaning he could gain access unseen by McKinney. He moved quickly to the door, opened it, and entered.

He walked through the empty office to the far end. There on the floor was the long, slim cardboard box, which he had seen the stocky guy putting into the back of McKinney's pickup earlier.

Two other bulkier cardboard boxes stood next to it.

Johnson walked to a water cooler near the door and filled a cup. Out of the corner of his eye, through the doorway, he could see that McKinney and his helper were preoccupied with ensuring that the huge drill bit was boring correctly into the wooden beam.

It was obvious what was going on here.

Johnson reached into his pocket and removed two of the

microchip GPS tracking devices he had brought from Belfast. He pulled the protective seal from the black self-adhesive pad on one tracker and pulled open the cardboard flap at one end of the long box.

There was no doubt. The soft black case inside was designed to hold a rifle. There was a heavy-duty zipper, which Johnson tugged slightly open so he could slip his hand inside, just to make certain.

Yes, there it was; he could feel the cold steel end of the barrel.

Johnson took a penknife from his pocket, made a slit in the soft padding inside the case, and stuck the tracker inside it. He zipped up the bag and reclosed the box. The tiny tracker would not now be obvious unless someone inspected the rifle case carefully and spotted the slit.

Then Johnson repeated the exercise with another tracker at the other end of the box, this time undoing a zipper to what felt like a gadget storage pocket, just in case the first one failed.

Less than a minute and the job was done.

He briefly eyed the other cardboard boxes. He guessed there was probably other weaponry or ammunition in them, too. Should he put trackers in them, too? he wondered. But unlike the rifle, they were heavily taped up, and it would take too long.

On the edge of the desk was a printed sheet. Johnson stepped over to take a look. It was a bill of lading, which he knew was a document signed by shipping lines when they picked up goods for loading. He glanced down the sheet. The section describing the goods read "wooden beams." Above it, the consignee was named as "O'Malley's Timber International, Dublin Port." The delivery date stated was January 24. Presumably this was for the cargo that McKinney was going to ship, with the weaponry stowed in it. Or could it be for a different, possibly innocent, order from this clearly busy warehouse? He would have to try and verify that somehow, and the tracker devices would help with that. There was nothing else of relevance on the sheet.

Johnson picked up the cup of water that he had filled and took a sip, just as McKinney appeared at the door, his hands on his hips, forehead furrowed.

"What the hell are you doing in here?" McKinney asked in an even, slightly menacing tone. He looked steadily at Johnson.

"Just getting a drink, as you can see," Johnson said, looking McKinney directly in the eye. "Why?"

McKinney glanced down at the boxes on the floor, then back at Johnson. "Who are you?" he asked.

"Night shift," Johnson said.

"Night shift? But they start at ten."

"Just coming in early. The supervisor told me to get in. Need any help?"

McKinney shook his head. "What's your name, and who's the supervisor?"

"Wright, Callum Wright. My supervisor is Tom Kurtheim. And yours?"

"Never you mind," McKinney said. "Callum Wright, did you say your name was?"

"Yes," Johnson said.

McKinney ran a hand through his hair. "Out, now. Go on, feck off out."

The Irishman clearly hadn't lost his Ulster invective, nor his accent. However, Johnson was relieved that he apparently hadn't realized his night shift security man shouldn't be there at all.

Johnson shrugged. "No problem, man, calm down. I'm going. You sure you don't need any help?"

The Irishman just gazed at him.

Johnson strode out of the office, past McKinney, and out the warehouse main door.

There he cut a left, across the now snow-covered parking lot, back toward where Fiona was still waiting behind the pickup truck.

She was holding a small camera pointed at the shipping container.

"Come on, let's get the hell out of here," he said.

* * *

Tuesday, January 15, 2013
   Boston

It was odd, Patrick thought, that the security barrier into the Pan-American Timber Products complex was up.

The truck onto which the shipping container was loaded, complete with its illicit cargo, had left ten minutes earlier, and the guard should have lowered the barrier again immediately.

McKinney had intended to drive out of the gates and then home, before the snow had really started piling up. Now, however, he decided to check with the guard that everything was okay before leaving.

He pulled over to one side and braked to a halt, then jumped out of the cab and strode into the prefabricated security office inside the vehicle gate entrance.

A jolt ran up his spine when he saw the chaos inside the hut. Papers, pens, folders, and stationery supplies were strewn all over the floor, and two drawers had been pulled out of the desk and left upside down on the floor.

McKinney instinctively moved back into the doorway and scanned the room looking for intruders. It was only when he noticed a slight movement in a dark corner behind the fridge and heard a muffled grunting sound that he saw a man lying on the floor.

He walked over, bent down, and turned the security guard over. A cloth that had been fastened in place with duct tape was stuffed in the man's mouth, and his arms and legs were bound tight, also with tape.

McKinney quickly released the guard, who was having difficulty breathing. It took him a few minutes to recover sufficiently to tell his boss how he had been attacked by a man and a woman who had conned him with a story about car breaking down, had knocked him out, and had then bound and gagged him.

McKinney immediately thought about the night security guard he had seen. What was his name, Callum Wright? He knew that the night staff had been instructed to check in at the hut before starting their shift, and he knew that Wright had turned up early, because annoyingly, he had barged into the warehouse.

"So why didn't the night shift guard, Wright, see you when he checked in for his shift?" McKinney asked. "He came in early, didn't he? And where is he now?"

The guard looked confused. "No, Callum hasn't turned up yet. His shift doesn't start for another quarter of an hour. He's never early. And you're right, he always comes in here to check in, have a quick chat, when he starts."

It was then that McKinney realized.

The guard was unable to give McKinney a description of the man because he said he'd been hit from behind and had immediately blacked out. The woman had long dark hair, was slim, good looking. Beyond that he couldn't remember much.

It definitely wasn't a straightforward burglary, despite the chaos in the security office, which McKinney was now certain was a red herring. No burglar would have come so brazenly into the warehouse, bluffing his way in and out under the pretext of having a drink of water.

So who the hell was the man, and would he have realized what McKinney was actually doing? He doubted it because when he thought back, the man hadn't seen him doing anything more than drilling into a wooden beam. The rifle had been on the floor of the office but was in a zipped bag and a cardboard box. Nonetheless, it was worrisome.

CHAPTER TWENTY-FIVE

Saturday, January 19, 2013
  Belfast

The one-and-a-half-hour surveillance detection route Johnson and Jayne took around Belfast and its surroundings prior to their meeting with O'Neill in some ways seemed excessively long.

But after the shooting of Donovan and the discovery of the tracking device on his wife's car, Johnson didn't want to take any chances, particularly as O'Neill had arranged to hold the meeting at an MI5 safe house, which he let slip was code-named Brown Bear. The last thing he wanted to do was give its location away to any watching dissident terrorist.

"It's good practice. If you'd seen what I'd seen, you wouldn't question it," he said, after Jayne finally hinted that he had driven far enough.

Eventually Johnson was satisfied they were black, or free of any tail, and headed into Newtownards, about thirteen miles east of Belfast, where Brown Bear was located in the middle of an anonymous area of modern housing.

The snowstorm in Boston, which had intensified the morning after Johnson and Fiona had left the timber yard, had delayed Johnson's return to Northern Ireland and also had prevented Fiona from getting back to her *Inside Track* offices in Washington, DC.

Finally he managed to get on a flight to Dublin, where Jayne met him and drove him back to Belfast.

In the meantime, Jayne found a new apartment, also on Falls Road, only a few hundred yards away from the one belonging to Donovan that they had vacated.

It took two days to arrange a meeting with O'Neill, who was working long hours at MI5 in preparation for the G8.

Johnson and Jayne parked near a large secondary school half a mile away from Brown Bear and walked to the house, which was across the road from a park where children were playing with a dog and riding bikes.

In contrast to their previous meeting, O'Neill had the hollow-eyed, drawn look of a man who had not had a good night's sleep for some while. Hardly surprising, Johnson thought, given that one of his old buddies had recently been gunned down in his own house.

His hair was greasy and unwashed, he had at least two days' worth of stubble, and there were food spills on the front of his sweatshirt.

"Come through, this way," O'Neill said hurriedly. Before closing the front door, O'Neill glanced swiftly and unobtrusively up and down the road.

Johnson insisted that the three of them sit well away from the windows, at the rear of the house in the kitchen. He folded his arms and glanced across at O'Neill. "Are you all right?" he asked.

"Not really," O'Neill said. "But I can't afford to dwell on it. Now, what have you got for me?"

Johnson briefed O'Neill on what had happened in Boston and gave details of the incoming cargo from McKinney.

The snow in Boston hadn't prevented the departure of the vast container ship *Evans's Girl*. Johnson had worked out which ship it was after a check online to corroborate the brief details in the bill of lading he'd seen and then a phone call to the port to confirm that *Evans's Girl* was the only container ship bound for Ireland from Boston at that time. Its destination was Dublin Port.

Thankfully, both the GPS tracking devices that he had stuck inside the rifle case had worked as intended, confirming his research to be accurate.

Johnson tapped on an app on his phone and showed O'Neill a map, on which two small icons—showing the trackers—were currently at a point on a background of blue, a thousand or so miles directly south of Greenland. The ship was about a third of the way through its 2,800-mile journey across the Atlantic.

Next, Johnson took out his laptop and logged onto the remote-camera monitoring website so he could show O'Neill pictures from the devices he had planted in Duggan's house and underground complex.

O'Neill's eyes widened a little. "You put cameras in Duggan's place? That's sticking your neck out."

"Someone's got to," Johnson said, pointedly. "At least if Duggan puts the stuff in his bunker—which is admittedly unlikely—we've now got a good chance of knowing about it."

He gave O'Neill the username and password for the monitoring site. "Might be wise for you to have access to this, just in case I have to go back in there."

"Joe didn't come here to sit on his ass," Jayne told O'Neill.

"And neither did I. If it's the G8 that Duggan's targeting, we've only got nine days to sort this out, and we're running out of opportunities."

Johnson smirked to himself. Jayne was struggling to contain her exasperation at what she saw as lethargy from the MI5 man.

Jayne drummed her fingers on the table. "I'm assuming that police failed to pin anything on him over Moira's murder, otherwise we'd have heard something?" she asked.

"Correct, unfortunately," O'Neill said. "As I expected, Duggan had plenty of alibis. A pub landlord, a takeaway restaurant owner, a farmer. All three of 'em said he'd been in Newry that night and had spent time with them. See, that's what you're up against. There were no forensics. He's a clever bastard. Maybe it wasn't him who did it. Maybe he got one of his cronies to do the dirty work. But there was nothing on them, either. They're all obviously well trained. The crime scenes people and forensics are still doing tests, but I'm not holding out much hope, frankly."

"Okay," Johnson said, trying hard to avoid sighing. "In that case we're back to the G8." He showed O'Neill a copy of the draft schedule for the school visit he had found on the USB drive taken from Duggan's house. "What do you make of that?"

O'Neill read it. "It's obviously been leaked from the police, probably the chief constable's office. Nobody else would have this detail at this stage. The problem is that it doesn't help us hugely."

Johnson knew what he meant. All it proved was that someone had stolen the document and leaked it. In terms of pinning charges on Duggan, it was next to useless, despite giving a clear indication as to what his thinking might be.

"We still need to catch him in the act," O'Neill said.

"Which brings us back to why I went to a lot of trouble to recruit an agent close to Duggan."

"Can I ask who?"

"I'll tell you sometime."

"But is he going to give us what we need?"

"That's the million dollar question," O'Neill conceded. He shifted in his seat and pursed his lips. "Stopping a few pipe bomb attacks on policemen based on his information doesn't really count for much if we're missing out on the big fish."

"Like the chief constable," Johnson said.

O'Neill nodded. "It's extremely frustrating. I'm due to meet him later this afternoon, actually. So let's see what we get. I'm not optimistic."

"Are there any others in the brigade, apart from your agent, who you know?" Johnson asked. "Any who might help you?"

O'Neill ran briefly through the brigade members, mentioning Liam McGarahan, who he understood to be the brigade's intelligence officer, and Danny McCormick, thought to be the quartermaster. "I don't think they'll turn informer, though."

Johnson nodded. "Okay, then. So the question is, who's next for the bullet? Big fish or little fish?"

O'Neill leaned back in his chair and shook his head. "I've no idea. Could be me—or you."

* * *

Saturday, January 19, 2013
Belfast

Dennehy steered his blue Vauxhall cautiously out of Belfast

city center and out along Newtownards Road, where British union flags fluttered in people's gardens and unionist slogans were painted on walls. Someone had even daubed a concrete bollard with red, blue, and white paint.

The huge yellow arches of Samson and Goliath, the twin gantry cranes that towered more than three hundred feet above the Harland & Wolff shipyard away to his left—the yard that built the *Titanic*—caught Dennehy's attention. The cranes stood like sentries on duty, watching and seeing everything going on down below, including, he knew, the odd tout passing information to police and intelligence service handlers in homes, pubs, cafés, and parks.

He flicked on his windshield wipers to deal with a splattering of raindrops as he drove past the tall spire of St. Matthew's Church on his right, a rare Catholic enclave standing defiantly in a Protestant landscape, and then on past the Great Eastern pub with its UVF flag outside.

Dennehy tried to keep a close eye on his rearview mirror, as he always did when he ventured into East Belfast. These days he was never sure whether he was under surveillance and if so, who might be watching him.

It could be one of Duggan's volunteers on the brigade side. The OC definitely had him on his list of suspects, he knew that. But equally, it might be someone working for O'Neill's colleagues within MI5. Increasingly, Dennehy felt caught between the two, slowly squeezed under the expectations that were put on him, with no easy or obvious way out.

He felt ill-equipped to deal with it: the subterfuge, the surveillance, and the risk of exposure. He was an electrician, not a trained spy, and although O'Neill and his previous handler had given him some instruction in street craft, like how to check for surveillance and evade detection as he went for meetings with his handlers, he knew that he wasn't a natural at it. He felt too nervous, and he was certain that the likelihood of detection was greater than it should be.

If he were honest with himself, a year of being GRANITE was more than enough.

Dennehy flicked the Vauxhall sharply and suddenly right down Albertbridge Road, then took a left and then another left onto Beersbridge Road before turning right onto Hyndford Street.

He checked his mirror. The only vehicle in sight was a black Volvo 4x4 a couple of hundred yards behind him, with two bikes mounted on a roof rack.

Dennehy was now as confident as he could be that he had no tail. He parked near Greenville Park before walking through it, past the bedraggled bowling green, the tennis courts, and the football stadium.

He sat on a bench and pretended to make a phone call but used the moment to make a final check for any sign of surveillance. The only other people in the park were two young men on the far side messing about on mountain bikes, trying to do wheelies.

Dennehy stood and walked on until he drew near to Orangefield High School on Cameronian Drive. There, sitting fifty yards from the entrance, in a familiar dark blue Ford Mondeo station wagon, was O'Neill.

Dennehy opened the front passenger door and climbed in. O'Neill was wearing a blond wig and a pair of glasses with tortoiseshell frames.

What's all this about?

"You're in the clear, no tail?" O'Neill asked, his forehead creased with worry lines, his black leather jacket done up tightly, a maroon scarf wrapped around his neck.

"Certain as I can be," Dennehy said. "You're taking no chances, are you? Nice disguise."

"Can't afford to. How are things?"

Dennehy leaned back against the headrest and momentarily closed his eyes. "Shit. Duggan's on the warpath. He knows he's got a tout, and I'd say I have to be near the top of his list, if not at the top. Feckin' stressful."

"All right, well, stress goes with the territory. You know that. You're doing a good job, but I need more, frankly, as I've told you before. If you can do that, I'll look after you," O'Neill said. He always said that, but Dennehy was not confident that he meant it. What did "look after you" mean in practice? Dennehy doubted it would amount to much.

"Okay, come on, then. What you got?" O'Neill asked, his voice staccato and sharp.

Dennehy switched his attention back to his MI5 paymaster. "One thing," he said. "I've been told there's a pipe bomb planned across at Irvinestown, Enniskillen, Wednesday morning, first thing. It's a copper, a Prod. I don't have the road."

"Are you involved in it?" O'Neill asked.

"Indirectly. I'm picking up some gear from a cache and then doing a drop in Hannahstown. I'm standing in for another volunteer who was originally detailed to do the job. That's it."

"Okay, I'll make sure you get a clear run in and out, and then we'll tail whoever does the pickup from you in Hannahstown after that. We can check which cops live in Irvinestown and alert them."

"Right."

O'Neill tapped his fingers on the steering wheel. "But that's not what I'm really interested in right now. I'm more focused higher up the tree. Is there anything going on around the G8?"

"Nope. Nothing G8, nothing else at all right now."

"Are you 100 percent sure? No weapons, ammunition coming in from anywhere, being moved across borders, or anything like that?"

"Yes, I'm sure," Dennehy said.

He glanced at O'Neill, who was giving a thousand-yard stare out the windshield down the road, where two guys on bikes had just disappeared around the corner. It was obvious he didn't believe what he'd just been told.

Dennehy swore under his breath.

CHAPTER TWENTY-SIX

Wednesday, January 23, 2013
  Forkhill

Dennehy sensed his wife's presence, despite his closed eyes, as he tried to settle his mind before yet another meeting with Duggan.

When he opened his right eye, Tess was standing there, leaning against the doorframe, legs crossed, holding a sheet of paper in her hand.

"What the hell is this?" she said in a level tone.

In his armchair, Dennehy opened the other eye and studied the piece of paper she was wielding across the other side of the living room. It was creased and torn and bore an Ulster Bank logo at the top.

He knew immediately what had happened. *Shit, the bloody laundry basket—my jeans.*

"Twelve and a half thousand bloody pounds. More than a thousand a month for the past year. Why didn't you tell me?" she said. "I thought you'd told them no?"

He had known for some time that she suspected, even knew, deep down. It was probably his mood swings, his occasional evasiveness about his whereabouts. But he had found it hard to tell her, and she presumably didn't want to ask, not without anything concrete to go on.

So it had been like the elephant in the room, casting a dark shadow over their lives, yet undiscussed, unmentionable. Now there was no more ducking the issue, not anymore.

"How else am I supposed to pay the mortgage, pay for you and the kids, keep us going?" he said.

"No wonder Duggan's got it in for you. Does he know?"

"No. I don't think so. Well, I'm not sure. He suspects, but he suspects all of us."

"What, because of all the jobs that have been scuppered?"

He nodded.

"Do you have a death wish or something? Is this MI5 who's paying you, or the police?"

She was sharp, his wife. "Five. But they're raging angry too, because of the chief constable and because I can't tell them everything. I've explained I'd be a dead man by now if they'd stopped it happening, but they're coming under the cosh—I think they're under pressure to explain it to the top brass."

Dennehy sighed and put his head in his hands. He looked up at Tess from beneath a furrowed brow.

"It's money," he said. "But I don't think it's worth it anymore. It's a mess, a real mess. Feels like the pips are squeaking."

He heard a chair scrape on the floor upstairs. His children, Becky and Tommy, would be downstairs in a minute to get their coats on before heading to school.

Tess pressed her lips tightly together and lowered her voice. "Why don't you pull out, just stop, and we can get out of Ulster, maybe go to the south of England, even Spain, and get our life back. You've done your bit."

Dennehy gave an ironic laugh. "They won't let me, not that easily. It's hard for them to get people like me. I held out for a long time—you know that. Three years they were trying. And the money's handy, too, you can't argue, with me not working now. How would we manage otherwise?"

"You're a fool, Martin, a fool. It's more about how are *we* —and I'm talking about me and the kids—are going to manage if Duggan finds out? Tell me that."

* * *

Wednesday, January 23, 2013
  Slieve Gullion

The hulking dark outline of Slieve Gullion rose up, specter-like, behind the parking lot as Duggan climbed out of his Volkswagen, his mood reflective of the dark clouds that hovered over the peak.

He strode over to the other two cars, where his brigade cohorts Danny McCormick, Liam McGarahan, and Kieran O'Driscoll were standing with Dennehy.

Duggan had spent the previous few days in a state of anxiety.

First, a week earlier, had come the call from Patrick, deep into the night Boston-time, telling him that there was a possibility the plan to smuggle in the Barrett and the remaining cigarettes in the second shipping container might have been compromised.

There had been an apparent burglary by someone posing as a night worker at the Pan-American Timber Products warehouse, and McKinney thought that the imposter had walked past him into the office just as he was drilling out one of the wooden beams to hide the gun.

McKinney was fairly certain that the gun hadn't been spotted, but he told Duggan he was letting him know as a precaution. And he couldn't give a good description of the night worker, who had been wearing a pair of company overalls and a cap, other than to say he was tall and had some short gray hair showing beneath the cap.

But as the days had gone on, nothing had happened, and Duggan's stress levels eased, helped by the safe arrival in Dublin of the first shipping container from Colón, with its cargo of five million cigarettes hidden behind timber. It had gone through customs unimpeded and had been swiftly processed, the cigarettes taken to a number of distributors who moved them on to their final destinations. The cash had already started to pour in.

But then, that morning, there had been some bad news.

Duggan had heard that the carefully laid plot to take out a Protestant police constable in Irvinestown, Enniskillen, using a pipe bomb attached underneath his car, had been discovered that morning, and an army technical team had been mobilized.

Within minutes, the road outside the constable's house had been blocked off, armored vans were everywhere, and they'd sent in a robot to defuse the device, which had then exploded. It had wrecked the car but injured nobody.

Duggan had seen it all on the TV news before leaving home.

The constable, who had remained safely in his house with his wife and two teenagers, was interviewed. He seemed shaken, but that was as far as it went.

It was the same plot about which Duggan had briefed McCormick almost two weeks earlier so arrangements could be made to retrieve the explosive and materials from the cache at Dundalk.

The rest of his brigade looked warily at him as he approached the group. He knew they would all be aware of Irvinestown by now.

"Bad news, boss," McGarahan said. "Irvinestown, I mean."

"Yeah, bad news," Duggan said as he joined the group, standing deliberately between McCormick and Dennehy. "Some bloody tout leaked it."

The visitor parking lot at Slieve Gullion Forest Park was virtually guaranteed to be empty in mid-January at any time of day. That was why Duggan had chosen the spot, more or less equidistant from their respective homes.

Duggan felt angry but confused. He knew that McCormick was the only one in the brigade who had known about the Irvinestown job; he was therefore the obvious suspect.

But on the other hand, Duggan had also been sent some video footage that morning that caused him to slam his kitchen door so hard that the catch had broken.

He decided to start with the video and took his cell phone from his pocket. "Here, look at this, all of you feckers. I had an interesting video clip sent to me only this morning by one of our volunteers who lives up in Belfast."

The other four men gathered around him and looked over his shoulders at the screen.

Duggan tapped on his videos app and pressed play. A slightly shaky video began to play, showing a young man on a bike as he cycled down a road, then attempted to do a wheelie. Next to the bike was a dark blue Ford Mondeo station wagon and a sign that marked the entrance to Orangefield High School.

"Ignore the guy on the bike," Duggan said. "Just focus on that car. Who do you see inside?"

Duggan glanced at Dennehy, standing next to him, whose eyes widened slightly. Duggan could see him trying to control his facial muscles.

"Looks remarkably like you, in that car, Martin, doesn't it?" Duggan said, lowering his tone a few notes. "Sitting chatting to a blond guy in a black leather jacket. Weird."

"When was that?" McGarahan asked.

"Last Saturday, up in Belfast," Duggan spat.

Duggan folded his arms and looked at Dennehy.

Dennehy shook his head. "You've got it wrong. I was talking about some work. If I was touting, like I've told you before, you wouldn't have got away with bringing down the chief constable's chopper, would ya? You'd be staring at the inside of a Maghaberry cell by now, defending your ass against all comers, that's what you'd be doing."

Duggan ignored him.

"That's two now in the space of the last week or so. First the moped volunteer up in Lurgan, he gets stopped by the police. Now this one," Duggan said. "Okay. Just tell me who the other man in the car is."

"It was someone I was talking to about getting electrical work," Dennehy said, glancing at McCormick, who remained silent. "I'm without a job at the moment, remember? I need work."

Duggan suspected he was lying. He had already instructed his volunteers in Belfast to run a check on the car license plates, which hadn't come back yet. He wanted to give Dennehy a chance to confess, though; he enjoyed hearing confessions. And he also enjoyed watching people stew.

"Right," Duggan said. "You won't mind if I have some checks done on who that car belongs to and who was inside it, then."

Dennehy shrugged. "It's a construction company boss, Dave Biggins. I've known him for years. We were chatting about a new housing development he's got a contract for. He needs electricians."

"Okay," Duggan said. "There's another thing, Martin. When I got back home two Saturdays ago after the police had finished quizzing me about Moira—and what a waste of time that was—me and Liam here went into the barn. And the shaft cover down to the den was off. I think someone had been down there. Was that you?"

Dennehy shook his head. "Definitely not. Haven't been down there in a long while."

Duggan spat on the ground. "There was somebody down there. If not you, then who? The American investigator?" He clasped his hands behind his back and walked away a few paces, visibly thinking.

The leaden skies started spitting raindrops, and the top of Slieve Gullion disappeared in a gray mist. But Duggan didn't seem to notice.

He turned and stroked his chin. "I've got a little job for you, Martin. It won't take you long. Should be an easy one for a man of your caliber."

There was silence as Dennehy stood with his arms folded, and McCormick, McGarahan, and O'Driscoll exchanged glances with each other.

The rain was really starting to come down; it was the kind of intense rain that kept Ireland green. And it was driven by a fierce wind that had gathered strength moving across the Atlantic.

"What I want you to do," Duggan said, "is a hit. And the guy who I want the hit done on works for MI5 in Belfast. Name of Brendan O'Neill. Perhaps we can talk about it soon."

He scrutinized Dennehy's face closely for a reaction.

There was definitely a twitch, and did he blanch a little? Duggan was certain he did.

There was a short silence. "Right," Dennehy said. "When do you want to talk about it?"

Duggan actually didn't want to talk about it at all. He just wanted to see Dennehy's reaction. He turned and headed back toward his Passat.

He stopped after a couple of strides and turned around. "I'll let you know. It'll be soon. Anyway, are you all coming across to the Cross Square for a beer?"

He was referring to the Cross Square Hotel in Crossmaglen, where they often gathered. It was a republican stronghold.

McGarahan and O'Driscoll nodded, but Duggan couldn't help but notice that McCormick looked down at the ground before glancing up and also nodding.

"Yeah, I'll come too," Dennehy said belatedly.

Duggan turned and continued toward his car. He was determined to get to the bottom of what had happened. And he was certain that he would get to the bottom of it, because these guys had nowhere to run.

* * *

Wednesday, January 23, 2013
  Crossmaglen

Duggan placed three pints of Guinness on the table, the third held precariously between the tips of his fingers. Then he went back to the bar to fetch the other two.

The Cross Square Hotel, a twenty-five-minute drive from Slieve Gullion, was busy for a late afternoon on a Wednesday. A group of folk singers sat in one corner, guitar cases stacked on the floor, having come in for a beer after their practice session at someone's house.

Two old men wearing stained and threadbare gray suits sat in deep discussion near the door, and a group of girls drank wine and cider, laughing, giggling, and swapping stories about guys they knew.

Duggan, McCormick, McGarahan, Dennehy, and O'Driscoll were all at a table near a flat-screen TV mounted on the wall.

There was a sports program on with a slot about the high-flying local Gaelic football team, Crossmaglen Rangers, which was playing in the semifinals of the All-Ireland Senior Club Football Championship next month.

The club's ground was just down the road from the Cross Square, and a few supporters were among the crowd in the bar, judging by the cheers when a short interview with the club chairman had finished.

After the sports slot, the news started. The second item was about the increasing violence being perpetrated by dissident Republicans in Ulster and the possible impact on the upcoming meeting of the G8 at Enniskillen, which was due to start five days later.

Duggan blanked out the noise from the bar and focused on the TV newscaster. He hadn't really been expecting that the shooting down of the PSNI helicopter and the killing of Eric Simonson might result in the cancellation of the G8 or a decision by some senior leaders not to attend. That would amount to bowing to terrorism. But he couldn't be certain.

The program started with a short interview with the Northern Ireland assistant chief constable, Norman Arnside, who was confident that the event would be a success and assured that all measures had been taken to ensure there would be no terrorist activity.

Then the newscaster moved on to introduce a clip from

Barack Obama's White House press conference, in which a journalist asked if he was worried about the security situation in regard to his forthcoming Belfast visit.

Obama, who was standing in front of the usual American flag and White House logo, leaned forward at his lectern and spoke deliberately and slowly into the microphone.

"The progress made in Northern Ireland toward peace over the last fifteen years has been remarkable," Obama said. "It underlines my belief that the clenched fists of terrorism will never win out, and that determination to wage peace is trumping it every time. Nationalism is something I understand, but terrorism is something I don't. Change in Northern Ireland will be brought about by democratic means —so it will only happen if a majority of the people want it. The G8 meeting in Northern Ireland will underscore all of that and show that the province is a place in which the world, in which America, can safely do business. So no—I am not worried about the rise in activity."

Another journalist piped up. "So will you cancel your visit to Belfast, Mr. President?"

"Definitely not, never," the president said.

The newscaster finished by saying that confirmation had been received that both the UK prime minister and the US president would spend time with the new acting chief constable for Northern Ireland for discussions about the security situation. The senior policeman was also expected to accompany them to some of the planned receptions in the province, as a show of unity and as a vote of confidence by the political leadership in policing in the province.

With that the newscaster moved on to another item.

There were a few jeers in the bar.

One of the two old men called out, "Asshole Yank, what does he know about us?"

One of the men sitting among the folk singers, who was

holding a guitar, turned around. "The new copper in charge knows nothing either. He won't last in that job, like the last one, in the chopper."

McGarahan and O'Driscoll nodded their approval.

"He's right," McGarahan said. "He's got no right to be commenting on our business. We've all been sold down the feckin' river by the politicians, but he wouldn't know anything about that."

He paused and looked at Duggan. "And what does the Dentist think?"

Duggan took a sip from his pint of Guinness. "The Dentist thinks that the G8 is gonna be a real opportunity," he opined.

"An opportunity for what?" O'Driscoll said.

Duggan gave a thin-lipped grin but didn't reply.

CHAPTER TWENTY-SEVEN

Thursday, January 24, 2013
   Belfast

Johnson was scrolling through the video links from Duggan's house when he saw something that made him sit up and take notice.

Duggan was visible on the monitor, working in the kitchen on the MacBook. The picture was in black and white, but Johnson spotted something that he had briefly seen when he had opened the lid of the laptop in Duggan's house, but it hadn't registered with him at the time.

Then he had forgotten it in the rush to install the cameras and the chaos of his escape from the underground bunker.

He turned to Jayne. "Come and look at this," he said, pointing to the screen. "I'm so stupid. That computer you can see Duggan using. I found it when I went in there and booted it up, but it was password protected, so I couldn't get into it."

"Yes, you told me. And what's your point?"

"It's a MacBook with a light blue cover."

"Yeah, so what? Come on, don't go cryptic on me."

"Well, this might be purely coincidental," Johnson said, "but remember when we met Beth Doyle, she said there'd been a burglary at the start of last year and that her husband's laptop had been stolen?"

Now it clicked into place for Jayne. "A MacBook with a light blue cover. I remember."

Johnson nodded. "Exactly. And there's something else. See that sticker on the corner of the keyboard?"

"A ladybird."

"Yes. That could definitely identify it. I need to see Beth again. I'm just wondering if that might be her husband's laptop." He took a screenshot of the video, in which the laptop and its ladybird sticker were clearly visible.

"If it is, then how the hell would Duggan have got it?" Jayne asked.

Johnson shrugged. "No idea."

Jayne had already arranged to catch up with Noreen and a couple of her other old contacts from MI5 that morning. She was also due to collect a rental car, a white Toyota Corolla, so that they could work independently and also have a backup vehicle, if needed. They agreed that Johnson would visit Beth alone.

As soon as Jayne left, Johnson took the M1 to Portadown and made his way back to Beth's house.

Since their last meeting, she seemed to have done nothing about his request to see copies of her husband's journal. He had texted her a few times and had received either noncommittal answers or none at all.

So a face-to-face meeting might be more productive, he felt.

Beth seemed a little flustered to see Johnson on the doorstep. She fiddled with her glasses and twiddled the hair around her ears in an embarrassed fashion before inviting him in.

"I'm sorry, Mr. Johnson, I did ask my son to get those scans done, but he's been very busy. I'm not sure he was enthusiastic about handing them over. They're all quite personal," she said.

Personal. What does that mean? He decided not to pursue that further, just for the time being.

"I understand," Johnson said, "but would you mind taking a look at this?" He took his laptop from his bag and showed Beth the screenshot he had taken of Duggan sitting at his desk tapping at his computer.

"Do you recognize that laptop?" Johnson asked.

She stared at the screen. "That's my husband's laptop. See that little round ladybird sticker on the top of the keyboard? My granddaughter put it there. That's his, definitely. How did you get this picture?"

"You said it had a pale blue cover," Johnson said, ignoring the question. "Well, I've seen the machine, and it definitely has a pale blue cover. That sticker confirms it, then. You might want to know that the man using it, I believe, is the man who shot your husband."

"Who is it, then?" Beth asked.

"I can't say right now," Johnson said. "First I need to confirm what I'm suspecting. And I need those journals to get to the bottom of why it happened and whether anyone else might be in danger. It's critical."

He didn't mention that he had already found out where her son, Archie, lived in London. Nor did he say that if Archie didn't cooperate, he wouldn't hesitate to carry out an illicit visit of the type that he had carried out several times during his career. That could wait until the next step.

"I wish you'd tell me who you think it is, but okay, I'll try again," she said. She looked irritated.

"Please do."

Johnson left. As he climbed into his car, his phone pinged with a short message from O'Neill. *Met my agent recently (FYI it's Dennehy). He says nothing currently planned for the G8. Likely bullshit but letting you know.*

It had to be bullshit, Johnson thought. He called Fiona to update her on the progress. He was aware from the exchanges of emails and text messages they'd had over the previous few days that she was busy writing analysis articles and stories in advance of the G8, but the task of covering the event had been given to the Dublin and London correspondents of *Inside Track* as well as the deputy editor and the international affairs correspondent. Fiona wasn't going to be traveling to Belfast for the meeting.

"That helps us," Johnson said. "You'll be free to go back to Boston and track down McKinney, when the time comes."

"Yes, but this is going to be all in the timing," Fiona said. "I obviously don't want to approach him and alert him until you've found a way to reel in Duggan at your end. As soon as you've done your bit, then I can press the button. I've briefed my editor here, and he's very keen on the story. It'll be huge for us. Then it'll be over to the police at this end to haul him in and press charges."

"Agreed," said Johnson. "I'll give you an update if you hang on."

He clicked onto the tracking app that was linked to the GPS tracker hidden in the rifle case en route from Boston.

The two small icons representing the trackers showed that the ship was well up the east coast of Ireland and was very close to Dublin.

"Looks like the ship's going to be docking soon," Johnson told Fiona. "I'm going to head down there with Jayne. I'll keep you informed. Wish us luck—we may need it."

* * *

Thursday, January 24, 2013
  Dublin Port

The green, blue, orange, brown, and yellow shipping containers were stacked five high and were being moved around like children's building blocks by the giant automated gantry cranes that ran nonstop in the container terminal.

A group of run-down industrial buildings stood on the other side of the road, all peeling paint, cracked cement, and weather-beaten fascias.

Dock workers in fluorescent orange and yellow jackets watched and chewed gum as the display of well-organized, heavy-duty logistics continued behind them, and a seemingly never-ending parade of trucks carrying shipping containers went in and out of the port, belching black diesel fumes.

They had taken both cars to Dublin Port to give them more flexibility and for security purposes, in case they came under surveillance or were threatened.

They parked next to each other across the road from the container terminal, next to a rusty chain-link fence that separated the road from an oil tank farm. Jayne locked her newly acquired white Toyota and sat in Johnson's black Ford.

Johnson knew from the app on his phone, which he had mounted on a dashboard holder, that the container holding the rifle had arrived. The two icons glowed bright and motionless on the map of the port area.

But he had no idea precisely where in the chaos of the terminal it was or on which of the myriad of trucks it was being loaded.

He and Jayne decided to sit tight and wait until it was on

the move. Then they would, by process of elimination, be able to track its movements. At least, that was the theory.

Johnson muttered dire warnings about likely having to wait deep into the night and fetching soup to keep them warm. He put some melancholy jazz and blues on the car stereo.

But Jayne, who seemed to have some prior knowledge of how modern ports operated, contradicted him sharply. Once fleets of cranes got to work on modern container ships, they were unloaded very quickly, she said, with an air of authority.

"I knew a guy who captained one of those ships," Jayne said. "He said that the life of a seafarer is no longer what it used to be, back when they had days in port while ships were unloaded. Now it's automated and quite boring."

"Knew a guy?" Johnson said. He folded his arms and looked the other way.

Jayne turned out to be right about the unloading time.

After less than three hours, Johnson made yet another check on the phone. Then he sat quickly upright and shoved the ignition key into its slot.

"The circus is on the move," he said.

They watched the screen as the two icons moved slowly out of the port in the direction of the M50 divided highway, which led toward the ribbon of the M1 heading to Northern Ireland.

"You lead, I'll follow," Jayne said. She jumped out of the Ford and got back into her Toyota.

Johnson reached over, removed the Beretta from the glove compartment, and placed it in the door compartment next to him. Then he started the engine and steered the Focus in the same direction, Jayne on his tail.

The container truck was probably a mile or two ahead of them, Johnson estimated. By the time they reached the tangled major road junction north of Dublin, out near the airport, where the M50 merged into the M1, the gap had been closed.

Which truck was it, though? There were a few freight trucks carrying shipping containers on the highway. Johnson tried to remain level with where he thought the icons were.

Gradually, as they passed more junctions, the traffic peeled off and thinned out. Now there were just two trucks visible, both unbranded, both a few hundred yards ahead, one carrying a rusting yellow container, one a blue.

Johnson dialed Jayne on his cell phone, still in the dashboard holder. "We can't afford to screw up here. I think it's the blue one," he said.

"Yep, okay," she said. "Leave this phone connection open so we can talk."

At the next junction, the truck with the yellow container took the exit. The blue one continued on the M1.

"Just keep a distance," Jayne said, her voice distorted over the cell phone connection. "We've no idea whether one of their guys is in the cab or not. Don't want them to realize they're being tailed."

Two junctions farther on, the truck took the exit and then, after three miles, headed into an industrial park, where it turned into a timber yard with a sign that read O'Malley's Timber International.

"The boss at the timber company is obviously on their payroll," Johnson said. "Have to hand it to these guys. They're organized."

Johnson drove into a DIY warehouse parking lot next door and reversed into a space so he could see from the rear car window through a gap in the bushes and the steel security fencing into the timber yard behind. Ten seconds later, Jayne did likewise, parking next to him. She slipped out of her car and into his passenger seat.

The container truck, about 150 yards from where Johnson

and Jayne were parked, was backed up against a raised loading bay. Next to it, four large unmarked white vans waited, almost in formation, their rear doors open at the same level as the bay.

"Shit, this is a military operation," Jayne said.

Johnson nodded. "That's precisely what it is."

The large steel gates to the timber yard had been closed. Johnson counted eighteen men, working in groups of six, who were removing the heavy wooden beams from the container Johnson had seen being loaded the previous week in Boston. All of the beams, apart from four that were placed to one side, were taken to a covered area and stacked.

The four beams that stood separately were loaded into one of the white vans.

"Got the plate of that one?" Jayne asked. "I'm guessing those four are the ones with the toys."

Johnson nodded and tapped a note into his phone.

The men stopped for a break. Several of them smoked, and some urinated against the fence at the back of the yard.

Johnson could now see the men more clearly. "That one over there on the left, lighting his smoke, that's Duggan. Definitely. I recognize him from the video footage we saw," he said.

Another man, carrying a flashlight, began to walk around the perimeter of the yard, looking closely at the bushes. He drew near Johnson's car.

"Best get well down. Though he'll not see through these darkened windows anyway," Johnson said. They both slid down in their seats until their heads were well below the level of the seat backs.

The beam from the flashlight shone straight into the car, paused for a few seconds, and then moved on.

When they next dared to look, the men were hard at it

again. Most of them had their coats off and a couple were down to their T-shirts, despite the cold.

This time, instead of beams, they were carrying plain brown cardboard boxes, roughly two feet long, and loading them into the other three vans. One of the men paused, broke open one of the boxes, and began to remove some of the contents, passing small packets around to the other workers.

"What the hell!" Johnson said after he'd watched them for a few minutes. "Those are cartons of cigarettes. Thousands of them."

Several of the workers removed cigarettes from the packs and lit up.

"Unbelievable," Johnson said. "So presumably, they smuggle the smokes in to fund the arms deals. They won't be paying any import duty. It amazes me how much of this stuff gets straight through the ports."

Jayne snorted. "There's no way they can inspect all those containers. To open one, unload it, and inspect it properly would take hours. You'd be damned unlucky to get caught. They probably just write it off as bad luck if it happens. The customs people make a PR meal of it when they do catch someone, but the reality is, those are the tip of the iceberg."

The unloading operation continued for another hour or so. Then the men gathered together, and the man Johnson was now certain was Duggan handed out small brown envelopes to the others. They then dispersed to cars parked around the yard.

The truck holding the shipping container eventually drove off.

Johnson checked the GPS tracker app on his phone again, to make sure the rifle case was still in the yard. The two icons glowed at him reassuringly from the screen.

"That's it, then, job done. They've paid the guys. We just need to make sure we follow the right van now."

Someone opened the gates to the yard, and the cars drove off. Next, the three vans holding the cigarettes left.

The two icons remained stationary on Johnson's phone screen map.

There were two men left in the yard, one of them Duggan. They climbed into the van Johnson knew contained the four beams—and presumably the rifle—and moved slowly out of the parking lot.

Johnson started the car but left his lights off and didn't move until the van was around the corner.

Once Jayne was back in her Toyota and ready to follow, he accelerated away. They only turned their lights on once they were back on the main road.

Johnson dialed Jayne on his cell phone, then switched back to the tracking app. "It looks like he's heading back toward the M1," Johnson said. "Just need to make sure we don't lose this asshole."

CHAPTER TWENTY-EIGHT

Thursday, January 24, 2013
  South Armagh

Once on the divided highway, the white van accelerated rapidly into the night, its red tail lights weaving between lanes as it passed slower-moving traffic. But it never went much over the speed limit.

Johnson hung back at least four hundred yards behind the van as it cruised north past Drogheda and then Dundalk.

It was now past eight o'clock and the traffic was sparse, with an occasional truck still heading north and a few cars coming south, presumably commuters heading back home to the Republic from Belfast.

North of Dundalk, without indicating, the van suddenly veered down an off-ramp signposted Carlingford.

Johnson accelerated to follow, Jayne still in position just behind.

The van sped around a traffic circle, and within seconds they were on a narrow country road.

Johnson quickly noticed that whereas the van had closely stuck to the speed limit on the highway, presumably to avoid any attention from the police, now it ran flat out down a dark, twisty lane with little passing space.

He gripped the steering wheel and forced himself to concentrate. The van driver clearly knew these lanes well.

"Looks like he's running," Johnson said to Jayne over his cell phone.

He rounded a bend too quickly, came very close to a hedge, and then downshifted into third gear to give himself more control. "It's possible he's realized he's being tailed," Johnson said.

"Maybe," Jayne said, her voice sounding distant over the hands-free loudspeaker system. "Probably more obvious now we're off the motorway. Why else would he be gunning it?"

Johnson realized he hadn't updated O'Neill, so he temporarily ended the call with Jayne and dialed the MI5 man. But O'Neill's phone, after ringing a few times, went to voice mail.

Bare trees and hedges flashed past in the white light of the Ford's headlights. Here there were no road markings, and Johnson was forced to focus on the shoulders to give himself a navigation point as he came in and out of the frequent sharp bends.

The van was about three hundred yards ahead of them now. They took a sharp left just after a farm and then a right at a large white-painted pub on a corner, where the lights were all on but the parking lot was empty.

A minute later came a crossroads warning sign and a stop sign immediately afterward.

But the van hurtled over the junction without slowing, Johnson following, still some distance behind.

Immediately after the van passed, a car came from the left side of the junction, a green Land Rover came from the right, and they both braked to a halt a couple of feet from each other right in the middle of the crossroads, blocking it completely.

There was no reason for the two cars to have stopped. There had been no accident, no collision. Johnson glanced in the rearview mirror and could see that another Land Rover had emerged from a driveway to block the road behind him, separating him from Jayne, who was stuck behind it.

In front of him, the drivers of the Land Rover and the car had both jumped out and appeared to be arguing.

Johnson knew instantly that this was some kind of setup, either a tactic to allow the van to get away or, possibly, to take him out. He decided in an instant what he would do. He braked hard to avoid smashing into the Land Rover but then steered hard right, then sharply left, and rammed his foot down on the accelerator, scraping the driver's side of his car on some brickwork as he forced his way through the narrowest of gaps between the Land Rover and a wall at the corner of the crossroads.

As he drove up the road, he glanced in his mirror. The two men were scrambling to get back in their vehicles.

Johnson redialed Jayne's cell phone.

"Jayne, are you still there behind me?" Johnson said, his voice suddenly reedy and tense.

"Yes, but I'm stuck behind that bloody Land Rover. It's not moving. What the hell's going on?" Jayne's voice was breaking up over the cell phone, and he was down to just one bar showing on his reception indicator.

Johnson pounded his hands on the steering wheel and checked the GPS on his phone. The coverage on that also appeared intermittent, but then the green dot moved, showing that the tracker inside the van was now pulling well away, moving fast and heading north.

"Sonofabitch," Johnson shouted. "It's a setup. It's been fixed. Get out of there, fast as you can, Jayne."

"No, the bloody Land Rover's still blocking me, I'm going to . . ."

But Johnson didn't hear the rest of Jayne's sentence as he lost the signal on his phone completely.

"Shit," he muttered to himself. "We're screwed here."

Johnson felt he had no choice but to follow the van even if it meant leaving Jayne behind. She would have to catch up later, although navigating through dark country lanes with no cell phone signal was not ideal.

He was forced to slow down to study the GPS tracking app on his phone as best he could while keeping his car on the road. The van now appeared to be at least a mile or so ahead and seemed to stop briefly before taking a right-hand fork.

Johnson put his foot to the floor and sped down a straight stretch of road.

Now the clouds over the Irish countryside cleared, revealing a full moon, and suddenly the road rising up ahead of him was lit with an eerie white light that reflected off the blacktop.

Johnson took the next right, following the tracker, but after half a mile, the road surface deteriorated alarmingly, with large holes visible. The GPS had stopped farther down the lane, just in front of him.

A couple of hundred yards ahead, a huge heap of black gravel and concrete waste loomed in the high-beam headlights, right in the center of the road, completely blocking it.

It's a dead end. What the hell?

The GPS was indicating right where the heap of gravel was. This couldn't be right. It was a disused lane, which clearly functioned as a dumping ground or storage area for road repair materials.

Johnson braked and peered through the windshield. He noticed in the headlights a long, slim cardboard box lying on the heap of gravel, right where the GPS was showing the tracker to be.

Except there won't be a rifle in it any more. Idiot.

"Shit, I'm screwed here," Johnson muttered to himself. He flung the car into gear and executed a rapid three-point turn.

Duggan and his cronies must have found the GPS trackers, shoved them in the box, and junked it on the pile of gravel. But now he was a sitting duck for an ambush.

Johnson, his adrenaline now in overdrive, accelerated back down the lane. A few seconds later, he had to slam on his brakes again. In his lights he could see, at the side of the road, what appeared to be a dead fox.

He was certain it hadn't been there when he had driven the other way, just minutes earlier. Or had it?

Oh, shit . . . I'm going for it.

Johnson let the clutch up and accelerated hard past the fox. He was about fifteen yards past it, the car whining at high revs in second gear, when there was a massive bang and a flash from behind him that lit up the fields and trees on both sides of the road.

Fragments of glass from the rear windshield sprayed past him into the front of the car, and he felt the back end skew sharply sideways as the force of the blast caught it.

Johnson lost control of the Ford, which hit a large hole in the pavement and then speared into a ditch at the right side of the road, where it rammed hard into a tree.

He felt his head bang into the side window and there was a rushing noise in his ears. He wanted to move his hand but couldn't.

He blacked out.

* * *

Thursday, January 24, 2013
  South Armagh

For just a second or two, Jayne thought she was dealing with some thoughtless farmer who had decided to turn his Land Rover around in the road without checking for approaching traffic.

But she quickly realized it was a classic old IRA countryside roadblock tactic. During her stint in Northern Ireland in the early '90s she had twice been caught up in almost identical maneuvers.

Jayne grabbed her Walther from the glove compartment.

Her thought was confirmed by Johnson, who shouted over the crackly cell phone connection that it was a setup. She then heard him say he was on the move again, moments before the phone connection was completely lost.

Obviously Johnson's car was being deliberately separated from hers. And assuming Duggan and his dissident buddies organized the roadblock it didn't take much imagination to work out what the next step was likely to be.

Jayne quelled the temptation to bang on her horn.

Instead, she put the gun on her lap, rammed the white Toyota into reverse, and backed it into the gateway of a field on her right.

The car wheels spun in the mud as she accelerated back in the direction she had come, away from the roadblock, all the while expecting to hear gunshots and feel the impact of rounds hitting the car's bodywork.

But there was nothing.

Within seconds she had rounded a bend and was away. She had no idea whether Johnson was safe or whether he had managed to get back on the tail of the truck carrying the tracking device and the sniper's rifle.

But she knew one thing: she and Johnson were now headed in opposite directions down a dark country lane in south Armagh that appeared to be bristling with dissident terrorists.

* * *

Thursday, January 24, 2013
  South Armagh

Johnson came around when the car door was yanked open and his head, which had been resting against it, lolled sideways.

He found it impossible to focus. All he could see was the black, shadowy figure of a man who grabbed him forcibly by the arm and pulled him out of the car onto the muddy shoulder of the road, then lashed his hands together tightly behind his back.

The man pulled Johnson to his feet, but the ground wobbled as if an earthquake had struck, and he crashed straight back to earth.

"Shit," a voice said, in a broad Irish accent. "Here, Liam, help me get this bastard into the van."

Johnson blacked out again.

The next time he came to, his chin hit the wooden plywood floor of a large van. A bandage or some long, thin piece of cloth was wound around his head, holding another piece of cloth in his mouth.

By the dim glow of an interior light, Johnson saw a man watching him, his back to a partition that separated the driver's cab from the rear. He was sitting on four huge wooden beams—the ones which had come from Boston.

Johnson's first thought was of Jayne. *Did she get away or*

was she somehow trapped too? He hadn't heard gunshots, but the cell phone connection had terminated abruptly. It was impossible to know what had happened.

The van bounced as it rattled over a bump in the road, then lurched to the left, moved forward more slowly, and finally came to a halt.

The driver turned around and looked through the glass window in the center of the dividing panel. It was Duggan.

"Blindfold him, get him into the house, then get him downstairs. We'll keep him in the den. And have you got his stuff?" Duggan shouted.

"Yes, boss," the man sitting on the beams called. He held up a plastic bag that Johnson could see contained his phone, the Beretta, and his wallet.

The man picked up a piece of ripped towel and tied it around Johnson's head, blindfolding him.

Johnson heard the back doors of the van open; then he was pushed out of the back and told to stand. This time he was able to do so without the earth disappearing from under him, but his head throbbed and felt distinctly wet from where it had bashed into the side window of the car.

Someone grabbed him by the arm and propelled him forward. He sensed that they had moved indoors, and then a man ordered him to walk down some stairs. He was maneuvered into position, then pushed.

At the bottom, he took a few more steps. Then came another order. "On your knees, then crawl straight ahead when I tell you, Yank."

Johnson did as commanded.

He knew he was now going into the tunnel at Duggan's house, through the bookcase door and hatch door, heading from the house to the den.

He tried to picture where he had left the microcameras, wedged between cinder blocks, and prayed that the batteries were holding up. The instructions had given an estimated battery duration between charges of around seventeen days, but how accurate that was, he had no idea.

A boot hit Johnson hard in the backside. Without the use of his hands, which were still lashed behind his back, he lost his balance, toppled forward, and hit his chin on the floor.

"Crawl, come on, lift yourself up, you asshole, and crawl," That was Duggan's voice from behind him.

Johnson complied but found he could move only slowly forward.

He could hear somebody else crawling ahead of him, presumably another one of Duggan's gang, and others behind.

After what seemed like an eternity, he felt his knees move off the carpet squares and onto solid concrete.

A voice came from in front. "Stand up."

Again he did as told.

Someone untied his blindfold.

He was in the den, its grim, gray cinder block walls illuminated by the two bare bulbs. It looked exactly as it had on his previous visit.

The man who stood next to him ran a hand through dark, dank hair and rubbed the blue-black stubble on his chin. He held a Browning 9 mm pistol in his right hand.

Johnson looked back at the hatch to the tunnel just as Duggan emerged, also holding a Browning.

Duggan instructed Johnson to sit on one of the wooden chairs that stood against a wall.

Then Duggan sat on the office chair, put his Browning on the desk next to him, and swiveled to face Johnson. "Okay, you fecker," he said, pausing to cough. "You've given us some hassle. But now you've screwed up. You'll be staying here for a while, where you can't cause us anymore trouble, until we can decide what to do with you. You want to explain what the hell you're doing, poking your nose in?"

He spoke in a flat, quietly menacing tone but with no sign of anger.

Strange, Johnson thought. There was no reference to any suspicion that Johnson had been in the den or tunnels before.

"Look," Johnson said. "I'm an outsider here, but it's obvious even to me that what you're trying to do isn't going to work. I know you've taken out a few guys, but it seems to me that times have moved on. The ship's sailed—you're not going to somehow get the politicians to do a U-turn by plugging a few coppers or prison officers."

Duggan ran the back of his hand across his nose.

"You don't know what you're talking about," Duggan said.

"Probably not, but—"

"First, you haven't a clue what I'm trying to do."

"Tell me what you're trying to do, then."

"You know shit about life here, how it's been destroyed by the Brits over the past few decades. The politicians have made us all slaves to a shit peace settlement that ain't going to last just to get themselves a few years of power, a nice pension. It's built on sand."

"Doesn't look that way," Johnson said.

"Listen, find out how people feel, don't believe the politicians. Our country is our country. We're Irish Catholics, not British Protestants. Nothing's changed since 1916—nothing. My grandfather, Sean, died in the cause, in '57, and so did my father, Alfie, in '84."

"If you carry on, you'll be next. That what you want?" Johnson asked.

"I want to smash the idea of British rule as the normal thing around here. If we just lie down and accept it, it'll become a reality, eventually. We're not having that. Like my old math teacher at school used to say, what's twenty-six plus six? Answer: one."

It took Johnson a second to realize that Duggan was

referring to the twenty-six counties of the Irish Republic and the six of Ulster: a united Ireland.

"Forgive me," Johnson said. "I'm trying to figure out how shooting a prison officer and a policeman and an investment company guy and a security company boss is going to help. And I'm not going to mention your stepdaughter."

"Who says I shot them?"

Johnson didn't respond.

The light cast by the bare electric bulbs cast stark shadows, making Duggan's eyes appear like large black bullet holes in his head.

Duggan picked up his pistol, then stood and turned to his colleague. "That's enough talk. Liam, let's get the American tied up on that mattress. He can stew down here for a bit."

"Okay, boss."

"Then I need to call the quartermaster, let him know what's going on, and speak to Patrick. We need a meeting to decide what to do with this guy. Or rather, when to do it."

Duggan looked at Johnson. "It'll be slow. But we're underground here, so you'll be able to scream as much as you like."

CHAPTER TWENTY-NINE

Friday, January 25, 2013
Newtownards

Jayne knocked at the door, then rang the bell. There was no response, so she tried again, and again.

She checked her watch. It was almost one o'clock in the morning. Brown Bear, O'Neill's safe house in Newtownards, remained silent and in darkness, just as his main home in Belfast had been when she had stopped there half an hour earlier. All the street lights, apart from one, had gone out.

A car approached at speed from the other end of the street, slowing markedly as it passed the house. From the driver's window, a white face peered at her, illuminated by a pale green glow, presumably from a dashboard instrument panel, and the car crawled slowly on toward the nearby school.

Jayne felt deeply uncomfortable hanging around on the doorstep. She swore and took her phone from her pocket.

After escaping the roadblock, she had spent nearly an

hour in the dark driving a circuitous route around Forkhill, Drumintee, and on the main N1 road that ran from Dublin to Belfast. She had absolutely no idea where Johnson was, although her immediate fear, given the roadblock, was that the dissident Republicans might have trapped and executed him.

She tried several times to call Johnson, but each time his phone went straight to voice mail. *The person you are calling is not available. Please leave a message.*

Eventually she conceded defeat and headed back to Belfast, trying several times en route to contact O'Neill, also without success. His phone too went straight to voice mail, so she decided to drive to his house.

Jayne had memorized the log-on details for the video monitoring website Johnson had been using to view the feeds from Duggan's underground bunker. Johnson had also given the details to O'Neill when they had visited him at the safe house. It was now critical to check the video feeds as quickly as possible.

Standing on the doorstep, she tried calling O'Neill one more time. But yet again, there was no reply.

She left another message asking O'Neill to call her back urgently as Joe had run into serious problems.

Where the hell is the guy?

She walked back to her car and tried to tee up the video monitoring website on her phone. But the 3G cell phone connection was just too slow, and eventually the site crashed.

After two more tries, she gave up, started the car, and drove back toward Belfast. Clearly, if she were going to mount a search for Johnson, she couldn't do it single-handed.

Yet she felt unable to call the local police. Even now, the idea of bringing in local coppers whose heavy-handed approach would likely torpedo any chance they had of trapping Duggan seemed like a nonstarter to her.

Jayne turned on the car radio, only to find syrupy late-night love songs. It wasn't what she wanted to hear. She reached over and firmly pressed the off button.

By 1:40 a.m. she was back at the apartment on Falls Road, her head buzzing despite her tiredness.

Jayne again tried logging on to the monitoring site, but even though she was now on a broadband connection, the feeds still refused to load. Exasperated, Jayne tried calling both Johnson and O'Neill one final time, but both calls went to voice mail.

She immediately sent an encrypted email to Alice Hocking, one of her oldest and best friends at the UK Government Communications Headquarters in Cheltenham, asking if she could put a trace on Johnson's phone as soon as she got into work in the morning. In theory, Alice shouldn't carry out such a check, given that Jayne was no longer employed by the SIS and didn't have official access to GCHQ's expertise. But she knew that Alice would be able to slip the query through at some point. It was a long shot: if Johnson had been trapped by the dissidents, it was almost certain they would have removed the SIM card and battery from his phone. If he was still free, then by morning he would have called or messaged her anyway—she was certain of that. But it was worth a try.

Once the email had been sent, there seemed to be no other option but to try and get some sleep and then regroup in the morning.

All Jayne could hope for was that perhaps by then, O'Neill would have surfaced, and they could jointly come up with a plan.

If not . . . then what? Jayne had no answer to that question.

* * *

Friday, January 25, 2013
  Forkhill

Two miles from where Johnson was lying incarcerated in the underground den, Duggan was standing in a corner of the drafty barn owned by his brigade machine gunner, Pete Field.

Field, who still had a swagger about him after forcing the emergency landing of the chief constable's helicopter three weeks earlier, was the only other real gun enthusiast in the south Armagh brigade. He looked after his DShK heavy machine gun just as meticulously as Duggan did his Barrett M82.

And like Duggan, Field was still, remarkably, a cleanskin who had never been convicted of a crime north or south of the border.

That was one reason why the four huge oak beams with their valuable contents had been taken to Field's property for safekeeping after their long journey from Panama via Boston.

Now came the task of checking the weapons, test-firing them, and removing them as quickly as practicable to a safe cache, whose location was to be determined by the brigade's quartermaster, Danny McCormick.

Duggan and Field walked to a decorator's trestle table, on which a five-foot-long, one-foot-wide soft black carrying case lay.

Duggan had a momentary flashback to Christmases of long ago: the surge of anticipation and the excitement at unwrapping a new toy. He unzipped the case, flipped open the top, and took out the unassembled components of an almost-new Barrett M82A1 .50-caliber rifle.

His friend McKinney had done a good job in sourcing the weapon at such short notice, even if it had cost him seven and a half thousand bucks. The rifle looked as though it had hardly been used, its matte gray paint free of scratches or marks.

Duggan ran his hand lightly, almost sensuously, across the upper receiver and placed it on the table, then did the same with the lower receiver. Then he slid the long, slim barrel from the transport position to the firing position, clipped the upper and lower receivers together, put the lock pins in place, and pulled the bolt back. He wasn't expecting to find ammunition in the chamber but checked anyway, out of habit. Then he flipped off the safety and pulled the trigger. He gave a thin-lipped smile of satisfaction at the loud click when the firing pin came forward.

It had taken just a couple of minutes to transform the rifle from being in pieces to fully assembled.

Duggan picked up the weapon. It weighed more than thirty pounds, and that was without the Schmidt & Bender scope and ten rounds of ammunition. Probably forty with all that attached, he estimated.

Quite apart from the weapon's power, its flexibility, transportability, ruggedness, and—ashamed as Duggan sometimes was to think it—the *looks* of the Light Fifty were what he loved about it. Even the recoil after firing was minimal for such a large, powerful gun.

Duggan felt relieved to have it, given the job he had in mind: the margins for error would be minute, and there would likely be no second chance. It would probably be a one-shot opportunity, he knew. But with this baby, he wouldn't have to worry about the bolt not chambering the next round properly, unlike with his old M82.

"Beautiful. Pity I can't find a woman like this," Duggan said, stroking the barrel slowly. Field laughed, despite having heard the joke several times before. He used the same quip when talking about his DShK.

Duggan's phone beeped. He pulled it out of his pocket

and read the WhatsApp message, which was from McKinney. *Has the second batch of sweets arrived at the corner shop? Can we have a quick chat on the phone?*

Duggan groaned inwardly. Fair enough. McKinney wanted to ensure the second shipping container had arrived safely. But inevitably he would want to discuss what the rifle was going to be used for, who was on the hit list, and the risk-reward factor involved.

From his throwaway pay-as-you-go cell phone, he sent McKinney a text message containing the number of the old telephone that Field kept in the barn, the same one Duggan had used several times for his covert conversations between the two of them.

A minute later, the old phone burst into life, with its museum-piece double bell ring that jarred the quiet of the barn. Duggan walked to the wooden desk and picked up.

"Patrick, how are you?"

He then turned toward Field and inclined his head, indicating silently that the volunteer should leave him alone to conduct a private conversation. Field obediently turned and left the barn, pulling the door shut behind him.

"Dessie, I assume the second container's arrived. No drama, I take it?" McKinney said.

"Not quite that simple," Duggan said. "We received the goods last night, but they came with a few unexpected extras."

Duggan outlined how, following McKinney's tip-off about the burglary at the Boston timber warehouse, they had been especially vigilant and had become suspicious that they were being tailed out of Dublin. Then he shared how a search of the box and bag containing the Barrett had revealed two tracking devices, and how the swift, well-executed actions that followed had resulted in the capture of Johnson.

McKinney was silent for a few seconds, then swore. "That

could have been him who broke into the timber yard, then. What are you going to do with him now?" he asked.

"I'll give him a grilling to find out what the hell he's doing, why he's been after us, and who brought him in. Then I'll have to get rid of him, obviously. He's already seen too much," Duggan said. "But I need to focus on the G8 right now. Liam's going to take care of Johnson for the time being. He's locked up in the den so he can't do any damage."

There was a low whistle on the other end of the line as McKinney exhaled. "What's your plan for the G8? It had better not be Obama . . ."

"Still working it out, Patrick." There was a weary note to Duggan's tone.

"If you're going to take Obama out, I might as well close up this end of the operation completely, there'll be so much shit flying around," McKinney said, his voice rising a fraction. "You realize you'll screw all fund-raising out of America for the whole republican movement if you hit him. We won't get another cent out of the US. It's been hard enough these past few years. People are tired of the violence, Dessie. You do this and public opinion will be burned. And I'll be burned with it—there'll be a witch-hunt, I'm telling you."

Duggan looked up into the dark roof of the barn. It was something that had crossed his mind, not that he was going to admit it to Patrick.

"You've gone native, Patrick. We all know that. And you know very well it wouldn't affect our cigarette imports. That's where the money's coming from these days, not from rattling a tin around the pubs and bars in Boston like in the '70s and '80s. Anyway, I'm not telling you what I'm going to do, certainly not over an open phone line."

There was a pause at the other end of the line. "There'll be no one here to discuss anything with if Obama goes," Patrick said.

* * *

Friday, January 25, 2013
 Forkhill

The odor of damp cement dust had invaded Johnson's nostrils, and he could detect no other scent. He lay helpless on the double mattress, his ankles bound with thin, strong climbing rope to metal rings fastened into the concrete floor. His wrists were similarly bound to what looked like rock-climbing pitons that had been hammered into the wall behind him. They were immovable.

Johnson watched silently by the light of a single dusty bulb as a spider almost as big as a drinks coaster inched its way up the wall beside him and disappeared into a gap between two cinder blocks.

The man Johnson knew as Liam appeared at intervals, accompanied by a man whom he called Martin, who was chunkily built with dark hair, a mustache, and a black leather jacket. Johnson recognized him immediately as the man he had seen with Duggan attacking Moira in Belfast, almost three weeks earlier. Ronnie Quinn had identified him as Martin Dennehy.

Johnson also remembered O'Neill referring to McGara-han, thought to be the intelligence officer. This must be him, then.

And Dennehy, Johnson now knew, was also O'Neill's agent inside the south Armagh brigade. He was therefore his best hope.

But Johnson never got the chance to speak to Dennehy alone. Whenever he came into the bunker, it was always with McGarahan.

Even if Dennehy had showed up by himself, and despite

him being O'Neill's agent, Johnson felt it would be foolish to think he could trust him, because clearly O'Neill couldn't.

McGarahan and Dennehy quickly fell into a routine: McGarahan would stand there, his Browning pointed straight at Johnson, while Dennehy untied him.

Then Dennehy would push Johnson, always backed up by McGarahan and his Browning, into a small cinder block cubicle behind a door made from lightweight brown plywood. Inside the cubicle there was a pear-shaped pan set into the concrete floor—a rudimentary squatting toilet—together with a bucket of water for sanitary purposes.

McGarahan and Dennehy carried out a similar double act for serving food: Dennehy untied Johnson while McGarahan stood guard. So far, every meal had been identical: a plate of baked beans on toast, served up with a glass of water.

Johnson weighed his chances of overpowering one or the other of the Irishmen. Despite his heavily graying temples and weather-beaten face, McGarahan's forearm muscles resembled lines of steel rope, and his shoulders were the size of a New England Patriots linebacker. Dennehy looked like more of a target, heavily built but more obviously fat than muscle and, in Johnson's judgment, less mentally alert. But quite apart from the fact that Dennehy was never alone, attacking O'Neill's agent could prove badly counterproductive.

At least the Irishmen hadn't left Johnson gagged. Duggan doubtless assumed that nobody could hear him if he shouted out anyway, so it would make little difference, Johnson thought.

But that was where they were wrong, Johnson hoped. He prayed that the two microcameras he had planted at either end of the underground den a few days earlier were working, and that O'Neill was monitoring from his laptop. Maybe Jayne too, if she'd managed to escape the roadblock intact.

Johnson knew that the cameras were positioned in a way so that they wouldn't show into the deep recess where he was lying tied up. The viewing angles weren't wide enough for that, and Johnson cursed himself for not having placed more cameras around the bunker.

But he knew that, providing the cameras remained functional, every time McGarahan allowed him out into the main area of the den, he should be visible. He just had to hope that these occasions coincided with O'Neill when viewed his monitor, or that he or Jayne would review the stored footage for signs of his whereabouts.

What Johnson really needed was an opportunity to speak into the camera and microphone more directly, and the only time he could do that was when McGarahan and Dennehy untied him and he was in the main part of the bunker.

But what to say, and how? If he said anything obvious, the Irishmen would immediately smell a rat and gag him again— or worse. Then he'd be screwed. Rather, he needed to get McGarahan and Dennehy into a conversation and work his messages for O'Neill into that, somehow.

The problem was, the two Irishmen remained virtually silent, other than issuing the occasional curt instruction in a deep, gruff Irish brogue. Neither seemed willing to get into a conversation.

So the next time McGarahan and Dennehy took Johnson out of the recess for a visit to the toilet, he decided to throw a grenade into the proceedings.

Johnson stopped right in the middle of the main floor area and turned to McGarahan, who helpfully was standing only a yard or two from where he had placed the micro-camera in the wall.

"This bunker," Johnson said. "Don't you and your boss Dessie Duggan worry it's going to be raided by the police or maybe the security services?"

"Shut the feck up," McGarahan said. He waved the barrel of his Browning toward the stall. "Get in there, use that toilet, and do your business. You've got thirty seconds before I tie you back up." He nodded toward the sheet of plywood that formed a makeshift door to the squatter toilet.

Johnson shrugged and walked into the stall, shutting the door behind him. While he was in there, he heard a loud scraping noise as the hatch door from the tunnel opened.

He heard McGarahan's voice. "Okay, Dessie. The American's just using the toilet in there."

The unmistakable, low-pitched, even tone of Duggan's voice came back in response. "Right. Is he behaving?"

"I guess," McGarahan said. "I just had a little rant from him about us being caught down here by police."

Duggan snorted loudly. "He won't be ranting for much longer."

"What's the plan?" McGarahan asked.

There was a pause, then Duggan said in a lower tone, "Nothing immediately. I need to focus on Project Gyrate for now. After that, I'm thinking we'll take him to Davy's pig farm. There'll be no trace of anything once the animals have finished with him."

Johnson felt the skin on his scalp tighten involuntarily. Then he heard the loud ring of a cell phone.

CHAPTER THIRTY

Friday, January 25, 2013
  Belfast

O'Neill woke at his house in Holywood with a strange sense of foreboding. He tried to tell himself it was just because of the hangover he was suffering after the previous evening's whiskey session with an old army friend. They had started at six o'clock and he had gotten home at ten. But he knew the sense of dread he was feeling was due to more than that.

O'Neill had turned his phone to silent when he had gone to bed at about quarter to eleven and had inserted his earplugs, as usual. He didn't want to be woken unnecessarily, especially by his boss, when he was too drunk to make much sense.

Now, at just after quarter past seven in the morning, he grabbed the phone from his bedside table to find a string of missed calls that had come in between 11:08 p.m. and 1:44 a.m.

One of the calls was from his mother and seven were from

Jayne Robinson, who had also left two messages. He dialed into voice mail.

Brendan, it's Jayne here. It's urgent. Joe's gone missing down in south Armagh. His phone's off. To cut a long story short, there was a roadblock, which I'm certain was Duggan and his gang, who we were tailing. We were separated and Joe went off the radar. Call me as soon as you can.

The second message was in a similar vein.

O'Neill sat up straight in bed and drank the glass of water that stood on his bedside table. *What the hell?*

He calculated he had now not heard from Johnson for six days, not since their discussion about the remote cameras at Willows Farm.

He too had tried calling Johnson's phone a few times the previous night, returning a missed call. But the calls had gone straight to voice mail, and although he had left a couple of messages, Johnson hadn't called back.

When O'Neill remembered what Johnson had said about the shipment from Boston and his brief reference to possibly needing to get back into the underground bunker at Duggan's place, Jayne's news sounded ominous.

He dialed Jayne's number and tried to preempt any angry reaction to his failure to pick up her urgent calls by apologizing profusely.

There was a short silence at the other end of the line.

"It wasn't just the calls," Jayne said, eventually. "I was knocking on your front door at half past midnight, and on the safe house door. But there was no answer. Where the bloody hell were you?"

O'Neill ran his hand through his hair. "I think I was just exhausted. I've been working around the clock. I must have been out for the count."

He decided not to mention the whiskey session or the earplugs. Jayne didn't seem the type to be sympathetic about such unprofessionalism.

"Right," Jayne said. "First we need to check the video and sound feeds from the cameras Joe put in Duggan's bunker and house. I couldn't get them to work last night. There has to be a fair chance that Joe's in there."

O'Neill agreed. Keen to appear proactive, he invited her to come around to his house as quickly as possible to formulate a plan.

While he was waiting for her to drive over, he went to his small study and logged on to the secure video monitoring website to view the feeds from Willows Farm. Slowly the grid of outputs from the cameras loaded, but none showed any activity.

Twenty minutes later, Jayne stood in his kitchen, her brow furrowed, her hair rather askew, while he brewed some strong coffee.

"So sorry I screwed up last night," he said. "And—"

"Brendan, yes, you did. But forget it. Let's move on," she said, her voice level and businesslike. "We need to work out where we go from here, and we need to do it quickly. Otherwise Joe's going to be history."

She was correct on several levels. And O'Neill felt as though it wasn't just Joe who was at risk of becoming history. For most of his career, Brendan had negotiated his way around the bear traps and snake pits of life in the large, highly political organization that was MI5 by keeping his head down and doing a decent job. But he had been assisted on many occasions by a sharp antenna for looming trouble, a gut feeling that had enabled him to take preemptive action.

He had been working flat out, twelve hours a day, on projects related to security around the G8 meeting, now only three days away. Once it had become clear that the event was definitely going ahead, despite the killing of the chief constable, pressure had mounted on MI5 and the police to ensure the event was not going to be disrupted by terrorists.

The nightmare scenario, of course, was an attack on one of the world leaders in attendance.

And the man who loomed largest and darkest in O'Neill's consciousness was Duggan, for a whole variety of reasons. If O'Neill had a bad night's sleep, it was invariably due to some dream involving Duggan.

Despite the workload, O'Neill logged on a few times every day to the video monitoring website Johnson had shown him. On each occasion, the grid of black and white screens, showing the outputs from the cameras hidden on Duggan's property, showed no activity.

O'Neill took his coffee and led Jayne to his office, sat in front of his PC, and pulled up a chair for her. He began to flick through the outputs from the various cameras, starting with those in Duggan's house.

This time, at last, there were signs of activity. O'Neill sat bolt upright. The two cameras placed in Duggan's kitchen didn't show any people, but one of the breakfast barstools was pulled back, and a full mug of tea or coffee sat on the work surface, along with a half-eaten banana. Behind the mug lay an Apple laptop computer with its lid open. O'Neill flicked on the sound feed, but there was only silence.

He scrolled down the grid of video screens. The next outputs to appear were from the other rooms in Duggan's house. In the main bedroom, the duvet was folded back, and a couple of shirts and a pair of trousers were strewn across it. But nobody was in sight. In the underground tunnels, again there was no sign of movement and no sound.

Finally O'Neill reached the two outputs from the cameras in the den, which appeared side by side. What he saw and heard made his stomach drop. There in the center of the screen stood a man holding a handgun, while a few feet away, speaking on a cell phone, was someone O'Neill had never met but whose face he knew well from photographs: Dessie Duggan. There was a third man in the picture, and this one O'Neill knew very well: GRANITE.

O'Neill turned up the volume on the sound feed and heard Duggan's voice.

"He won't be ranting for much longer."

"What's the plan?" asked the man O'Neill didn't recognize.

There was a loud crackle on the sound feed, but O'Neill clearly heard Duggan's response. "Nothing immediately. I need to focus on Project Gyrate for now. After that, I'm thinking we'll take him to Davy's pig farm. There'll be no trace of anything once the animals have finished with him."

O'Neill looked momentarily puzzled at Duggan's reference to Project Gyrate, but it took him all of a few seconds to realize that the reference was probably to the G8 meeting. He glanced at Jayne, whose lips were pressed tightly together, her eyes glued to the PC monitor.

Then Duggan's phone rang. O'Neill watched as he answered the call and then paced around the den, speaking into the device. Despite the occasional click and whistle of interference and flashes of black and white across the video feed, he could easily distinguish what was happening and being said.

"Gyrate's a goer?" Duggan asked. "Good, I was worried the council would put the blocks on it." There was a pause as Duggan listened to his caller. Then he spoke again. "Yeah, I've got him down here, tied up. He's going nowhere . . . Okay, I'll speak to you later." He put the phone back into his pocket.

O'Neill watched as both cameras showed what looked like a makeshift door, a rough piece of board on hinges, swing out into the den. Suddenly Johnson appeared from a recess, pulling up the zipper of his trousers.

"Shit!" muttered Jayne, under her breath. "They've got him."

O'Neill felt a thin film of sweat appear on his brow. He wiped it with his shirtsleeve.

Immediately, the unknown man pointed his gun straight at Johnson's chest, and Duggan stood with his hands on his hips, staring at Johnson, while GRANITE did likewise.

Duggan glanced at both of his colleagues, then nodded toward Johnson and said, "Get this bastard tied up again. I need to go. I'll call you later."

With that, the camera at one end of the den showed Duggan as he opened the hatch door, which squealed loudly as the bottom of it scraped across the floor, and disappeared through it.

The man with the gun indicated with a nod of the head to Johnson that he should move. O'Neill watched as Johnson walked to one side of the den and vanished into the blackness of a side area, GRANITE close behind him. Presumably, the dissidents were keeping Johnson in a kind of anteroom or side area inside the den not covered by the cameras Johnson had put in place.

By now O'Neill's initial shock at what he was seeing had given way to a rising anger, which he felt in the shape of tension across his shoulders, increasing blood pressure pressing on his temples, and a blinkered, relentless focus on whatever had triggered the emotion.

"Bloody GRANITE," he said. "Why the hell hasn't he told me about this? Asshole."

"GRANITE?" Jayne asked.

"Dennehy," O'Neill said. "My bloody agent in there. Not the one with the gun, the other guy."

News of Johnson's incarceration was exactly the sort of

thing O'Neill was paying GRANITE for. Yet, despite the warnings given to him, he made no phone call, sent no text, no email.

This was the last thing O'Neill needed. He had enough on his plate without trying to work out a way to exfiltrate Johnson from a certain death trap.

Jayne leaned back in her chair and tugged at her chin. "Do you think he meant what he said? About the pigs, I mean."

"Yes."

There was undoubtedly little time to play with. O'Neill had heard of cases where the IRA had disposed of victims' bodies by feeding them to pigs before, but had never worked on a case where it had been proven.

"We've got a dilemma," O'Neill said, almost thinking aloud.

Jayne looked at him and raised her eyebrows.

"I mean, do we send in the police to pull Johnson out and arrest Duggan?" he said. "There's obviously enough evidence just from this video footage to nail him on kidnap and unlawful imprisonment. But—"

"But you want more, you mean?"

"Yes."

"Terrorism charges, then. Is that what you're after?"

O'Neill nodded. He needed to catch Duggan in the act of plotting and carrying out an act of terrorism. He wasn't going to share with Jayne his dilemma: whether he should take yet another risk now—in the same way he had with the sliver of intelligence he had obtained prior to the death of Chief Constable Eric Simonson—or report what he knew to the authorities immediately.

But Jayne saved him the trouble. "I know what you're thinking," she said. "And my view is, if they had an urgent reason to kill Joe quickly, they'd have done it by now. So as he's still alive, we should go and pull him out. We'll be quicker and nimbler than the cops. They'd be all over it like a swarm of wasps. It'd be a complete mess, and Joe would probably get gunned down in the cross fire. I work a different way."

She studied him from below lowered brows, as if assessing his capabilities, he thought.

"Are you up for that?" she added. "But we haven't got any time to play with."

It wasn't an ideal scenario, O'Neill thought. The concept of trying to mount an exfiltration operation to get Johnson out of a bunker guarded by a bunch of dissidents wasn't his number one option. But it was probably the only one he had right now. Jayne was right about them having no time. And she seemed to be an extremely capable pair of hands.

O'Neill nodded at her. "Yes, I agree. I've got to go into the office this morning, but let's get things moving this after-noon. I need to speak to GRANITE urgently."

Then he glanced at the monitor screen and swore again as GRANITE walked back into the frame. *The stupid bloody tout's going to pay for this.*

* * *

Friday, January 25, 2013
  Belfast

In the space of just two weeks, Arthur Higgins had wielded his magic welder's wand and, as Duggan had expected, had delivered to order.

Arthur was one of a group of craftsmen, engineers, mechanics, financial types, and managers the Real IRA could call on for a wide variety of services when required.

True, the roster of helpers wasn't as long as in the heyday of the Provisional IRA in the '70s and '80s, but it continued to provide whatever skills might be required for a particular project.

Anyone looking at Duggan's white VW Transporter van from the outside would not notice anything different from similar models scuttling around Belfast delivering bread to corner shops or car parts to repair garages.

But inside, it looked quite different. There was now a false ceiling, comprising a solid sheet of steel supported by three cross-struts, that stretched three-quarters of the way from the rear of the van to the front. This false ceiling was approximately three feet lower than the real ceiling, leaving a cavity big enough to accommodate a person. The thin but rigid steel sheeting was more than strong enough to support the heaviest of individuals.

Just behind the dividing panel that separated the driver's cab from the cargo area, two footholds had been welded to the dividing panel. This allowed someone easy access to climb into the ceiling cavity, the rear part of which had been turned into a sniping platform using a combination of foam cushions and wooden supports.

A small door in the dividing panel gave access to the rear cargo area from the driver's cab.

Most critically, a hinged flap, approximately eight inches square, had been installed in the outer skin of the van body, above the rear doors, and was accessible from the ceiling cavity. It could be opened from inside the van and used as a kind of rudimentary gun port for a sniper lying on the false ceiling.

Duggan gave a nod of approval, although he knew he would have to fiddle around with the platform and customize it to his own requirements because Arthur didn't have a clue about that kind of thing.

He slid the Transporter into first gear and drove slowly

out of Arthur's unit on the industrial park, turned right, and followed the road out onto Falls Road.

Behind him in the cargo area of the van was his Yamaha Grizzly four wheel drive quad bike. Arthur had created a lightweight aluminum platform, three feet long and two feet wide, from tubing and sheet metal, which was clipped to the existing black metal rack on the Grizzly, mounted behind the driver's seat. The aluminum platform could also be detached and rested on the ground or other flat surface.

Either way, the device would form a usable platform for a sniper's rifle—not perfect, but good enough to provide a solid base.

The Grizzly was secured by ratchet tension straps secured to four anchor points Arthur had welded to the van's floor.

The silence emanating from the rear of the van told him that the anchor points were doing their job well: the Grizzly was being held firmly in place. Arthur had also, as requested, provided two metal ramps that could be anchored to the rear of the van, allowing the Grizzly to be driven in and out of it.

All in all, Duggan was very happy with the work that had been done, for which he had recompensed Arthur with used bills out of brigade funds.

The other items in the rear of the van were the ghillie suit and two vinyl sheets—one much larger than the other—that Duggan had collected from Francis Conaghy's unit in the industrial park.

Francis had used the high-definition aerial drone photographs and his own expertise to devise a suit that not only fitted perfectly but, in Duggan's opinion, would mesh almost seamlessly with the heather and grasslands on Black Mountain. If necessary, he could cut some additional vegetation and weave it into the green netting to which the artificial grasses were stitched. But he thought it would probably be unnecessary.

Francis had also produced a small ghillie that Duggan could drape over his rifle barrel to disguise it.

Now, though, Duggan had another task to complete: a meeting with Fergus Kane, his mole at the Police Service of Northern Ireland. Duggan certainly didn't want Kane to know about the work done to the Transporter, or even that it existed. So he negotiated his way down Falls Road, past the giant Milltown Cemetery on the right and the Belfast City Cemetery on the left, and cut a left up Whiterock Road to his large storage garage, where he had left his blue VW Passat.

Above the garage was a one-bedroom studio flat Duggan sometimes used as a crash pad when he was in Belfast. It was comfortable and well equipped and a far better option than a hotel. He had bought the flat and garage two years earlier for what had seemed a bargain price following a plunge in the Belfast property market in the years following the global financial crisis of 2008.

Having swapped vehicles, Duggan drove west out of the city up to Black Mountain, where he and Dennehy had previously met Kane almost three weeks earlier. He spent an hour walking along the footpaths near the television tower, gazing down at the city below, weighing up the terrain, calculating angles, and working out possible timings. Using his Vectronix Terrapin range finder, he double-checked the measurements he had made on his last visit. At intervals, he tapped a few notes into his cell phone.

That done, Duggan drove back down the hill to the Lámh Dhearg Gaelic football club parking lot, just off Upper Springfield Road, with Black Mountain and Divis now behind him. There he pulled in next to the main gates and waited, the green expanse of the sports field stretching away in front of him behind the low-slung white clubhouse.

The location was well off the beaten track, and they were unlikely to be seen there.

Ten minutes later, a black Ford Fiesta came up the hill, slowed as it reached the gates, and turned in. Kane parked next to Duggan's car, climbed out, crouched, and quickly slid his small frame into the Volkswagen's passenger seat.

Duggan glanced sideways at Kane and didn't waste time on pleasantries. "So, you got what I asked for last time?" He didn't bother to reiterate the shopping list of details he'd requested relating to the Obama and Cameron community visit.

Kane glanced around him and over his shoulder before pulling a piece of folded paper from his pocket. He unfolded the sheet, smoothed it, and held it out between the two front seats. "This is it," he said, pointing to a series of timings written with neat, small handwriting in blue ink. "I'm not saying this is set in stone—you know what these high-level political visits are like—but I think this is going to be more or less how it's going to run, provided there's no rain on the day."

Kane's eyes flickered between Duggan and the sheet of paper, his right hand twitching in his lap, his left knee moving continuously from side to side.

Duggan leaned over and scrutinized the sheet. "Ten minutes for the football? Is that definite? It's not likely to be squeezed down?"

Kane shrugged. "I think not. They're keen to do it. There'll be television cameras in there, a battery of press photographers."

Duggan peered at a list that Kane had written down of key personnel who were expected to be at the event to chaperone the international leaders. All the major Northern Ireland political leaders were there: Gerry Adams and Martin McGuinness from Sinn Féin, Gerry Robinson, the first minister and leader of the Democratic Unionist Party, Alasdair McDonnell, leader of the Social Democratic and Labour Party. The list went on.

Duggan's finger traced down the list. At the bottom it came to rest next to three names under a neatly underlined heading: Senior Police.

"Campbell," Duggan said softly, his finger moving fractionally back and forward against the first of the three names.

"Yes, you know he's been acting chief constable. He's going to be confirmed in the job tomorrow," Kane said. "So it'll be all sorted before the G8. He's my new boss."

Duggan scratched his chin. "So he'll definitely be at the school too, I assume. Will he be watching the football along with the rest of them, Obama and so on?"

"Yeah, Campbell's a big football fan," Kane said. "He's bound to be there. A big Linfield supporter." He was referring to one of Belfast's best-known teams, a Protestant club, whose home ground was Windsor Park, where the Northern Ireland national team was also based.

A thin smile flickered across Duggan's face.

* * *

Friday, January 25, 2013
  Belfast

By eleven o'clock, O'Neill was sitting at the back of a meeting room on the first floor of the Holywood headquarters building listening to a senior MI5 officer from London droning on about the importance of watching out for other threats apart from dissident Republicans during the G8 summit meeting.

In principle, he agreed with the sentiment. It was true

that groups such as Al-Qaeda presented a very different threat than the dissidents and would come from a different angle if they did try to make a move. It would certainly be a bigger, more sophisticated attack, if it happened, so it was indeed crucial not to become too blinkered and parochial, here in Northern Ireland, as the speaker argued.

But in practice, O'Neill knew with absolute certainty that the threat wasn't going to come from far afield. It would be local.

His mind was far from the material under discussion, but he robotically took a few notes and sipped his cup of tea, which was getting cold.

He knew that, more than ever, he was walking a tightrope. There were suspicions in some quarters, including from Jeff Riordan, who headed the MI5 office in Northern Ireland, about the way he had operated and continued to operate following the chief constable's death. This was despite the united front that, thankfully, his immediate boss, Phil Beattie, was still presenting.

But O'Neill knew that if he were caught compounding his earlier error over the chief constable and were thought to be yet again withholding vital information about dissident activity—this time the kidnap and imprisonment of an American citizen—it would spell the end of his career.

True, in the case of MI5, it might not have the same fatal consequences as if he were caught by the dissidents, but losing his job would feel like a death of sorts.

It now felt like a matter of principle. He needed to nail Duggan—but in a way that would lead to his prosecution for the worst of his crimes, so he got what he deserved. He needed to have him caught in the act, about to attempt murder in a major act of terrorism—something that would see him go to prison for a very, very long time.

It simply wouldn't do to have him in court on a lesser

charge such as kidnap or false imprisonment, for which he might be released on parole after a relatively short time. The risks attached to that would be too great—for personal reasons that O'Neill had always kept very private.

Before his thoughts could wander any further, O'Neill almost spilled his tea into his lap as his phone vibrated in his pocket. It was an incoming text message.

He took the device from his pocket and examined the screen.

Then he sat up and swore under his breath.

"MAYBE TITANIC," read the message, all in capitals.

It meant GRANITE's cover was possibly blown.

CHAPTER THIRTY-ONE

Friday, January 25, 2013
  South Armagh

After spending three hours driving a circular surveillance detection route around various quarters of Ulster—through an industrial park in Ballymena, a housing estate in Derry, the back streets of Omagh, and a succession of country lanes in south Armagh—Jayne was confident there was nobody, neither dissident Republicans nor MI5 officers, tailing them.

Following O'Neill's instructions, she arrived at their destination. It was the same farm lane, he explained, where he had met GRANITE three weeks previously, right in the depths of the south Armagh countryside, near the point where a narrow country road crossed the border with the Republic, hidden away behind a wood.

The meeting had taken on a new urgency following the message O'Neill had received that morning from GRANITE, which he showed to Jayne when she picked him up from the Tesco supermarket near his home.

Jayne edged her Toyota Corolla up the lane, pulled off the track onto a piece of rough ground next to a long-abandoned farm tractor, and turned off the engine. Now all they had to do was wait.

O'Neill seemed just as worried about a surveillance operation by his MI5 colleagues as he was one by the Real IRA.

Jayne held off from asking why for as long as she could, hoping that he would volunteer the information. But eventually she felt she had to ask the question. It was obvious some internal issue was bothering him, and if there were a risk that could compromise what they were trying to do, she needed him to tell her.

"Is there something I should know about—why you're worried about the office tailing you?" she asked.

His hesitation told her all she needed to know. She wasn't going to get the full truth.

"It sounds as though GRANITE's already in trouble," he said. "I just need to do everything possible not to compromise him further. You know the rules of running an agent."

"You mean, there are people in MI5 who might be happy to see him sacrificed as long as they get their information?" she asked. If so, it would be a familiar story of tension between an agent handler and those further up the internal management chain who wanted to bolster their CVs. She herself had experienced similar situations within the SIS.

"Yes. He's in position to tell us if there's an operation planned on any of these G8 leaders," O'Neill said. "And that might be from Obama and Cameron downward."

After a few minutes Jayne saw a navy blue Astra crawling up the lane toward them.

"That's him," O'Neill said.

GRANITE reversed in next to Jayne's car. She studied him as he got out. Dennehy had a mustache and floppy mop of dark hair with gray streaks and he was wearing the kind of black leather jacket that seemed ubiquitous all over Northern Ireland.

He climbed into the rear seat of the Toyota and shut the door. "You're lucky to get me," he said. "All manner of shit is flying around."

The conversation proved to be less awkward than she had feared. GRANITE kept things factual, unemotional, and told it how he saw it. He spoke rapidly, as if he wanted to get the meeting over with as quickly as possible—which was without doubt the case.

First he dealt with the situation in the bunker. He outlined exactly where Johnson was being held, what the conditions were like, and responded to O'Neill's questions about the options for an exfiltration operation.

GRANITE took a piece of paper and a notebook from O'Neill and sketched out a rough map of the layout of Duggan's den and the maze of tunnels that linked to the diesel tanks and the house.

Jayne didn't tell GRANITE she already had a map of the underground complex that Ronnie had given to Johnson. But she noted with some relief that GRANITE's diagram matched Ronnie's. This man wasn't obviously trying to set them up, though she would definitely take further precautions.

"Your best bet is in and out through the emergency exit in the field," GRANITE said, "so you're going to get covered in cow shit. The problem is that Duggan is in and out of that den all the time, quite unpredictably. Could be anytime. If he catches you, you're going to be fed to the pigs alongside Johnson, you know that? If he's in a good mood he might shoot you first."

GRANITE sank into his seat, tilted his head back, and closed his eyes. Jayne guessed he was mulling over the consequences if Duggan discovered what he had done. In that instance the pigs would be the end game, not the opening act, of his punishment.

"And what about the message you sent me?" O'Neill asked. "How serious is it?"

"Feckin' serious. I'm on a short list of two for the pig trough, and the only reason there's two on it is because I got smart," GRANITE said. He went on to explain how the information he had previously passed on to O'Neill about the Irvinestown pipe bomb—which had saved the policeman's life—had come from McCormick, who was now a prime suspect in Duggan's eyes.

"It's a matter of time—this is the end," GRANITE said softly, his eyes still closed. "You realize that, don't you? I'm gonna need an exit out of here, a safe house, a change of identity, a new house for me, Tess, and the kids. There's no way I'm gonna be able to ride this one out with Duggan. If you take Johnson out of there, he'll know it's me who's given them away."

GRANITE opened one eye and looked at O'Neill. "If you can't give me that, you're serving me with a death sentence."

In that moment Jayne felt sympathy well up inside her for Dennehy, who appeared to be an honest man and was probably doing what he was doing to feed his family.

"That's assuming we don't trap Duggan," O'Neill said. "If we do, which is my immediate intention, your problem has gone away."

Jayne felt tempted to contradict the blatant lie from O'Neill about trapping Duggan immediately but kept her mouth shut for fear of making him look like a fool. It didn't take long before she felt bad about it.

"What if you don't trap Duggan?" GRANITE asked.

"I don't know," O'Neill said.

Jayne assumed from her own knowledge that it would be difficult for O'Neill to request a safe house somewhere in the south of England, a new identity, police protection, a resettlement package, and a payoff for not just GRANITE but his entire family without extremely good reason. He would have to give extensive details about his dealings with his agent and the information and value received from him. The cost of such resettlements was huge, not least for housing, and the budget was restricted. The police and MI5 had done it before, a few hundred times since the Troubles began, but it was always an uphill battle through bureaucracy to make it happen.

She felt torn. She desperately needed GRANITE to stay in place until Johnson was rescued. Doubtless O'Neill was more worried about the G8 than about Johnson, given that Dennehy might be able to provide the vital snippet of information that could save the life of the president or the prime minister.

Jayne knew exactly where GRANITE was coming from. Why would any man take the risk of informing on violent dissident terrorists—for which certain death was the punishment—unless the intelligence service committed to whisking him out if his cover were blown? No matter that the monthly salary he collected was keeping his family afloat. Not that GRANITE was probably being paid much anyway, in relative terms, given the risks he was taking.

She tried to imagine how GRANITE was feeling right now. Was O'Neill issuing him a death sentence by ignoring his pleas? But then she told herself to harden up. They all had a job to do.

"I'll tell you what I'll do," O'Neill said, momentarily closing his eyes. He clearly hated these conversations. "I'll go and discuss it with Phil, my boss. You met him. I'll see what is feasible."

Jayne leaned forward. "The important thing now is to get the details of this rescue operation nailed down," she said.

She and O'Neill ran through the options and timings and signals that GRANITE might be able to give them when the time came to go in. Eventually, after an additional half hour of discussion, they agreed on a plan.

GRANITE hesitated. "If you need any more guidance, go and see a guy up the road in Forkhill who knows this place. Ronnie Quinn."

Jayne fought to stop her eyebrows from rising. This really was a tight-knit, interlinked community in south Armagh. Everyone seemed to know everyone else.

"Ronnie Quinn? Who's he?" O'Neill asked.

"He used to be one of Duggan's favorites," GRANITE said. "He did all the building work on the underground complex. But they've grown apart. He'll help you—might even go in there with you if needed." GRANITE gave him Ronnie's address.

"I have to go," GRANITE said. "Been here too long already. I'll be in touch when and if I can." He climbed out of the Toyota and got back into his car.

As Jayne watched GRANITE drive away down the lane, she glanced at O'Neill.

"It's been a while since I've had to get my hands dirty on this kind of job," he said.

"Me too."

"I keep thinking, wouldn't it be easier just to let the police take care of it?" he said. "I could be at home, watching TV, or enjoying a quiet beer, while they steamed in."

Jayne said nothing.

"Anyway," he went on. "Interesting that he mentioned this guy Ronnie Quinn. I spent quite a lot of time in the early and mid-'90s trying to recruit him as an agent. Never managed it."

Jayne turned to look at him. "Bloody hell, so you just lied to him. Several times," she said. "I visited him with Joe only a couple of weeks ago. He gave us a map of the underground complex at the farm."

"You're joking?" There was a note of disbelief in his voice.

"No, I'm not," Jayne said. "Ronnie was an angry man. He was close to Duggan's ex-wife, his stepdaughter's mother. And Duggan had his stepdaughter killed, from what I can gather. So why did you lie about Ronnie to GRANITE?"

O'Neill shrugged. After a few seconds, he said, "I think you're right about the stepdaughter. Maybe that's why Ronnie's changed his allegiances since I saw him last. We'd better go and see him."

* * *

Friday, January 25, 2013
Forkhill

The noise of the hatch door scraping against the floor woke Johnson from a restless sleep. He lifted his head and looked up to see Dennehy appearing through the entrance from the tunnel, closely followed by McGarahan, carrying his Browning as usual.

The two Irishmen stood at the foot of the mattress; then Dennehy crawled across it and untied Johnson's wrists and legs while McGarahan remained still, his gun pointed directly at Johnson's chest.

"You can get up for a few minutes, walk around, take a piss," McGarahan said. He looked steadily at Johnson, who waited for Dennehy to get out of the way, then shuffled on his backside to the edge of the mattress.

After yet another four-hour stint of lying motionless on the mattress, Johnson's knees, ankles, and hips were feeling stiff and immobile. It took a few seconds to get them working properly again.

He walked slowly around the den. This was a new development. They hadn't invited him to walk around before, so why now? It wasn't clear.

Johnson shuffled across to the recess on the other side of the main room, a mirror image of the one his mattress was in. As he had noticed on his previous, brief covert visit, this one had a dartboard mounted on the gray cinder block wall. Six darts were stuck into the board; three of them had flights in the orange, white, and green colors of the Irish Republic flag, the other three the American Stars and Stripes.

Stuck on the wall next to the dartboard, Johnson also noticed the sheet of paper he had seen before. Someone had used a black marker pen to write a series of letters across the sheet. Some of them were crossed out in red ink. The paper was riddled with small holes where darts had clearly been thrown into it. It had obviously been pinned to the dartboard at some point and used as a target.

Johnson stared at the sheet. ESGJWDMDBOCC. The letters that were crossed out, all peppered with dart holes, were deleted in pairs, and the only letters left untouched were BOCC.

"What are you doing?" Dennehy asked, his voice rising a little. "Walk, don't stand. I'm not going to have a game of darts with you. This is your pissing and exercise time. You've got three minutes."

Johnson turned and walked into the toilet stall and shut the door behind him, then undid his belt and pulled his pants and shorts down. The squatter toilet stank, although the surrounds were clean. Maybe the drainage system, presumably to the same septic tank used by the house, wasn't working properly.

A few minutes later Johnson was tied up again on the

mattress. His legs and backside hurt and he realized he could get bedsores.

Dennehy peeled two bananas and fed them to Johnson, without speaking. Then Dennehy put a plastic beaker of water to Johnson's lips and instructed him to drink. This was humiliating. Why not let him eat the banana and drink the water while he was untied? Johnson mentally cursed his captors.

Once the two Irishmen had gone, closing the hatch door behind them, Johnson's thoughts went back to the sheet of paper on the wall next to the dartboard.

What did the letters signify? Were they something to do with darts? A competition? A knockout, in which the loser was crossed off? Sets of players' initials?

If nothing else, it had given him something to think about that took his mind off his situation and the possible fate Duggan had lined up for him. He lay there, staring up at the gray concrete ceiling.

A large spider, the same one he had seen earlier, scuttled out of a crevice located part of the way up the wall and slowly made its way to the ceiling, where it came to a halt, as if resting after the exertion of its ascent.

Johnson again tried to mentally compute the chances of success if he attempted to overpower Dennehy the next time he was untying his wrist and ankle restraints. But although he liked his chances, Dennehy's colleague McGarahan appeared to be fully concentrating on his task as an armed backup. That wouldn't work.

Johnson still wasn't able to work out what was going on in Duggan's mind. Why was he doing what he was doing? Why had he killed the men he had?

The more he thought about it, the more he was sure he had been coming at the problem from the wrong angle. He and Jayne had spoken to the victims' wives, but he was growing increasingly certain that the key lay with them. If he ever got out, they would be his first port of call for another visit.

But that seemed a big "if." It was a damn pity he hadn't been able to get hold of Will Doyle's journals. He still felt Beth hadn't told him all she knew, and the same went for some of the other victims' wives.

CHAPTER THIRTY-TWO

Saturday, January 26, 2013
  Belfast

The text message from GRANITE was short and to the point. *Saturday night Duggan dining in Cross 8pm. Your best chance.*

Jayne looked at the phone that O'Neill pushed across the table at her.

They had been sitting in the early morning blackness of his kitchen in the Holywood area of Belfast, sipping cups of strong coffee, the room illuminated only by a single lamp, when the missive had arrived.

At least GRANITE was doing what he had promised, Jayne thought. She had taken up O'Neill's offer of a bed in his spare room, viewing it as more practical if they were going to properly plan a rescue operation.

Jayne immediately recognized the opportunity. "How long would it take him to get back to the house from Cross, if he were tipped off or if there were an alarm or something?" she asked.

"A quarter of an hour, maybe a bit more. It's around ten or eleven miles."

"Is that going to give us enough time to get him out?" Jayne asked.

O'Neill shrugged. "It'll have to," he said.

Although Jayne preferred to keep any exfiltration operation small and not involve officialdom, she was nevertheless curious about the lack of coordination between O'Neill and his superiors at MI5.

She knew that normally, any MI5 officer contemplating the type of operation they were considering would liaise with everyone from the head of MI5 in Northern Ireland downward. They would have a full team in support from A4, the section within MI5's A branch responsible for surveillance, as well as A1, the technical operations team that got involved in covert entry, and the police.

"Have you still not discussed any of this with your boss?" she asked.

"No, I can't," O'Neill said. "It's just going to open too much of a can of worms. I might regret it, but I don't have a choice right now."

Jayne shrugged. It suited her.

The two of them had a quick discussion about the choreography of the operation. Then O'Neill swapped a couple more text messages with GRANITE to make arrangements for exchanging green or red go-ahead or danger signals, information, and timings.

Jayne and O'Neill studied the two maps of the underground complex drawn by Ronnie and GRANITE. Obviously, entering through the barn, as Johnson had done earlier, would be too risky; they needed to use the emergency exit under the cattle trough in the field.

They tried to calculate distances, their likely crawling speed in confined underground tunnels, and the inevitable delays generated by three people being involved in the return journey.

Jayne could see they would need some help to create, if needed, a distraction somewhere on the farm complex, diverting the attention of Duggan's gang away from the emergency tunnel entrance in the field and the underground complex. That would hopefully give them enough cover to get in and extract Johnson.

Either she could go into the tunnels, with O'Neill creating the diversion if required, or vice versa. The only other alternative was for them both to go in and enlist Ronnie's help to create the diversion. But how much could they rely on Ronnie? He was old, and it was uncertain how he would perform in a high-pressure situation.

"This might sound paranoid, but do you think there's any chance we're being set up?" Jayne asked.

"I don't think so. But what other option do we have, anyway? There's no time to resolve it. We'll just have to take precautions. Actually, I'm pretty certain GRANITE's not setting us up."

He was right about one thing—the clock was ticking.

Jayne started to run through the equipment they would need, like vehicles and communications and surveillance gear.

She suggested making another check on the feeds from the hidden cameras planted at Willows Farm.

This time, instead of the eleven cameras that had shown up on the grid the previous day, there were now only eight. The one in the kitchen ceiling in the house appeared to be out of action, as was the one in the master bedroom and another in the tunnel.

Jayne swore. On the positive side, if the cameras had been discovered, then the ensuing thorough search would have found the others. That had not happened. So she assumed the batteries were dying. How long would it be before they all faded? After all, it was now two weeks since Johnson had planted the devices.

"We'll have to hope the two cameras in the den stay live," Jayne said.

O'Neill nodded. "Yes, they're critical."

He clicked onto those two cameras, which were thankfully still operational, but there was nobody in the shot and nothing coming over the sound feed. Jayne rubbed the back of her head. She hoped the quiet simply meant Johnson was tied up in an area of the room they couldn't see.

After they each showered and ate a quick breakfast of cereal and toast, she began to sketch out a possible plan of action.

"We're going to need some gear," Jayne said. "I don't know if you can put your hands on the kind of stuff I think we'll need."

"Tell me what you're thinking of."

Jayne ran through a short list of items and explained what she had in mind. To her surprise, O'Neill said he had all of them.

Once they had each packed a small bag with warm clothing and raincoats, he drove her to a lockup garage half a mile from his safe house in Newtownards that he rented for cash. The garage, which looked nondescript from the outside, had an external door that was slightly rusty in places and had an impressive array of dents, as if someone had been throwing a golf ball against it. But once O'Neill lifted the external door, Jayne could see there was a high-security, pull-down metal shutter door inside it, secured by three padlocks. No burglar would easily gain entry.

O'Neill unlocked the door and they went inside. He turned on a light and locked the door behind them. From a rack, O'Neill pulled down two black plastic bins and removed the lid from one of them. Inside were three packs of orange-colored material tied up in clear plastic bags.

Jayne took a step back. "Semtex!" she said. "Where did you get that?"

"Don't ask," O'Neill said. "Remnants from some long-ago raid on an IRA arms cache south of Enniskillen. I just kept it. Thought it might be useful one day. Just don't tell anyone."

The other bin held electrical wire and the other components Jayne had requested. O'Neill transferred the contents of both bins into two large black backpacks, then stowed the bags in the trunk of his car, along with the tools Jayne had specified.

Finally, O'Neill drove south onto the N1 and headed toward Forkhill.

Just over an hour later he nosed his car cautiously down the gray gravel lane that led to Ronnie's house and parked carefully behind some thick conifer trees, which shielded the Mondeo from the sight of anyone driving along the road.

Ronnie looked surprised to see Jayne but greeted her warmly, then turned to O'Neill and stood looking at him, visibly trying to work out exactly where the MI5 man fitted into the jigsaw puzzle of his memories.

"I remember you. Mother of God, you're back for another try, are you?" Ronnie said, taking a step backward. He peered at O'Neill from the gloom of his darkened hallway. "You don't give up, do you?"

O'Neill shrugged. "I don't forget either. I've got a problem and I was hoping you might be able to help me out."

"A problem? Duggan, I assume," Ronnie asked. "Same as her." He nodded toward Jayne.

"You're on the right track," O'Neill said.

"You'd better both come in, then," Ronnie said, turning to Jayne. "Where's Joe?"

Ronnie made three mugs of tea and then sat in silence while Jayne and O'Neill outlined what they suspected Duggan was doing and how he was holding Johnson at Willows Farm.

"The bastard killed Moira," the old Irishman said, surveying Jayne and O'Neill in turn from beneath a set of black, bushy eyebrows. "So you can be sure I'm going to help you as much as I can."

"At last," O'Neill said, in a dry tone. "Better late than never."

Ronnie ran a hand through his silver-gray hair. "It would seem so. But just explain to me exactly why you're doing this."

"Simple. Joe's a very old friend of mine," Jayne said. "We stand by each other."

"Yes, and Johnson's been prepared to stick his neck out to investigate Duggan," O'Neill said. "Okay, he's a professional and he's being paid, but nonetheless, he's taking big risks. And he was working for an old friend of mine, Michael Donovan, who was shot dead—almost certainly by Duggan. I feel I owe it to Michael to complete the thing."

Ronnie chewed at the inside of his right cheek. "Okay. So this Michael Donovan. Why would Duggan have wanted to take him out?"

O'Neill shrugged, then took another sip of tea, looking evenly at Ronnie from across the top of the mug.

Ronnie sat back in his chair. "I see. Whatever." He sighed and then finally said, "Okay, I'll help you. What do you want me to do?"

Jayne began to explain her plan to rescue Johnson and the part Ronnie would need to play in assisting them.

* * *

Saturday, January 26, 2013

Forkhill

The short midwinter day had long ended by the time Jayne, O'Neill, and Ronnie drove up the long country lane through northern County Louth toward the point where the Irish Republic ended and Ulster began.

Jayne again opted for a circuitous route to approach Willows Farm from the south, partly to avoid being spotted or recorded on camera and partly to ensure that there was no surveillance, including any from MI5.

O'Neill confided that he could never feel confident that he wasn't being watched by his employer and therefore took all possible precautions on the assumption that he was. Before leaving Forkhill, he removed the SIM card and battery from his cell phone and switched to a new pay-as-you-go card, which he slotted into a brand-new, basic Nokia phone.

Jayne watched him switch his phones around with approval. At least she was dealing with a professional.

Rain splattered across the windshield in irregular, occasionally violent squalls. The wind was audibly gathering momentum, whistling its way into every tiny crevice of O'Neill's Ford.

Once they drew within a mile or so of Willows Farm, Jayne directed O'Neill to turn off his lights and cut to the right through the same gate she had used on her previous visit with Johnson, and to park in the same location behind the stack of silage rolls.

"Can we contact GRANITE and check what's going on?" Jayne asked

O'Neill used his burner phone to send a short message to GRANITE. *Car's in the garage now, going for a walk.*

Back came a reply. *Fine. Dog's eating his dinner. Weather outlook's still good. Will let you know if rain clouds approaching.*

There was no questioning that the weather metaphor was anything but literal. Jayne and O'Neill zipped up their black waterproof walking jackets and put on the two black backpacks containing the Semtex and other equipment O'Neill had taken earlier from the storage garage in Belfast.

Ronnie was dressed in similar gear but had no backpack. He had the look of a man who lived on exercise, nuts, and berries. Jayne had growing confidence that he could do what was required of him. In any case, his local knowledge was about to be put to the test.

"We'll take the same route I used last time," Jayne said. "It worked well and gave us a good vantage point over the farm. Always best to take the high ground, every time."

She knew from years of experience how to approach such situations, albeit from in her more distant past, when she had worked on special undercover surveillance operations in territories across Europe, including Northern Ireland. It was definitely preferable to the desk-bound drudgery of her recent SIS role.

Jayne pulled the waist strap on her backpack tight. That was enough talking. Now was the time for action; any conversation would be kept to the bare, absolute essentials.

She turned and led the way up the side of a hedge toward the wooded ridge at the top of the slope, where she turned left and followed the tree line, ensuring that they were several yards below the actual ridge in order to avoid their silhouettes being visible against the sky from below. O'Neill and Ronnie followed closely behind. None of them spoke until they had covered the mile or so that took them within sight of Willows Farm, several hundred yards below them. The light from two ground-floor windows at the rear of the farmhouse was visible, together with an outside light that appeared to be somewhere in the farmyard.

Another sharp squall of rain hammered against them, driven by a westerly wind, as they came to a halt.

"We'll move together down the hill and against the hedge, then we'll separate at the bottom," Jayne said. Ronnie and O'Neill nodded, their heads bowed, jacket hoods pulled tight in an attempt to keep the rain out of their faces.

They walked slowly down the side of what she knew from her previous visit was a cow field. As the trio walked, the cattle became visible at the bottom of the slope, huddled together next to a fence that kept them out of the farmyard.

"That's your entry point, underneath that water trough," Ronnie murmured, pointing at a black outline that rose in front of the herd of cows. "That's where you get covered in shit."

Jayne didn't need telling. She remembered how badly Johnson stank on his return from the previous mission.

However, she was looking for something else. She scanned the farmyard and the space at both sides of the farmhouse. Eventually she saw what she was looking for, barely poking out from the left side of the house.

She patted the backpack that was slung over her shoulder; it contained the Semtex, cable, blasting caps, and an infrared-controlled electronic detonator that she and O'Neill had packed in his garage that morning.

It felt like she was winding the clock back twenty-five or thirty years to the type of disruptive or diversionary operation she used to get involved with in Afghanistan during the '80s. She had planned it in great detail with O'Neill, so there was no need for much talk now.

They were close to the fence separating the field from the farmyard.

"Can you check with GRANITE if it's all clear and ask him if the security camera feeds are monitored?" she asked O'Neill.

He took out his phone and sent another text message to GRANITE. *Just finished my walk. Are the kids asleep? And is anyone watching TV?*

Jayne waited impatiently for a reply to come in. She certainly didn't want to venture around to the front of the house if there were a danger that someone might emerge from the building at the wrong time. Five minutes passed by. There was still no response.

It began to rain again, sheeting sideways at forty-five degrees. This was a pain in the backside in one respect but could be helpful in another. *Come on, GRANITE.*

After another ten minutes, O'Neill held up his phone screen toward her, sheltering it from the rain with his backpack. *Kids asleep now. Were awake before. Nobody watching TV.*

"Give me a few minutes," Jayne murmured. "I'll be back."

She moved to the end of the clump of gorse bushes, climbed over a wire mesh fence, and made her way down the far southern side of the farmyard, past the rear wall of the barn where she knew Johnson had previously entered, thus avoiding the camera mounted on the front. She moved into the shadows of some thick evergreen bushes that ran down the left side of the farmhouse.

She stopped and looked for what she guessed would inevitably be in place. There it was, mounted on the house wall, its lens directed toward the front of the building. Even better, she could see that there was an inch or two of exposed cable coming from the camera before it disappeared into the wall. She reached into her backpack and removed a pair of wire cutters they'd packed back at the garage.

The camera was either static or permanently trained in one direction, which again worked in her favor. She dropped to a crouch and, ignoring the hammering rain sluicing into her face, moved quickly to the house wall. There was a wire trellis below the camera, which looked just about strong enough to bear her weight. It was the only option.

She put one foot on the bottom wire, grabbed another wire above her head, and tested it. It didn't give way, so she climbed up to the next wire. Again it held fast.

Three more wires up, and Jayne, her hair now saturated, was able to reach the short length of cable that ran from the back of the security camera into the wall. She worked one of the cutter's blades behind the cable, then squeezed the handles hard. Eventually it sliced through the wire.

Jayne descended back down the wire trellis and dropped lightly onto the flagstone path that ran around the outside of the house.

It was unlikely that anyone would come out of the house in this weather to check the camera, even if they noticed it wasn't functioning, which—based on GRANITE's message— seemed equally unlikely.

From the base of the trellis, she made her way along the side of the house, dropping to all fours and crawling beneath two windows. Finally she emerged at the front, now only twenty yards away from the road. Here was a stretch of gravel driveway that formed a parking and turnaround area for cars. And there, standing only a short distance from the front door, was a gray Audi station wagon. It was parked sideways, which Jayne realized would allow her to work on the vehicle while remaining unseen on the opposite side from the house.

Now the rain was accompanied by occasional claps of thunder. The noise also neatly covered up the sound of her footsteps on the crunchy gravel.

She moved swiftly to the side of the car farthest away from the house, dropped to her knees, and removed equipment from her backpack. Working with her hands under the shelter of the car, she first placed a plastic bag—which held a small slab of Semtex to which were taped two slim tubular blasting caps—under the rear passenger side wheel.

Next she began unreeling a length of yellow and blue cable attached to each of the blasting caps as she stepped over to some bushes between the driveway and the fence that separated the property from the road.

There she connected the cable to a small black electronic detonator with a radio antenna, which she hid in the bushes, and scraped some gravel over the cable so it was invisible to all but the closest of examinations.

That done, she made her way back alongside the house and over the fence and rejoined O'Neill and Ronnie in the corner of the field. As she did so, the rain suddenly stopped.

O'Neill gave her a grin and a look of approval. The idea of using old IRA weaponry against the Republicans had clearly left him with a distinct feeling of satisfaction.

Jayne's thoughts were less political and partisan and more practical in nature. They might need a diversion, and she had set one up. There was a long way to go before this operation was finished.

Jayne said nothing but gave a quick thumbs-up signal. She reached into her backpack, removed a small device that looked like a walkie-talkie, with a keypad and an antenna sticking out from the top, and handed it to Ronnie.

She just hoped that he had memorized the code, as instructed. The intention was for the device now positioned under the Audi to be deployed in a very specific way. If required, it would create an emergency diversion during the extraction mission, but otherwise it was meant to be used only when they got Johnson out, to provide cover while they made their getaway.

It would also have the advantage of decommissioning the dissidents' most obvious means of road pursuit, although

Jayne assumed there were other usable vehicles in the surrounding outbuildings.

There had been no further communication from GRANITE inside the farmhouse, so Jayne assumed the den remained unguarded. She needed to make sure, though, so she took her cell phone from her pocket and logged onto the monitoring website where she could view the outputs from the minicameras inside the underground complex.

Gradually the video feeds loaded, although at a much slower rate than on O'Neill's PC. After a few minutes, only four were showing. One was in the kitchen, where GRANITE was visible, his back to the camera, apparently reading a book. There was one from the living room, which showed nobody, and two from the tunnel, again with no sign of activity. There were no outputs from the den. Jayne cursed and tapped on the refresh button. But still only four cameras appeared to be working.

"Shit," Jayne murmured.

"What?" O'Neill asked.

"Video links to the den are down."

Jayne used her hand to brush away the rivulets of rain-water dripping onto her cheeks from her wet hair.

She reached inside her backpack and removed a small headlamp that she pulled over her forehead. Realistically, she knew she had no choice. "Okay, screw it. Let's go in."

CHAPTER THIRTY-THREE

Saturday, January 26, 2013
Forkhill

Thoughts of the punishment beatings and tortures handed out to IRA informers over the decades were foremost in Johnson's mind as he lay in the semi-darkness and the damp on the mattress in Duggan's underground den.

Cigarette burns, electric shocks to the genitals, repeated submersion in a freezing cold bath, hanging upside down from beams, iron crowbars used to break ribs, and the notorious six-pack—bullets to ankles, knees, and elbows.

Not easily depressed, Johnson had slipped into a kind of downward spiral triggered by his own thoughts. He tried to remind himself they were only thoughts. None of it had actually happened. So why dwell on it, fearing something unknown. Surely Duggan would have acted by now if he actually intended to torture him.

The problem was, Johnson had no way of discerning Duggan's thoughts or plans.

He had also lost his sense of time. Dennehy and McGarahan had confiscated his watch and phone, so other than mealtimes, there was no way of marking what hour of the day it was.

Johnson assumed it was evening. The two Irishmen had come and gone with the usual plate of baked beans on toast, accompanied by a cup of water. There had been no sign of Duggan all day, which made Johnson think he must have gone off somewhere, because previously he had been in and out the whole time.

The extended toilet break offered the previous day, which had allowed Johnson the chance to examine the dartboard, had proved a one-off. Since then he had been marched straight across to the stall, pushed in, then escorted back to the mattress immediately.

Was O'Neill able to see any of it via the hidden cameras? Again, there was no way of knowing.

Johnson sighed. He couldn't just carry on passively accepting this; he needed to think of a way to engineer more time in the main area so O'Neill would be able to see him if he viewed the feed.

But he struggled to devise a workable plan.

As he lay there, he wondered what Jayne was doing. He hoped she escaped from the roadblock and presumed she hadn't been trapped by Duggan. Otherwise she would likely have been brought into the bunker too. One thing was for sure: if she was free, he could rely on her doing everything possible to get him out.

Johnson's mind drifted back to another time with Jayne, in entirely different circumstances, in Islamabad, the capital of Pakistan, in 1988. At the time, they were both working for intelligence services, she for the British Secret Intelligence Service, MI6, and he for the CIA.

Their affair had been a brief one: covert meetings in each

other's apartments, snatched moments in cars and cafés, and occasional restaurant meals, dressed up as contact-building exercises. It had not gone down well with Johnson's boss, Robert Watson, who was the station chief in Islamabad, part of the CIA's Near East Division. Someone had tipped him off, and he had flown into a rant about the irresponsibility of it, asking Johnson what he thought might have been the implications had it been a Russian honeytrap.

The affair had started around the same time as an incident in March 1988, when Johnson and his CIA colleague and close friend Vic Walter were on a covert mission out of their Islamabad station into Afghanistan.

They managed to avoid the occupying Russian forces and get themselves black, free from surveillance, for a planned meeting in the Afghan city of Jalalabad with a top-level source Johnson had recruited, an Afghan mujahideen commander.

The meeting ended unexpectedly after a warning about an imminent raid by the KGB. Johnson and Vic managed to escape, but ran into a KGB sniper. Johnson pushed Vic into a doorway, saving him, but a round hit the top of his right ear, leaving him with a nick, a scar for life.

Johnson subsequently shot the KGB sniper during a dramatic gunfight, causing a huge diplomatic upset. Pakistan's Inter-Services Intelligence agency demanded to know why the CIA was recruiting its own agents in Afghanistan and running covert operations in the country, rather than sticking to protocol and working through them, as had been agreed.

Johnson never got to the bottom of how the meeting with the Afghan commander had been compromised, but he suspected a leak from the US embassy in Islamabad. Maybe even from Watson.

Anyway, the Jalalabad incident was a black mark in Johnson's file. It devalued his reputation at CIA headquarters at

Langley and, when combined with his affair with Jayne, resulted in Watson having him fired in September that year.

Johnson shook his head free of the thoughts that gripped him. Why was he now dwelling on yet another negative point in his otherwise successful career? It was a bad habit he seemed unable to lose. And the deeper the trough he was in, the worse this tendency became. It fed on itself.

He lifted his head and gazed across the main area of the den to the recess on the other side, where the dartboard was.

Then, suddenly, out of the stillness and darkness of the bunker, he detected a noise from an unseen source, around the corner at the far end of the room, out of Johnson's line of sight. It was a faint scraping sound, like a fingernail on a sheet of sandpaper, but in the stillness and silence of the bunker, its sound was magnified and made Johnson jump.

Was it a rat?

The noise came again, louder and more prolonged this time. After several seconds, a now wired Johnson recognized exactly what it was: the hatch door at the other end of the den was opening. The one that led to the diesel tanks and the emergency escape.

Somebody was coming in. And it wasn't Dennehy or McGarahan.

* * *

Saturday, January 26, 2013
  Crossmaglen

Duggan glanced at his watch then sipped his pint of Guinness. He drummed his fingers on the bar at the Cross Square Hotel and swore quietly to himself.

He was there to meet his quartermaster, McCormick, for

a quick drink and some dinner and to discuss storage arrangements for the newly arrived Barrett M82.

But McCormick was already half an hour late and every time Duggan called him, his call went straight to voice mail. Normally McCormick was the most punctual of people, so this was a little disconcerting.

Duggan tried to focus on the Gaelic football highlights program on the wide-screen television on the wall facing him. But he was struggling to concentrate. There were suddenly too many decisions to make, and Duggan, usually quick to weigh the best course of action in most circumstances, was feeling a little overwhelmed.

The G8 meeting in Belfast was due to get underway in two days, and there was a lot to sort out. The equipment he needed was now in place, including the rifle, but Duggan would prefer to have at least a couple more sessions with it to ensure he was fully comfortable with the setup.

Generally, the Barrett was spot-on, but there was a little side-to-side trigger movement that he wanted to tighten up. That would mean dismantling the trigger mechanism. The trigger pull weight also felt a little heavier than he was used to, so he was planning to shorten the firing spring a little to achieve a crisper release.

It shouldn't be a problem. He would make the adjustments when he got home and then do another set of tests in the morning.

The Transporter van and Grizzly quad bike that Arthur Higgins had adapted were safely stashed in the storage garage off Falls Road up in Belfast, but Duggan wanted to spend a couple of hours ensuring that the shooting platform in the false roof of the van was set up exactly as he wanted.

And then he now had the headache of deciding what to do with Johnson—a headache he could have done without.

Disposing of him would be time-consuming, not least in

ensuring all tracks were covered. It required considerable thought and planning. And time was a commodity he was short of. It was easier just to leave him where he was until the G8 was over and he had time to resolve the problem properly and thoroughly.

Duggan's phone rang. It was McCormick.

"Dessie, sorry, buddy, I'm not going to make it tonight. Had a bit of a run-in with the wife, and it's blowing all hot and cold here. Problem is my daughter needs fetching from over Armagh way, and my missus is refusing to do it."

Duggan drummed his fingers harder on the bar top. "For feck's sake, Danny, get a grip. When your wife starts grabbing you by the balls and pushing you around like one of those radio-controlled cars, you're in trouble. You're a letdown. I've been standing here nursing a pint for the past forty minutes waiting for you."

"Sorry again, boss. I owe you one. Can I come over to your place tomorrow morning instead?"

"Too right you owe me one. Okay, tomorrow at ten."

"Thanks, and I'll see you tomorrow then," McCormick said.

Duggan ended the call and looked around the bar. There were a couple of other people he knew in there but nobody he wanted to sit and have dinner with. Neither did he feel like sitting by himself. He hated doing that.

Years ago, before the Good Friday agreement and the republican movement was generally unified, he would have had any number of the old guard, the Provisionals, coming up to him, keen to share a pint and a chat.

These days many of the old guard in south Armagh still lived somewhat in fear of the Provisional leadership such as Thomas "Slab" Murphy. And accordingly, they kept their distance from dissidents such as Duggan and his guys and maintained their slight air of disapproval. Not that it bothered Duggan. He'd always gone his own way, in any case.

Duggan sighed. He decided to go home and eat one of the microwave meals he had stored in his freezer. He sank the remains of his Guinness in one gulp and strode out of the bar.

Thirty seconds later, Duggan was in his Volkswagen, en route home, an hour and a half earlier than he had planned.

PART FOUR

CHAPTER THIRTY-FOUR

Saturday, January 26, 2013
 Forkhill

Johnson smelled them before he saw them.

The sickly odor of cow shit spread rapidly across the bunker and into the recess where he was lying. There was the faint sound of footsteps squeaking slightly on the concrete floor of the bunker.

He remained absolutely silent, his head up as far as he could lift it given his wrist restraints, watching and listening.

Who the hell is it?

Then a few seconds later, Jayne's head appeared around the side of the wall and immediately jerked back in surprise. She uttered an involuntary, "Oh."

Johnson immediately fell back flat onto the mattress in relief. "Thank you, God. Good work. Can you cut these cords? Let's get the hell out of here."

Jayne stepped forward, followed by O'Neill. Both of them were wearing headlamps that were turned off, and their trousers dripped a liquid, brown slurry, with a stench that made Johnson retch.

She removed a small Swiss army knife from her pocket, opened the knife blade, and crawled onto the mattress.

"Sorry it took me a while," she said. "We saw what was going on from the video feed earlier. The cameras are dead now."

Jayne sliced through Johnson's bindings. "We've not got long," she said. "Duggan has gone to Crossmaglen, meeting someone for dinner or something, but I've no idea when he's back."

"How do you know?" Johnson said.

"Dennehy."

Johnson stood up but realized that his feet and lower limbs felt dead. "Circulation's gone," he said. "My feet are numb." He shook his legs until they began to tingle and gradually the feeling came back.

"Have you two got any backup?" he asked.

"Yes, Ronnie Quinn," Jayne said. "He's outside."

Johnson paused for a fraction of a second in surprise. He could ask the questions later. "Gun?"

"Yep." She patted her hip, where the gun was stuffed into her belt, beneath her jacket.

"Okay, let's move," Johnson said. "I've done this trip before. O'Neill, you lead the way, Jayne can go second, I'll bring up the rear. What time is it?"

O'Neill looked at his watch. "Eight-thirty."

"Just one thing, quickly," Johnson said. He pointed to the sheet of paper pinned on the wall next to the dartboard. "What do you make of that?"

O'Neill looked irritated as he glanced at the piece of paper. "We can't waste time with this. I've no idea what it's about." He peered more closely, then shook his head.

Johnson turned to Jayne. "Can you snap a photo of this

sheet with your phone, Jayne? I've just got a feeling it might mean something."

Jayne removed her phone from her pocket and took a quick picture.

O'Neill was already walking over to the hatch door at the rear of the bunker. "Come on, let's go." He dropped to his knees at the tunnel entrance, clicked on his headlamp, and began to crawl in, followed by Jayne.

Johnson followed, pulling the hatch door shut behind him, just as he had done on his previous visit. There was little doubt in his mind that his two minders would return to the bunker very soon. Even though Dennehy was working with O'Neill, it was extremely unlikely he was going to do anything or behave in a way that would give himself away to his colleague McGarahan. So assistance from that quarter was unlikely.

They quickly reached the first diesel tank storage room and filed past the giant green tank through to the next tunnel.

"It's like a bloody fuel factory down here," Jayne said. There was an electronic humming noise coming from a square box in the corner of the room, which had two-inch pipes entering and leaving it, and the sound of diesel dripping into the tank was clearly audible. The smell of fuel was overpowering.

When they had passed through the second diesel tank room, the going got tougher. The heavy rain of the previous few hours had left the floor of the third and final tunnel section even more waterlogged and boggy than on Johnson's first visit. As the trio crawled through, the filthy mix of water, cattle urine, and dung reached up to their thighs, saturating their trousers, shoes, and socks.

At least when they reached the shaft that led up underneath the cattle trough, O'Neill and Jayne had already removed the heavy metal manhole cover, so all three of them were able to climb out and lie flat in the mud. The rain had started hammering down again, and Johnson jumped at the sudden sound of a clap of thunder, which seemed to come from almost overhead.

Johnson, exiting last, pulled the manhole cover back into place. Thankfully the cattle were gathered in the far corner of the field, not around the water trough.

"Ronnie's over in the corner of the field. We'll check we're clear, then run, low as we can, over to him next to those bushes," Jayne said.

The three of them crawled into the open and knelt there for a few seconds. "Okay, let's go," Johnson murmured. They ran at a crouch across the field, O'Neill in the lead, until they reached the black shadows cast by a group of sprawling evergreen bushes.

Ronnie was waiting. He nodded silently with a thin-lipped smile of recognition at Johnson.

As they arrived they caught the high-pitched whine of a fast-moving car in low gear heading up the lane on the other side of the farmyard, the glare from its headlights strafing the leafless trees like a black and white nightclub strobe. Its brakes screeched, and the car headlights appeared in the gap at the right-hand side of the farmhouse, where the driveway led into the farmyard. They now pointed like searchlights, straight into the field toward them, picking out the rain that continued to pour down.

On the far corner of the left side of the farmhouse, a powerful outside light suddenly came on. Now Johnson could see another car, which looked like a gray Audi, left of the house.

The headlights of the first car went off and a man jumped out, shouted something inaudible, and started running toward the house before disappearing from sight behind it.

O'Neill tapped Ronnie on the shoulder. "Give me that remote control," he said.

Ronnie looked at him. "What for? I don't think we should—"

"Just give it here," O'Neill interrupted.

Ronnie shrugged, reached into his jacket pocket, and handed over what Johnson recognized, from the branding on the front, to be a radio-controlled remote trigger device. *Surely he's not going to?*

"What the hell are you doing?" Johnson asked.

"Jayne wired up that gray Audi over there," O'Neill said. "That's Duggan who's just climbed out of the other car. He must know you've escaped. That's why he's driven in fast like that. We need a distraction."

"Hang on a minute," Johnson said, "that sounds like a bad idea. We don't need to do that, we can—"

Jayne interrupted. "No, don't trigger it now, Brendan. We don't need to."

"Just leave it to me," O'Neill said.

A few seconds later, a running figure emerged at the left side of the house, next to the gray Audi, yanked the door open, and jumped into the driver's seat. The car's engine roared.

"That's Duggan," O'Neill said.

Before Johnson could reach him, O'Neill punched three of the buttons on the front of the trigger device.

A fraction of a second later, an ear-ripping blast tore into the night sky, echoing up the hillside, as a ball of orange engulfed the Audi. A mushroom of fire rose above the spot where the car had been, and a column of rapidly rising smoke followed.

"Got the bastard. Come on. Let's get the hell out of here," O'Neill said. He turned and led the way up the sloping field toward the ridge at the top.

* * *

Saturday, January 26, 2013
  Forkhill

It was after eleven o'clock by the time Johnson, Jayne, O'Neill, and Ronnie arrived back at Ronnie's house. They were soaked from the rainstorm that had continued as they trekked back to O'Neill's car.

They had to take another circuitous route, via several villages south of the border, to get themselves safely back to Ronnie's house in Forkhill.

By that stage Johnson was struggling to contain himself, although he said nothing. *What was Brendan thinking of?*

Ronnie invited them in, despite Johnson's concerns that the older man was compromising himself and potentially risking a dissident republican reprisal beating if others in the south Armagh brigade found out about his role.

"Screw 'em," Ronnie said. "You come in, clean yourselves up. I'll make you a bit of food."

"As long as it's not beans on toast, that'd be great," Johnson said. "But I'm worried we're putting you at risk. We can't stay long."

"Nah," Ronnie said. "They don't suspect me, anyway. I'm not in the game. They wouldn't look twice in my direction. They think I used to be one of Duggan's mates and I'm harmless."

Johnson asked Ronnie to put the regional television news on to see if the blast at the farm had been registered, but there was nothing. Johnson wasn't surprised. The farm was some distance from the nearest neighbors, and the heavy rain and thunder claps would doubtless have muffled the sound of the explosion. There would be few casual passersby along such a remote country lane to witness the damage. And the dissident Irishmen would hardly be reporting the blast to the police, no matter how serious the damage.

Johnson knew that Duggan could never have survived the explosion at the farmhouse.

One thing was certain: Johnson was pleased his finger hadn't been the one on the detonator. That could eventually lead to serious trouble for O'Neill, Johnson guessed, from any one or all of several different sources—primarily MI5 and the police. Not to mention the media.

And right now, Johnson's view was that O'Neill deserved all he would get. He had blown any chance there was of hauling Duggan into court. To set up an explosion as a potential distraction was one thing. But to trigger it when it was going to blow someone to pieces, even a terrorist, was quite another.

That wasn't Johnson's way of operating.

He turned to Brendan. "I can't thank Jayne and you enough for getting me out of that shithole. But I don't get why you blew him up?"

O'Neill looked him straight in the eye. "You don't know these people—I do," he said, his voice level. "If I hadn't done that, we'd probably be swinging upside down in Duggan's barn on a meat hook by now, with jump leads attached to our balls. That's where you'd be, if I hadn't got you out of there."

Johnson shook his head. "What you did isn't the answer," he said.

O'Neill leaned forward. His eyes were a little red around the edges, his skin almost gray. "Why don't you just be thankful you're out of there. It's easy for you, coming in from outside. You can walk out anytime you like. For us, we're stuck here with kids in schools, families, roots that have been put down. We're dealing with a helluva stressful situation, issues that go back decades, and it's bloody complicated."

Johnson felt like starting an argument but refocused on the immediate practicalities. He needed to get himself and Jayne back to Belfast. Then he needed to rent another car and report the previous one stolen—which he had decided was the best course of action—buy another phone, and obtain a new SIM card.

In a wider sense, did the events of that evening spell the end of his investigation, assuming Duggan was now dead? Johnson weighed the question. In some respects, yes, but there was still an active dissident republican brigade in south Armagh that was certain to continue operational activities and almost as certain to continue illegal imports of tobacco and weapons unless action was taken.

So the answer, in the short term, was no. He would like to finish the job. He had already been working without pay since Donovan's death, so he might as well carry on. Money had never been his main incentive in life. But truth, justice, and professional pride were definitely still all at stake.

Johnson munched his way through the makeshift supper of cheese sandwiches and tomatoes that Ronnie had hurriedly put together, then leaned back in Ronnie's threadbare armchair and closed his eyes momentarily.

His captivity at Willows Farm had lasted two days, but it had seemed much longer. He suddenly felt extremely weary, but in the same moment he realized he hadn't been able to check for messages, either text or voice, that might have been left on his phone, which had been confiscated by Duggan.

He asked O'Neill if he could borrow his phone to call his message service and dialed in.

There was only one voice message: it was from Beth Doyle, who said that she had obtained photocopies of her husband's handwritten memoirs from her son, Archie, but that she had second thoughts about handing them over and asked that Johnson give her a call.

Johnson gazed at the ceiling and groaned to himself. Despite the chaos of the previous few days, the journals remained on his mind. Nothing was ever straightforward, especially when he needed it to be.

The thought reminded him about the sheet of paper pinned next to the dartboard.

"Jayne, can you email me the photo of the sheet of paper down in the bunker, please?" Johnson said.

She nodded.

O'Neill stood and surveyed the room. "We'd better get moving back to Belfast. I've got a feeling a shitstorm's going to erupt tomorrow."

CHAPTER THIRTY-FIVE

Sunday, January 27, 2013
Belfast

The morning news bulletin on BBC Radio Ulster was heavily focused on the security clampdown that was well underway in advance of the G8 meeting, due to begin the following day.

Cars were subject to random searches on their way into the city center, causing traffic backups. There were spot checks on hotels, and armed police were posted at key strategic points around Belfast, the newscaster said.

But there was nothing about a dissident Republican being killed in a car explosion on a farm near Forkhill.

Johnson flicked off the radio and glanced around the apartment just off Falls Road that he and Jayne had returned to in the Toyota, which they had picked up from O'Neill's house in the early hours of the morning.

Despite his tiredness, Johnson had woken at eight o'clock after just six hours of sleep, his head immediately buzzing, his adrenaline flowing.

He instructed his cell phone company to disable his old SIM card and walked to a shop just along the road where he bought himself a new one, together with a phone. Then he restored all his data from a backup of his old phone on his laptop and sent messages to his key contacts with the new number.

That done, Johnson rented another car, this time a black Mazda 323, from a different company and took a taxi to go and collect it. The process of reporting the previous one stolen would have to wait—he had no time for the inevitable bureaucratic nightmare.

Now he could get back to business. He made two mugs of coffee and put one of them on the table in front of Jayne.

"We need to go see Beth," Johnson said. "She left a message saying she's having second thoughts about handing the copies over."

"You think these memoirs will help us, do you?" Jayne said. She raised one eyebrow and sipped her coffee.

Johnson shrugged. "Don't know. But there are things going on here that I don't understand. My feeling is there are issues that go way back. People aren't prepared to talk about them openly—Donovan didn't and he died. O'Neill won't either. So maybe this will give us a way in. Don't know. Might be wrong."

"It's worth a try, I agree," Jayne said, to Johnson's relief.

Twenty minutes later, Johnson and Jayne headed back to Portadown for the third time. He hoped that Beth was at home. He didn't call ahead for fear that she might disappear.

The storms of the previous night had blown out, and the skies over Northern Ireland were blue and almost cloudless; only large pools of water on the road gave a clue as to the turbulence.

On the way into Portadown, they drove past a billboard on which some dissident republican graffitist had sprayed a sniper rifle crosshairs symbol, the letters IRA, and a slogan in huge black-painted letters: "We only have to be lucky the once."

Beth answered the door and did something of a double take to see them on the step. In contrast to their previous visits, she looked unkempt. Her gray hair hadn't been brushed, and there was a tea stain on the front of her white blouse.

"I had a real difficulty in persuading my son to send these copies," Beth said. "He said he thought they were sensitive, and having read through them again, I can see why. I was up into the early hours reading them, trying to decide what to do, whether to let you see them or not. I now don't think I'm going to."

"Could we at least discuss it?" Johnson asked. "And indoors. We don't want your neighbors to hear."

She looked down at the ground and held the door handle tightly. "I don't know," she said and looked back up at Johnson, who attempted a smile.

Then, slowly, she opened the door and indicated for them to enter. Once she shut it behind them, Johnson gathered himself and mentally ran through his argument.

"Look, Mrs. Doyle," he said, in as even a tone as he could manage. "This is not about your husband, it's about something much bigger. It's about the whole principle of justice and the process of securing it."

"Don't give me that kind of high-moral bullshit," Beth said, shaking her head.

"It's not bullshit. Things have happened which are very wrong, both legally and morally, and I really need your cooperation in ensuring that we do the right thing. It's that simple. I don't know what's in that journal of your husband's, but I'm certain it will help us understand what has happened. If they give us just a fraction of information as we try to find out what happened to your husband, then we should take them; otherwise we're at risk of impeding justice."

Beth narrowed her eyes, as if in pain, and clicked her tongue against the roof of her mouth several times, clearly undecided.

She led the way through to her kitchen and picked up a yellow folder from a rack, then clutched it across her chest with both arms folded against it. "I would like a commitment from you to keep the contents confidential, away from the media or journalists," Beth said. "The only reason I'm going to let you see these papers is because I want to get to the bottom of what happened to Will. But I don't want to stir things up and put my family in danger."

"You have my word that I'm not going to give anything to journalists," Johnson said. "There have been enough casualties during this inquiry, and no, I don't want to see anymore either."

"Thank you," Beth said. "In that case, let's sit down and you can go through it. I would rather you read it here first, so we can discuss it, rather than you take it away."

She led the way into her living room and handed over the folder.

Johnson took it and looked inside. There were a few photocopied sheets taken from a handwritten journal, which he quickly flicked through. "This is all of them?" he asked.

"No, this isn't all of them. These are just the ones from 1984."

Johnson looked at Beth. "So why just 1984? I didn't ask for any specific year."

"It's the year you're probably going to be most interested in. You'll see when you read them." There was a note of finality in Beth's voice that said she didn't want to answer questions.

Johnson shrugged and sat on the sofa. He took out the

papers and began to read. The sheets were copied at high resolution, which made the precise, neat handwriting easy enough to read.

December 15, 1984

Another day chasing the S.Armagh brigade's finest. Got my new motor, a Cavalier, from the 14th South Det bleeps this morning after they'd finally finished fitting it out with the usual array of toys— mikes, comms gear, covert video camera gear, tiny earpieces, engine cutout switch, brake light off switch, bulletproof panels, glass, etc. You name it—this car's got it. Gadget paradise. So went out after lunch with Gazzer for the regular surveillance sweep around Forkhill, Cross, etc. Different route, different routine, every time. No Special Forces with us today for a change, as they're all on roadblock planning duty. They plan, we deliver. A blitz planned for next few days—they want us to nail Alfie Duggan, somehow. He's been on the run well over a year now from Long Kesh. The problem has been finding him. He's clever, often one step ahead, on the move. But he's had too many hits since getting out—three soldiers dead in the last three months, all long-range, 7.62mm rounds. It has to be Duggan. So patience is running out. The plan has previously been to arrest him. They wanted to catch him red-handed and nail him then so they can double his sentence. But like I've always said—bullshit, why bother? That's not going to happen. How many more soldiers' lives first? So plan B's swinging into action—Conman's masterminding it with Eric's help. It makes more sense to me.

December 17, 1984

The tech boys gave us a briefing today on the new covert cameras now live in Bandit Country. Twenty-two of them, all with pin-sharp pics giving on- to two-mile views. Remarkable pieces of kit. There were twenty-five, but three have been found and "disabled" by the S.Armagh brigade already!! Idea is to use these to ID targets. The hope is Alfie D's going to break cover pre-Christmas to see his wife/son. It's a waiting game. We're certain he's being moved around safe houses—so he has to break cover sometime. The Don and Brenner not happy today at being stuck in (separate) car boots operating surveillance cameras in Drumintee and Cullyhanna, respectively, for five hours in the freezing cold, locked up more or less in the dark, where they can hardly move. Tough life. Crucial job, though. Probably it'll be me tomorrow. Can't fecking wait. Not.

December 18, 1984
Things now hotting up. Roadblock in place for much of the afternoon near our Bessbrook Mill base. It's going down with the locals just about as well as you might imagine. The S.Armagh brigade retaliated with their own roadblock outside Forkhill. We left them to it—no point in starting a shooting match when we've got bigger fish to fry imminently, hopefully. The whole Det's on a leave ban, a couple of people even recalled from holidays, and going into full operations mode now. Method we're using to find Duggan is to concentrate on his son, Dessie, on the basis that he's going to lead us to Alfie before too long. We put a tracking device on Dessie's Land Rover Defender a week ago —we stole the vehicle off his driveway for an hour or so at 3 a.m., replaced it with another identical Land Rover with the same plates, just on the off chance he did wake up and look out of his window (unlikely), then after the device had been installed on the original, put it back again. Neat.

December 19, 1984
The call came at just after one in the afternoon when the speaker

system at Bessborough blasted out a loud "Standby!" It was unsched-
uled—obvious something was moving. Sure enough, once we got into
the operations room for a briefing, the pictures on the monitor screens
from the covert cameras told their story. Everybody was focused on
the one hidden in a tree on the Coolderry Road, down near Larkins
Road and Slab Murphy's farm. The operator zoomed in. Feck me if
there wasn't Alfie Duggan, Dessie Duggan, who was climbing out of
his tracked Defender, and a guy nobody recognized with long black
hair and a beard. We watched as they walked up the field, set up
behind some bushes well away from the road with a sniper rifle that
looked like an FN, and began a practice session. The operations officer
running the show, Harry, stood up and pointed to six of us: me, Eric,
Conman, the Don, Brenner and Gazzer. "You lot, in my office now."
I'd never seen him do that before—so I knew we were handling a deli-
cate job. And Harry didn't want the rest of them to know what the
game plan was, either. After about five minutes in Harry's office, I
knew why. "I've had enough of being screwed about by this Alfie
Duggan," Harry started off by saying. So I virtually predicted what
he was going to say next. The order was to set up a roadblock to catch
Duggan on the way out, where the Coolderry Road went through a
wood. Officially, we were to search and arrest him. But then Harry
gave the unofficial follow-up. "Of course, he'll go to pull a gun, at
which point you don't feck about. I'm not saying this, but you shoot
the shit out of him. You know what I mean?" He looked meaningfully
at each of us, right in the eyes. "It'll be collective, nobody responsible,
okay? I'll back you to the hilt if needed." And that's pretty much how
it happened. About fifty minutes later we were in position and had
the block set up. An operator back at Bessborough was in our ear,
watching off the video screen. So after the practice session was
finished, we heard that the third guy, with the beard, vanished in the
other direction toward Larkins Road and the Republic. But Harry
seemed to know that Alfie would come our way, and so he did, in a
green Rover 3500. It came around a sharp bend, moving fast. The
driver saw our roadblock, and I thought for a second he was going to

try and drive through it. But he braked hard at the last minute and
stopped. We went three to each side of the car, all of us with Heckler &
Koch HK53s, some with SIG Sauer P220s in our belts as well. Of
course, Duggan didn't go to pull a gun—he was putting his hands up.
But he still copped it. All of us let rip, virtually simultaneously,
though I think it was Conman who fired first. Everyone else was half
a second behind him. My God, the car was shredded, and Duggan
splattered all over it. But we did find an FN FAL in the back seat at
his feet, so that was all right, then; it justified everything, no problem
at all. Seriously? My guess is there'll be hell to pay over this at some
stage.

That was where the photocopied excerpts ended. Johnson,
his scalp feeling as though it had been pulled tight as a drum,
looked up at Beth, who sat with her arms folded across her
chest, staring at him, eyes wide, not speaking.

Johnson's brain was about to pop as he processed the
implications of what he had just read. It was now obvious
why Beth had been reluctant to pass the diary to him, given
her husband's role.

But he was focused more on the other people who had
clearly been involved in the murder of Alfie Duggan.

Who are they?

"Thank you for letting me see this," Johnson said. Beth
was clearly frightened about what would happen next. He
leaned forward and looked her in the eye. "I can see exactly
why you've been worried about it, but let me say this—you've
done the right thing. It's important."

Beth nodded at him, still not speaking.

"There's one very crucial thing I need to know," Johnson
said. "Did you know the men your husband is referring to?
The ones whose names and nicknames he's using."

"Only Gary Joyce. That's Gazzer," Beth said, a slight
tremor in her voice. "We were friends with the Joyces. They

were the only friends we really had out of the 14th, and that was years afterward, when we became proper friends. So I know Gary worked with him. The others I don't know."

Johnson looked back at the journal. That left four others.

Eric? That was most likely a real name, not a nickname. The Don? Definitely a nickname. Brenner could be either a surname or a nickname, and Conman was obviously a nickname.

Then something flashed across Johnson's mind.

You can call me the Don, like most people. No need for Michael.

That was what Donovan had told him on his arrival in Northern Ireland, more than three weeks earlier. Johnson had continued to address him as Michael, but the nickname had lodged in his brain. It was probably a coincidence. Or could that possibly be whom Will Doyle was referring to?

"Did your husband ever mention a man called Michael Donovan? And did he call him the Don?" he asked Beth.

She wrinkled her forehead, searching the recesses of her memory, and gazed at the floor. "Might have done. It sort of rings a bell. But it was a long time ago. I can't be sure." She shrugged and looked up.

Johnson felt he had been here before in his career, many times. Facing a jigsaw puzzle with pieces missing and no obvious way of filling in the gaps. But that was how he had built his reputation—building connections in his mind and finding solutions, even when they were elusive.

Another thought then crossed Johnson's mind—an image of the sheet of paper stuck to the wall next to the dartboard in Duggan's underground bunker. He was suddenly certain that one of the sets of letters that he had seen crossed out had been MD. Michael Donovan?

"Jayne, do you have the photo you took of the sheet stuck next to Duggan's dartboard, please?" he asked.

Jayne looked at him and raised her eyebrows, then took

her phone from her pocket and flicked through a series of images before holding one up in front of Johnson.

He stared at it, then at the journal, his mind now working at full speed. "MD. Crossed out," he said, thinking out loud. And if Michael Donovan was crossed out, was that a reference to his shooting?

He looked at the other initials on Jayne's photo. WD. Crossed out. Will Doyle? It had to be. Then there was GJ, also crossed out. Gary Joyce, Gazzer. Both Will and Gary had been shot dead by a sniper.

Now he was making headway. So who was the Eric referenced in the journal? Johnson looked back at Jayne's photograph again.

The other set of initials that had been crossed out was ES. Could that be Eric somebody?

Jayne opened her mouth as if to speak, then closed it again. Johnson noticed the movement.

"What?" Johnson asked. "You thought of something."

"Yes. ES. Is that Eric Simonson?"

"My God." Johnson leaned back in his seat.

Of course.

Then he knew.

"Shit," Johnson said, lowering his voice. "They're all reprisal shootings, then. Dessie Duggan, avenging the murder of his father back in '84."

But who was BO? Which presumably had to be the Brenner referenced in the journal. Surely not Brendan O'Neill?

But if true, it would explain perfectly why O'Neill had been so quick to push the detonator button when he saw Duggan climbing into the Audi at his farm. It was an opportunistic act of pure self-preservation. He saw a chance and took it.

Johnson's mind went back to the document on the USB

flash drive he had taken from Duggan's kitchen, which also had the initials BO on it. *Brendan O'Neill, or Barack Obama? Surely Obama, but . . . ?*

But there was one set of initials and one nickname Johnson couldn't place. He was about to ask the question when Jayne voiced it for him.

"Beth, do you know who CC might be?" she asked.

"No idea," she said. "These were Will's old army colleagues. I never met any of them at the time. It was all hush-hush because they worked in intelligence. I only met Gary years later, like I told you."

"It's probably the one nicknamed Conman in your husband's journal," Johnson said.

But again Beth shook her head. "Sorry, I don't know."

Johnson had to see O'Neill immediately to talk through what he had learned. It would be a tough conversation.

The phone vibrated in his pocket. He took it out and answered the call. It was O'Neill.

Before Johnson could speak, O'Neill jumped in. "Joe, I've just heard that both Martin Dennehy and Danny McCormick were found dead this morning by the roadside. Sounds like both were classic touts' punishment killings. Tortured, naked, shoes off, bags on their heads."

CHAPTER THIRTY-SIX

Sunday, January 27, 2013
Belfast

Johnson and Jayne waited for O'Neill in a coffee shop a couple hundred yards away from the Sunflower pub, where Johnson had seen Duggan and Dennehy attack Moira more than three weeks earlier.

As the barista poured hot milk to make the cappuccinos they had ordered, Johnson glanced up at a television in the corner. A regional television news bulletin was underway, and a report about the explosion at Duggan's house was just beginning.

"So the police and firefighters must have finally been called in by someone," Jayne said.

Johnson's ears pricked up as the reporter told how a rabbit's foot charm, attached to a key ring, had been found at the scene of the incident. The rabbit's foot had a small metal plate attached, on which was engraved the name Alfie Duggan and a date, December 19, 1984.

Police were assuming the rabbit's foot had belonged to Alfie's son, Dessie, who was thought to have died in the explosion, the reporter continued. Police were going to have DNA tests done on the remains of the body in the car in order to confirm this.

Just then, O'Neill walked into the coffee bar and saw the tail end of the report. He walked up to Johnson and raised a ragged set of black eyebrows. "I heard all this on the car radio as well. So Duggan's definitely dead."

"Hmm," Johnson said. "It seems that way. But if that's true, then who killed Dennehy and McCormick?"

O'Neill shrugged. "Don't know. Could have been someone else in the brigade taking reprisals for Duggan. The person I'm sorry for, really sorry for, is Dennehy, and also his family. There have been a lot like him over the years. He tried to do the right thing, but it doesn't take much. One small mistake."

Johnson felt suddenly humble and sad. Dennehy had paid with his life for passing on information that would save other lives—including, Johnson was well aware, his own.

But at the same time Johnson had a sense of unease about what O'Neill had said.

"I'm not so certain that Duggan's definitely dead," Johnson said.

O'Neill shrugged. He ordered a cappuccino from the coffee bar cashier and pointed toward a free table in the corner of the room.

Johnson pursed his lips as he turned and walked toward the table, O'Neill and Jayne close behind.

"And if by some chance it wasn't Duggan in the Audi, who was it?" Johnson asked. "The only obvious one is Liam McGarahan."

O'Neill nodded. "Suppose so, but I'm certain it was Duggan. I saw the way he was running. It was the same man who got out of the other car and then ran behind the house."

Jayne shook her head. "You can't assume anything. Duggan could just have dropped the rabbit's foot anytime. Doesn't automatically mean he was in the Audi."

O'Neill shrugged again, then exhaled slowly. "I don't know. Bollocks. This is turning into a monumental screwup."

That was something of an understatement, Johnson thought wryly. The G8 was due to begin the following day, and with President Obama and Prime Minister Cameron leading a bunch of world leaders into Belfast for the event, it had great potential to screw up significantly further yet. O'Neill might assume Duggan was dead, but Johnson felt he couldn't afford himself the same certainty.

"I know how you feel," Johnson said, feeling a moment of sympathy for the MI5 man. "Same thing happened to me in Afghanistan, a long time ago. I lost an agent when a meeting went wrong."

"Not a good feeling."

"No, it's not," Johnson said. He paused. Perhaps now was the time to drop the bombshell. "Look, I need to put something to you, and perhaps you can just come clean with me here."

He watched O'Neill carefully as he shared how he had just come from visiting Beth Doyle and the details he had read in her husband Will's diary. As he spoke, O'Neill kept a straight face, but he swallowed a couple of times, and there was a look in his eyes.

"So, the name Brenner, in Will's diary, and the initials BO on the piece of paper in Duggan's bunker—that's you, isn't it?" Johnson asked.

This time O'Neill couldn't prevent his eyes widening a little. "What the hell," he said slowly. Then his voice leveled out again, although Johnson was certain his face blanched a little. "Take my advice and don't jump to conclusions about what you don't know, given that you've come here with no background about all the shit that's gone on here over the years."

He looked obliquely at Johnson. "And remember this: what you've read in Will's notes, that's one man's view, not the way I remember it," O'Neill said. He wiped his hand across his mouth, a thin film of sweat visible on his forehead.

"Okay, so what was your view of it, then?" Johnson asked.

"You can't know what it was like back then," O'Neill said slowly. "It was a bloody pressure cooker that we were living in down in south Armagh. Every day we would go out on patrols, not knowing whether we'd come back, whether we'd get a bullet between the shoulder blades, between the eyes. It drove us all gradually insane. Some guys couldn't sleep, couldn't concentrate. It got to us all; it was just that some didn't show it."

He looked Johnson straight in the eyes. "It was because of the snipers. You didn't know whether they were there or not. It meant that you couldn't walk at the side of the road because of the risk that someone might have planted a bomb under a drain or behind a wall. And you couldn't walk in the middle of the road, because then you were a sitting duck. Alfie Duggan was the king of 'em all. And the thing was, after he escaped from Long Kesh, he still kept going, still kept taking us out." Here he wagged his forefinger slowly around the room, looking first at Johnson, then at Jayne. "Took us out. One. By. One."

Jayne nodded. "Can't argue with that," she said. "I saw it all at firsthand. There were a lot of young soldiers sent over here who just lacked the expertise, lacked the experience to deal with it. There was a bunker mentality."

"Yes, but what you did, both in '84 and last night, was kangaroo court justice," Johnson said, matching O'Neill's gaze. "Why not just arrest Alfie that day, put him back in Long Kesh? He wouldn't have come out again, would he?"

O'Neill gave a derisive laugh. "Well, yes, he would have. He'd have been out as part of the Good Friday agreement, wouldn't he, as it happened, like all the other IRA killers who were let out at that time. But let's put that to one side. That day, it was the red mist that got us all. It was pent-up anger at seeing friends and colleagues gunned down, murdered, day after day. It just all poured out."

Johnson didn't tell O'Neill that he was never going to persuade him of the merits of that point of view, no matter how long and hard he tried. Now was not the time for a debate about ethical soldiering.

The issue of what he would do about O'Neill and his role in Alfie Duggan's death would have to wait. That had suddenly become the elephant in the room.

Instead he ran through the list of five of the six sets of names and nicknames mentioned in Doyle's journal, confirming with O'Neill that they were all who he assumed they were. O'Neill confirmed them all.

"Then that leaves one person," Johnson said, his voice lowering slightly in pitch as he spoke. "CC. Who is CC? I'm guessing he's the person nicknamed Conman in Will's journal," Johnson asked.

"You've not worked that one out yet?" O'Neill asked. "Conor Campbell. Deputy chief constable before, under Eric, now confirmed in the top job as of two days ago. The only other realistic internal candidate was Norman Arnside."

Of course, how did I miss that, Johnson thought. He now vaguely remembered hearing something on the radio about Campbell's appointment as acting chief constable, but somehow the connection with the nickname and initials hadn't registered with him.

"It was all over the news," O'Neill went on. "Him and Simonson worked hand in glove for years. They got out of the army together, only a couple of years after the Duggan shooting. They joined the police together, got promotions more or less in tandem. He was always called Conman."

"So now you and him are the only two on Duggan's list still standing," Johnson said. "And if by some remote chance Duggan wasn't in the Audi when you blew it up, then . . ." His voice trailed off. He didn't need to say anymore.

Johnson leaned forward. "This was why Donovan brought me in, wasn't it? He wanted me to get to Duggan before Duggan got to him. It wasn't really about his business at all."

O'Neill gave a slight nod. "He never discussed it with me, but I guess you're correct, up to a point. But his business was taking a hammering; that was no lie."

Johnson knew that a significant number of British army soldiers had been prosecuted for killing Republicans during the Troubles. But plenty of them had escaped justice, as had very many Republicans responsible for the deaths of hundreds of police and troops in Northern Ireland.

"What happened to the police files after Alfie Duggan was killed?" Johnson asked. There *must* have been files, he knew that. Any killing by security services would have a file of some kind, and there had been inquiries into some of them.

O'Neill explained that the police facility at Carrickfergus, eight miles northeast of Belfast, was a high-security site where most of the files of that type had been stored. "But a lot of files went missing from Carrickfergus around that time and during the '90s," he said. "Some of them implicated people right up to the very top—and I don't mean just the top of the army units out there or the MI5 teams. I'm talking about right to the top politically, at Whitehall and Westminster, as well as Belfast and Dublin, because official policy was that the army and police should operate according to the letter of the law. In practice, certain politicians effectively allowed all kinds of illegal things to go on."

"Blind eyes were turned, you mean?" Johnson asked.

"A lot of blind eyes, I can tell you. Thing was, we were hanging, drawing, and quartering ourselves by writing everything down. The IRA certainly wasn't doing that. And it wasn't a game you could win by sticking to the law, especially if you were running agents, like me. If you wanted to protect your agent, you had to let certain IRA operations go ahead, which might involve innocents being killed. If you stopped an IRA operation, you left your agent open to being killed as a tout. It was a no-win situation then, and it still is. That's why some of the files disappeared."

"Disappeared?" Johnson asked.

"Yes. Stolen, taken, whatever. Once people knew that inquiries into some of these killings were starting, like the Stevens inquiry that everyone's heard of, it became obvious that stones were going to be turned over and uncomfortable truths uncovered. So there were some odd incidents. There was an unexplained fire in a Carrickfergus incident room where investigators were going through files, many of which were destroyed. There was a burglary. So who knows—maybe the files relating to Alfie Duggan were among those that vanished."

Johnson was aware that the British government had commissioned three different inquiries by Sir John Stevens into the role of state security services in the killings of Irish nationalists. But as far as he was aware, the Alfie Duggan killing had not been among them.

He glanced at Jayne, who raised her eyebrows. Maybe her friend Noreen, who had worked at Carrickfergus, might know something about the missing files. He made a mental note to ask her later—he didn't want to raise that question in front of O'Neill.

"What about Dennehy's death?" Johnson asked. "You

stopped a few IRA operations on the back of his information, and Dennehy lost—he got shot."

"Welcome to Northern Ireland," O'Neill said. "Fifteen years since the Troubles supposedly ended."

He was right, Johnson thought. Dennehy's death summed up the cynicism and sadness of the region's recent history.

And how can I really understand it?

Johnson nodded slowly. "Okay, let's try and look forward," he said. "When I was in the bunker, I heard Duggan referring to Project Gyrate and talking about Gyrate being a goer. It was obvious to me he was talking about the G8."

O'Neill nodded and told how he had listened in via the hidden cameras and had also heard that conversation.

"So what are we going to do about Campbell?" Johnson asked. "Is he going to be out on public duty during the G8? And what are the arrangements for the likes of Obama and Cameron? If by some chance Duggan's not dead, then they're all going to be irresistible bait, aren't they? He could take out a US president and Campbell in one go. Or someone else in the brigade might be capable of handling a sniper rifle, even if Duggan's dead."

"Yes, that's a fair point," O'Neill said. "I'm certain there's going to be fortress-strong security for the G8. It's what goes on around the fringes that worries me—for instance if they have a walkabout or community visit or something planned as part of the agenda. That's usually the case, and that's the weak point. I've not seen an agenda, but I'm trying to get one."

"Why don't we just go and talk to Campbell?" Johnson asked.

"We could," O'Neill said. "But Campbell won't want to touch this with a ten-foot pole. He'll pretend it's not happening, like he's done, and Eric Simonson did, for the past twenty-nine years, and just hope for the best."

A little like O'Neill was doing now, Johnson couldn't help thinking.

"What about someone further down the PSNI, then?" Johnson asked. "Maybe an upcoming deputy or assistant chief constable who thinks it might be a chance to make his name. Tell them what we know."

"We can do that," O'Neill said. "But I've been there before—they're an arrogant bunch and they're yes-men. They won't want to do anything to upset the newly appointed chief constable—they'll be licking his backside, not trying to poke a sharp stick in his ribs. They don't like to listen to us at MI5 because they think they're doing a good job and they've got all the bases covered. There's no love lost. In fact they don't like to listen to anybody. So don't think that as an American you can just walk in there out of the blue and they'll listen. Second, it could open a massive can of worms if they start probing into what happened down at Duggan's farm—for both of us, not just me. I mean, you broke in there and planted a surveillance kit."

"That was about doing something for the greater good," Johnson said. "Could be an even bigger can of worms if they start digging into what Campbell did in '84." He leaned back and stared at O'Neill. "And into what you did, for that matter."

"There's no proof. No files. No witnesses. Four out of the six are dead." O'Neill shook his head and stood up. "You could say that was for the greater good, too. Alfie murdered a lot of soldiers."

O'Neill turned to face Johnson. "I need to go," he said, "but I'll tell you what I'm going to do. I agree we should try with Campbell. I'll call him to chat about this and at the same time try and find out what the plan is for the G8. Then I need to go and try to explain to my boss why and how my main agent in the south Armagh brigade ended up dead in a ditch. I'll call you later when I know more." He walked out.

Johnson watched him leave, then leaned toward Jayne. "Surely if there were files that linked Eric Simonson and Conor Campbell to a questionable incident, such as Alfie Duggan's death, neither of them would have been appointed chief constable?"

"Yes, correct," Jayne said. "But if the files had disappeared, then who would know? Thing is, everyone knows that the Historical Enquiries Team has been doing a poor job on some of the cases, especially where it involved the military or the police killing Republicans. They're the ones who should be 100 percent rigorous with this kind of thing, but they're not."

Johnson knew that the HET, set up in 2005 within the Police Service of Northern Ireland to investigate more than three thousand unsolved murders committed during the Troubles, had been the subject of some controversy. There was deep skepticism that it was delivering the kind of justice that bereaved families deserved, at least in terms of deaths allegedly caused by security services.

"Well, we'll have to make damn sure they're 100 percent rigorous this time around," Johnson said. "Not sure how, but we'll give it our best shot."

* * *

Sunday, January 27, 2013
  Belfast

O'Neill hadn't spoken to Conor Campbell in more than ten years and had exchanged emails only twice during that time, to update each other's contact details. And in the eighteen years prior to that, they had exchanged words no more than a couple of times.

There had been no falling out. They had both made up their own minds that keeping a distance was the safest way to play it. Burying their heads in the sand and trying to pretend that what had happened was not real was the only way to keep going.

Now, though, Campbell was in full listening mode. He had responded to a short text message from O'Neill by calling back within minutes on his secure cell phone.

O'Neill, who had returned to his Holywood home, described what had happened at Willows Farm and gave a summary of the contents of Will Doyle's diary, as described to him by Johnson.

"We both know what Duggan was doing, Brendan, taking us out one by one, but he's almost certainly dead now," Campbell said. "That's solved our problem, because I don't think the Doyle journal is going to stand as proof against us of what happened on Coolderry Road that day."

"Agreed," O'Neill said, "It's just a dead man's diary." He paused for a second, then added, "So how long will it take to confirm that Duggan died down at Willows Farm?"

"The DNA tests will confirm it," Campbell said. "It will just take a day or two."

"Yes, I saw him run from one side of the house, then reappear on the other side and get into the Audi," O'Neill said. "There was no mistake. It was definitely him."

"I'm certain you're right," Campbell said. "What does Johnson think? He was there too."

"Johnson saw it all, but he thinks we shouldn't automatically assume anything."

"Yes, well, if he were alive, it would be tricky," Campbell said. "I wouldn't be able to arrest him unless I got something rock solid pinned on him. We couldn't have him wriggling off the hook and then shooting off his mouth in court or to the media about me, you, and the others killing his father. Then we become the offenders, not him. The last thing we need is for him to turn the tables on us like that."

"So what would you do, then?" O'Neill asked.

"We'd have to catch him when he's ready to shoot," Campbell said. "That's where we've consistently failed all these years—we've not had the hard evidence. Nobody's ever caught him with a gun, not even a sniff of residue, not a cartridge shell. He's not like most of these dissident jokers. He's old school. And people in south Armagh still won't give evidence against anybody—they're all running scared. But that's all immaterial anyway, because I'm sure he's dead."

O'Neill knew that Campbell was correct about the reprisals against touts and informers and indeed anyone prepared to testify against violent dissidents. The dissidents had ensured that the culture of fear across the rural population hadn't gone away with the Good Friday agreement. The fate of Dennehy was a prime example of that and made it even more unlikely that ordinary people would risk all by giving evidence.

"Right," said O'Neill, "what about security for the G8, then? Obama and Cameron and the others? Just in case."

"I'm not concerned about the event itself," Campbell said. "We're encircling the venue. Nobody's going to get near it."

"Okay, what about when the politicians are in transit or doing things outside the actual complex?"

Campbell hesitated. "We've not made anything public, so this is strictly confidential, but we do have a school visit planned, Whitefield Integrated Primary School. Obama, Cameron, and a couple of others are going, with me in tow. They'll watch and join in a short game of kids' football on the playing field for a photo op, then they'll go inside and they'll each make a speech for the TV cameras. Aim is to show how things are normalizing around here. But again, that'll be watertight. The whole area for a mile around the school will be cordoned off. Travel to and from the place will be in armored cars. We'll have snipers, dogs, bomb squads, you name it, all around the place. The Obama team will have its own security detail, of course, and we've made arrangements for that. So it should be fine. The media won't be told until first thing tomorrow morning, but that won't be a problem for them as they'll have crews mobilized anyway."

The two men agreed to keep in touch as needed over the coming hours, effectively giving O'Neill a hotline to Campbell that bypassed his bosses at MI5, whom he decided to keep out of this particular loop, at least for the time being.

"Just in case this guy Joe Johnson needs to get hold of me urgently, or if he finds out anything else, give him my secure number," Campbell said. "I need to go now. I'm due in a meeting to run through G8 arrangements."

O'Neill gave Johnson's cell phone number to Campbell and ended the call. He sat thinking for a few moments. Then he called Johnson, gave him a summary of the conversation he had just had with the new chief constable, and passed over Campbell's number.

"Campbell and I both believe Duggan's dead," O'Neill said. "So you only call Campbell in absolute emergencies if you find out anything that changes that view."

He agreed that he would call Johnson at about five o'clock that afternoon and hung up.

O'Neill checked his watch. He needed to walk up the road to the newsstand to pay the bill for his daily delivery of *The Times*. It was worth it to be able to sit and enjoy his breakfast while digesting the day's news.

He also needed to pick up some shirts from the dry cleaner next door to the newsstand before heading into the office for his own departmental pre-G8 briefing.

Five minutes later, O'Neill had his shoes on and made his way out of the house, through the housing estate, and onto the main road.

He stopped on the corner and scrutinized the screen on his phone, pretending to tap out a text message but using the opportunity to carry out his normal countersurveillance checks.

Satisfied that there were no signs of a tail, he crossed the road and made his way past the school on his right and a few more houses, then toward the arcade of shops, set back from the road. As usual there were a couple of white vans parked on the road right outside the dry cleaner, which O'Neill knew did contract work for hotels and restaurants in the area. Drivers were often delivering and collecting linen, so O'Neill ignored them.

There was another van, a Volkswagen with a high roof, parked on the other side of the road, about a hundred yards away. It was only when he gave it a second glance, as a small child on a scooter appeared from behind it, that he realized there was something different about it.

CHAPTER THIRTY-SEVEN

Sunday, January 27, 2013
  Belfast

Duggan held his position rock solid, keeping his right eye fixed firmly on the reticle in his scope, which was pointed directly at the center of O'Neill's chest. He relaxed his entire upper body and consciously slowed his breathing.

The barrel of his Barrett M82A sat neatly a couple of inches inside the hinged flap at the back of his white van, and the opening was just large enough for Duggan to get a good view through his scope.

O'Neill continued to walk up the road toward the dry cleaner's shop, as Duggan had expected.

The MI5 man, surprisingly to Duggan, had made the mistake of getting into a routine, visiting the shop over a number of previous Sundays at similar times, something that had been noted by one of Duggan's brigade volunteers.

Now he was about to pay the price.

Almost unconsciously, Duggan tightened his finger fractionally around the trigger.

Then Duggan noticed O'Neill glance at his white van. A few seconds later, he looked up again, and this time the glance became a stare.

Duggan knew instinctively that O'Neill, as a trained intelligence officer, had spotted the square black hole on the back of the white van and realized there was something wrong and would dive for cover.

Indeed, he saw him brace himself, preparing to throw himself sideways behind an adjacent wall.

But Duggan was too quick. His finger was the only part of his body that moved as it pulled the trigger.

There was a sharp bang, followed immediately by another as Duggan fired a follow-up shot, just to be sure.

But it was unnecessary.

O'Neill's body was catapulted backward several yards as the first round slammed into his chest. The second hit him in his lower torso, but by then the damage was done.

* * *

Sunday, January 27, 2013
  Belfast

"We've got to find out what happened to those original files on the Alfie Duggan shooting," Johnson said. "That's the key to it. You said your friend Noreen used to work at Carrickfergus. Would she be able to find out?"

He paced to the other end of the kitchen and turned to look at Jayne, who shrugged.

"It's a hell of a long time ago. We're talking the '80s. What's the likelihood of them still being anywhere? If they went missing twenty years ago, it's highly unlikely. But I'll give her a call and see what she says."

She disappeared into the living room to make the call but came back two minutes later. "Noreen's not answering, so I left a voice mail. Hopefully she'll pick it up and get back to me."

Johnson switched his focus to O'Neill. It was strange that he hadn't called back following his planned conversations with Campbell and with his boss.

When seven o'clock passed and O'Neill still hadn't called, Johnson started to get a feeling that something must have happened. He called O'Neill's cell phone three times in twenty minutes, but each time it went to voice mail.

He was about to try Campbell instead when Campbell saved him the trouble and called him.

After the briefest of terse introductions, the senior policeman got straight to the point. "I've just heard that Brendan O'Neill has been shot dead, not far from his home. Apparently on the way to the newsagent. I had assumed, like Brendan, that Duggan had been killed down at his home. But now I've changed my view, although we're still waiting for DNA tests. Either way, I need to meet you, urgently."

Johnson swore. "Oh, shit. That's five." It was unbelievable. If he were to rank the people he had encountered on his visit to Ulster in terms of perceived ability to look after themselves and for street awareness, O'Neill would have been at the top. What the hell had happened?

Campbell refused to discuss it any further on an open phone line. "You'll have to come into our HQ. I think we should meet face-to-face. Only problem is I won't have long, probably ten minutes maximum. I'm right under the cosh here—we've got eight thousand officers policing this G8, nearly half of whom have been drafted in from other forces, and there's a massive security operation going on. It's a logistical nightmare, so as you can imagine, I could do without this going on."

The chief constable instructed Johnson to hold the line while he got his personal assistant to arrange a car to collect Johnson, who insisted on bringing Jayne along, and the two men agreed to meet an hour later.

It was now clear to Johnson that Campbell, following his earlier conversation with O'Neill and O'Neill's death, had decided he had no choice but to trust and confide in him.

By just after eight o'clock, Johnson and Jayne were sitting side by side at a wooden table in a small interview room at the PSNI's headquarters on Knock Road, East Belfast.

"This should be interesting," Johnson whispered.

A few minutes later a large barrel-chested man strode in and introduced himself as Conor Campbell. Johnson shook hands and introduced Jayne. "She's ex-MI6, did a stint here for a few years in the early '90s. Works freelance now."

Campbell nodded at Jayne. "That helps. I don't think we ever had dealings though, did we? I was far more junior back then."

"No," Jayne said. "That's one thing that's changed. Congratulations. But there's still a lot that hasn't."

Campbell grimaced. "That's one way of putting it. It's unfortunate that we've got a determined nutter who just happens to have a certain lethal capability and, seemingly, a strong motivation." He sat down across the table from the two of them and began by briefly describing the reports on O'Neill's shooting.

"I'm astonished Brendan wasn't taking more precautions," Johnson said. "I said to him there was no certainty Duggan had died."

Campbell ran a hand through his short iron-gray hair and shrugged. "Maybe he got complacent. I don't know," Campbell said. "But that's beside the point. It's happened. The thing is, if this is Duggan, I need to get to the bottom of how he did it before tomorrow. I'm worried he might want to repeat the trick—but this time with Obama and Cameron."

"It had crossed my mind," Johnson said, as dryly as he could manage. "Not to mention yourself."

Campbell's face twitched and his eyebrows rose. "Yes, well, you're right, but I'm not the first priority here. Look, we've got people down there where the shooting happened, crime scene investigators, detectives, but it's really a skeleton team, frankly, because every spare officer is tied up on the G8. We're at full stretch—beyond full stretch. And from what I've heard, the people we do have down there have made no progress since they arrived. I haven't got the time to get involved in this, and anyway, I don't want to start showing a big personal interest in O'Neill right now. I can't afford to, and it would look odd when I've got the G8 on my plate. So I need you to do something, if possible."

Johnson guessed what was coming next. "Go on," he said.

"You're an investigator, Brendan told me, right?" Campbell said.

"Yes, that's right. But war crimes, not necessarily homicides." Johnson looked across at Jayne, who was staring at him, scratching her chin.

"Never mind that," Campbell said. "Are you able to get down there and just see if you can talk to a few people, local residents. You'll have to knock on doors. Be honest, say who you are, a private investigator. Whatever. Just don't pretend you're a policeman, obviously. I want someone who might have seen what happened. Where the gunman was. Where he was hiding. Because it's quite possible he could try and use the same method tomorrow. And God forbid if the US president or the UK prime minister is shot dead on my patch. He can take me out but not Obama."

Campbell paused. Now he was breathing heavily; his

already florid face and fleshy neck had gone a deeper shade of red. He folded his arms and surveyed Johnson from across the table.

Hardly surprising he was stressed, Johnson thought, but to have a chief constable making this kind of request of a non-policeman, not to mention someone he had previously never even met—it seemed scarcely credible and spoke volumes about the trust Campbell clearly had had in O'Neill's vote of confidence in Johnson.

"Okay," Johnson said. "Leave it with us." He glanced at Jayne, who nodded. He took from Campbell the address where the shooting had taken place.

Johnson decided that if Campbell wanted to work with him, he should reciprocate. The issue of what to do about the Alfie Duggan killing could wait—Campbell clearly wasn't going to raise it. So he told the chief constable about the draft G8 community visit schedule on the USB flash drive that he had obtained from Duggan's house during his covert visit two weeks earlier.

"Bloody hell," Campbell said. "I won't ask you why you were in Duggan's house, but you're telling me Duggan had that?"

"Yes. It looks like you've got a mole in your camp."

"Too damn right it does. And obviously, if Duggan's had the draft document, he's most likely had the final details."

"Right," Johnson said. "So where is this visit happening, then?"

Campbell tersely ran through Obama and Cameron's short visit scheduled for the following afternoon. The timetable remained identical to the draft document that Johnson had seen.

"Don't you want to rethink this?" Johnson asked. "Why not just cancel this school visit? You can tell the public the security risk is too high and the president's life is under threat."

There was a pause. Campbell placed his hands behind his head and leaned back. "No, can't do that. Absolutely not. That would be giving in to these dissidents, and nobody in the Northern Ireland Assembly is going to stand for that, not with the world looking on. It would be the opposite message from what we're trying to convey, which is that things are normalized here now. I've been confirmed in this job only a couple of days, and I'd be on a hiding to nothing if I even suggested it. I've already got enough enemies gunning for me inside and outside the force. I'd probably get fired on the spot. They'd say it's my job to police and manage the risks, and I think we're doing that. Yes, I'm worried, of course I am. You can doubtless tell that. But I do think we've covered all the bases."

You might be about to be fired anyway, Johnson thought. But he let the chief constable continue.

Campbell stopped and looked at his watch. "Look, we're going to have to break off. I've got a crucial meeting I need to run to now. Let's keep in touch."

Campbell stood and shook hands again. "We've got the biggest bloody security operation ever seen in Northern Ireland for this G8. We're just going to have to trust in it." He nodded at Johnson, then Jayne, and strode out of the room.

Johnson glanced at Jayne. "Looks like we're going to play at being police detectives for an hour or so," he said.

* * *

Sunday, January 27, 2013
  Belfast

. . .

Jayne surveyed the crime scene. Under the glare thrown off by some temporary floodlights, four uniformed police officers and two forensics experts in white suits were working inside an area cordoned off with white plastic tape. There was a white tent, presumably over the spot where the body fell. But that was it. No other officers were visible.

"I think it would be better if I do this," Jayne said. "Nobody's going to talk to an American. Not one going door-to-door. It's a unionist area. They'll be okay with a Brit calling on them."

Johnson nodded. "Makes sense."

Jayne climbed out of the car and walked toward some houses that overlooked the shops where O'Neill had been gunned down.

She got short shrift at the first four doors she knocked on, all of them belonging to neat semidetached redbrick houses.

An old man who came out of the first house looked at her suspiciously. "We don't like talking to spooks around here, especially British ones," he said after she had introduced herself. "I don't mind the local police, I know them, but they haven't been in yet. Sorry, but I'll wait and speak to them."

At the second, a stressed housewife wearing a cooking apron and carrying a baby, whose dog was barking inside the house, sighed deeply. "It's not going to make any difference, love, what we say. I didn't see anything anyway. I was changing the baby's nappy when I heard the bangs outside. I'm assuming it was a dissident shooting, but they never get caught or prosecuted, do they?"

She received similarly negative responses at the next two. By this time she was beginning to feel not only discouraged but conspicuous as well.

At the fifth house, across the road from the dry cleaner's shop, a youngster in his late teens answered the door. When

Jayne asked for his parents, he replied in the negative but then asked who she was. So she explained, briefly.

"You're investigating the shooting?" he asked.

"Yes, that's right," Jayne said.

The boy shook his head and folded his arms. "No, I was busy upstairs," he said in a low-pitched Belfast accent.

"Okay, thanks anyway," Jayne said. She turned to leave and took a couple of steps down the path.

Then from behind her, the youngster spoke again. "Actually, I think I might have seen something." She turned. He had lank, dark hair that needed shampooing and a black T-shirt with a *Grand Theft Auto* logo on the front.

Jayne refocused on the youth and walked back up the path. "What did you see? Anything could be useful."

"I was looking out of the window when I saw a white van parking across the road, one with a very high roof. A Volkswagen Transporter. I know that because my uncle's got one. I thought it must be a dry cleaning van and didn't take any notice. Then ten minutes later, I looked again, and at the back, there was a square black hole at the top that hadn't been there before. I thought it was one of those police speed traps. We sometimes get them on this road because it's straight and people go fast. But it looked different and had no police markings on the van."

The boy paused and looked at Jayne. "The next thing I know, as I'm looking at this van and the black hole, trying to work out what it is, there's a flash at the hole, a massive explosion, then another one, and I look down the road and there's a guy lying there, blood everywhere. About fifteen seconds later, the van starts up and drives off. And that's it. Someone must have called the police, and the ambulance, and they came straightaway. Since then it's been crazy out there."

Jayne knew immediately what had happened. It must have been Duggan, operating from a specially adapted van, set up as a mobile sniping platform. She remembered from her time with the SIS in Belfast that IRA sniper gangs of old had used similar tactics.

"Thank you very much, that's very helpful," Jayne said. "You were very observant. Is there anything else you noticed? Did you see the driver of the van and can you remember the registration plates?"

"Sorry, no. I didn't see the driver, and I didn't think to check the plates. I should have done that." The boy now looked downcast.

"Don't worry. Did you see any markings on the side of the van? Any logos, company names, that kind of thing."

"No, not on the side I saw."

"Fine," said Jayne. "Police might come around and inter- view you as well and ask similar questions, but that's normal procedure."

Jayne said goodbye and left. As she did so, her cell phone rang. It was Noreen.

"I got your message," Noreen said. "You're clutching at straws, you know. So many of those files just vanished or were burned in a fire we had at Carrickfergus."

"Yes, I realize that," Jayne said.

"And you realize that there's not a cat in hell's chance that either of those two guys would ever have been appointed chief constable if there was any whiff of this kind of thing hanging around them? I think it's a nonstarter."

"Yes. Okay, point taken. Thanks, Noreen."

Jayne made her way back to the Mazda, where Johnson was waiting.

"I got some info. Duggan was in a white van," she said. She described what the boy in the house had told her.

Johnson pushed his head back against the driver's seat headrest and closed his eyes momentarily. "Okay," he said. "There's lots of VW Transporter vans but can't be too many high-roofed ones. I'll let Campbell know. Maybe there's a chance they can put the call out and pull it in before Duggan does more damage."

Jayne glanced at him. "I don't like to say this, Joe, but if Duggan's as smart as he seems, the van is almost certainly tucked away in some garage, off the road and out of sight. If he's adapted it to allow him to use a rifle through a flap in the back, he's going to want to keep it away from close scrutiny."

Johnson nodded. "True. Unless he's actually using the damn thing."

She suggested that he should check the feeds from the cameras he had planted in Duggan's house, on the off chance that the batteries in one or two of them might still be working. It seemed unlikely after more than two weeks but worth a look. At least it might show whether Duggan had returned to Forkhill, which she thought might be the case, or was still out elsewhere, which would be a more worrisome scenario.

The feed on Johnson's cell phone took a long time to load, as usual, but only one camera at Willows Farm remained functional: the one in the kitchen he had hidden between two saucepans on a high shelf. The others in the house and in the underground bunker and tunnels were completely dead.

Jayne peered over Johnson's shoulder to look at the screen. The kitchen appeared to not have been used recently. Two coffee mugs stood upside down on the draining board. The countertops were clean and tidy. A dishcloth had been hung over the tap to dry. The laptop with the blue cover that had been stolen from Beth Doyle's house was no longer there.

"Where the hell has the bastard gone?" Johnson said. He tugged at the small hole on the top of his right ear.

"It's more about where he's going to strike from—if he's going to strike," Jayne said. "Not where he's gone. I get the feeling that Campbell wants to catch him in the act with his big bloody gun, not sitting in a coffee bar without a shred of evidence on him. It's a high-risk, high-reward strategy."

Her phone rang. It was Noreen again.

"I just remembered," Noreen said. "I've got a vague recollection that the investigation team at Carrickfergus, the Stevens inquiry people, took copies of the files to Nottinghamshire police headquarters for safekeeping. I might be wrong, but I think my colleague Sarah arranged it. But that would have been in 1989. I've no idea what happened to the files after that."

"Bloody hell. Is there any chance of finding out more?" Jayne asked, her voice rising a few tones. "If they had back-ups, surely they would have investigated anything significant in those files, even if the originals had gone?"

There was a short silence. "That's where you're wrong," Noreen said. "They just didn't. The inquiry ended up being more limited than people expected. There were whispers that many files weren't touched at all because people in high places pulled strings to put the block on many investigations."

"What about the Historical Enquiries Team, then?" Jayne asked. "Surely it's their job to go through all those files?"

"It is their job—but they've been completely overworked, unable to spend enough time on files, and ineffective in many ways."

"Well, do you have any contacts in Nottingham you could call to find out?"

"Doubt it. If Sarah did the work, as I recall, she might have one. There was a liaison lady whom I dealt with sometimes. But I've no idea if she's still with Nottinghamshire police. I'll see if I can dig up her number. It was a long time ago."

Jayne thanked her and ended the call.

"Did you get all that?" she asked Johnson, who had been

leaning in close to her, his cheek nudging against the top of her head, trying to listen to Noreen's voice.

"Mostly. Sounds like a long shot. But perhaps our only shot as far as Campbell's concerned."

* * *

Sunday, January 27, 2013
Belfast

Johnson knew he wouldn't be able to sleep unless he came up with something that would advance this investigation before he went to bed. It was almost midnight, and time was rapidly running out.

He lifted the lid of his laptop once again and skimmed through the collection of files he had put together over the previous three weeks. He ended up focusing on the one labeled "Visit."

Johnson grasped the edge of the table with both hands, suddenly realizing with great irritation that he had missed a trick. There had been no useful electronic footprint, no helpful metadata, in the document containing the draft details of the Obama school visit that he had obtained from the USB flash drive at Duggan's house.

But if the flash drive had been handed to Duggan by the mole inside the Police Service of Northern Ireland, then maybe there was a possibility that the person's fingerprints were still be on the plastic housing.

Johnson grabbed his phone and tapped out a secure text message to Campbell.

Think you should get flash drive from police mole fingerprinted. It might ID him and trail might lead to Duggan. I have the drive here. It's mostly been in a plastic bag. Joe.

A minute later, Johnson's phone rang. Campbell sounded exhausted, his voice flat and fading.

"Good thought," Campbell said. "I'm losing the plot—should have thought of that straightaway. We'll get the thing straight over to the Fingerprint Bureau, and they can check it out overnight."

Campbell said he would have a car sent immediately to collect the device from the apartment where Johnson and Jayne were staying on Falls Road.

"Any progress in the hunt for Duggan's van?" Johnson asked.

"Nothing. He's obviously gone to ground."

"Yes, but I'm certain he's not at his house."

"What makes you think that?" Campbell asked.

Johnson sighed. Now he was going to have to confess. He explained how, during the same covert visit when he obtained the flash drive, he had planted surveillance cameras inside Duggan's property, one of which remained serviceable.

He heard Campbell swear under his breath. "I don't want to know," he said.

"Okay, I'm not telling you. It's about the greater good," Johnson said. "I'm not going to bore you with the details now. I'll tell you when this is over, but he had me imprisoned in his underground bunker for two days after we tracked him smuggling cigarettes and a sniper rifle in from the US. Jayne and O'Neill rescued me."

There was silence from Campbell. Johnson decided to change the subject; Campbell was unlikely to be too happy with a US civilian running some sort of unofficial crime detection operation on his own patch, behind his back.

And Johnson knew Campbell would be even less happy if

the PSNI's Historical Enquiries Team—set up in 2005 to investigate unsolved murders committed during the Troubles of the '70s, '80s, and '90s, including those committed by British Army soldiers—were to turn its attention to the shooting of Alfie Duggan in 1984. That was a card that Johnson could play if needed.

Shortly afterward, a plainclothes policeman knocked at Johnson's apartment door, produced his ID, and took away the flash drive in a secure plastic bag.

Johnson felt that, barring something unexpected materializing in the morning, this was his last hope of getting to the bottom of what Duggan's plan was for the next day.

Before he went to bed at about half past one, Johnson made yet another check on the remaining video surveillance camera at Willows Farm. Nothing had changed in the kitchen, nothing had been moved. The same empty coffee mugs were still on the draining board. It was obvious to Johnson that Duggan was spending the night somewhere else, preparing for the following day.

CHAPTER THIRTY-EIGHT

Monday, January 28, 2013
  Belfast

Johnson's phone awakened him at just before five-thirty. It was Campbell, who clearly had spent even less time in bed than Johnson.

The overnight tests and checks run by the PSNI's Fingerprint Bureau on the USB flash drive had come back in, Campbell told him.

After running them through the system, a match had been found for Fergus Kane, the public affairs officer responsible for the force's relationships with the various government agencies across Northern Ireland and in the Republic.

Although not a policeman, Campbell said, Kane had visited major crime scenes on several occasions and had therefore been routinely fingerprinted for elimination purposes by the forensics teams. That meant his prints were in the system.

Two officers had been dispatched to arrest Kane and haul

him in for questioning, Campbell added. A search for the white van Duggan had been using had so far drawn a blank and was proving difficult without a registration plate number.

"I'm going to be snowed under dealing with politicians and G8 officials today, as you can imagine," Campbell told Johnson. "So I've briefed my assistant chief constable, Norman Arnside, who's responsible for crime operations. He'll be your main contact today, but either he or I will keep you updated if there are more developments."

Johnson slid out of bed. He didn't envy Kane, whoever he was. Police interrogation methods doubtless differed from those employed by dissident Republicans, as the fate of Dennehy had demonstrated. But nonetheless, he would have an extremely unpleasant experience, with Campbell on the war path.

He was about to go and wake Jayne when she emerged from her bedroom.

"I just had a thought," Jayne said, before Johnson had a chance to tell her about Kane. "If Duggan had his van adapted as a sniping platform, then somebody must have done the work on it."

"Good point," Johnson said. "But the problem is, how many outfits are there in Ulster that can do that sort of work? Probably dozens."

"Actually, it's unlikely to be many," she said. "Most don't want to work with violent dissidents. Maybe whoever modified the van is on the PSNI watch lists."

"But would Duggan confide in someone like that? Wouldn't he just ask for a job to be done and not explain what he was going to do with the vehicle afterward? And why would the person know where Duggan was?"

Jayne shrugged. "Don't know. That's second-guessing. Let's find out. Anyway, I can't think of anything else constructive we can do right now to resolve this."

Johnson grabbed his phone. "Okay. I'll contact Campbell; why don't you try your friend Noreen. And ask her if there's any progress on those files in Nottingham."

He tapped out a text message to Campbell. *Can we get a list of car repair shops, welders, etc., who might have IRA/dissident allegiances and might have had the ability to turn Duggan's van into a sniper platform?*

A reply came back a few minutes later. *Will try and get someone onto this. Good thought.*

"*Try?*" Johnson said out loud.

* * *

Monday, January 28, 2013
*   Belfast*

Duggan kicked the rear tire of the Grizzly quad bike and stood hands on hips. He turned to O'Driscoll, who had arrived at the garage just off Falls Road five minutes earlier. "Feckin' welder. If you need a job doing, do it yourself," he said. He looked at the sniper's platform on the back of the Grizzly and kicked the tire again.

His anger was only partly due to the defective welding job. The rest was down to his ongoing fury, which had hardly dissipated over the past couple of days, over Johnson's escape from his bunker and the death of his IO, McGarahan, in the car blast outside his house, which had also blown in all the windows on the front of the property.

He knew very well he could have been the one in the Audi.

But Duggan tried to put that out of his mind and focus on the issue at hand. A joint on the underside of the aluminum plate, where it was joined to the tubes, had become detached, which meant the sniper's platform wobbled when Duggan tried to rest his Barrett rifle on it. It was just about usable, but it certainly wasn't conducive to the kind of accuracy that he was going to require later that day. A wobble at the wrong moment could torpedo the entire operation.

"Bollocks," Duggan shouted, louder this time. There was no alternative. He was going to have to pop back to Arthur Higgins' garage and have him do an emergency repair.

O'Driscoll climbed up into the back of the van and carefully placed the five-foot-long black case containing the Barrett next to the dividing panel that separated the cab from the cargo hold. He picked up an AK-47 assault rifle from the floor, placed it next to the Barrett's case, and covered both weapons with an old tarp.

Once O'Driscoll had gotten out, Duggan put the metal ramps at the back of his VW van back in place and climbed into the seat of the Grizzly.

O'Driscoll turned toward him. "Dessie, don't you think that, just maybe, this welding cock-up is a sign. Maybe we should just abort this job. It's not looking good to me, not after Johnson escaped. He's bound to have alerted the cops and every other man and his dog—they'll all be looking for us."

"They won't be looking in the place we're going," Duggan said. "And anyway, the way I've planned it has taken the risk out of it."

He had to admit to himself that O'Driscoll had a strong point. But Duggan wasn't going to say so. His finance director was an intelligent man but wouldn't have been his first choice for this kind of hands-on operation. Anyway, Duggan's reasons for wanting to complete this particular mission ran very deep inside him. It was personal.

Duggan started the Grizzly and then slowly maneuvered it up the ramp into the back of the van.

Then he secured the quad bike with tension straps, closed the van's rear doors, and clicked his remote control to open the electric door to the garage.

Duggan, as he drove across the city, felt far more apprehensive than he normally did on jobs. His biggest concern was that someone might have seen his van parked near the spot where he had shot O'Neill and that police had put out an alert for it. Although more police cars than usual were patrolling, white vans were everywhere too. Which was exactly why Duggan had bought such a ubiquitous vehicle in the first place. When the tight-fitting sniper flap at the rear of the van was clicked into place, it would take a close examination to distinguish it from any of the others out on the streets. In any case, that morning he had also put on a fresh set of plates, stolen by one of his volunteers from an identical van at an accident repair center the previous week.

Less than ten minutes later, without having noticed any police surveillance, the two men were outside Higgins's unit on the industrial park. As Duggan had expected, the large vehicle entrance to the garage was already open. He knew Higgins was an early riser.

"Just leave this to me. It could be tricky," Duggan said to his colleague.

"Because of Dennehy?" O'Driscoll asked.

Duggan nodded. He strolled into the garage and raised a hand when Higgins looked up from his workbench. But the older man didn't return the greeting. Instead he stood staring and slowly removed his large polycarbonate welding glasses.

Duggan stopped when he saw Higgins's reaction.

Higgins slowly walked up to him. "You bastard," he said. "What the hell? I wasn't expecting to see you here again, after what happened."

"Whoa, hold on a minute," Duggan said. "What are you talking about?"

"What d'you think I mean. Martin Dennehy. That's who I'm talking about."

Duggan stared at him. "Don't make accusations when you don't have any proof."

"I don't need proof. I know what happened," Arthur said, almost choking on the words.

"No, you don't. Anyway, he was a tout. A complete tout. In the pocket of the Brits. He had what was coming to him. I warned him several times."

"Bullshit," Higgins said. "You're a liar. I don't know what you're doing here, but just get out of my yard. Go on, move. Out, now."

"I need a repair done first, on that welding job you did. You didn't finish it properly. A joint's come undone," Duggan said in a level tone.

"No way. You'll have to get somebody else to do that for you. I'm not touching it." Higgins folded his arms and stood, legs apart, staring Duggan in the eyes.

Duggan shook his head, reached inside his jacket, and took out a Browning pistol, which he pointed at Higgins. "You'll do it now," he said quietly.

Higgins slowly unfolded his arms and raised his palms in front of him. "There's no need for that. Leave it here, I'll do it, then. You can collect it Wednesday. I've got something urgent I'm trying to finish today." He nodded at the workbench behind him.

"Nope, it's got to be now, right now, buddy."

"Today? Why today?"

"Because I've got a job I need it for."

* * *

Monday, January 28, 2013
  Belfast

. . .

Once the welding repair had been completed to Duggan's satisfaction, he took a circuitous route through Belfast to his next destination, first driving southwest along the Anderson-stown and Stewartstown roads before cutting a sharp right northward toward Hannahstown.

His encounter with Higgins had left him feeling uneasy. He never planned to force the old man to do the welding repair at gunpoint. After all, Higgins had been a loyal servant to the republican movement over several decades. But Duggan had no other option.

Arthur's relationship with Dennehy must have been closer than Duggan had imagined.

"What you going to do about Arthur now?" O'Driscoll asked. "I hope he doesn't start playing silly buggers."

Duggan shrugged. "I'll sort it out with Higgins, talk him around. He won't do anything stupid."

BBC Radio Ulster, which Duggan had tuned into on the van radio, was focused on the G8 meeting. There were interviews with political leaders, commentators, and other random analysts, who queued up to give their interpretation of what the event signified in terms of Irish politics and the regional economy.

Duggan steered the van past the Lámh Dhearg Gaelic football club, just off Upper Springfield Road, and continued out of the city and up the hill until he reached a junction signposted to Black Mountain and Divis, off to the right.

There he took a narrow, potholed road past a few houses and small farms, where cows and horses grazed. The number of trees diminished rapidly the higher he climbed, and the landscape turned to moorland.

There was only one car at the Divis and Black Mountain National Trust tourist parking lot, a rough expanse of concrete near the top of the hill. It probably belonged to a dog walker, so there was nothing for him to worry about there. He turned right, the giant TV transmission aerial now ahead of him, and drove another few hundred yards along a single lane until he reached the empty, much smaller parking lot next to the low-slung stone coffee shop, which was closed. It was the same place where he and Dennehy had met Kane at the beginning of the month.

Duggan pulled into a space in the parking lot, making sure he could see back down the road where he had come from, and glanced at his watch. It was quarter past ten. Despite the unplanned visit to Higgins he was still on schedule.

Now he needed to wait for the man to arrive. He knew from the reconnaissance trips he had carried out over the previous couple of weeks what the guy's timetable was almost certain to be. He also knew that the presence of white vans in the coffee shop parking lot was unlikely to attract any attention: they were there every day because of ongoing maintenance work.

"He'll be here by about half past. You can set your clock by it," Duggan said.

A couple of miles or so to the south, three helicopters flew slowly over the city of Belfast, which was spread out far below them at the base of Black Mountain. Another helicopter was stationary, hovering somewhat nearer to them, over the boundary between the Whiterock and Highfield areas where the school visit was due to take place later that day.

"The police chopper guys'll be getting nervous now, ahead of the G8," O'Driscoll said.

"So they should be," Duggan said. "Doubt they'll be looking up here, though." Sure enough, the helicopters remained in a steady formation over the city itself, sweeping across from east to west, roughly in a line that appeared to follow Falls Road.

To Duggan's relief, there was no sign of rain and none was forecast, although there was a blanket of white clouds above them, with only the occasional break that allowed the sun to shine through. There was little chance of the school football match being called off for bad weather.

Just over a quarter of an hour later, another white van appeared in the distance near the National Trust parking lot and slowly made its way up the lane to the small coffee shop parking lot. Duggan sat up in his seat.

The van, a Mercedes Sprinter, turned into the parking lot and came to a halt twenty yards away from Duggan's vehicle, its rear doors pointing toward him. The driver, who Duggan recognized from his previous reconnaissance trips, got out, walked around to the back of his van, and opened the rear doors. Inside he could see the same pale green quad bike with a storage box attached that he had seen the man using before.

"Time to move, Kieran boy," Duggan said. They had previously agreed that Duggan would make the initial contact with the van driver, and then O'Driscoll would follow.

"Yep. Go for it," O'Driscoll said.

Duggan pulled his woolen hat down over his forehead and ears, put on a pair of black-framed plastic glasses, and opened his door. He walked toward the man, who was dressed in a yellow high-visibility waterproof jacket with the words *Belfast Landscaping* emblazoned across the back in black four-inch-high capital letters.

"Hi, mate," Duggan said. "Are you on path repair duty again today?"

The man jumped slightly, turned around, and looked at him. "Yes, that's right. Why?"

Duggan removed his Browning from his pocket and pointed it at the man. "Not today, you're not. You can take a break. Day off. Throw your phone and the keys for the van and that quad bike on the floor."

The workman's eyes widened, and he raised both hands to above shoulder level. "What is this? I haven't done anything. What's this all about?" His voice rose sharply.

"You've done nothing, and nothing will happen to you provided you do exactly what I tell you," Duggan said. "Now put the phone and keys on the floor."

The workman slowly reached into his pocket, removed his phone and two sets of keys, and threw them on the ground.

"Good," Duggan said, as he picked up the keys. "Take that jacket off, then get into the van, slowly, and lie down behind that quad bike."

The man slowly removed his jacket and climbed into the van, just as O'Driscoll appeared at Duggan's shoulder. When the man was flat on his back behind the quad bike, O'Driscoll climbed in and secured his wrists and ankles with white plastic ties while Duggan pointed his pistol at him. Then he removed a piece of cloth from his pocket, stuffed it in the man's mouth, and wound some thick masking tape several times around the man's head to hold the gag in place.

That done, O'Driscoll fetched some thin rope from Duggan's van and lashed the man's wrists to the frame of the Mercedes on the passenger side, at about a foot above floor level, and his ankles to the frame on the driver's side at a similar height.

"That'll stop him from banging on the floor to attract attention," O'Driscoll said. Duggan nodded his approval. "Yeah, good idea."

Duggan threw the man's yellow Belfast Landscaping jacket to O'Driscoll. "There you go, team jacket. Stick that on," he said. There was another matching jacket lying on the floor, but Duggan ignored it.

He grabbed two shovels, a rake, and a fork from a rack on

one side of the Mercedes and threw them out of the back of the van.

Then he took a ramp that was lying on the van floor, put it in position, climbed onto the quad bike, and started it up. He slowly reversed it down the ramp onto the parking lot.

Finally Duggan shut the Mercedes van door and locked it.

"Right. We need to go and do some hard labor," Duggan said, picking up the tools he had thrown out. "Path repair work." He grinned at O'Driscoll and threw him the quad bike keys. "At least, you can do the hard labor. You drive this guy's quad, and I'll get the Grizzly out of our van."

CHAPTER THIRTY-NINE

Monday, January 28, 2013
  Belfast

It was Noreen who got back to Jayne first. She sent a list of potential vehicle mechanics and welders with known republican links who might have carried out the customization work on Duggan's van.

Noreen had run a search through the files on MI5's system and had come up with a list of four possibles, all small one- or two-man businesses.

One, based in Derry, was a vehicle repair garage run by a known Republican who had been active in the past. Another was a commercial truck customization business based in Antrim, and there were two in Belfast, fairly close to each other, in the Andersonstown area.

Johnson leaned over Jayne's shoulder and scanned down the list she was reading on her phone. The note from Noreen said these were just the most likely candidates, known to have done work for dissidents previously. She had restricted the list to those four, given that time was critically short. But she added that there were lots of other options she could have included in a second tier of names.

"We're just not going to have time to get to places like Derry or Antrim," Johnson said. "We need to be here, so let's try the Belfast ones." He pointed to the two bottom names on the list.

"Agreed," Jayne said. "Let's get moving."

"She's obviously not made any progress on the Nottingham files?"

"No, otherwise she'd have mentioned it."

The clattering of three police helicopters flying low overhead in a slow-moving formation accompanied their ten-minute journey down Falls Road and then Glen Road, to the Andersonstown suburb.

The first business, McCague's Body Shop, was tucked away in a dilapidated corrugated steel unit in a plot sandwiched between Glen Road and Shaws Road. Outside, two rusty cars were propped up on bricks, minus their wheels, and a black puddle of sludgy engine oil had gathered in a dip in the concrete yard.

Johnson and Jayne got out and banged on the large steel vehicle entrance and on a small side door. But there was no response, and the unit looked deserted.

"We haven't got time to hang around. Let's move on. Next one," Johnson said.

Jayne gave him directions to the next business, Arthur Higgins Welders, in an industrial park about two miles from McCague's.

The three helicopters sweeping across the center of Belfast had now been joined by a fourth, which was hovering over the suburbs slightly farther to the west.

The industrial park was somewhat run-down but busy. Cars and vans were parked outside most of the units, and men were loading and unloading vehicles with boxes and crates.

They found Arthur Higgins Welders in the corner, next to a Chinese food importer. At least this one was open. Johnson parked the Mazda outside, and they walked in through the vehicle entrance.

There was only one person inside: a gray-haired man in blue overalls who was watching a small Ford van as it rose slowly on a mechanical vehicle inspection platform. When he saw them, he pressed a big red button, and the platform squeaked to a halt; then he walked slowly toward them, his lips pressed together.

"Can I help?" the man asked, looking at them from beneath bushy eyebrows that were lowered so far Johnson could only partly see his eyes.

"We're looking for Arthur Higgins," Johnson said.

"You've found him."

"Okay, good," Johnson said. "I'm really sorry to bother you, as I can see you're very busy here, so I'll be as quick as I can."

"Right."

"We're actually investigators, private investigators, just trying to locate someone you may know. So just a quick question. It's about a man named Dessie Duggan."

Higgins's eyes flickered and his chin jerked a fraction. "You're American. What sort of investigators are you, and why are you looking for Duggan?"

Jayne cut in. "We're private investigators, nothing to do with police or intelligence, but it's related to the G8 meeting. We need to find Duggan for security reasons, and we gather that he's had some welding work done on a white van. So we're just checking people who might have helped him with that work. It's him we would be interested in, definitely not the person who did the work."

Higgins looked first at Jayne, then at Johnson, through gray eyes surrounded by a spiderweb of wrinkles. He looked like a veteran chess player, calculating his next move, Johnson thought.

"He might have been here, yes," the old man said eventually.

Johnson breathed in sharply. "Okay, when was that?"

Higgins looked at his watch, a cheap black plastic digital device. "I'd say about an hour ago."

Shit! Johnson tried to calm his thoughts. He felt surprised that the man had given him that much information. "An *hour* ago? Had you done some work for him on the van before that?"

"Yes," Higgins said. "A couple of weeks ago."

"Right. A Volkswagen Transporter, by any chance, plain white, no markings or logos on it?"

"That's right, a tall VW. Not the normal height, and no markings."

"And the work you did, that involved putting an opening, a flap, in the back, did it?" Johnson asked.

Arthur shrugged and said nothing for several seconds. Then he said, "Might have done."

"Thanks, that's helpful to know," Johnson said. "And can you remember the plate number?"

Higgins groaned and closed one eye, clearly trying to recall the number. "I think it was a 55 plate, but beyond that, I can't remember. Had no reason to make a note of it."

Johnson had enough detail about the van, but a key question remained unanswered. "Why did he come back this morning?" Johnson asked.

"That was to do with another job I did for him at the same time," Higgins said. "Some welding had come undone, and he came in and insisted I fix it immediately."

"And was the welding work also on the van?" Jayne asked.

"Nope. That was on a quad bike, a Yamaha Grizzly, a big beast. The welding work I did for him was to install a flat rack on the back of it, a kind of detachable platform made of black metal sheeting. The sort of thing you could strap boxes to—it was flat. He had the Grizzly in the back of his van."

A quad bike. What the hell? Johnson tugged at the old injury at the top of his right ear. "Did he say where he was going or what he was going to do with the quad?"

"He said he had a job on today, that's all. That's why it was urgent," Higgins said. He folded his arms and chewed at the inside of his cheek.

"Did he say what?" Jayne asked.

"Nope. I wasn't really in a position to ask too many questions."

"Why?" Jayne asked.

"Because the bastard was pointing a bloody gun straight at me at the time."

Jayne looked at Johnson and raised her eyebrows, then glanced back at Higgins. "And you don't know any more than that about what he's intending to do? No hints?"

Higgins shook his head. "No. None at all."

"So what color was the quad bike?"

"A dark green color," Higgins said.

It didn't make any sense at all to Johnson. If Duggan was going to make a quiet, stealthy attempt to assassinate one or both of the main leaders of the western world or Conor Campbell, then using a noisy quad bike as his means of transport surely wasn't the way to go about it. Where the hell was he going to use a quad bike in the city? And for what? *A platform?*

He checked his watch. The G8 school visit was due to begin in forty-five minutes.

CHAPTER FORTY

Monday, January 28, 2013
Belfast

As soon as Johnson and Jayne left Higgins, Johnson sent a text message to Campbell to update him. But instead of a reply, he got a call two minutes later from Arnside, the assistant chief constable.

Arnside wasted no time with pleasantries beyond explaining that, as Johnson had assumed, Campbell was now fully occupied dealing with the Obama and Cameron visit.

Johnson gave Arnside a quick verbal account of the conversation with Higgins and details of the dark green quad bike with the custom-built platform on the back. "The big question now is why Duggan needs a quad," Johnson said.

"Yes, agreed. I assume he needs it for access to somewhere. Hold the line." Johnson heard Arnside barking orders, presumably into a police radio, first to what sounded like helicopter control, then to the armed response unit.

Arnside came back on the line. "I'm at Falls Park on a

chopper, but I want you to go to the school, as I'll be traveling there soon. By the time you get to the school we'll have decided on a plan. You'll find heavy security, but I'm instructing them to let you pass. Have you got passports with you?"

"Yes, we have."

"Okay. Just show them at the checkpoints," Arnside said. "Get there as quickly as you can, and call me if you pick up any more information." He asked Johnson to confirm his car registration plate, gave him his secure cell phone number, and then hung up.

Johnson and Jayne got back into the Mazda and set off. It was clear to Johnson, once he got back on Falls Road and within a couple of miles of the Whiteside school and city center, that the security operation underway in Belfast was of battlefield dimensions. The place was now crawling with police vehicles, motorcycle cops, armed officers at makeshift checkpoints, and dogs with their handlers.

Johnson went through a police checkpoint but then pulled onto the side of the road next to a small supermarket on Falls Road, just a few hundred yards before the next checkpoint, which he could see ahead.

To him, Arnside's instructions sounded intuitively wrong.

"What *are* you doing?" Jayne asked. She sounded exasperated.

"This doesn't feel right," Johnson said. "There seems little point in us going to the school when Duggan's likely to strike from farther away."

What had Moira told him, when they were sipping whiskey on her sofa. The conversation seemed like months ago now.

His friends called him the Dentist because they said he was so accurate, he could take out a tooth from a mile away.

"Maybe. But where, though?" Jayne said. "Police seem to

have all the bases covered. He wouldn't get near the place with that van of his, surely?"

Johnson shook his head. "No, he wouldn't." He leaned back against the driver's seat headrest. "At least, you wouldn't have thought so. But he's done it before, obviously. That's why they've never caught him. A clever bastard."

He scratched his chin and glanced at Jayne. "Come on, think. Now's the time for some brain work. What are his options?"

"Well, if he's a sniper, he needs a line of sight to his target. I'm thinking high-rise tower blocks, apartments, offices."

"Agreed. But why does he need the quad bike? That's the issue. Unless it's for escape purposes, to get down narrow alleys or something," Johnson said. "Anyway, let's drive on and see if we can spot any buildings within range that he could operate from."

He continued through four more police checkpoints, each time producing his and Jayne's passports and giving Arnside's name as a reference, until he got onto Springfield Road, within half a mile of the school. He pulled onto the side of the road again.

Johnson shook his head. "There's nothing. I don't see any obvious building where he could operate and stand a hope of escaping. The taller blocks of flats are too far into the city." He got out of the car and walked a few yards down the road, took out his phone, and used his maps app to calculate the distance to the taller buildings near the city center.

Jayne also got out and leaned back against the car door, her arms folded.

Two marked police BMW X5s roared past at high speed, sirens blaring, up Springfield Road toward the school. Behind them, three police motorcycle police followed at a slightly less frantic pace. To the east of the city, a large helicopter took off and headed toward them. As it drew nearer, Johnson recognized it as a Chinook.

"I'm guessing that's a mile to the city," Jayne said. "I think one of those tower blocks would have to be the favorite. That was where the snipers on both sides sometimes operated from when I was based here."

"No, it's a mile and a half," Johnson said, peering at his phone screen. "I just don't see it working. And it still doesn't explain the quad bike."

He turned around and glanced up at the hill overlooking Belfast, Black Mountain, which stood behind him.

Jayne saw him looking up. "No, that's even farther away. There's no way," she said.

But Johnson wasn't thinking about the distance. Rather, the image of Black Mountain from this angle reminded him instantly of what he had seen lying next to the Leon Uris novel on the kitchen countertop in Duggan's kitchen during his first solo visit to the house. It was a large-scale Ordnance Survey map of Black Mountain. The photograph on the map's cover had been almost identical to the view he was now looking at.

"Sonofabitch, it's the mountain. That explains the quad bike," Johnson said softly. He turned to Jayne. "I remember now. I saw a detailed map of the damn mountain in Duggan's kitchen. Where else would he get a clear line of fire from around here? There's nothing. It's the only option. Yes, it looks a hell of distance, but how far is it actually?"

Johnson went back to the maps app on his phone and tapped away for several seconds. "I think that ridge up there is probably a mile from the school. Less than it looks. And the key thing is the height. It gives him an angle, a line of sight."

"True. But none of the other shootings have been that far,

and surely the police would have the mountain covered," Jayne said. "The helicopters would be watching it."

"You would expect so. But I'm going to call Arnside and ask."

Johnson dialed the number for Arnside, leaving his phone on loudspeaker so Jayne, standing next to him, could hear. He briefed Arnside quickly on his thoughts and the map he remembered seeing.

Arnside sounded confident. "We've covered the mountain, had choppers flying over it regularly and patrols up there. It's a very long distance, and more to the point, it's very open and exposed. If anyone tried anything up there, the choppers would see him. There's no cover, not even any trees; it's all grass and moorland. I'm certain he would want to get nearer and have more cover. It's a damn long shot from up there."

"I see your point, Mr. Arnside," Johnson said, "but the kind of terrain you've described might explain *exactly* why he needs a quad bike. Can you do another security sweep of the mountain, just to be sure? There's nothing to lose, is there? All we're looking for is a white van and a quad."

There was a pause. Then Arnside sounded suddenly decisive. "Why not? You're right, there's nothing to lose. Let's do the sweep. Turn around and come back to Falls Park right now. You can come on board my chopper—you might have something to add to the party. Where are you?"

Johnson gave a brief description of their location.

"Falls Park is only three or four minutes from there," Arnside snapped. "Quick as you can. I'll call you back in a minute. I need to prime the crew."

Johnson and Jayne climbed into the car. He knew exactly where Falls Park was, as they had passed by it on several occasions. He started the engine, did a U-turn, and accelerated with a squeal of tires back in the direction they had come from.

Johnson was speeding along Falls Road when Arnside called back. Jayne picked up Johnson's phone and accepted the call, putting the device on speaker so Johnson could hear and talk.

"The crew's preparing for takeoff, so you need to move," Arnside said. "There's space for only one, so I can't get your colleague on with you. Can she drive the car back to the school?"

Jayne leaned toward Johnson's phone and spoke. "It's Jayne Robinson here. Yes, that's fine, can do."

"Good. Get moving. I'll see you at the park. You can't miss us. I'll tell our guys at the gate to let you through." He ended the call.

Jayne's phone beeped. She read the message.

"That was from Noreen," she said. "She's got hold of that old contact at Nottinghamshire police. Apparently they've found a file in a vault there she thinks is the one we need. But get this—they can't release it without the authority of the Northern Ireland chief constable."

She slapped her hand against the car seat. "What a joke. He's never going to give consent. Not when it could mean signing his own downfall. We've got no chance."

Johnson sighed. "We'll have to sort that out later." He turned sharp right toward the park. Time was running out.

He wasn't looking forward to getting into a helicopter. The last time he'd been anywhere near a Police Service of Northern Ireland helicopter, he'd seen it shot down and the chief constable shot dead. Duggan's work.

* * *

Monday, January 28, 2013

Belfast

Duggan parked the Grizzly about thirty yards south of the gravel path in the middle of a stretch of heather and grass. This was going to be the risky part: getting safely into position without being spotted from the air.

He glanced up at the police helicopters that were still hovering in a formation of three a couple of miles away, where Falls Road wound its way toward the city center. Another helicopter hovered nearer to them, about a mile away, above Whitefield Integrated Primary School, where the president of the United States was expected soon.

But none of the aircraft seemed interested in what he was doing on Black Mountain. As he watched, one of the trio over the city center peeled away and descended, landing in or near Falls Park, Duggan guessed. That helped—one less pair of eyes in the sky to watch him.

Duggan removed the long black case containing his Barrett and ammunition from the rack at the back of the Grizzly, together with two other bags. One of them contained the two vinyl sheets, the other the ghillie suit.

He unclipped the aluminum sniper platform and pulled on the ghillie suit, which—to his surprise—fitted him perfectly.

A few minutes later Duggan was in position about twenty-five yards away from the Grizzly.

Observers from the air would be unlikely to give the Grizzly a second glance, unless they came very close to it. It was covered with a vinyl sheet imprinted with a high-definition photograph of the heather and grasses that Duggan had taken using his drone on top of Black Mountain. From above the Grizzly would appear to be simply a mound of earth covered in vegetation.

Duggan placed his portable sniper's platform on the heather and covered it with the smaller vinyl sheet, which bore a similar imprint to the larger one.

The ghillie suit made him look like a walking, talking bush made of heather and blended perfectly into the terrain. Even a trained eye would have struggled to spot him once he was horizontal.

He lay flat next to the platform with his Barrett—draped with the small ghillie—resting on it.

Over the years Duggan had found that it was the small touches, the attention to detail, that had kept him free and undetected in the various operations he had carried out. The ghillie for the rifle barrel and the high-powered twenty-seven magnification Schmidt & Bender scope mounted on top of it were important. In nature, there are no straight lines, and the human eye is naturally drawn to man-made items with defined edges such as rifles and platforms. By disguising the barrel, Duggan was maximizing his chances of going undis-covered.

He glanced over his shoulder. There, fifty yards away, O'Driscoll, wearing the yellow Belfast Landscaping jacket, was pretending to be busy with his shovel. Next to him stood the company quad bike with its storage box of equipment. Any police helicopter that had surveyed the mountain over recent days would not notice anything different about the man going about his low-key path maintenance work. He was part of the scenery. Indeed, the eye would be drawn to him and away from anyone else nearby—which was Duggan's intention.

Ideally, Duggan would have liked O'Driscoll to act as spotter for him, working with a high-powered spotting scope to check the target and whether he had hit it or not. But to do that in such an open position was extremely risky and significantly raised the likelihood of being seen. Instead he would have to rely on his own eyes and judgment.

Duggan unfolded the inverted V-shaped rifle bipod and adjusted it until the height of the barrel felt comfortable and correctly positioned, with sufficient pressure on it to avoid the rifle hopping around when he fired. That would be particularly important with no spotter—he would need to ensure the rifle stayed as stable as possible immediately after firing so he could continue to get a clear enough view through the scope to know whether he had hit or missed.

He set the sixteen-inch variable power scope to its highest magnification of twenty-seven times, placed his right eye a few inches back from the powerful scope, and rotated the eyepiece until the playing field of the Whiterock school far below him came into sharp, close focus. Now that he could see every detail of his target area, he moved the reticle until the crosshairs were in the center of the football goalposts.

Duggan had already zeroed the rifle following his previous visit to the mountain, setting up the scope for a distance of 1,610 yards. That was the distance his Vectronix range finder had shown from his firing position to the school, allowing for the downhill angle.

Now he needed to fine-tune his settings to allow for wind speed and direction. He took his Kestrel 4500 meter from his pocket. The size of a phone handset with a miniturbine set into the top to measure wind speed, it would calculate all the ballistics settings he would need, based on the details he had already inputted for his gun, including the scope, the reticle, and the .50-caliber BMG rounds he was using.

To Duggan's relief, there was only a slight wind, even on the top of Black Mountain. The Kestrel confirmed this, showing a breeze of two miles per hour traveling right to left as he faced his target. Duggan expected that, down at the school, the breeze would be even less.

He adjusted his scope, turning the windage turret on the side of the device to shift his aim slightly to the right, to take into account the wind conditions.

As he did so, Duggan's thoughts drifted back to the twist of fate that had brought the stolen laptop with the pale blue cover into his possession, thanks to a simple house burglary at Will Doyle's house, carried out by a junior brigade volunteer a year earlier.

The volunteer had later found on the laptop a copy of Doyle's journal from his time in the British army in 1984 and had immediately realized the link to Dessie Duggan.

When the youngster had arrived on Duggan's doorstep, carrying the laptop and its incriminating contents, Duggan suddenly had found himself, after years of searching, with all he needed to identify the killers of his father, Alfie.

Duggan had expected a long battle to identify all six. But he had given the same volunteer the task of obtaining that detail, and within days, the young man had wormed his way into the British army's human resources archives via yet another volunteer in the department and had come up with a roster of men in the unit operating in south Armagh at that time. After that, matching names between the roster and Doyle's journal had been easy. Of the six soldiers, five were now dead. And the sixth was about to meet a similar fate.

Duggan's only regret was that he had had to remove the risk that the brigade volunteer might tell other people what he had found on the laptop. He therefore killed the young house burglar and fed his body to the pigs at Davy's farm.

Duggan shook his head, as if to switch his train of thought, then relaxed and concentrated once again on the view through the scope.

Now all he had to do was wait for his target to arrive.

CHAPTER FORTY-ONE

Monday, January 28, 2013
  Belfast

One second, the twin engines of the Eurocopter EC145 were idling. The next, a high-pitched whine penetrated the earphones Johnson had just put on. The aircraft bellowed and clattered, and a couple of seconds after he had fastened his safety belt, it took off, leaving his stomach behind on the ground.

The Police Service of Northern Ireland chopper was the same model Duggan had shot down in Crossmaglen. Johnson clutched the side of his seat on the left side of the helicopter and glanced at the pilot and copilot up front, sitting straight-backed in front of the cockpit display, which was shrouded by a black hood.

He glanced at Arnside, an athletic-looking man of about fifty, who sat opposite on the right of the cabin, looking anxiously out of the acrylic glass that surrounded the cockpit and cabin.

The other two seats were occupied by armed officers dressed in black, wearing body armor and carrying what Johnson recognized from their compact, distinct outline as Heckler & Koch G36C assault rifles, with holstered pistols on their waists. It crossed Johnson's mind that none of their body armor would be effective against a .50-caliber round.

The helicopter rose sharply, banked off to the left, and accelerated toward Black Mountain, which Johnson estimated was probably a mile and a half northeast of their takeoff point.

As they rose, the sun broke briefly through the clouds, casting a bright swathe of light over the Harland & Wolff shipyard and its giant twin yellow cranes in the eastern part of the city to their right, before disappearing again seconds later.

Arnside turned toward Johnson. "You'll hear the external feed on your headphones coming from the guys on the ground down at the school. That's Hotel Victor."

Already the Eurocopter was at the same height as the mountain and crossing the line of green trees at the foot of the escarpment which rose up to over twelve hundred feet above sea level.

"We're looking for a white van and a dark green quad bike with a flat black platform attached to the back," Arnside reminded the crew over the intercom. "Keep going. We'll check out the road to the transmission tower."

The chopper continued for several more seconds, until the copilot spoke again over the intercom. "There, sir, ahead, there's two white vans in the car park at the top."

Arnside leaned forward. "I see them. Can you pull in close and go lower so we can take a look?"

The pilot nodded, and the chopper slowed and descended until it was hovering perhaps a hundred and fifty feet above the two vans.

"No markings on either van, sir," the copilot said.

"Yes, that's what we were told, it's got no markings," Johnson said. "But one van, not two."

"Sir, I've seen vans here a few times in recent weeks when I've been overflying between base and the airport," the copilot said. "I've seen men doing repair work on the paths and walkways."

Arnside nodded. "Okay."

This was wasting time. There was clearly nobody in sight near the vans. "A sniper's not going to be operating from here," Johnson said. "If he were going to use the mountain, he'd be on the edge of the ridge, overlooking the city. Not here where he can't see anything."

"Yes," said Arnside. "Agreed. Get over to the edge. We'll take a sweep down the ridge."

The chopper rose, turned half a circle, and accelerated back toward the city. As soon as it reached the edge of the ridge, where the ground dropped sharply away toward Belfast far below, the pilot did a left turn, slowed, and at a height of about two hundred feet, began to follow a footpath that tracked the top of the ridge, with the city below now to their right.

A message from someone on the ground crackled in Johnson's ear. "Police Four Five, this is Hotel Victor. We have Renegade arrival on site in two minutes. Over."

Johnson looked at Arnside, raised his eyebrows, and mouthed, "Obama?" The assistant chief constable nodded.

Arnside spoke into his headset microphone. "Hotel Victor, this is Police Four Five. Roger that. We checked the Black Mountain car park. There are two white vans, no personnel visible. Now sweeping the ridge south to north. Over"

A reply came back. "Police Four Five. This is Hotel Victor. Roger that. Over."

After a mile or so Johnson could see the path curled back around to the left, away from the ridge and toward the tall television transmission tower farther to the northeast, away from the city.

Then the copilot called out. "Man down below there, working." His voice rose sharply. "And he's got a bloody quad bike parked on the grass near him."

Both Johnson and Arnside leaned forward. A man was indeed working on the path, spade in hand, shoveling gravel from a heap at the side of the path and spreading it over the path.

"Keep her steady," Arnside said. "Let's take a look at him."

Johnson watched as the man stopped work, leaned on his spade, and stared up at the helicopter hovering above. Then Johnson switched his attention to the quad bike, which was parked a few yards off the path. It was pale green in color.

"Nothing obviously suspicious," Arnside said.

"No," the copilot chipped in. "Looks like one of the men I've seen up here working on this path over the past few weeks. Same uniform, same logo. Same pale green quad bike. We're looking for a dark green quad, right?" The workman was wearing a yellow jacket that bore the logo Belfast Landscaping in large black letters on the back.

"Hang on a minute," Johnson said. "There's one quad bike and one man, but there were two large vans back at the parking lot. Have you noticed whether there's been two vans there every day?"

"I think just one, from memory," the copilot said.

"Can we just move the chopper a little closer to it so we can have a look?" Johnson asked.

Nobody replied, but the pilot edged the Eurocopter forward until it was directly above the unoccupied quad bike, which to Johnson looked like any other quad he'd seen and had some kind of storage box on the back, containing tools.

It was definitely not a flat black rack of the kind Higgins had described.

Another message came over the intercom from someone in the network down on the ground. "This is Hotel Victor. Expecting Renegade arrival in thirty seconds. Over."

"I don't think this is what we're looking for," Arnside said. "We'd best keep moving and check the rest of this ridge. Time's almost run out on us. Keep going."

The pilot, who had swiveled to look at Arnside, turned back around again to look out his windshield and reached for the cyclic stick in front of him. He nudged it forward to get the aircraft moving ahead again, causing the nose to dip a little. As he did so, the sun broke through a gap in the blanket of clouds above them.

The angle of the helicopter gave Johnson a clearer view of the stretch of ground south of the gravel path. That was when he saw something that caught his attention.

The sun shining from the south suddenly cast a large dark shadow from what looked like a mound of earth, covered in heather and grass. It was out of character with the rest of the flat, featureless terrain. Before the sun had come out, there was no shadow, and the mound had been almost invisible.

"Hang on a minute," Johnson said into his headset microphone. "What's that mound down there, where the shadow's coming from." He looked at Arnside.

"*What?*" the policeman barked.

"The shadow from the mound of heather," Johnson said.

Over the intercom, the voice of the police officer on the ground crackled into Johnson's ear. "This is Hotel Victor. Renegade now on site. Repeat, Renegade now on school site. Over."

The pilot, listening on the intercom, nudged the cyclic back again and got the chopper back into a hover, then turned it so Johnson had a clearer view below.

The copilot picked up a set of binoculars and focused on the mound. "Looks like a tarpaulin, not actual heather. It's a flat surface," he said.

Johnson caught a glimpse from the side angle of the shadow again, and this time it was obvious. The shadow had an edge that was almost straight, not the kind of outline that would be thrown off by a mound of earth.

"There's a cover disguise thing on top of something there," Johnson said, his voice rising. "It's a camouflage. Is it a sniper platform in there?"

Arnside reacted instantly. "Shit. Get the chopper down, *now,*" he shouted. He turned toward the two armed officers and addressed them by their call signs. "Delta, Zebra, get out the second we touch down. Everyone else, seat belts off and hit the floor if you can."

The pilot began to lower the aircraft rapidly toward the rough carpet of heather, moss, and grasses. Seconds later, it touched down with a bump, lurched sideways, and came safely to rest.

The helicopter's doors clicked open, and the two armed officers leaped out of the right-side door.

"Delta, focus on the sniper hide. Zebra, check the path repair guy first," Arnside shouted.

"Roger. He's leaning on his shovel," Zebra replied tersely.

As he spoke, from somewhere outside the helicopter came a sharp explosive crack—the unmistakable sound of high-powered rifle fire—that was audible even above the noise of the engines. The shot was followed immediately by another.

Both armed officers flung themselves to the ground. One rolled a few yards to the right of the helicopter, the other rolled to the left out of Johnson's line of vision, somewhere under the helicopter. He saw the man on the right lying prone on the ground, gun in hand, and then there was a loud clatter of semiautomatic fire as they raked the mound with bullets.

The rounds shredded the rear part of the cover and sent a shower of fragments of what looked like dark green plastic spiraling up into the air, partially revealing more green and black metal beneath the cover. Then the firing stopped, and Johnson watched through the Eurocopter's windshield as the officer who had been out of his sight under the helicopter ran to the contraption, dived to the ground at the side of it, and yanked off the remains of the cover.

Underneath was a dark green quad bike. But there was nobody on it and certainly nothing that resembled a sniper platform.

"What the hell's going on?" muttered Arnside over the intercom.

"Sniper somewhere," Johnson said. "I heard it. You must have done too."

"Yes, but where the hell is he, then?" Arnside paused a moment, then pressed a button on his handset. "Hotel Victor, this is Police Four Five. We have a potential crisis situation on Black Mountain, repeat, a crisis situation on Black Mountain. Suspect Tango activity in the vicinity. You will need to—"

But Arnside never completed his sentence. Instead he was overridden by another voice that burst through Johnson's headphones.

"This is Hotel Victor, repeat, this is Hotel Victor. We have a man down on school site. Repeat. We have a man down. Over."

* * *

Monday, January 28, 2013
  Belfast

. . .

The clattering of the helicopter engines behind Duggan grew nearer, causing him to tighten his jaw muscles. He didn't want to turn around to look in case the movement gave away his hidden position inside the ghillie suit.

But he knew it had to be a police chopper.

Now what? Was it just a routine flypast, a box-ticking exercise? There had been nothing to suggest the police had any reason to come looking on Black Mountain.

It was true that Johnson's escape from the underground bunker had given Duggan a lot of concern, but the more he thought it through, the more he was certain there was nothing that could possibly lead the American investigator here. The two men he believed to be touts and who might have steered either Johnson or the police in this direction were dead.

From the air, there could be nothing that might make the helicopter crew think O'Driscoll was anything other than one of the ordinary workmen who had been on the site for some time. And Duggan was very confident that his ghillie suit meant there was nothing to give away his position from the air.

The helicopter will go away soon.

The problem now was, if he allowed himself to be distracted, he was likely to miss the narrow window of opportunity he needed.

Duggan kept his eye firmly fixed on the reticle in his scope. Through the eyepiece he saw a group of six police motorcyclists approach the school gate, followed by a posse of black BMW X5s, three Chevy Suburban SUVs, and two enormous Cadillac limousines flying the American flag. There were more 4x4s and motorcycle police riding behind.

This was it. A greeting party of about fifteen people, some

whose faces Duggan recognized, others he didn't, congregated at the school gate. The men were mostly wearing smart black suits and ties, some of them with overcoats, others without. There were five women, all wearing coats of various hues.

One man stepped forward and opened the passenger side doors of one of the Cadillacs as soon as the motorcade came to a halt.

The noise of the chopper behind Duggan was now deafening, but he could tell it was still hovering well above the ground. He just had to hope the ghillie suit was doing what it was intended to do.

Duggan focused hard on the rear door of the Cadillac, but he was unable to get a clear line of sight because of the people who were partly obscuring the car. It was like peering through a forest of dark coats.

He saw one dark-haired man climb out of the rear door nearest to him. That looked like David Cameron, the British prime minister. He could also see on the other side of the car another man getting out, presumably Barack Obama. Then he caught a glimpse of a man with short iron-gray hair emerging from one of the BMWs.

Conor Campbell.

The man on the far side of the Cadillac, definitely Obama, moved around the back of the car. He was accompanied by three men, one of them Gerry Adams, the Sinn Féin leader. The other two, with dark glasses, looked like Obama's Secret Service security detail.

Adams joined Cameron, and the two statesmen appeared to exchange a joke. Then they both turned as Campbell began ushering them between the other members of the greeting party, who separated to allow them a clear path through the school gate and into the parking lot. Behind them walked three men who were quite clearly Obama's security detail.

Duggan's finger, held loosely on the trigger of his Barrett, tightened imperceptibly.

He moved his reticle a fraction to the right until the crosshair rested on the center of his target's chest.

As he did so, the pitch of the helicopter's engines behind him changed suddenly. And in that moment he knew it was going to land.

Shit.

His plan—to wait until the group down on the school playing field was stationary—was not going to work. He couldn't wait. Indeed, this was going to end one way or another in a manner he had not intended.

But he had to finish the job.

Maybe it's my time to join the martyrs—Bobby Sands, Jim Lynagh, and the Loughgall Eight, the south Armagh brigade volunteers, Fergal Caraher. And Alfie.

He fought hard to calm himself, to go through his routine to try and relax and lower his heart rate. Though the process was engrained in him, just like his ability to ride a bicycle or drive a car, it was now proving difficult.

The line of sight to the three men became clearer after they passed through the tall blue steel school gates and onto the black tarmac of the parking lot. Duggan noticed Obama's tie flutter a little to his right; there must be a slight breeze down there, he thought, and instinctively adjusted his aim a fraction to compensate.

Now the three men were suddenly in the clear: Obama, Cameron, and the man he was going to kill—Campbell.

Duggan consciously relaxed again, despite the raucous clattering of the helicopter behind him. He tightened his finger on the trigger and then, almost without effort, pulled it back.

The Barrett recoiled a little as the .50-caliber BMG round left the barrel.

He missed Campbell. Instead, right behind him, one of the dark-suited security detail, wearing dark glasses, suddenly collapsed. Duggan caught a glimpse of a spray of red behind the man.

Feck!

Duggan had been here before. He knew from experience exactly what would happen next. There would be a second, maybe two at most, before realization dawned, and then there would be a well-drilled operation that would see the remaining security screaming at the political leaders, shielding them with their own bodies, and hustling them away to safety.

Either way, the window of opportunity to get in another shot was minuscule.

Campbell was half-turning to see what had happened behind him when Duggan pulled the trigger again.

CHAPTER FORTY-TWO

Monday, January 28, 2013
Belfast

Johnson could see from his position in the helicopter that Delta, the armed police officer crouching on his haunches next to the wrecked quad bike, was confused. With his shoulders visibly taut and his weapon at the ready, he surveyed the ground in front of him, facing toward the city of Belfast that was spread out far below. Then he looked left and right.

"Delta, what do you see?" Arnside asked.

"Can't see anything out here," came Delta's voice through a crackle of electronic distortion over the intercom, into Johnson's ear.

"There's definitely someone out there," Arnside replied, his forehead creased, eyes flicking from side to side. "We all heard the two bloody rifle shots. Can't be far away."

"But there's nowhere to hide," Delta replied.

As he spoke, there came the staccato rattle of semiautomatic gunfire from somewhere to the right of the Eurocopter.

Johnson looked out the window just in time to see the black-clad figure of Zebra, the second officer, who had been in a prone position to the right of the aircraft, slump facedown to the ground.

There was a slight pause, then more gunfire and a series of loud bangs from the front right side of the helicopter. Several holes appeared in the laminated side windows and windshield as bullets raked the right side of the fuselage. Johnson saw the pilot's head jerk forward, a spray of blood splattering the cockpit.

"Shit! It's the bloody path repair guy," yelled Arnside, looking out of the window behind the helicopter. "He's up there with a rifle. Delta, hit him."

Johnson watched as the officer code-named Delta swiveled around in his position next to the damaged quad bike and simultaneously flattened himself to the ground to a prone firing position, his assault rifle out in front. A second later, he opened fire in the direction of the path repairman, out of Johnson's sight behind the helicopter.

When the firing stopped, Arnside cut in. "Delta, did you get him?"

"No," muttered the officer. "He's flat on the ground. Couldn't get a clear shot."

Johnson looked back at the cockpit. The pilot's body, on the right, was slumped at forty-five degrees, his head a bloody mess. Johnson couldn't see if the copilot, in the left-hand seat, had been hit or not.

A second later there was another loud gunshot, followed immediately by a huge bang as the rear end of the quad bike next to Delta disintegrated into splinters of metal and plastic. A loud moan came over the intercom.

Delta lurched backward from the quad and fell on his side, motionless.

"Delta, are you okay?" Arnside shouted immediately. "What the hell was that? Delta? Do you read me? Delta?"

But there was no response.

Another massive bang followed, and the front windshield of the Eurocopter exploded, as did the window on Johnson's left. He instinctively ducked for cover behind the seat in front of him and glanced at Arnside, who had also ducked. There was a loud crackle from the intercom, but nobody spoke.

After a couple of seconds Johnson raised his head. The right-hand side of the Eurocopter's bubble-like windshield now had a large hole, surrounded by a white area and a dense spiderweb of cracks emanating at all angles across the entire width of the laminated glass

A similar hole had been bored through the cabin window to Johnson's left.

Suddenly, through the damaged windshield, beyond the motionless figure of Delta and the destroyed quad bike next to him, Johnson caught sight of a figure rising and then running full tilt through the heather, like an apparition from a horror movie, with trails of greenery and bracken billowing behind from his back. A cap he was wearing had similar camouflage materials attached, and he was carrying a long rifle in his right hand, which also trailed green camouflage.

Duggan.

Johnson unclipped his safety harness and opened the cabin door next to him on the left side of the helicopter, out of sight of Duggan, who was running away on the right side of the aircraft back toward the workman and the other quad bike on the path.

Got to stop the bastard.

As Johnson was climbing out of the Eurocopter, there was another series of gunshots and a couple of bangs from the top of the aircraft, right above the cabin, followed by an excruciating metallic squealing and groaning sound. The rotor hub mechanism had been hit. Then came another similarly loud bang from the rear of the helicopter, toward the tail. It was unclear whether it had been Duggan or the path repairman who had fired the shots.

Johnson jumped down to the ground and rolled sideways away from the helicopter toward the still figure of Delta. After a few yards he began to crawl as fast as he could until he reached Delta. The police officer was breathing, although he was unconscious, presumably as a result of being hit by some fragment on the side of the face, where a large gash was bleeding heavily.

Johnson grabbed Delta's HK G36C that was lying next to him and checked the selector. It was turned to E, the semiautomatic setting. That would do.

Then he ran back toward the Eurocopter, whose main rotor blades were now drooping on one side at an angle; the central hub that was mounted on top of the cabin was visibly shattered where the rounds had smashed into it. The smaller tail rotor was also smashed in the center where another round had cannoned into it. The helicopter was out of action.

Crouching as low as he could while continuing to run, Johnson made his way to the rear of the chopper.

As he did so he heard the raucous sound of a quad bike engine firing up. As soon as he had a clear sight around the back of the Eurocopter, he could see the quad bike with two men on it accelerating rapidly along the gravel path away from him in the direction of the parking lot.

Another few seconds and Duggan and his colleague would be out of sight on their way back to the parking lot and their getaway van.

Johnson dropped to one knee, pulled the compact, spare frame of the Heckler & Koch up to eye level, squinted through the sight, and took aim at the lower rear end of the fast-moving quad bike.

He slowly pulled the trigger, squeezing off a burst of rounds that all missed and realized he needed to adjust his aim fractionally. This time there was no mistake.

The quad bike suddenly veered off the path to the left, down the slope, then somersaulted, throwing its occupants into the heather, and came to rest upside down against a large rock.

The two men who had been thrown off the quad bike were lying motionless near the machine.

* * *

Monday, January 28, 2013
  Belfast

"Think you got the bastard," Arnside said as he dropped to the ground from the stricken Eurocopter's cabin door. He glanced at the body of Zebra, lying ten yards away, and set off immediately at a jog toward the spot where the quad bike had veered off the path.

Johnson, still carrying the Heckler & Koch, stood still for a second. Killing Duggan was the last thing he wanted. He set off after the assistant chief constable, who pulled a pistol from the holster at his hip as he ran.

He nearly twisted an ankle when his foot slipped sideways as he ran across the rough heather, but he recovered and made it to the gravel path just a few seconds after Arnside, who was moving at a speed consistent with his obvious fitness.

With a hundred yards to go, Johnson felt acutely aware

that they were both sitting ducks if Duggan was still able to use his Barrett.

But as they drew nearer, he could see the prone figures of the two men, lying a few yards away from each other on the ground. Duggan, in his ghillie suit, was closest to them, about ten yards off the path, and the other man, in the yellow Belfast Landscaping jacket, was slightly farther away.

Johnson kept his eyes glued to them, watching for any sign of movement as he ran. As they drew nearer, Johnson saw Duggan fling an arm into the air, and he almost pulled the trigger of the H&K. But he held off as the arm sagged back down again.

From behind him he heard the clatter of another helicopter approaching.

Johnson sighed in relief when he saw the long outline of the Barrett M82 lying on the ground several yards away from Duggan. Then he spotted another rifle, an AK-47, just off the path ahead of them, which the other man presumably had used to shoot Zebra and the pilot.

Duggan was writhing on the ground, facing away from them. He was clearly not a threat. The other man wasn't moving.

As Johnson and Arnside approached, Duggan rolled over to face them. Despite the ghillie suit and a swathe of camouflage paint on his face, Johnson could see he had a large cut above his right eye that was gushing blood.

"You can just feck off," Duggan said, staring at them, the whites of his eyes standing in sharp contrast to the dark paint and blood that surrounded them. "Bloody hell. Bloody police. Go on, feck off."

That was when Johnson noticed a distinct smell of petrol coming from the quad bike, which was wedged upside down at a forty-five-degree angle against a three-foot-high rock a few yards away.

Fuel was dripping from the back of the machine, in which a few bullet holes were visible. One tire had a large ragged gash in it, which had presumably caused the crash. Johnson reflected momentarily that maybe he hadn't lost all of his old shooting skills. But then he stiffened as he realized the risk from the leaking fuel.

Arnside removed one of two sets of handcuffs that were clipped to the black duty belt around his waist, bent over Duggan, and expertly secured both hands behind his back.

Then he walked to the other man and did likewise.

Duggan looked up at Johnson. "You feckin' asshole," he said. "You've just let another killer cop off the hook, you realize that?"

He must have missed, then.

"No, you're wrong," Johnson said. "If you're talking about Campbell, he's not off the hook. Far from it."

Arnside turned around. "What are you talking about? What's that about Campbell?"

"I'll explain in a minute," Johnson said.

Behind them, the thudding and clattering of the incoming helicopter engine got rapidly louder. Johnson turned to see the machine, identical to the one Johnson and Arnside had been in, descending onto a flat area around the path, roughly fifty yards away. The heather and grasses were being flattened and blown in its downdraft. Another helicopter was following it, and he heard the wailing of sirens in the distance.

As soon as the chopper landed, one of the cabin doors opened, and three armed policemen dressed in black jumped out and ran to where they were standing.

"What's the update?" Arnside said tersely.

"One American Secret Service officer dead down there, sir. He's a member of the president's security detail," one of the men said.

Johnson's stomach flipped over. Another man dead in the course of doing his job.

"The president? The PM?" Arnside asked.

"Both secured but shaken."

Johnson stepped forward. "And what about your chief constable?" he asked.

"A round just missed him by a hair's breadth, I'm told."

Johnson breathed a sigh of relief. He glanced down at Duggan, who lay staring up at them, blood still pouring from the cut over his eye.

Arnside's police radio burst into life.

"Police Four Five, this is Hotel Victor, do you read me? Over."

Arnside took the radio off his belt and pressed a button. "This is Police Four Five. We have two Tangos secured on top of Black Mountain. Both are injured but not critically. We are going to fly them back to base in Police Four Six, which has just landed here. They will then need medical assistance before we deal with them. Our pilot has been killed, Zebra is dead, Delta is injured, as is the copilot, I think. We need urgent medical help for them, too. Over."

"This is Hotel Victor. Roger that Four Five. Will send in a chopper urgently. Over."

Arnside replaced the radio on his belt and turned to one of the armed officers. "Okay, Pete, can you get these two in the chopper? We'll take them back to base."

He looked down at Duggan. "I am arresting you on suspicion of the murder of a United States Secret Service officer, and there may be other charges to follow. You do not have to say anything, but it may harm your defense if you do not mention, when questioned, something which you later rely on in court. Anything you do say may be given in evidence. Do you understand?"

Duggan gazed up at him from beneath lowered black eyebrows but said nothing.

"Do you understand?" Arnside repeated.

"What I understand," Duggan said, "is that your chief constable is a killer—he and his army death squad mates murdered my father in cold blood. He's the one you should be arresting. Not me."

He paused, then added in a tone that mimicked Arnside's. "Do you understand?"

Arnside paused for a moment and glanced at Johnson, who nodded almost imperceptibly.

"This is the only way of getting any justice around here," Duggan went on. "All you police and army feckers just look after your own, sweep it under the carpet, pretend it never happened."

Johnson shook his head. "Actually, that's where you might be wrong," he said.

Two of the armed officers lifted Duggan to his feet, each supporting him under an armpit, and frog-marched him to the helicopter.

Johnson glanced at the Barrett rifle, which was still lying on the ground. He walked over and studied it.

Arnside followed and stood beside him. "So what's all this about the chief constable?" he asked.

Johnson stared at him. "You mean you've really no idea?"

"No, I don't."

Johnson raised his eyebrows. "Okay, well, what he said all appears to be true," he said. "Campbell was one of a group from 14th Company, the Det, who gunned down Alfie Duggan at a roadblock of some kind near Crossmaglen in 1984. Dessie's shot the rest of the soldiers who were involved. Campbell's the only one left."

"Bloody hell."

"Yes, exactly."

Arnside looked uncertain. "Is it provable?"

"My understanding is that there was a file made after the Alfie Duggan shooting that named the members of the unit that were present," Johnson said. "The file disappeared from Carrickfergus during some mysterious burglary more than twenty years ago, and—"

"Yes, I know about that burglary," interrupted Arnside. "I was working there at the time, as were Campbell and . . ." His voice trailed off.

"As well as Campbell? Campbell was working at Carrickfergus when the burglary took place?"

Arnside's eyes took on a glazed look. "Yes. And not just Campbell. He was friends with Eric Simonson, who was also there."

"They were both working at the facility?" Johnson asked.

"Yes, it wouldn't have been all that long after they moved from the army to the police—a few years, maybe, I don't know. They were obviously quite junior guys in the RUC at the time."

This is it, Johnson thought. *I've nailed them.*

He fought to remain composed. "Okay, well, did you know that copies of those files had been made before that burglary by the team investigating various shoot-to-kill incidents involving the army in Northern Ireland and had been taken to Nottinghamshire police headquarters as a backup?"

"No."

"And because the investigation was shelved, people seemed to forget about the backup copies, which have sat in a locked basement room in Nottingham ever since."

Arnside put both hands on his hips and scrutinized Johnson. "You're joking?"

"No, I'm not. I found out about it from a source at MI5 who just happened to have worked at Carrickfergus back in those days and knew the person responsible for arranging the backup copies."

Arnside pursed his lips as the implications of what he was hearing sank in. "So you're telling me I might need to go and make arrangements to have my boss arrested?" he said, his voice slowing to a crawl.

Johnson nodded.

"You do realize that could amount to career suicide," Arnside said. "I can't do that without it being absolutely bloody watertight."

"I think in reality, it's likely to be taken out of your hands," Johnson said. He guessed it would be elevated up to government level.

"Hmm, possibly. However, one thing you might not be aware of is that as part of my assistant chief constable's role, I have responsibility for the financing and resources of the Historic Enquiries Team, and I take responsibility for any case referred by that team to the PSNI for further investigation and possible prosecution."

Johnson put his hands on his hips. Now it was his turn to feel surprised. "So you're telling me it's your job to sort these cases out?"

"Basically, yes."

Both men turned around as, behind them, the helicopter's engines rose sharply in pitch. The pilot increased his revs further, and a few seconds later, the machine was airborne and heading toward Belfast.

Johnson turned back to the assistant chief constable. "I think you'll find the case is watertight," Johnson said. "I don't know about career suicide. Actually, you might find yourself with a promotion sooner than you think."

EPILOGUE

Monday, February 4, 2013
  Belfast

Johnson glanced at his watch: ten minutes to go before the press conference was due to start, and the last time he had looked, the school hall had been already full of journalists, TV cameras, radio mikes, and bustling police public relations officers trying to make order out of chaos.

Initially he had been astounded that the Police Service of Northern Ireland had decided to return to Whitefield Integrated Primary School, the scene of the planned killing of Campbell and the place where one of Barack Obama's security detail had met his demise just a week earlier.

But the more Johnson thought about it, the more it made sense. The location symbolized not just defiance toward terrorism but determination to build peace between Protestants and Catholics across the sectarian divide.

Arnside explained to Johnson that when it was established, the intention had been for the new school to accommodate an even balance of children from both arms of the Christian faith. And so far it was doing its bit to ensure they grew up together knowing integration as a normal part of their daily lives, not plotting how to kill each other.

He wanted to use the school at the press conference as an example, a vision, of how he saw Northern Ireland society evolving in the wider sense.

Fiona had wanted to fly to Belfast for the press conference to tie up the loose ends from her end of the investigation, given that police had arrested McKinney in Boston the day after the Black Mountain shootout. But to her annoyance, her editor had instead delegated the job to *Inside Track*'s London and Dublin correspondents who had been in Belfast for the G8. However, Fiona had led the way on coverage of the drama and had a major exclusive story, followed up globally, on the cigarette and arms smuggling that had been going on.

Johnson turned to Arnside, who stood in the school classroom just off the main hall, sipping a cup of tea and reading through the scripted statement he had prepared for the TV cameras.

The statement, which surprisingly had not been leaked to the media, was a lengthy one.

It reiterated in precise terms the catalog of murder charges laid at the door of Dessie Duggan, following the killings over recent months of Eric Simonson, Gary Joyce, Will Doyle, Michael Donovan, Brendan O'Neill, Martin Dennehy, Danny McCormick, and the still unnamed US Secret Service officer. He was also to be charged with the attempted murder of Campbell and of procuring the murder of his own stepdaughter, Moira McKittrick.

Kieran O'Driscoll was to be charged with the murders of Zebra and the pilot of the Eurocopter, conspiring to murder

Campbell, and aiding and abetting in the murder of the US Secret Service officer.

The police had decided, after lengthy deliberations, against charging Duggan with conspiracy to murder, or the attempted murder, of Barack Obama and David Cameron. After a lengthy questioning of Duggan, they had come to the conclusion that assassinating them hadn't actually been part of the plot.

But all that was old news, as far as the waiting journalists in the adjoining room were concerned. It had been splashed all over the newspapers, had been the top news story on every international television channel, had dominated radio and online news for the past week, and had been among the highest-trending stories in Twitter's history.

The new revelations, which Johnson knew would be pure media dynamite once released, were contained in the second part of Arnside's statement.

It went into considerable detail about an alleged crime committed in 1984—the cold-blooded shooting on Coolderry Road, south Armagh, of Alfie Duggan, by a unit of six soldiers.

Only one man—the now suspended chief constable of Northern Ireland, Campbell—was to be named on the charge sheet for that murder, Arnside was preparing to announce. The simple reason for that was that he was the only one still alive out of the six alleged perpetrators. The other five were all among the victims of Alfie Duggan's son, Dessie.

The missing incident file that had been recovered from Nottingham did no more than briefly describe the Alfie Duggan shooting and list the names of the army personnel present. It drew no conclusions and apportioned no blame. But it did corroborate the detail of who took part in the incident, as described in Will Doyle's journal, which had now become a smoking gun.

Finally Arnside looked up from his sheaf of papers. "This is going to cause an absolute shitstorm," he said.

Johnson resisted the temptation to roll his eyes. Neither he nor Jayne, who stood next to him, had ever seen anything like it. And neither, he suspected, had the media audience in the hall who were about to receive the details.

Six army officers had gotten away with the shoot-out for nearly three decades, thanks in part to the fact that two of them had become top policemen in the force that was responsible for prosecuting such crimes.

Johnson didn't envy Arnside at having to face the media on this one.

"How exactly are you going to explain the twenty-nine-year delay in getting to the bottom of this?" Jayne asked Arnside.

The policeman pressed his lips together. "I'll just have to come clean, as far as I can, anyway—I'm very limited in what I can say now that Campbell's being charged. Otherwise I'm at risk of prejudicing the whole prosecution. I'll have to admit the conspiracy by him and Simonson and then confess to a cock-up by everyone else in monitoring what was going on."

Johnson nodded. "The problem you've got," he said, "is explaining how those files at Carrickfergus could have been stolen by them in the first place and then how the copies could sit untouched in a box in Nottingham all this time without anyone realizing."

"Yes, and there is no explanation," Arnside said. "The Historical Enquiries Team has done a damn good job in locating almost all the files and papers relating to past crimes of this kind. How they missed these, I have no idea. If it was due to any instruction by Simonson or Campbell, then we'll get to the bottom of that and add it to the charge sheet."

Johnson glanced at Jayne. The fact was, although the HET

had its own director, the entity was part of the PSNI, and many of its investigators were former policemen from Northern Ireland. He knew there had been allegations that the HET had different, softer procedures for investigations involving former police, military, or security services members who were accused of crimes against terrorists than it did for those who were members of the IRA or loyalist terrorist groups. Who knew what orders Campbell and Simonson had given behind closed doors.

However, the Campbell case was too high-profile to be swept under the rug. It had already been passed over to the PSNI's Crime Operations Department, which Arnside had been heading, and there was every likelihood that the investigation would be taken over by an outside, independent police force from England.

But there would inevitably be an enormous political outcry, too, both in Northern Ireland and in London, where senior politicians would try to capitalize on the situation, as ever.

"You'd better make sure you keep the heat on your investigators," Johnson said. "I want to see justice done after all that effort."

Arnside nodded. "But I don't want it to derail the peace process," he said. "That's my worry; both sides will use it as an excuse to restart hostilities." He jerked his thumb toward the group of journalists, who were visible through the glass panel in the classroom door. "I'd better go and face the music."

Johnson and Jayne watched as he opened the door of the classroom and strode across the school hall to where a lectern had been placed for him to make his address. In front of him were rows of seats, all occupied.

The room fell silent as Arnside placed his notes on the lectern, cleared his throat, and began to speak.

As he did, Johnson's thoughts drifted to the innocent victims, not just those who had lost their lives but the wives left as widows, like Norma Simonson, Beth Doyle, and Susan Joyce; the children left fatherless, like Becky and Tommy Dennehy; and those who had died trying to do the right thing, like Moira. Especially Moira, whose memorial service was being held in two days. Johnson and Jayne were definitely planning to attend.

Jayne seemed to read his thoughts. "None of this makes any sense," she whispered.

"No sense at all," he said. "All I can say is, we've made a difference. We've brought it out into the open. Now it's up to others."

What had O'Neill said at Ronnie's house, after their escape from the bunker? *It's easy for you, coming in from outside. You can walk out anytime you like. For us, we're stuck here with kids in schools, families, roots that have been put down. We're dealing with a helluva stressful situation, issues that go back decades, and it's bloody complicated.*

Yes, complicated it was. But Johnson knew one thing: his work was showing how futile, how unproductive, how destructive all this sectarian hostility and fighting in the name of nationalism, unionism and religion really was.

For Northern Ireland, substitute any number of other countries and regions around the world. Johnson knew there were similar situations almost everywhere that different peoples, tribes, factions and religions coexisted. War crimes were often the result. And as long as Johnson could continue doing what he was doing to catch the perpetrators, he would.

* * *

BOOK 4 IN THE JOE JOHNSON SERIES: STALIN'S FINAL STING

If you enjoyed **Bandit Country** you'll probably like the fourth book in the Joe Johnson series, **Stalin's Final Sting**, which is another investigation into dark crimes from the past. It is available on Amazon—just type "Andrew Turpin Stalin's Final Sting" into the search box at the top of the Amazon sales web page.

To give you a flavor of **Stalin's Final Sting**, here's the blurb:

Ex-Cold War spies bite back . . . The darkest secrets of a Russian oligarch—a legacy from Stalin. A hidden batch of the CIA's Stinger missiles. And the insatiable Afghan thirst for revenge.

Ex-CIA war crimes investigator **Joe Johnson** is sucked into an inquiry which delves into the deadly world of Soviet and US undercover operations in Afghanistan during the 1980s—and mysterious connections to current US and Russian politics.

Johnson and his ex-MI6 colleague Jayne Robinson find themselves pursuing a Russian oligarch with strong links to Putin and a past he would rather keep hidden —and an Afghan mujahideen bent on the most blood-thirsty revenge.

The investigation is thrown awry by Johnson's crooked former CIA boss, now on the run, and by a miscalcula-tion of the dangers lurking in the Hindu Kush moun-tains, ridden with heavily armed Taliban insurgents.

The story reaches a raw climax in Brooklyn, Manhat-tan, Moscow, and Kabul, as Johnson battles to over-come the powerful forces lined up against him, including former KGB agents.

Stalin's Final Sting is a gripping thriller—the fourth in the Joe Johnson series—with some twists that the reader will never see coming.

* * *

ANDREW'S READERS GROUP AND OTHER JOE JOHNSON BOOKS

If you enjoyed this book, I would like to keep in touch. This is not always easy, as I usually only publish a couple of books a year and there are many authors and books out there. So the best way is for you to be on my Readers Group email list. I can then send you updates on the next book, plus occasional special offers. There's no spam and you can unsubscribe at any time.

If you would like to join my Readers Group and receive the email updates, I will send you, **FREE**, the ebook version of another Joe Johnson thriller, *The Afghan*, which is a prequel to the series and normally sells at $2.99/£2.99 (paperback $9.99/£9.99).

The Afghan is set in 1988 when Johnson was still in the CIA. Most of the action takes place in Afghanistan, then occupied by the Soviet Union, and in Washington, DC. Some of the characters and story lines that emerge in the other books have their roots in this period. I think you will enjoy it!

The Afghan can be downloaded **FREE** from the following link:

https://bookhip.com/QHCLTZ

If you only like reading paperbacks you can still sign up for the email list at that link. A paperback of *The Afghan* is for sale on Amazon.

You should also enjoy the other thrillers in the Joe

Johnson series, if you haven't read them yet. You may find it is best to read them in order, as follows:

Prequel: *The Afghan*
1. *The Last Nazi*
2. *The Old Bridge*
3. *Bandit Country*
4. *Stalin's Final Sting*
5. *The Nazi's Son*

To find the books, just type "Andrew Turpin Joe Johnson thriller series" in the search box at the top of the Amazon page — you can't miss them!

IF YOU ENJOYED THIS BOOK PLEASE WRITE A REVIEW

As an independently published author, through my own imprint The Write Direction Publishing, I find that honest reviews of my books are the most powerful way for me to bring them to the attention of other potential readers.

As you'll appreciate, unlike the big international publishers, I can't take out full-page advertisements in the newspapers or place posters on the subway.

So I am committed to producing work of the best quality I can in order to attract a loyal group of readers who are prepared to recommend my work to others.

Therefore, if you enjoyed reading this novel, then I would very much appreciate it if you would spend five minutes and leave a review—which can be as short as you like—preferably on the page or website where you bought it.

You can find the book's page on the Amazon website by typing 'Andrew Turpin Bandit Country' in the search box.

Once you are on the book's page, scroll down to 'Customer Reviews', then click on 'Leave a Review.'

Reviews are also a great encouragement to me to write more.

Many thanks!

THANKS AND ACKNOWLEDGEMENTS

I would like to thank everyone who reads **Bandit Country**—which is my third novel in the Joe Johnson series, following on from **The Last Nazi** and **The Old Bridge**. I hope you enjoy the book and that it proves entertaining and even informative.

As always, there have been several people who have helped me through the long process of research, writing, and editing. My main early "beta" readers this time were my brother Adrian, Warren Smith, Dave Payne, Mark Farrar and David Cole—thanks to all of you.

But I also have a growing team of advance readers who go through my books at a later stage, just prior to publication, and have been able to give me a few useful pointers and have spotted the odd error. If you would like to join my Advance Readers team, send me an email at andrew@andrew-turpin.com and let me know. Make sure to tell me a little about yourself — including what part of the world you live in and the type of books and authors you like.

Adrian also again helped with the graphics for my website and reader emails as well as providing good encouragement generally. Writing can be a lonely business sometimes!

I used a different team of editors for this book. Kevin Smith and Jon Ford gave me some very helpful feedback and ideas for improvement in the earlier stages, and then Chrisona Schmidt did a very good job at the line-by-line copy editing stage. Thanks to all of them—the responsibility for any remaining mistakes lies solely with me.

Damonza, my cover designers, again did an excellent job.

AUTHOR'S NOTE

As a teenager during the 1980s, the conflict in Northern Ireland was never far from the headlines and the television news bulletins. I still have fairly clear memories of watching stories about car bombs, street fighting between the IRA and the British soldiers, and sniper attacks.

My interest in Northern Ireland deepened while studying history at university, and I ended up writing my final year dissertation about attempts by David Lloyd George's British government to impose conscription in Ireland during the First World War in 1918—when all of Ireland was governed from Westminster.

The initiative, which failed, simply helped fuel a rising tide of republicanism that by 1921 had resulted in independence for what is now the Republic, with Northern Ireland remaining part of the United Kingdom.

Since then, I've remained interested in events across the Irish Sea, and so it seemed almost inevitable that I would turn to this fertile source of fiction for one of my Joe Johnson stories.

Despite many public inquiries, much of what happened in Northern Ireland during the conflict between the IRA and British security services remains shrouded in doubt and uncertainty. Nothing was ever black and white—perfect for a war crimes investigator who is determined to deliver justice, but who also recognizes the deep-rooted, historic nature of sectarian and nationalist sentiment and the difficulties involved in determining who is on the side of right.

It is not necessary to read very deeply into the history of The Troubles before coming across accounts of the events on November 22, 1975. On that day, the south Armagh brigade of the Provisional IRA attacked a British army observation post

at Drummuckavall, near Crossmaglen, on the border between
the Republic of Ireland and Northern Ireland. Three British
soldiers were killed in the shooting, which came nine months
after the Provisionals had declared a ceasefire.

The following day, the British government's Secretary of
State for Northern Ireland, Merlyn Rees, referred in a statement to "the bandit country of South Armagh." The tag
stuck and has been widely used by the media ever since in
connection with the southern part of County Armagh.

The third Joe Johnson thriller, entitled *Bandit Country*,
is set in a Northern Ireland landscape which, two decades
after the 1998 Good Friday peace agreement, still does not
match up to the vision laid out at that time.

The on-going conflict between violent republicans, who
want a united Ireland, and unionists, who want Northern
Ireland to remain part of the United Kingdom, still simmers
away and explodes into violence at fairly regular intervals.
During 2017, there were about sixty shootings and over thirty
bombing incidents by dissident republican terrorists, princi-
pally the New IRA, as the largest group is known. Some of
the attacks were directed at police officers and police
stations.

Generally speaking, it is not violence of the type that
disrupts people's lives day after day as it did at the height of
the Troubles in the '70s and '80s. But the New IRA now
represents the biggest threat since its bigger, older, brother—
the Provisional IRA—ended its campaign in the 1990s. The
New IRA is adept at sourcing explosive and weapons, and
efforts to combat it continue to consume a large amount of
time, resources, and funding among the police and intelligence organizations in the region.

Bandit Country is set in 2013. But little has fundamen-
tally changed since then, and as is often the case in communities where nationalism and sectarian conflict are hard-wired

into the culture, it is likely that these issues will be at the forefront for years and decades to come.

In that sense, it is hoped that the book might spur readers with little knowledge of the history of Northern Ireland to find out more, and to watch developments there as they unfold in the future with new interest.

One major issue now is how the border between Northern Ireland and the Irish Republic will be structured once Britain has left the European Union, while the Irish Republic remains inside it. Some senior police and security experts fear that a "hard" border, with checkpoints, might become a new target for the dissidents.

Finally, I should note that as Joe Johnson, the lead character in this series, is from the United States, and most scenes are from his point of view, it makes sense to use American spellings and terminology in most cases, rather than my native British. Any mistakes in this respect are mine alone— please do point them out to me.

BACKGROUND READING AND BIBLIOGRAPHY

There is a large pile of background reading on Northern Ireland sitting on my hard drive and on the shelf in my small writing den. The task of combing through it in a search for interesting fragments that could be incorporated into a fictional story has been fascinating, and the list below represents only a small sample of the whole.

I really need to start with a huge thank you, but also an apology, to one writer in particular—Toby Harnden, currently the Washington bureau chief of *The Sunday Times*. He wrote a seminal non-fiction book in 1999—the original *Bandit Country* — on the conflict in Northern Ireland, and south Armagh in particular, built around his experiences and research as a correspondent in the region.

I spent quite some time trying to locate a copy of Toby's book, but failed, and ended up emailing him and asking for help. He very kindly let me see a copy and I quickly realized why it is held in such high regard.

It is immensely well-researched, written in Toby's usual engaging style, and is packed full of colorful material about some of the IRA's most notorious leadership figures in south Armagh, such as Thomas "Slab" Murphy, as well as facts and analysis. It proved an invaluable source of background information and ideas for me as I battled to construct my plot.

Hopefully he will see it as a huge compliment that I've also stolen his title. *Bandit Country* was a tag coined in November 1975 by the then British Secretary of State for Northern Ireland Merlyn Rees to describe south Armagh, and has been widely used ever since.

I struggled for a long time to think of a good alternative for this book, and despite toying with several options, I just couldn't come up with anything that matched the stark Wild West imagery conjured up by the original tag. Given that Toby's book is non-fiction, and was written a long time ago, and is not available as an e-book, I hope he will forgive me for my lack of original thinking. I certainly have a very long way to go to match the 100,000 worldwide sales that his book achieved—if anyone wants to drill much deeper into the history and background of the conflict in Ulster, I would thoroughly recommend it as a starting point. It is possible to find copies of the paperback edition at the Bookfinder website: http://www.bookfinder.com/

It is also possible to read the full text of the book at Toby's own website, http://www.tobyharnden.com/

Apart from that, there were several other excellent books which also provided me with a deep seam of background material and ideas.

Mark Urban's book, *Big Boys' Rules*, available at http://www.amazon.co.uk/dp/0571168094, gives a detailed account of struggles by British security forces and the Royal Ulster Constabulary to combat IRA terrorists in Northern Ireland. It examines in particular the tactics employed by undercover units within the Special Air Service (SAS) and 14 Intelligence Company. Operations mounted by these small, specialist units resulted in the deaths of thirty IRA terrorists between 1976 and 1987, according to Urban, some of them in planned ambushes. During the same period the regular army killed nine IRA men.

Charlie One, by Sean Hartnett, available at https://www.amazon.co.uk/dp/B01M0SUN1A, is a first-hand account of counter-terrorism operations run by 14 Intelligence Company. Hartnett gives a fascinating insight into intelligence gathering, decision-making processes, and tactics employed to combat IRA operatives across Northern Ireland during the Troubles.

There is a graphic account within Iain Cobain's book, *The History Thieves*, available at https://www.amazon.-co.uk/dp/B01DTT5TO0, about attempts to sabotage inquiries by Lord Stevens into the killings of various IRA terrorists and the role played in these deaths by British army intelligence officers in the Force Research Unit and the RUC's special branch. Cobain also details the extent of collusion between certain members of the army's Ulster Defence Regiment and loyalist, or unionist, terrorist groups, in mounting lethal operations against republican terrorists.

Stakeknife, available at https://www.amazon.-co.uk/dp/B009SS4NGC, written by former army intelligence officer and Force Research Unit member Ian Hurst under the pseudonym Martin Ingram, gives a detailed account of life running agents inside the IRA and the life-and-death decisions that had to be made daily in order to protect those sources. As Hurst spells out, sometimes there were very stark, dark, choices to be made—literally allowing some informers to be killed in order to protect others who were seen as more valuable. I tried to reflect a little of this in Bandit Country. This book also details how British security forces colluded with loyalist terrorist units.

In terms of fundraising by republican forces, a House of Commons Northern Ireland Affairs Committee report in 2012, *Fuel Laundering and Smuggling in Northern Ireland,* is enlightening. Its focus is on the extent of cross-border tobacco and fuel smuggling between the Republic of Ireland and Northern Ireland. The report is available at: http://www.publications.parliament.uk/pa/cm201012/cmselect/cmniaf/1504/1504.pdf

The *Miami New Times* website carried a graphic account of how one tobacco smuggling gang was caught as they transported millions of cigarettes from Miami to Dublin as part of an IRA fundraising operation. Go to: http://www.

miaminewtimes.com/news/black-market-cigarettes-miamis-new-vice-6365502

There is much material available about British security forces' tactics in combating IRA sniper gangs. For example, the *UK Elite Forces* website details the operation by the SAS in 1997 that resulted in the capture of one gang at a farm complex near Crossmaglen. The gang had been responsible for the deaths of seven soldiers and two policemen. See: http://www.eliteukforces.info/special-air-service/sas-operations/ira-sniper-team/

The ongoing catalogue of violent dissident republican attacks on British security targets, particularly policemen and police stations, is well documented by the BBC, which maintains a timeline of incidents dating back to 2009. Go to: http://www.bbc.co.uk/news/uk-northern-ireland-10866072

Efforts by the Police Service of Northern Ireland to tackle the problem have been outlined by media, including The Belfast Telegraph, who ran a useful article about the anti-terror unit which can be found at: http://www.belfasttelegraph.co.uk/news/northern-ireland/psni-antiterror-unit-runs-68-cases-30935183.html

The formation of the New IRA in 2012 as a fresh grouping of republican organizations was widely documented, but was reported initially in an article in *The Guardian* newspaper. See: https://www.theguardian.com/uk/2012/jul/26/ira-northern-ireland-dissident-republican-groups

I have centered my story around a meeting of leaders of the G8 group of industrialized countries in Belfast. There actually was a G8 meeting in Northern Ireland in 2013, at the Lough Erne golf resort, but it took place in June of that year, not January, as portrayed in my book. Barack Obama did attend, along with David Cameron, and they both visited a school, but it was in Enniskillen, not the fictional Belfast school depicted in my book. The BBC has an account of Obama's visit to Northern Ireland at: http://www.bbc.co.uk/news/uk-northern-ireland-22889607

ABOUT THE AUTHOR AND CONTACT DETAILS

I have always had a love of writing and a passion for reading good thrillers. But despite having a long-standing dream of writing my own novels, it took me more than five decades to finally get around to completing the first.

The Last Nazi is the first in the **Joe Johnson** series of thrillers, which pulls together some of my other interests, particularly history, world news, and travel.

I studied history at Loughborough University and worked for many years as a business and financial journalist before becoming a corporate and financial communications adviser with several large energy companies, specializing in media relations.

Originally I came from Grantham, Lincolnshire, and I now live with my family in St. Albans, Hertfordshire, U.K.

You can connect with me via these routes:

E-mail: andrew@andrewturpin.com
Website: www.andrewturpin.com.
Facebook: @AndrewTurpinAuthor
Twitter: @AndrewTurpin
Instagram: @andrewturpin.author

Please also follow me on Bookbub and Amazon!

https://www.bookbub.com/authors/andrew-turpin
https://www.amazon.com/Andrew-Turpin/e/B074V87WWL/

Do get in touch with your comments and views on the books, or anything else for that matter. I enjoy hearing from readers and promise to reply.

CPSIA information can be obtained
at www.ICGtesting.com
Printed in the USA
LVHW111344071219
639772LV00001B/144/P

9 781788 750059